THE DARK LORD'S DESIGN

DAWN OF WIZARDS
BOOK THREE

JEFFREY L. KOHANEK

FALLBRANDT PRESS

PUBLISHED BY JEFFREY L. KOHANEK and FALLBRANDT PRESS

www.JeffreyLKohanek.com

ALSO BY JEFFREY L. KOHANEK

Dawn of Wizards

The First Wizard

Paragon of Solitude

The Dark Lord's Design

Fate of Wizardoms

Eye of Obscurance

Balance of Magic

Temple of the Oracle

Objects of Power

Rise of a Wizard Queen

A Contest of Gods

* * *

Fate of Wizardoms Boxed Set: Books 1-3

Fate of Wizardoms Box Set: Books 4-6

Fall of Wizardoms

God King Rising

Legend of the Sky Sword

Curse of the Elf Queen

Shadow of a Dragon Priest

Advent of the Drow

A Sundered Realm

Fall of Wizardoms Boxed Set: Books 1-3

Fall of Wizardoms Box Set: Books 4-6

Wizardom Legends

The Outrageous Exploits of Jerrell Landish

Thief for Hire

Trickster for Hire

Charlatan for Hire

Tor the Dungeon Crawler

Temple of the Unknown

Castles of Legend

Shrine of the Undead

Runes of Issalia

The Buried Symbol

The Emblem Throne

An Empire in Runes

* * *

Runes of Issalia Bonus Box

Wardens of Issalia

A Warden's Purpose

The Arcane Ward:

An Imperial Gambit

A Kingdom Under Siege

* * *

Wardens of Issalia Boxed Set

2ND AGE

GALFHADDEN

TALASTAR

DROVARIA

THE INCULTUM

DOMUS SKRAI

DOMUSI

DOMUS RA

DOMUS HEX

SEA GATE

KROTAL

THE STAGNUM

HOOKED POINT

GREAVESPORT

SYLVANAR THE VALE

RIVERS END HAVENFALL

BARDS BAY

NOR'TAHAL

SHAI AELDOR

VAS AELDOR

AELDORIA

THE AGROSI

DIS AELDOR

TAHALA

WESTHOLD

RA'TAHAL

DARRISTAN SHILLINGS

EASTHOLD

THE GLACIA

INCULTI INFINITUS

JOURNAL ENTRY

All eras have a beginning and an end, and when the sun sets on one age, the subsequent dawn announces the birth of another. What occurs during those dark moments between is the stuff of legend.

Although the world was unaware of its significance, the moment magic first flowed through human veins signaled the end of the second age. This young man turned wizard swiftly grew into his role, honed his craft, and was prepared to leave a mark upon the world. Then, a powerful prophecy struck, one foretelling a great darkness that would sweep across the land, consuming all life in its path.

To stave off certain doom, this young man, alongside a few trusted companions, set off on a dangerous quest that eventually led them to a lost and lonely tower hidden amid the frozen wastes of the distant south. This tower was home to a dwarf unlike any other, a paragon of magic who perceived a great need for his vaunted abilities. With the fate of the world in the balance, he would press his thumb against the scale in the hope of tilting the outcome in favor of this young wizard. But the darkness had already come, and in that darkness lurked an enemy the world had yet to fully comprehend.

The fate of the world dangled over the edge of a precipice. The first wizard and a small band of heroes sought to stave off disaster. Could they, somehow, persevere? Or had the die already been cast?

Read on and discover the truth behind the most stunning outcome in the history of our world. By the time our tale draws to a close, a new age will have dawned.

The era of the dark lord begins.

Source unknown

CHAPTER 1
EMBARKING

"I need to leave." Saying the words was more difficult than Ian Carpenter expected.

Winnie, who lay beneath him, reached up and touched his cheek. "When will you return?" Her emerald eyes pleaded for him to stay.

He leaned into her touch, gently pulling her hand to his mouth and kissing her palm. "I do not know."

"I could come with you."

Part of him rejoiced at the idea of having her by his side, but his travels had been fraught with danger. *If she were killed because of me...*he banished the idea before tears emerged. *Is this love?* He did not know. For years, he had thought he loved Rina, but the dreams, both day and night, which had once featured the golden-haired beauty were now graced by Winnie's auburn curls.

"It will be dangerous." He hoped the intensity in his voice would avoid an argument. "You cannot imagine the danger, the monsters...the evil that lurks outside the walls of this citadel."

She opened her mouth to speak but he pressed a finger against her full, red lips.

"I know what happened in Shillings. If you recall, I also was abducted and forced into slavery. While individual freedom is a precious thing, you were never truly at risk of dying. The worst of it came when Rysildar took over this tower. The Drow singer was a cruel and demanding monster, but some monsters are worse than others."

Her green eyes hardened, and she pulled her hand back. "Would you keep me locked in a jar like some fancy bauble?"

Ian sighed inwardly. He had hoped to end the argument, not start a new one. "I do not own you, Winnie. I will never try to control you. I am merely saying that there is no need for you to place yourself in unnecessary risk. Do you even know how to defend yourself in case of an attack?"

His response earned him a grimace. "I suppose not."

He leaned in and gave her a peck on the lips. The kiss was a brief reminder of their night together, portions of which were spent with him in tears and her consoling him. Urgency and concern tugged at him. "If we keep it up, I will never leave."

"Would that be so bad?"

"Not for us, but I have responsibilities, and I am concerned about my mother..." The message from Nor'Tahal hadn't left his mind since Korrigan had read it to him the day before.

"I pray she is well."

"As do I." He stood and cinched the sash around his waist. It was a shimmery white, in stark contrast to the dark red robes he had selected for the day. The robes covered his body from neck to ankles, leaving his boots and hands exposed. "I need to see her as soon as possible, which is why I must go."

"I will be here when you return." She pouted, pulling the bedsheet up to cover herself. "You will return, won't you?"

"Yes. I promise." He walked to the bedroom door and pulled it open, turning for a last glance after he stepped out.

She had rolled to her side, to face him, the sheet clinging to her curves. "I...think I love you, Ian."

He opened his mouth to reply, but no words came out. Her declaration bounced in his head, erasing all other thoughts. Unable to speak, he simply closed the door and stood on the landing with his eyes closed. *Is this love?* he asked himself again. No answer came.

Unsettled, he descended the curved staircase running along the tower's outer wall. By the time he reached the ground level, three stories down, he had regained his composure. He was not alone.

"Ah." Parsigar groaned as he rose from a chair. The old dwarf leaned into his staff while his other hand pressed against his lower back. With a wispy white beard and bushy white eyebrows, he certainly appeared old, but few would guess his true age. "The young wizard makes his appearance."

Ian's older brother, Vic, turned from the window. "Finally."

Vic rubbed one of his broad shoulders while crossing the room toward Ian, the ripples of muscles visible on his bare arms. With brown hair, dark eyes, and sculpted facial features to match his athletic build, Vic easily attracted the attention of girls, something Ian had spent much of his teen years envying. That jealousy had eased of late, as Ian gained confidence in himself.

Lint, who stood no taller than the length of Ian's hand, sat on the end table with his tiny legs swinging relentlessly in a typical display of his endless energy. "Yeah. You lazy humans sleep away half the morning."

"That's easy for you to say," Ian replied. "Unlike you brownies, we humans require sleep. However, I'd be lying if I didn't admit I have been awake for some time now."

Cocking his head to the side, the brownie frowned. "Doing what?"

Ian's cheeks grew warm. "You never mind that."

"As I told you, Vic." Revita snorted from the sitting room sofa. "I knew Ian and the girl were having a morning tumble."

His cheeks turning red, Ian stammered, "I...we...I mean..."

She tossed her raven hair back and laughed. "You are even easier to embarrass than your brother."

"Vita..." Vic scolded as he stopped beside her.

"Oh, I am only having a bit of fun with him." Revita stood and patted Vic's cheek while wearing a familiar smirk on her coppery-skinned face. Turning, she straightened her black leather coat. Beneath it, she wore a black corset over a gray tunic. "I am ready to leave when you three are."

"Right, then." Ian gave a firm nod and walked over to the door, where three loaded packs leaned against the wall.

He hoisted a pack to his shoulder, pulled the door open, and lifted his gaze toward the pale blue sky. *Lionel. Come to me. We are leaving.* The sensation of excitement came through the bond between Ian and the fire drake. With that sensation came the feeling of direction.

Ian turned and narrowed his eyes while peering into the distance. A small, dark shape glided into view. It flew in from the south, sailed over the outer walls of Ra'Tahal, and then dove down, skirting the taller buildings before circling the tower. Ian turned in expectation, following the red and black fire drake as it drifted down and landed on his sleeve-covered forearm.

Stroking Lionel's head as he stepped back inside, Ian crooned. "There's a good boy."

He closed the door and noted that Vic and Revita had claimed the other two packs. Vic had already donned the harness over his cream-colored tunic and sleeveless leather jerkin, his pick-like weapon jutting up from over his shoulder. At the same time, Revita absently adjusted the silver bracer covering her right forearm. The bracer, along with the dagger strapped to her thigh, reminded Ian that she was more dangerous than one might guess. The couple gathered beside Parsigar, who leaned against his staff.

"Is everyone ready?" Ian asked.

"I was ready yesterday," Lint replied from the end table beside the old dwarf.

"Sorry, but without a night of rest, traveling as we are wouldn't have been possible." Ian lifted a finger. "Just remember that we are visiting Truhan's home. There, he is master and you need to treat him with respect."

Revita snorted. "That is asking a lot."

"Vita..." Vic chided.

"Do you remember how odd he was? How am I supposed to hold back comments if he says something ridiculous?"

"Just do it. We won't be there long, anyway."

She sighed. "Fine, but I doubt you'll get the same agreement from the pipsqueak."

Ian frowned at Lint, who grinned broadly. *She makes a fair point. The brownie doesn't respect anyone.* Any appeal Ian made to him was bound to go unheeded. Acknowledging that Lint was going to behave as he wished, Ian hoped Truhan would understand. So, he set his mind on his underground home beneath Mount Tiadd.

Fully rested after a solid night of sleep, he opened himself up and raw energy flowed in. The room grew brighter, the scents of flowers in the vase on the windowsill suddenly sharper, his senses overloaded while power coursed through his veins. Using a trickle of that power, he willed a construct to materialize before his outstretched arm. A disk of white light formed, made of intricate intersecting lines and exotic runes. Unlike typical constructs, which remained two dimensional, Ian bent this one around its axis until it became a globe. Through that globe, he channeled his magic while firmly imagining his desired destination, a chamber he knew well. A ripping sound broke the silence as a slice of light split the air before him, extending until it was six feet long. It then transformed into a circular window surrounded by sizzling energy. Beyond the opening was a massive chamber filled with stone columns that ran from the floor to a ceiling two hundred feet above. A brazier and scattered torches bathed the chamber in warm light.

"Go on," he said.

With a whoop, Lint leapt off the table, over the shimmering edge of the portal, and landed on the cavern floor before racing off. Vic took Revita by the hand and entered the gateway. Once the couple was beyond the opening, the elderly dwarf hobbled to it, lifted his staff over the lower edge, and stepped through. Last came Ian, with Lionel on his shoulder. Once beyond the gateway, Ian released the spell and it snapped shut with a pop that echoed in the massive chamber.

Revita peered up toward the platforms jutting out from the sides of the thick, stone pillars. Ropes dangled between the platforms, surrounding a maze of beams. "What is this place?"

"This is where I test my abilities." Ian pointed toward the center of the hall. "See the scorch marks on the columns?"

Everyone turned their attention to the blackened bottoms of the columns near the center of the room.

Ian explained, "That happened when I was experimenting with various fire-related spells."

Parsigar asked, "What spell caused that?"

"One that created a dozen tornadoes made of fire. Each was as tall as I am and moved in an unpredictable manner...until a few of them decided I was their target. I almost set myself on fire that day."

The old dwarf chortled. "My, my...I wish I could have witnessed that."

"Come on, you guys!" Lint's nasal voice carried across the massive chamber. He then darted into a dark tunnel and was gone.

Ian sighed. "Let's go before he gets himself into trouble."

They crossed the hall, and as they approached the tunnel entrance, a yip came from ahead.

"Help!" Lint cried.

Panicked, Ian flashed a worried look at his brother, then ran for the doorway.

CHAPTER 2

A TALL TALE

Alarmed by Lint's cry, Ian hurried along a short tunnel and emerged in another chamber. He stopped inside the doorway and quickly scanned his surroundings in search of the brownie.

Shelves packed with books covered the far wall of the study. Tables, chairs, and a ten-foot-thick column made of wooden slats occupied the middle of the room. The column ran from the floor to the twenty-foot-tall ceiling and consisted of hundreds of slots. Scrolls occupied dozens of openings in the lower portion of the column, while the rest of the compartments sat empty. A table covered in books was positioned between the column and the bookshelves. In front of the table squatted a handsome man with sculpted features, golden hair, and eyes that sparkled like seawater on a sunny day. Dressed in a fine black coat, black tunic, and black trousers, he remained crouched while holding a pewter pitcher upside down against the floor.

Still crouched, Truhan fixed Ian with a hard glare. "I assume you have a good excuse for bringing others here."

A small, muffled voice came from the pitcher. "Let me out!" Lint's tiny fists pounded on his metal cage.

"I will explain, Master, but can you please release my friend first?"

Truhan arched a brow. "You know this brownie?"

"Yes. His name is Lint." Approaching footsteps preceded Vic and Revita entering the study. Ian frowned as he realized what his master said. "How did you know he was a brownie?"

Truhan snorted. "Do you know any other humanoid creatures this small? Well, other than fairies, but since this one doesn't have wings, that seems unlikely."

"Like I said, he is my friend. Please let him go."

"Are you certain? Brownies are notorious for causing trouble."

Revita burst out laughing. "It certainly sounds like he knows about brownies."

Ian approached his master. "You can trust him. I trust him." In his head, he added *mostly*.

Truhan lifted the pitcher and stood.

Lint scrambled away, turned, and waved his fist in the air. "If you try that again, I swear I will glue your eyelids shut while you sleep!"

The man calmly replied, "What a very brownie like thing to say."

The threat caused Ian to wince. Bringing others to the secret lair was against his master's rules. He did not wish to stir any additional trouble. "Please ignore Lint. He means well."

"Where did you get the fire drake?"

Ian reached up and patted the creature on his shoulder. "This is Lionel. He and I are sort of..."

The tapping of a staff and scraping of feet had everyone turning toward the tunnel as Parsigar shuffled into view.

Truhan frowned. "Your brother and the thief, I recognize, but who is the dwarf?"

"I..." Ian recalled his quest to find the Paragon and his master's urging that Ian must do so at any cost. He walked over to the dwarf and rested his hand on his shoulder. "This is Master Parsigar. He has agreed to use his talents to aid our effort to save the world."

"You were to seek out the Paragon, not some old dwarf who is barely able to stand." Truhan rounded the table and sat in the chair.

Parsigar, who leaned against his staff, replied in a creaking voice, "You are speaking to the Paragon."

A moment of silence passed while Truhan stared at the dwarf. "That title was given to you by Gahagar?"

"It was."

The man narrowed his eyes. "You are extraordinary?"

"My king believed so."

He turned his gaze on Ian. "And how did you come to find this unusual dwarf?"

"Hold a moment," Parsigar said. "This discussion seems likely to be drawn out, and this old dwarf who can barely stand would prefer to sit."

"Very well." Truhan rose from his chair and crossed the room. "Let's visit the kitchen."

When the man walked off, Ian turned toward his companions. "Do not touch anything. Some objects are dangerous." He waggled his finger down at the brownie. "Did you hear me, Lint?"

"Yeah." The brownie pinched his already nasal voice. "Don't touch anything."

Revita waggled a finger at the brownie. "The last time you did so, we ended up fighting the statue of a massive, angry moarbear."

Lint planted his fists on his hips. "Are you going to hold that over me forever?"

"You do realize that was two days ago, don't you?"

The brownie waved it off. "Two days, two years, two decades, what's the difference?"

"For most people, those differences mean a lot." Ian headed across the room. "Come along and keep your hands to yourself."

At the far end of the chamber, he passed through another doorway that led to the kitchen. Similar to the other caverns, glowing orbs along the walls illuminated the space. Cabinets, shelving, and racks covered the wall to his right while a massive brick oven waited straight ahead.

Truhan was seated at the head of the table on the left side of the room. "Ian. Fill the teapot. I suspect our guests would like something to drink."

Revita leaned close to Vic and softly spoke just loud enough for Ian to hear. "Do you think he has any ale or wine?"

"Hush." Vic took her hand and pulled her toward the table.

Meanwhile, Ian lifted the tea kettle from a shelf, turned to the pump sticking out from the wall, and began to raise and lower the lever. Water poured out in bursts, slowly filling the kettle. With it full, he placed it on top of the oven. He then pulled a lever and an array of metal slots along the oven's top surface opened, which emitted heat against the bottom of the kettle.

Truhan said, "Now that we are settled, I would like to know what happened after you set out on your quest."

Ian slid his pack off his shoulder, set it beside the wall and pulled out a chair. The moment he sat, Lionel climbed down his arm and hopped onto his lap, where he curled into a ball. Absently stroking the drake's back, Ian considered where to begin.

"After leaving here, I found a boat that carried me downriver to Bard's Bay. That is where I happened upon my brother and convinced both him and Revita to join me. Before they could leave, I had to help them with a little problem of their own."

Truhan grunted. "What sort of problem?"

"Criminal gangs had taken over the city. They asked me to help get rid of those gangs."

The man furrowed his brow. "The free cities frequently change hands. Whoever is in charge is constantly at risk of being overthrown. Why bother?"

Vic spoke up for the first time. "The gangs controlling the city were ruthless, oppressive, and greedy. They held a foot against the throat of the people while taking every ounce of coin they could squeeze from them. How could we allow that to continue?"

"You would risk yourself for people who care nothing for you?"

Revita said, "It was my fault that the criminals took charge of the city."

Vic looked at her. "*Our* fault."

"No." She shook her head. "It was my fault. I was the one who freed the prisoners from the Carcera. Bard's Bay suffered for that decision."

Truhan arched his brow. "The criminals you released during the jailbreak were the ones who took over the city?"

"More or less," Vic replied. "You see, during our escape, they defeated the prison guards and freed everyone else. By the time Revita and I returned to Bard's Bay, Commander Kaden had been ousted and the city was in turmoil, which only grew worse as the seasons passed. We stayed, hoping to fix what we had broken, but two of us vs hundreds made the situation difficult to rectify."

Ian picked up the story. "When I arrived, one of the gangs had already been taken out, due to a clever ruse Revita and my brother pulled off. The largest and toughest gang remained in charge, so we recruited some help, formed a plan, and fought to reclaim the city. It was grim business, but we won the fight. When we left, a man named Essex had been placed in charge, and although the man had worked for Commander Kaden, he seemed to be more honest than his former employer." Ian hoped it was true, but time would need to pass for that to be proven – time that the world may not have. "If you recall, I originally set out for Havenfall, intent on finding the death speaker. So, with the situation in Bard's Bay resolved, we took a ship to the eastern shores of the Vale, intent on crossing it to reach the Sylvan capital. In the heart of that dangerous, wild valley, I found what I was searching for among fairies and brownies."

"Hold on." His gaze intense, Truhan leaned toward Ian. "Are you speaking of Fae Gulch?"

"That's right."

The man sat back with a snort. "I find that highly unlikely. The fairy village is protected by magic that makes it impossible to discover unless you are Fae yourself."

Ian wanted to ask how he had heard of Fae Gulch but instead chose to forge ahead. "In truth, I was abducted and taken there for violating one of their laws."

Lint piped up. "Ian brought fire to the Vale. I witnessed the whole thing. He should have died for that offense, but the elf princess saved him."

"The elf princess?" Truhan turned from Lint to Ian. "What elf princess?"

"Lint refers to Shria-Li, daughter of the king and queen of the Sylvan," Ian explained. "She had left her home in Havenfall and was living among the Fae."

"And this princess saved you? Why would she do that?"

"I had befriended her when she and her father visited Ra'Tahal last summer."

Truhan arched a brow. "Interesting."

Ian was uncertain how to reply to that, so he shoved it aside and continued his story. "Anyway, Shria-Li intervened and appealed to Tanaya, queen of the Fae, staving off my execution. Shortly after that, I discovered that Shria-Li was the death speaker."

In a rare display of surprise, Truhan flinched and blinked. "This person you sought was hidden in the one place a human could never find on their own?"

"Yeah. I guess."

"Yet, you ended up there anyway."

"Huh," Revita said. "Now that you say it, that was oddly convenient."

Truhan smirked and tapped the side of his nose before turning back to Ian. "Go on with your story."

"Well, I convinced the princess of the critical nature of my quest, but rather than travel by land all the way to Ra'Tahal, we decided to head to Havenfall. She would not explain how, but she promised the journey would take far less time going that route."

"From the Vale, Havenfall is in the opposite direction as Ra'Tahal."

"I said as much, but she was adamant. So, we recruited Lint to guide us through the Vale rather than risk those dangerous wilds on our own. During that journey, we came across this little guy." He stroked Lionel's head.

"I was going to ask about the fire drake."

"He is my companion. We are...connected."

"By your magic."

Ian shrugged. "I suppose so. The drake was in bad shape after being attacked by a giant willow."

"The widow willow?"

"You know of it?"

"I know how dangerous it is. How did you free it from the willow?"

"I sort of...destroyed the willow."

Truhan snickered. "Oh, that will piss him off for sure."

Revita asked, "Piss who off?"

"Never mind that," the man waved it off. "So, you destroyed the willow, rescued your pocket dragon, and then what?"

"We eventually made it to Havenfall." Ian recalled his argument with Fastellan but chose to omit that aspect of the story. "The next morning, we traveled to Ra'Tahal and met with King Korrigan."

"In one day?"

"Um..." *I promised not to reveal the secret of the portal stones.* "Yes."

"How could you have traveled such a distance in a day?"

"I will show you." Ian pushed his chair back, scooped up Lionel, and stood.

The drake raised its head, its eyes half open. Reaching out, Ian gathered his magic and crafted a portal. It opened to reveal the hall of testing, repeating the exact location of their arrival minutes earlier. Ian lifted Lionel and sent a thought. *Go. Fly through. Follow the tunnel and return to me.*

The drake extended its wings, sailed through the gateway, and continued across the spacious chamber. When Lionel faded through the dark opening at the far end, Ian dismissed the gateway. It collapsed in with a pop. A moment later, Lionel banked through the kitchen doorway and floated over to land on Ian's forearm.

Turning, Ian found his master's brows raised.

Truhan asked, "You have discovered a spell for translocation?"

"Yes."

"How?"

"I…" Ian recalled his promise to Shria-Li. "I cannot explain it exactly. It is one of numerous new spells I developed during my journey."

"I see," Truhan said evenly.

Anxious to avoid further questioning on the subject, Ian sat back down with Lionel on his lap and resumed his account. "When we arrived in Ra'Tahal, we appealed to King Korrigan to allow us into the catacombs below the Hall of Ancients. It took some doing, but he was able to gain us access. There, Korrigan led me and Shria-Li to Gahagar's tomb. She woke him and…"

"You actually spoke to Gahagar?"

Ian recalled the conversation with the dead dwarf's rotting, skeletal corpse. "It was a creepy experience, but yeah."

"And?"

"He told us that the Paragon was hidden someplace called the Tower of Solitude."

Truhan leaned forward and gripped Ian by the wrist. "You located the tower?"

"Yes, deep in the ice fields to the distant south."

"Ah," The man closed his eyes and sat back in his chair. He opened them and nodded. "So, that is where he hid it."

Ian asked, "You have been searching for the tower?"

"Many have searched for the tower."

"Why?"

Truhan furrowed his brow for a beat before replying, "Legend says that it is the home of the god, Vandasal."

Parsigar cackled. "Only sometimes."

"So, he does spend time there?"

"Yes," the old dwarf said. "But I rarely saw him. Oftentimes, years would pass before he would visit the tower's lower levels, and I was not allowed to venture in the upper reaches."

"I am not surprised. He has always been secretive, even with those he pretends to befriend."

Ian frowned. "How do you know this?"

Truhan leaned back and shrugged. "I have read as much in stories, but who truly knows what motivates a god?"

The old dwarf nodded. "Indeed."

"So, this tower is where you found Parsigar."

"Yes," Ian said. "But not until we overcame a few obstacles."

Vic snorted. "I'd call a fire breathing dragon, a deadly labyrinth, and a chamber full of killer statues more than obstacles."

"A dragon?" Truhan turned to Ian. "How did you defeat a dragon? They are immune to elemental magic."

"As I discovered. In fact, things appeared dire until I came up with the idea to use myself as bait and craft a gateway just before the creature ate me. It flew through the opening and smashed into a pile of rocks on the other side. Vic then spoke with the monster, who told us how to get inside the tower. Without that information, we might still be attempting to breach the building."

Turning toward Vic, Truhan asked, "You spoke with a dragon?"

"I did."

"Dragons are aloof and care little for the problems of others. Why would the dragon speak with a human like you?"

"We have a sort of...connection."

"I am curious as to how that could happen."

"So am I, but I assume it has something to do with me caring for a giant dragon egg and being there when it hatched."

Truhan stroked his chin in thought. "Incredible, but I believe you are correct." He turned to Ian. "That is quite the tale, but what do you intend to do now?"

Ian glanced at Vic, who nodded. "Vic and I need to visit Nor'Tahal."

"Why?"

"When we returned to Ra'Tahal with Parsigar, we learned that a messenger had arrived earlier that day from Nor'Tahal. There was an incident in the keep's kitchen." Ian's throat tightened. He wiped his eyes. "Our mother was injured."

"Your mother." Truhan sighed. "Is she well?"

Ian opened his mouth to talk, but tears emerged rather than words.

In a somber tone, Revita said, "She was burned. Badly."

Vic cleared his throat. Like Ian, he was obviously choked up but able to maintain more composure. "Their healers have been treating her, but we are urged to visit as soon as possible."

"I see." Truhan took a deep breath. "You intend to leave, then."

"Yes. Within the hour."

Ian wiped his eyes dry with the sleeve of his robes, sniffled, and took a deep breath. "We hoped we could leave Parsigar here."

"Speaking of the dwarf," Truhan turned his gaze on Parsigar. "You have found the Paragon, but how will that help fight the rising darkness?"

"Ah," Parsigar said. "I was wondering when you would arrive at that question."

"I was trying to be polite."

"All things have their time. Attempt too quickly or wait too long, either can result in error. The moment in which you act is often as important as the action itself."

Truhan narrowed his eyes. "I tell Ian the very same thing."

"You show wisdom. Since you were polite, I will now reveal my intentions." Parsigar raised his chin while stroking his thinning white beard. "I am a master of many crafts. Ian has appealed to me to use my skills to produce an item of power, to which I agreed. I have been watching while he utilizes his magic, but until I understand it, I am unable to begin."

Turning to Ian, Truhan said, "I can see why you brought the old dwarf here."

"Will you help him?"

"Help him understand your magic? In the entire world, there is likely nobody better suited to do so other than yourself. If you must be otherwise occupied, then I must do my part to ensure our success."

Relieved, Ian sighed. He had been worried about asking and was thankful for Parsigar broaching the subject as he had. "Now that it has been addressed, we need to leave."

TRUHAN FROWNED. "HAVE YOU EATEN YET?"

"No," Ian admitted.

"If you plan to travel to Nor'Tahal, you will need your strength."

Vic nodded. "Truhan has a point. Your magic will do us little good if you weaken from a lack of food."

A soft whistle arose, steadily growing louder. "It sounds like the tea is ready." Ian lifted Lionel off his lap and set him on the chair as he stood. With his concerns for his mother shoved to the back of his mind, he focused on the moment and asked, "Who would care for a cup of tea before breakfast?"

CHAPTER 3
NOR'TAHAL

With a full stomach and a pack on one shoulder, Victus Carpenter followed Ian, Lint, and Revita down a dark tunnel. The brief visit to Truhan's underground lair did little to alleviate his concern for his mother. Despite his outward calm, the idea of losing her was a constant ache that gnawed at his heart. He suspected his brother was troubled in a similar manner, but neither spoke of it. That was not their way. Instead, they both wore brave faces and laughed at jokes, pretending to ignore the pain.

The glass globe in Ian's hand emitted a pale purple glow that ate away the gloom and cast shadows along the tunnel walls behind him. The light revealed a dead end, blocked by a wall of stone. A bronze plate and sconce graced the wall to Ian's right. He approached the sconce, set the orb in it, and the light brightened five-fold. When he pressed his hand against the metal plate, a rumble shook the ground and the stone door blocking the route swung open. Daylight beckoned ahead.

The party passed through the opening, into a cave with the entrance partially blocked by a boulder. Once everyone was through, Ian closed the door and then led them outside. They slid between the boulder and the cliff wall before emerging on a flat shelf of gray rock, where they stopped to survey the horizon.

A thousand feet below, the plains of the Agrosi stretched out to the east while the peak of Mount Tiadd loomed behind them. The mountains to the north, the forest to the east and south, and the rolling fields of grass between it all painted a gorgeous vista.

Ian pointed southeast, toward a ridge barely visible through the haze of distance. "Ra'Tahal is located on that ridgeline."

Lint peered in that direction. "Isn't that where we were this morning?"

"That's right."

"How far away is it?"

"I can't say for certain, but it takes four days to reach it by foot." Ian then turned northeast. "That way is Nor'Tahal."

For a full minute, Ian stared in that direction, stirring Vic's concern for him. *He is worried about mother as well.* When Revita nudged Vic, he noted her nodding toward Ian, wordlessly telling him to intervene. He shook his head, preferring to avoid the topic. Her elbow jabbed him in the ribs, saying otherwise.

Rubbing his sore ribs, Vic turned toward his brother, who still stared into the distance. "Ian."

"Yes," Ian replied without turning.

"Are you alright?"

"I can't firmly recall what Nor'Tahal looked like. We will have to travel cross-country. I am seeking a unique marker for my first gateway."

"Oh," Vic was relieved to delay broaching the subject. "That's a good idea."

"There." Ian pointed toward a lonely oak resting on a hilltop near the edge of the plains. "I will target that tree."

When the portal appeared, Vic stepped through and waited while

Revita and Lint joined him, followed by Ian, who dismissed the gateway and sought a marker for the next.

VIC WATCHED his brother with concern. Although Ian claimed he was concentrating, he was quieter than normal and seemed to reply to questions with the briefest of possible answers. Throughout the day, Ian cast translocation spells, using the gateways to carry him and his party from one hilltop to another as they crossed the northern edge of the plains. Each leap covered one to five miles, which was far faster than any other form of travel, but the distance was considerable and Vic had to remind his brother time and again to take breaks to recover. He recalled how Ian's mind and body had shut down after he overextended himself in the past.

A river, its banks covered by trees and shrubs, ran along the Agrosi's northern border. Beyond the river, a tree-covered mountain range ran east and west, dominating the horizon. The group maintained a heading parallel to the river, using it as their guide. Vic recalled crossing that river during his prior visit to Nor'Tahal.

After hours of travel, the river turned north, and Ian adjusted accordingly. Four gateways later, a white bridge came into view. When Ian cast the next portal, the noise of rushing water came through the opening. As he often did, Vic stepped through the gateway first. With a single stride, he covered a distance exceeding two miles and emerged at the foot of a structure he had marveled upon seeing less than a year earlier. Made of alabaster stone with ornate murals carved into the walls along each side, the bridge was a work of splendor, but on this trip, the sight beyond the bridge is what held Vic's attention.

"There it is. Nor'Tahal."

Excited, Lint whooped and raced over the bridge while Vic, Ian, and Revita followed. A narrow gorge waited straight ahead, its walls covered in trees growing amid gray granite. A creek wound along the bottom of the gorge while a citadel built into the steep mountainside loomed above it. Dwarven warriors peered down from a wall bracketed by squat turrets.

The road split into routes leading east, west, and north, the latter winding up the side of the gorge opposite the citadel. The party followed switchbacks, rising above the gorge until the road came to a sudden end overlooking a crevice dividing the road from the fortress. Across a twenty-foot-gap was a tall, wooden door reinforced by thick bolts and strips of iron.

"Hello!" Vic shouted.

From the wall, a dwarf called back, "State your name and your purpose for visiting Nor'Tahal."

"I am Vic Carpenter. This is my brother, Ian...otherwise known as Barsequa Illian. We have come to visit our mother."

"Your mother?"

"She worked in the keep kitchen before..." The last word came out as a croak as Vic's throat constricted. Tears came, unbidden. He wiped them away and regained his composure.

"Who is the woman with you?"

"Her name is Revita Shalaan. She is my," Vic glanced at her. "She is my..."

Rather than help him out, she crossed her arms, arched her brow, and began tapping her foot. Somehow, Vic had backed himself into a corner, and he needed a way out. Unable to find a graceful way to complete his sentence, he tried a different route.

"She was among those who helped free Ra'Tahal from the Drow last year. She risked herself for your people. The least you can do is show her some courtesy."

The dwarf on the wall spoke to his companions, one of whom jogged over to the tower rising above the gate. Moments later, a cranking sound arose. The wooden door began to lower, creaking as it descended until it struck the near side of the chasm with a heavy thud. Lint darted across the drawbridge.

Vic glanced at his brother, who was staring through the citadel entrance, his expression somber. He reached out and lightly gripped Ian's arm. "I know this is hard, Ian. I feel as you do, but we must be strong...for mother."

Ian nodded numbly. "I know."

Dropping his hand, Vic took a deep breath to steel his own resolve. Somehow, he found the idea of seeing his mother in pain more difficult than rushing into battle. Concern held him back until Revita slid her hand into his. He turned toward her, but before he could thank her, she touched her finger to his lips, quieting him. Hand in hand, they headed across the drawbridge with Ian trailing, passing beneath the gate tower and into the citadel interior.

A busy square with a fountain in the middle welcomed them. To the left, right, and straight ahead were narrow streets bordered by walls and buildings of gray stone.

A dwarf dressed in studded leather armor stood between the citadel entrance and the fountain. His salt and pepper beard, wrinkles, and bushy eyebrows spoke of his age. The grimace he wore said more about his mood. The dwarf held one hand out before him. From that hand dangled a tiny person who kicked and spun while being held up by the back of his brown toga.

"Help!" Lint squealed. "Put me down!"

The dwarf said, "Is this little man yours?"

"I am no man!" Lint snapped back. "I am a brownie."

The dwarf's scowl deepened. "What in the blazes is a brownie?"

Vic approached the dwarf. "Master Ogglegon. It is good to see you again." The lie tasted bad on his tongue, but he thought it better to use honey than vinegar.

"You know me?"

"We visited last year, with Korrigan and Vargan."

"You refer to *King* Korrigan and *Captain* Vargan."

As Vic recalled, Ogglegon had been argumentative with Korrigan, showing him no love during that visit, yet he now stood up for the newly crowned king.

"Drop me, you big buffoon!" Lint swiped with his arms, as if trying to punch the dwarf holding him. Of course, he only found air since the dwarf's arm was ten times as long as the brownie's.

Revita said, "The brownie you are holding is our friend, Ogglegon. You can put him down. He won't be any trouble." She narrowed her eyes at Lint. "You *will* be good, won't you?"

Lint's arms dropped to his sides. "Fine. I will be good."

Ogglegon bent and dropped Lint the last foot. The brownie stumbled, turned and raised a fist.

"Lint..." Revita chided.

The brownie backed from the dwarf. "You are lucky my mistress is here to protect you."

"Mistress?" Ogglegon asked.

"Never mind him," Revita said.

With the situation in hand, Vic's thoughts returned to his mother. "We have come to visit Zora Carpenter. Can you tell us where to find her?"

"The cook?"

"Yes."

Ogglegon's scowl softened, as did his gruff tone. "She is in the healer's ward. I will escort you there."

When the dwarf turned away, Vic glanced at his brother. Ian's silence and numb stares worried him. Before losing sight of his escort, he took Revita's hand and led the party across the square and into a narrow street. Various scents came and went as they headed deeper into the hold, beginning with the delightful smell of freshly baked bread, immediately followed by the spiced aroma of roasted pig. Soon enough, the pleasant scents faded, replaced by a muskiness and the faint odor of manure. The party passed dwarves, goats, chickens, and pigs while on their way to the blocky, daunting keep at the rear of the complex. Instead of heading for the keep entrance, they walked toward a building at the base of the cliff wall. Made of gray stone, rectangular in shape, and only one story tall, the structure appeared rather plain compared to the rest of the city.

Their dwarven escort led them inside, where Vic stopped to survey the chamber.

A single room encompassed the building's interior, faint daylight emitting from dozens of narrow windows to the left and the right. A small bed stood below each window and a nightstand was positioned between each set of beds. Eight of the twenty-four beds were occupied. Dwarves, some sleeping, others bandaged, lay still. Those who were awake stared at Vic and his companions.

A person, his or her identity blocked from view, occupied a bed at the far end of the room. An elderly dwarf sat beside the bed, leaning over the patient.

Ogglegon spoke in a quiet voice. "I believe your mother is in the far bed. The healer seated beside the bed is Havaar. He has been waiting for you." With a nod, he walked back outside.

The door closed and silence crashed in. Vic's stomach churned at the thought of what might wait for him at the far end of the room. He forced his feet into motion, heading toward the dwarf bent over the bed. Having Ian and Revita at his sides offered a slice of solace. Dwarves and humans lying on the other beds watched silently as the three of them crossed the room.

As they drew near, the dwarf leaned back and released a deep sigh. Wisps of white hair draped down from the back of his otherwise bald head.

The old dwarf turned toward Vic and flinched. "Oh. You startled me." His white beard rested against his chest. Wrinkles marking the passing of many years framed his round face.

Vic glanced at the bed. A sheet covered the patient's body while bandages were wrapped around the head. He still could not tell if it was his mother. "Are you Havaar?"

"I am."

"My name is Vic Carpenter. This is my brother, Ian."

"Thank Vandasal you have finally arrived."

Vic swallowed the lump in his throat, yet his words came out as a weak croak. "We came for our mother."

Havaar turned toward the bed. "She was badly burned. It has taken all of our skill just to keep her alive. Had the holdmaster not insisted, we healers would have allowed her to pass days ago."

Fearing the worst was one thing. Realizing it was another. Unprepared for such dire news, Vic staggered and sat on the neighboring bed. Numb, he stared into space while memories of his mother danced through his mind. His father had died in an explosion only a year earlier. To lose his mother in a similar way...

Revita crouched in front of Vic, taking his hand. "I am sorry."

Vic turned to the dwarf. "Can she talk?"

"She sleeps deeply." Havaar shook his head. "I do not know if she will wake again. It has been days since she last stirred."

"So, this is it." Vic closed his eyes.

He did not want to cry. Fighting an angry villain or a terrifying monster was far easier than this. When he opened them, he found Ian standing on the opposite side of his mother's bed, his expression unreadable as he stared down at her. Ian reached out, gripped her scarred, blistered hand, and closed his eyes.

"Ian?" Vic waited a beat. "Ian? What are you doing?"

Silence.

Concerned, Vic stood.

Havaar gasped. "He uses magic. I can feel it."

Not knowing what to expect, Vic and the others watched and waited. Tense, quiet moments passed, and then his mother suddenly jerked. She stiffened and convulsed. Her eyes blinked open and she gasped.

With a glance toward each brother, only her eyes moving, a ragged whisper came out. "Ian. Vic."

Vic dropped to one knee and took her other hand, that one wrapped in bandages. "Hello, Mother."

In a scratchy, weak voice, she said, "Thank the good spirits." She paused. "You are here." She closed her eyes and tears emerged as she opened them. "I prayed... to see you one last time."

"We came as quickly as we could."

"I love you." She rasped. "You make me proud."

Tears came, unbidden, but Vic allowed them to track down his face. "You and Pa raised us to be good people. Without you, I don't know..." His throat tightened and the words refused to emerge.

Zora said, "I'm sorry,"

Vic shook his head. "Don't be sorry. It isn't your fault."

"The flames spread so fast... Kitchen workers were trapped. I tried to save them... The smoke was so thick..." she sobbed.

"You did the right thing, Mother."

"I should have run for help."

During the entire exchange, Ian's eyes remained closed while holding his mother's hand.

She rasped, "When you have children, tell them about me."

"I will. I promise." He wiped tears from his cheeks. "Does it hurt?"

"At first, it was agony, but now, I feel nothing."

For that, Vic was thankful. He pulled her hand to his lips and kissed it. "I love you, Mother."

She lifted a shaky hand, her exposed fingers stroking his cheek. "Be well, Victus." Tears filled her glossy eyes. "Follow your heart. It will not lead you astray."

"I don't want to lose you." More tears flowed down his face.

"I'm with you in spirit...in the form of a birdsong...a passing butterfly...the whisper of the wind." She gasped and shook. "My strength...it wanes."

Vic glanced up and found his brother shaking, his teeth clenched. Still, his eyes remained closed, his voice silent.

Zora softly said, "Your father waits. I now join him."

"Mother..."

"I love you...boys." Voice trailing off, her arm fell limp, her body stilling as she slipped away.

Ian dropped the other hand and staggered. Lionel's eyes rolled up and he toppled off Ian's shoulder to land on the bed. Stumbling backward, Ian fell against the wall and slid down to the floor. His head flopped over, and he did not move.

"Ian!" Vic cried.

Vic numbly stared out the window while the gloom of evening claimed hold of Nor'Tahal. His mother was gone, and he would miss her dearly, but his concerns had now shifted to his brother.

He turned from the window, his gaze lingering on his mother's bed. The sheet had been pulled up to cover her completely, and although her body was clearly still on the bed, there was an emptiness there, the sense that her spirit had moved on. He wrestled with sorrow threatening to overwhelm him and approached the bed adjacent to hers. The old dwarf seated beside it lifted his gaze to look up at Vic.

"I am sorry." Havaar shook his head.

"What ails him?"

"I do not know. His body is whole, but his pulse is weak, his breathing shallow. Despite my efforts, I receive no response."

Ian lay unmoving on the bed, with only the gentle rise and fall of his chest as a sign of life. The fire drake had been placed on the bed neighboring Ian's. Like his master, Lionel had been unresponsive for the past two hours.

Vic approached Ian, gripped his shoulder, and shook him. "Ian. Ian. It's me, Vic. Wake up."

The old dwarf sighed. "As I said before, shaking him will do you no good."

"Well, something must be wrong with him, or he would wake."

"When I delve to seek out his ailments, I find nothing except…"

"Except what?"

"It is as if his spirit is wounded."

"His spirit?" Vic spun toward the old dwarf. "How can that be?"

"I do not know."

"Can you heal his spirit?"

"I cannot." The healer shook his head, his eyes sad. "In fact, I have never even heard of such a thing."

The door to the Healer Ward opened, Revita stepped in and Lint skipped past her. A middle-aged dwarf with a thick beard and piercing blue eyes walked in.

"Targaron." Vic recalled the dwarf from his previous visit to Nor'Tahal.

Havaar stood and bowed as the other dwarf crossed the room. "Welcome, Holdmaster."

"There is no need for titles, Havaar. We are all friends here." Targaron stopped at the foot of Zora's bed. "I heard that she passed."

"Yes." Havaar gestured toward Ian. "Her son now teeters on the edge of death."

"Death?" The word had never tasted worse on Vic's tongue.

"His body is weak and does not respond to my magic. The longer this continues, the less likely it will be for him to return to us."

"But he has only been here for a few hours."

"The longer he is in this state, the less likely it is for him to recover. Should it persist and he slips any deeper, I fear he will not return."

Vic covered his eyes to fight off the tears. "How did this happen?"

With his mother's passing, Ian was his only remaining family. Now, he lay in bed, teetering on the edge of death. Vic had never felt so helpless.

An arm slid around his waist. He lowered his hand to find Revita standing there.

From his side, Revita softly suggested, "Perhaps it would be good to step away for a bit."

"And go where?"

"Targaron has invited us to dine with him. You need to eat."

"I suppose so." Although Vic's reply was apathetic, his stomach reacted to the idea with more enthusiasm, the rumble audible in the quiet room.

"See." Revita smiled. "Food will make you feel better."

"Ale as well." Targaron gave a firm nod. "In fact, I will open a new barrel."

Vic glanced back at Ian. Nothing had changed, nor had he expected it to change. "I guess there is nothing I can do here, anyway."

After being uncharacteristically quiet, as if aware of Vic's pain, Lint piped up. "What is ale?"

Targaron gaped down at the brownie. "You don't know about ale?"

"No. I don't think we have that in the Vale."

"Well, come along my little friend. You are in for a delightful evening."

The holdmaster headed toward the door while Lint skipped alongside him. Revita took Vic's hand and pulled him into motion. His feet followed without him giving thought. Still numb, he walked out the door, and although his body had left the room, his thoughts remained on his mother and brother.

CHAPTER 4
DEEP ROOTED CONCERNS

S hria-Li strolled aimlessly through the palace garden. The Tree of Life towered over her, the glow of its golden bark holding the shadows at bay. Many hundreds of feet tall and as broad at its base as a house, it was the largest tree in Havenfall, which was saying something, for the Sylvan capital was the home of the world's tallest trees.

The path brought her to the tranquil pool surrounding the tree. She knelt at the water's edge, rested her knees on soft, green turf, and leaned forward. The image of a female elf reflected in the still pool's surface – her pale hair held back by a headband made of twisted olive branches to expose her pointed ears, the sharply sculpted facial features of her race, and angled eyes of gold. Most would call her attractive. Some would even consider her beautiful. That face should not belong to her, for it felt like a mask. If one peered deeply into those eyes, they would find a troubled person, caught between the duty weighing upon her, the desire to be free and live life as she wished, and a third trait far darker and more disturbing.

"I was free once," she whispered to her reflection. "Even then, fate tracked me down and pulled me back in."

For Ian to find her in Fae Gulch, a secret place guarded by magic and buried in the heart of the Vale, nothing short of fate could have been behind their reconnection. Her time with the Fae had come to an end. Despite her wish to deny her dark ability, Shria-Li was forced to reveal herself as the death speaker.

"And now, I am back with my people and more trapped than ever before."

A female voice came from behind her. "Did you say something, Princess?"

Shria-Li rose to her feet and turned toward the speaker. A pair of armored palace guards, both female, stood ten strides away, watching. They were always watching. Each held a spear in one hand with the spear butt on the ground. "It was nothing, Daisha-Lu." She approached the two guards. "I am finished here."

Daisha-Lu, her hair hidden by a helmet that matched the blue of her eyes, nodded. "We will escort you back to your chambers."

Shria-Li's gaze shifted past the arches overlooking the garden, beyond the bulk of the palace proper, to the narrow tower jutting above and partially eclipsing the moon, bright against the darkening sky. That tower housed her private chambers – her prison.

In a tone that commanded respect, she said, "I prefer to visit the throne room."

"Princess, you know you are strictly forbidden to…"

She spun toward the guards and snapped. "I would speak with my father. If he is not there, we will look for him elsewhere." When the two guards looked at each other, she added, "You'll have to kill me if you wish to stop me."

Daisha-Lu frowned. "This goes against our orders. You know that."

"Orders given to you days ago."

"Yes, but that doesn't mean the orders have changed."

"Nobody understands the punishment issued by the king more than I, but now that he has had a few days for his anger to quell, I wish to appeal to him." Shria-Li sensed the guards' reluctance and altered her approach. "Admit it, you would prefer any assignment other than shadowing me day and night."

The two guards shared another look before Daisha-Lu nodded. "We will escort you to the king. I trust that you will bear the brunt of his anger rather than place blame upon us."

"You have nothing to worry about."

"Thank you, Your Highness." She gestured with her spear. "Let's go see if the king is still in the throne room."

They followed a curved path bordered by flowering shrubs, climbed the stairs to the terrace overlooking the garden, and headed down a walkway lined by arches open to the night. Opposite of the arches was a solid wall with sporadic alcoves occupied by tall vases from which golden trees bloomed. In her youth, Shria-Li used to hide in those alcoves. That was a simpler time, back before the weight of her obligation began to suffocate her. The terrace brought them to a shadowy corridor with light looming ahead.

The palace entrance hall was a grand space surrounded by doors and terraces. The trickle of water from a bubbling fountain echoed in the quiet hall. Cascading water flowed down a multi-tiered sculpture and spilled into a pool surrounding the trunk of a small tree. The tree's bark, branches, and leaves, all glowed with a golden aura that illuminated the hall with soft light. As a child, she had been taught that the entrance hall was the place where she was to turn serious, to remain quiet and to display respect before entering the chamber at the rear of the hall. Through nearby arches, the last moments of daylight bathed the palace courtyard in purple haze soon to turn black.

Shria-Li, trailed by her jailors, approached the throne room door. It stood open with a pair of palace guards bracketing it.

"Greetings, Princess," one of the guards said.

"I would speak with my father."

"The king and queen are inside, speaking with Captain Rozenne."

"I will wait inside, by the door." Before they could respond, she stepped inside. As expected, her shadowing guards joined her.

A pair of trees twice the size of the one in the entrance hall illuminated the throne room. The branches of those glowing trees extended toward the other and wove together to create a pair of seats elevated above a circular dais. On one throne sat her father, Fastellan. On the other was her mother, Tora-Li. Before them stood Rozenne, the new Captain of the Valeguard.

The trio in the throne room spoke softly, their voices all but drowned by the running water coming through the open doorway behind Shria-Li. The scene stirred a memory, back when Chavell was captain of the palace guard – back before he betrayed his oath by plotting to kill his own queen. At the time, the human girl, Safrina, had recently come to Havenfall, albeit against her will. *My, how much has changed since then?*

Rozenne bowed, turned, and descended the dais. With his winged helm in his arm, he climbed the sloped floor as he made his way toward the door. "Greetings, princess."

"Is all well with the barrier?"

"I..." He glanced backward. "I am sorry. I must go and meet with the evening squad before the shift change." Before Shria-Li had a chance to reply, Rozenne walked past, her own guards saluting him before he was gone.

While his lack of a response made her concerned, Shria-Li had her own problems, so she turned her attention back to the two people on the dais. A deep breath to fortify her resolve set her feet into motion. Her parents watched her descend along the sloped floor, pass row upon row of benches, and approach the dais, their eyes judging her in every way.

She stopped at the foot of the stairs and dipped her head. "Mother. Father. I beg you for a brief discussion."

Tora-Li arched her brow but remained silent.

"Shria-Li," Fastellan nodded. His golden eyes remained fixed upon her. Tall and lean with broad shoulders for his kind, chiseled features, and long platinum hair held back by his crown, most would deem him handsome, elven or otherwise. "If you have something to say, do so."

"I want to know how long you intend to keep me imprisoned."

Her father gestured toward the door. "We wish to speak with our daughter alone. You are dismissed for the evening." When the guards were gone, he turned his attention back toward Shria-Li. I see no bars holding you in. Regardless of how you might feel, a stay in the palace dungeon would be a much harsher sentence."

"Still, I have learned my lesson." Her gaze flicked to the twisted wooden staff standing between the two thrones. "Although I firmly believe I did the right thing, I will never again take the Staff of Life without your permission."

Her father reached for the staff and pulled it from its stand. "This staff is not yours or mine to do with as we wish. It is intended to protect our people. Not only did you defy me, but you were reckless in doing so. What if the city were attacked while you were away? What if the barrier had failed completely? What if..."

"I know." She took a breath, intent on remaining calm. "You don't need to make a list of what might have occurred. However, I tried to explain why it was critical for me to use the staff. As I told you, I am convinced I was in the right in this case, regardless of what you fear might have happened."

He pressed his lips together, preparing to berate her but was interrupted by Tora-Li.

"I commend you for having faith in your convictions, Daughter." Her mother smiled. The smile appeared forced, as if foreign to her. "We wished you to understand the gravity of your actions. Five days of close supervision with most of those hours locked in your quarters is sufficient. You are freed from this burden. I only ask that you avoid straying near the barrier and that you remain in Havenfall."

Fastellan's eyes widened. He thumbed his chest. "I am king."

Tora-Li snapped back. "And I am queen."

"We are to rule together…"

"Yet, you wish to chase after a human who is little more than a girl rather than honor your commitment to your wife."

Fastellan burst to his feet, the volume of his voice rising. "How long will you hold that over me?'

"I suspect until one of us dies. Maybe longer."

With his hands balled into fists, he stomped down the dais stairs, up the aisle, and through the exit. The door slammed shut behind him with a resounding boom.

Tora-Li stood and spoke with her chin held high. "I will tell the guards they can return to their regular duties."

"Thank you, Mother."

"Your liberty is your father's doing as much as my own. Had he been able to keep to his oaths, I would not be so quick to release you from your punishment."

Shria-Li frowned. "You did so just to spite him?"

Tora-Li straitened her pale, yellow skirts. "He has much to pay, to make up for how he hurt and embarrassed me. This is only one of a thousand lashes he can yet expect."

With the grace of a queen, she glided down the stairs and up the aisle. The door opened and drifted closed, the sound of it clicking shut barely audible.

The frustration of Shria-Li's brief incarceration was replaced by concern for her parents' relationship.

She plopped down to sit on the dais stairs and rested her head in her hands. "What am I going to do?"

There was no response.

CHAPTER 5
LONESOME

Safrina Miller followed a quartet of dwarves across Shadowmar Castle's grand hall and out of the massive double doors at the front of the building. She stepped out beneath a pale blue sky and pulled her cloak in tight to shield herself from the morning chill. Although it was the heart of summer, the evenings were cold and the air did not warm enough for her to shed the cloak until an hour or two after sunrise.

She stood at the top of the short run of stairs outside the front entrance. The castle courtyard was huge, stretching out before her up to the enclosing castle walls. It was paved in smoothed stone, with two sunken gardens surrounded by stone benches. Solitary columns and statues stood around those benches to create outdoor spaces for private discussions or moments of solace. At the midpoint of the walls to either side of the castle yard were staircases rising two stories to the top of the wall, along which two elven guards paced. Another pair stood by the open castle gate at the far end of the yard.

.   .   .

A DOZEN STRIDES from the front stoop where Rina stood, a score of dwarves gathered around a pair of carts. The dwarves spoke to each other in their native language while discussing their journey from Shadowmar to Shai Aeldor. At least, that is what Rina assumed. After many weeks of study and practice, she had grown comfortable in speaking Elvish, but the dwarves had an odd accent and their language, albeit related to that of the elves, remained beyond her.

The dwarves broke from their huddle. Two climbed into the seats of each cart while the others headed across the sprawling courtyard. Even as his comrades made for the castle gate, one dwarf – the only one among them who spoke fluent Elvish – turned and approached.

"Mistress Safrina," he said. "I want to thank you for your hospitality. Although we are saddened to leave you, we are eager to return to our homes and families."

"I understand Taskerbon. Were I in your shoes, I would be eager to depart as well."

"When King Fastellan returns, I trust that he will be satisfied, for all elements of the castle and the treasure chamber were completed to the agreed specifications."

"I am certain that he will be pleased with your work." She gestured. "Look at this courtyard. The statues and columns are a testament to the skills of your team."

"You are too kind." Taskerbon glanced over his shoulder. "As I said, we must go. Perhaps we will meet again."

"I pray Vandasal wills it to be so." Although Rina did not believe in the god, she had adopted the saying when dealing with the elves or dwarves who did believe in him.

"Well said." The dwarf walked off and waved over his shoulder. "Farewell, Mistress."

She remained on the castle stairs and watched as he caught up to his companions at the castle gate and crossed over the bridge spanning the chasm that divided the castle from the mountain. The elves manning the iron gate pushed it closed, the thud of the bar securing it conveying a sense of finality.

With a sigh, Rina turned and went back inside.

She closed the door and wandered to the center of the grand hall, where she stopped and listened. A heavy silence loomed. The sounds of workers shaping stone and hauling debris had filled those halls since her arrival a week earlier. Now, the dwarves were gone, leaving her alone with a dozen elven guards, most of whom were still asleep, one elven cultivator, and three human servants. The building might only be a quarter of the size of Havenfall Palace, but it was still massive for its limited inhabitants.

When first told that she would leave Havenfall for Shadowmar, Safrina had embraced the idea. Not only would she no longer be forced to face the queen's endless scrutiny but being far from Havenfall meant that she and Fastellan could be together, as he had promised her so many times. She pictured herself waking each day in his arms, standing on a balcony with his arm around her while watching the sunset, and cuddling with him before the fireplace on a cold winter day. Such musings filled her unoccupied hours, which were many. Too many. Fastellan had promised that he would join her soon, but with the days passing so slowly, it began to feel as if she may never see him again. Rather than bringing her closer to the life of her dreams, coming to Shadowmar had, thus far, only brought her aching loneliness. Having the dwarves gone as well only increased her feeling of unwanted solitude.

Rina advanced deeper into the hall, her slippered feet barely making a noise on the marble-tiled floor. As she passed the sitting area, she ran her right hand across the dark red velvet pillows along the back of the sofa. The three padded chairs across the sitting area were empty, the low table between them occupied only by a closed book on mountain wildlife. The mouth of the stone fireplace against the front wall stood dark and vacant, reminding her of an open maw, eager to consume the split logs stacked in the storage bay beside it. The door adjacent to the sitting area remained closed, the study behind it awaiting its master's return. Next door to the study was a parlor filled with books, weapons, and relics from around the world. Since her arrival at the castle, she had spent much of her alone time in that parlor, paging through books centuries old, most of which were written in Elvish with a handful crafted in her native language.

The long dining table across from the sitting area sat empty apart from a pair of dormant candelabras. A mere hour earlier, the table had been covered in plates, bowls, cups and crumbs from the dwarves seated around it. Rina already missed their jovial banter. She wondered if the vacant chairs felt the same sense of emptiness.

A pantry and a guest bedroom, both doors closed, lurked on the other side of the dining area. In the rear corners of the room, a pair of curved staircases rose up toward the castle's upper floors. At the midpoint between the two staircases, pillars bracketed an arched alcove. In that alcove was the most compelling feature of the complex – the door to the treasure chamber.

Rina approached the alcove. Aligning with the shape of the recess were a pair of doors forming an arch ten feet tall at the apex. The doors, painted black and reinforced by steel bands, were closed and would remain that way. She had been warned multiple times to avoid them. Even without the warning, the ominous text carved into the stone banner above the doorway would have given her pause. *Beware. He who enters with no right to pass shall die.*

She had pressed Taskerbon on three occasions, attempting to get him to reveal what secrets lurked beyond those doors. Despite her notable charms, which had never failed her before when males were involved, he remained steadfast that those secrets were not his to reveal.

"Mistress?" A voice called from her right.

"Yes?" Rina called back.

Footsteps came from the stairwell, and a woman wearing a gray dress and an apron emerged. She stood the same height as Rina but was twice her weight with brown hair, hazel eyes, and a plain yet kind face. "The guest rooms are all made. Is there anything else you require?"

"Thank you, Harriet. How are things looking in the kitchen?"

"Guster and Ned are almost finished washing the dishes. After that, Gus intends to begin making the mid-day meal."

Rina nodded. "Very well. All seems in order, so you may retire until it is time to eat. After our meal, I will let you know if anything else requires attention."

Harriet curtsied. "As you wish, Mistress." She then hurried up the stairs, her footsteps fading until she was gone.

The three human servants, each of them born to a life of slavery, appeared to quickly accept Rina as their mistress although she was not an elf. Rather than bringing her satisfaction, that position of power brought her additional guilt. *Who am I to command these people? They should be free to live as they wish.* Their deference toward her came with a cost. An emotional distance existed between Rina and the staff, making it clear that they would never be equals nor would they view her as a friend. That distance only increased her loneliness.

Without anything else to do. She wandered into the parlor and activated the enchanted lantern hanging by the door. Cool light bloomed and sent the shadows scurrying to the corners of the room.

Shelving covered three of the walls while two padded chairs and a circular table occupied the one nearest to the doorway. She approached one of the shelves, reached up, and randomly selected a book. The words *The Two Hundred Year reign of Bartellan the Wise* were embossed in the leather cover. With the book cradled against her, she curled up on the chair nearest to the lantern, opened the book, and began to read.

CHAPTER 6
GRUDGES

A pleasant north breeze cooled Shria-Li as she basked in the grace of Havenfall, the capital city of her people. She strolled down winding streets paved with flagstones, enjoying her reclaimed freedom. Elegant buildings connected by pale arches bordered the streets while trees and flowering shrubs grew amid the structures in a perfect balance of civilization and nature. Late morning sunlight gleamed off leaves of gold, copper domes, and white spires to create a stark contrast to the angled shadows and the deep blue sky. Birds tweeted, their song a harmony to the low thrum of people going about their day. Having grown up in Havenfall, she had often taken these things for granted. However, her newly arisen concerns about the future had her perceiving the world from a new perspective and forced her to appreciate the beauty and dignity of her people and their city.

The street she followed opened to a square surrounded by buildings and foliage. One side the square was busy with carts run by elves while human slaves purchased and carried goods back to the home of their owners. The sight reminded Shria-Li of Safrina. Until she had met the human girl, Shria-Li had not given much thought about slavery. It was merely a fact of life, as natural to her people as drinking water. The more she got to know Safrina, the more she became aware of the inherent inequity between elves and humans in her society. If the slaves were a subtle reminder, another sight across the square was a blunt one.

A building made of alabaster stone lay in ruins. A dozen men dressed in dust-covered clothing worked amid the rubble, using poles as levers to lift heavy chunks of marble into carts. A quartet of elves gripping shock lances with rounded tips monitored the slaves' progress.

A thriving apothecary filled with plants and herbs used to occupy the rubble-filled lot. The building had been one of the first places Shria-Li had taken Safrina after her arrival in Havenfall. Now, it was little more than a destroyed memory after a roc crashed down and collapsed its roof in. The sight of the ruins saddened Shria-Li, but the dirty, sweaty slaves forced to clean up the rubble broke her heart.

She turned from the scene, hoping to forget about it, but as she wandered back toward the palace, she found the injustice of the situation eating away at her like a parasite. It was as if her eyes were now open after a lifetime of walking among her people with them closed. Disturbed, she wondered what she could do to influence change. Slavery had become a core element of Sylvan culture, and she worried that it would take years or decades for her people to perceive it as wrong.

By the time she had finished mulling the situation over, she found herself strolling down a quiet palace corridor. Rather than head directly to her quarters, she decided she would pay a visit to her parents. First, she tried the throne room but found it empty. She then headed along a corridor leading outside.

In the palace garden, Valeria, High Priestess of Vandasal led a procession along a winding path bordered by lush, green shrubs covered in pink and purple flowers. The priestess wore the golden robes of her station, her white hair braided with spiraling strands of glowing, golden vines. A trail of seven clerics followed her, all female, all wearing robes of white. The procession took them to the water's edge, where the clerics spread out until all stood at the edge of the pool. Valeria raised her arms toward the massive tree looming above the garden, and then they began to sing. Their ethereal wordless aria filled the garden and produced tiny sparks of white light that danced amid the greenery.

The scene aroused memories of Shria-Li's testing ceremony – a ritual that had revealed her ability to speak to the dead. *The dark ability*, Valeria had called it before fleeing. A full year had passed since that fateful night, the same span since Shria-Li had last seen the High Priestess. *My parents are not here.* Shria-Li used it as an excuse to turn and leave, but deep down, she was terrified to face the high priestess.

She made for the nearest stairwell and ascended, intent on visiting the chambers her parents called home. When she reached the uppermost level of that portion of the palace, she heard shouts coming from the far end of the corridor. There, a quartet of guards stood outside the royal apartment. When Shria-Li drew near them, she found the chamber door closed. Shouting came from inside.

"Greetings, Princess," said one of the guards.

"What's going on?"

They looked at each other. "Perhaps you should see for yourself."

When the guards parted, she walked past them, opened the door, and stopped at the edge of the raised entrance of a spacious chamber. Opposite from where she stood, a wall of curved glass bowed out around an indoor garden with a bubbling fountain. A tree with golden leaves rose from the center of the fountain, the tree's upper reaches falling just shy of the ceiling, thirty-some feet above. Her father stood at one side of the room, picking armor off a rack beside an open door and then strapping it onto his body.

Near the fountain stood her mother, her arms straight and fists clenched at her sides. "You would abandon your people for your own selfish desires?"

He spun on her. "Selfish? It is you who is being selfish. Despite any promise I offer or gesture I make, you hold tight to the past and refuse to move forward."

"You were the one who broke vows and betrayed our marriage, yet you insist that I am the villain."

Fastellan grabbed his bracers off a shelf and clamped one onto his forearm. "You and I both know that our marriage was one of convenience. One we agreed to enter for the good of our people. We were to rule together and always put the good of the Sylvan first. Yet, in the past week, you have undermined my every action simply out of spite. In my eyes, that makes you the villain."

Her eyes flared in anger. "If I have caused you pain, I hope you understand that it is not nearly enough for what you have done."

"As you have made clear."

"So, rather than accept the consequences for your actions, you run away."

He finished strapping on his second bracer. "You do not allow me to share your bed. You spurn my every advance and show only contempt toward me when we are alone. I refuse to live in constant contrition with no hope for salvation."

"So, you choose to flee your responsibilities?"

"I choose to live a life of hope and joy rather than pain and torture, but it is not a choice of my own making. Your actions have driven me to this end." He picked his helmet off the top shelf, tucked it under his arm, and turned back toward her. "Rule well, Tora-Li. As of now, you are a queen without a king."

He stomped toward the stairs, ascended and walked past Shria-Li before disappearing out the door.

Stunned, Shria-Li had remained silent during the exchange. Only when he was gone and her mother's steely gaze met hers did she speak.

"What did you do, Mother?"

"I did nothing. It was your father's weakness that destroyed everything."

Pressing her hand to her head, Shria-Li tried to gather her thoughts. "Yet, when I took the Staff of Life against your will, you forgave me after a few days."

Her mother snapped. "His transgressions are a thousand times worse. I will never forgive him. Never!"

Shria-Li shook her head. "Then it is over. If you will never forgive him, why would he come back?"

Rather than reply, her mother crossed her arms and walked into her bedroom slamming the door shut. While the bubbling fountain filled the heavy silence left in her wake, it did nothing to sooth Shria-Li's heavy heart.

Her father's declaration to leave the city was reason enough to dismiss her concerns for her mother. She rushed to the door, opened it, and ran down the corridor. A descending stairwell took her to the ground floor and the corridor at the bottom brought her toward the rear of the palace. Upon reaching the door, she flung it open and stepped outside. With her skirts held up, she ran along a winding path to the stable yard, slowing down when she saw her father gesturing toward a pair of humans who were saddling his horse.

"Father!" Shria-Li called out as she reached the edge of the stable yard.

He turned toward her, his stern glare softening. "Shri." He frowned. "I am sorry you had to see that."

She approached and stopped a stride away. "I am sorry as well. If I did anything to make matters worse..."

He closed the gap and placed a hand on her shoulder. "You are not at fault in this. Do not assume blame, for none belongs to you."

"You are leaving." It was not a question.

"Yes."

"When will you be back?" Her voice cracked.

"I do not know."

"Where will you go?"

"I ride to Shadowmar."

Her next question came out as a whisper. "You go to see her, don't you?"

"I go where I am loved." Fastellan looked toward the palace. "I was an outsider when I married your mother and joined her in rule. Over the years, I thought I had gained goodwill among your mother's peers. Since my...transgressions, that has been erased. Your mother saw to that. If she had her way, every elf in Sylvanar would vilify me at every turn." He shook his head. "There is nothing here for me. Nothing except for you."

"You didn't answer me."

"I go to Shadowmar, and yes, Safrina waits for me there. There is no love for me here. Not anymore." He sounded sad. "Everyone wants to be loved. In this, I am not unique."

Spurned by his own wife, who did all she could to alienate him from his people, Shria-Li could not blame him for leaving. Yet, Safrina was her friend and for her to pursue Shria-Li's father felt like a betrayal of that friendship.

He gripped Shria-Li's shoulders. "Listen. You will always be my daughter, and I will always love you. Never will you be unwelcome in Shadowmar's halls. Come and see us when you are ready. Only then will my heart be full."

Turning away, he approached his horse, its saddlebags already packed, and climbed on. A stable hand gave Fastellan his helm, which he slid over his head. With a final nod toward his daughter, the former king of the Sylvan urged his horse into motion and rode off. He sat tall and proud in the saddle, swaying easily with the pace of his mount as sunlight gleamed off his gold and green armor.

Seeing the king ride through Havenfall had long been deemed as a proud and inspirational sight, yet all Shria-Li felt now was bitter sorrow. Tears streamed down her face as she watched her father ride away from the palace, never to return.

CHAPTER 7

THE RISING SHADOW

S tifling humidity caused Arangoli Handshaw to sweat. Profusely. With his back against a tree trunk, he sat beneath branches that spread out in all directions like a giant umbrella, casting him and his dwarf companions in shade. Even then, the heat and thick air constricted and choked the energy out of the small fighting squad. As he had countless times during recent days, Arangoli wiped the sweat from his brow. In his discomfort, sleep eluded him, yet he needed to rest. It would be another long night of travel. He shifted his position, but it didn't help, the uneven ground and the knots in the tree needling him to distraction. Eventually, he gave up on sleep, opened his eyes, and rose to his feet.

In the long grass before him lay the nine dwarves known as the Head Thumpers. Like him, each was dressed in armor, many of them wearing leather with metal plates, others in chainmail. Eyes closed, some slept on their sides, others on their backs. The rumble of snores came from more than one of the exhausted travelers. Those warriors had faith in Arangoli's skills and his ability to keep them alive regardless of the enemy they faced or their odds of survival. Even Arangoli had begun to believe that his team was invincible until a deadly confrontation four days earlier when Brannigan, one of his squad members, had fallen victim to the poisonous talons of a new and fearsome enemy. Orcs.

Although Arangoli was unfamiliar with the monsters prior to discovering them below the Drow city of Talastar, Brannigan's instant death to orc venom left a lasting impression. In fact, the incident had plagued him, lingering at the edge of his thoughts, day and night. Images of slashing talons, foaming mouths, and bleeding eyes haunted his dreams. It had taken days for Arangoli to acknowledge the startling truth. He was scared. It was a foreign emotion, and a feeling he would never voice aloud. Dwarves were a proud people, and Arangoli was a dwarf through and through.

Seeking something to focus upon rather than dwell on his fears, he lifted his gaze to survey the surroundings.

Yellow grass covered the rolling plains around him while, here and there, lonely trees dotted the landscape. Branches spread out at the top of each squat tree trunk, giving the trees the appearance of mushrooms with flat tops. Other than the grass wavering in the warm wind, nothing moved. To the east and just below the hilltop where the dwarves camped, a river cut through the grasslands and flowed north. A quarter mile upstream, a wooden bridge spanned the river. Moving slowly, Arangoli rounded the rather significant tree trunk, peering into the distance.

Brown and green mountains defined the southern horizon. The mountain range ran northwest and was known for its rocky cliffs and steep drops. To the west and north, grasslands stretched for many miles. A gravel road wound between rolling hills, splitting the grasslands as it wound its way toward the bridge.

The sun lingered in the western sky, the day gradually waning. Arangoli was anxious to resume their journey, but his crew needed rest, and he was reluctant to wake them before the sun touched the mountains to the west. Due to the heat, they had been traveling at night ever since departing from Talastar. The memory of the abandoned city caused him to turn his attention northwest. Although Talastar's dark walls were too distant to see, the sensations aroused by the eerie emptiness they had found in the abandoned Drow capital were too difficult to dismiss.

Then, something on the horizon drew his attention.

A black cloud bloomed. Even as he watched, the cloud spread. The formation was too dark to be a storm and too thick to be from a fire. The hair on his arms stood on end and a troubling sensation climbed his spine. Without a doubt, the gloom was unnatural and starkly troubling.

"Head Thumpers!" Arangoli bellowed. "Rouse yerselves!"

Dwarves opened their eyes and began to rise. Many stretched and yawned.

Gortch, his eyes at half mast, sat up, his thick, dark beard resting on his bulging paunch. He squinted at Arangoli while propping up his heavyset body with one arm. "The sun is still well above the mountains."

"Aye," Arangoli strode over to the tree trunk, squatted, and scooped up his pack and war hammer. "It'll be hot, but I'd prefer to get as many miles behind us as possible before nightfall."

"Why?"

"Look." A gesture toward the horizon drew everyone's attention.

Gloom, dreadful and dominating, darkened the northwest horizon.

"What is that?" Rax, a rather lean dwarf with a rapier on his hip, asked.

Pazacar, the wisest and eldest in the group, hissed. "It is the orcs."

"I agree." Arangoli nodded.

"Talastar must be over a hundred miles away."

"That is what I was thinking."

"This is bad." Pazacar gripped his staff tightly, his knuckles turning pale. "Whatever magic they used, it must be powerful to create a cloud that dark and of that scope."

The spread of the cloud had ceased, but based on the distance, it was easily five miles in diameter.

"Aye," Arangoli nodded gravely. "Which is why we need to refill our waterskins and head out."

Rather than wait for a reply or gauge if the others were ready, he set off with a swift stride making his way down to the riverbank.

Beneath the light of the full moon, Arangoli led nine dwarves along a gravel road bordered by grassy hillsides. The road ran parallel to the river, the rush of water coming from Arangoli's left while the dark, jagged shape of a mountain loomed to his right.

Nobody spoke. In fact, fewer than a dozen sentences had been uttered the entire night. Instead, heavy breaths, the clatter of armor, and the crunch of footsteps filled the otherwise silent evening.

The road alongside the river then turned south. Even in the dark, the silhouettes of two mountain peaks were visible.

"That must be the pass ahead." Arangoli said.

From his right, Pazacar said, "As I expected. We should reach it by dawn."

"Good." Fesgar's voice came from Arangoli's other side. "My back is sore and my feet are aching."

Rax grunted. "Stop your bellyaching. We are all sore and hungry."

"Especially, hungry." Gortch added.

"Especially you.

Gortch shrugged. "I'll not deny it. Just take care not to break a leg or something, Rax. I might be tempted to end your misery and cook you up. I heard scrawny dwarf on a stick is particularly tasty when slathered with butter."

A wave of laughter passed through the group, touching even Arangoli. *So long as they are exchanging barbs, things are not so dire.* A dark shape then passed before the moon. It was not alone. Squeals echoing in the night provided mere seconds of warning.

"Get down!" Arangoli shouted as he dove to the ground.

A winged creature sped over him, its wingspan eight or nine feet, its body the size of a dwarf. Dozens more sped right above where Arangoli lay. When they cleared, he rolled and scrambled to his feet.

"What were those things?" Rax stood and spun, his bow suddenly in his hand.

"Dire bats," Pazacar said.

Gortch grunted. "Vile beasts from what I hear."

In his training, Arangoli had studied deadly beasts. Any good warrior needed to understand the enemies he or she might face. Dire bats were known to prey on dwarves, elves, humans, or any animal that happened to be nearby. They hunted at night and traveled in colonies. One was not particularly dangerous, but it took mere seconds for a colony to swarm victims and strip flesh from their bones.

"Aye," Arangoli said. "Deadly as well."

Squeals came from the direction of the river, causing him to spin in that direction. He reached over his shoulder, gripped the war hammer on his back, and pulled it free. The moment his fingers wound around Tremor's leather-wrapped handle, he found a sense of comfort. The enchanted, ancestral weapon had never failed him.

"They are coming back!" He barked. "Weapons ready!"

Dark shapes came in fast. In the pale moonlight, the beasts were difficult to see until they drew near. At the last moment, Arangoli dove and swung his hammer. It clipped the wing of the lead bat, sending it twirling and crashing into the long grass. A steady rush of flying monsters sailed over the dwarves, some at no more than two feet off the ground.

As soon as the wave of monsters passed by, Arangoli hurried to his feet and looked around, seeking a defensible location. A rocky cliffside a few hundred feet from the road seemed their only option.

"This way! Run!" He burst into the long grass, heading toward the wall of rock.

A glance over his shoulder revealed his companions trailing by a few strides. In the sky beyond them, the bats banked and came at them from behind. They would not reach the cliff in time.

Arangoli stopped and held his hammer with both hands. "Form up behind me. Shields and weapons ready."

Armor and weapons clanked noisily as the dwarves gathered behind him.

The bats emerged from the darkness, sped over the road, and came across the grass. Arangoli readied himself. A thwap resounded as Rax loosed an arrow. A bat squealed and fell to the ground in front of the dwarves. The lead bat opened its massive jaw and came at Arangoli, who dropped to one knee and swung Tremor. The hammer struck the bat in the head and released a thump. The bat's momentum carried it into Arangoli, clipping his shoulder and knocking him on his back. A flurry of winged creatures flew over him, while squeals, shouts, and cries rang out as the dwarves fought back. When the wave was past them, Arangoli rolled to his feet.

"Get up!"

The other dwarves rose from the grass, two of them stumbling before finding steady footing. Four bats lay in the grass, one of which flopped on its back. A hard thump from Gortch's spike mace ended the beast.

"Get two torches ready, Fesgar. Everyone, follow me!" Arangoli raced toward the cliff with the other dwarves on his heels.

As they drew near the wall of moonlit rock, Arangoli spotted a dark recess. He raced straight for it and slowed to a stop at the edge of the moonlight. It was the mouth of a cave, twenty feet across and leading into darkness. Although it was too dark to navigate safely, standing in the entrance offered them a chance to fight back and avoid being flanked.

The peal of bats arose as the colony sped past the opening.

"Everyone form a line to my left and right. Attack anything that comes near. Fesgar, where are those torches?"

The dwarves lined up inside the cave opening. The bats turned and circled beyond the road.

Fesgar set two torches down and pulled out his flint. The striker caused a spark to flare, followed by another. It landed on the kerosene-soaked torch which burst into flames. He touched the second torch to the first and stood with them both held high. As the flames grew, a halo of amber illuminated his surroundings. Bats avoided light, so the torch might provide a reprieve, giving Arangoli and his team time to figure out their next step.

A mighty roar came from the bowels of the cave.

Arangoli spun around and gasped. "Oh, blazes. This is bad."

CHAPTER 8
A BAD SPOT

Gortch Onerslate spun around to peer into the cavern, its mouth illuminated by flickering torchlight. His friend and group leader, Arangoli, stood a few strides deeper in the cave. Beyond him, three sets of red eyes glowed in the dark recesses. Ferocious growls echoed in the chamber as those eyes drew closer. A massive beast covered in black fur stepped into the torchlight. It reminded Gortch of a wolf, except this wolf was the size of a wagon, stood twice the height of a dwarf, and had three heads.

Pazacar gasped. "Cerberus!"

Tales of the underworld were common among dwarven culture, often told by the priesthood and by those who sought to conjure waking nightmares during fireside chats. Dark, twisted creatures who feasted on the bodies and souls of the living were featured in those stories. Among those monsters was Cerberus, the beast who prevented damned souls from returning to the world of the living. As any practical dwarf was likely to do, Gortch had dismissed such tales as mere myth. To stand there, facing a beast of legend, made his prior denial seem ludicrous. Worse, if Cerberus and orcs were real, demons, darkspawn, and the Dark Lord himself all might be real as well. If all had, somehow, escaped the underworld...

The peals of bats came from outside the cave and drew his attention away from the monster.

The bats zipped past the opening, flying in both directions in a twisted, chaotic tornado of death just outside the cavern. Trapped between the massive, three-headed dog and the dire bats, the dwarves were in a bad spot. It was time for Arangoli to lead if they hoped to survive.

As if Gortch had spoken the thought aloud, Arangoli took charge and issued orders.

"Fesgar, hand a torch to Artgan, then I want you to join Paz and Orvatz outside." Arangoli pointed toward the tunnel opening. "You three are to keep those bats off our backs. The rest of you, form up in pairs and spread out in an arc. Each pair needs to target one of the dog heads."

Gortch knew his role. While Arangoli was their unquestioned leader, the Head Thumpers followed him largely because of the support Gortch displayed. In a demonstration of that support, he immediately hefted his mace and took position in the middle. "If we are to face this thing, what do you intend to do?"

"While you six distract it, I am going to slip around the back and attack it from behind." Arangoli eased to the edge of the cavern while Rax joined Gortch in the middle.

The other dwarves split up, two going to the right, two to the left, everyone gripping their weapons, ready to face a monster that likely outweighed the lot of them put together.

"If we are going to do this, let's do it." Rax, who stood at Gortch's side, drew his rapier and slashed through the air.

Gortch called out, "Hey, ugly arse! If you think you can, come and get us!"

The dog-like creature raised all three heads and howled. In the twenty-foot-wide confines of the cavern, the sound was enough to strike fear into the most hardened of warriors. The monster burst forward, its middle head snapping at Rax, who yipped, jumped backward, and slashed. His sword tip raked across the monster's nose. Despite the sharpness of his rapier, the cut barely broke through the black skin, leaving only a narrow strip of red.

Gortch took the opening to deliver an overhead blow. His mace struck the monster's neck with terrible force. The creature sharply swung its middle head toward Gortch, hitting him in the shoulder with enough force to toss him to the ground. He landed hard and rolled as a set of massive jaws snapped, barely missing him. Gortch made a backhand swing, scrambling to his feet. The mace missed the mark when the beast yanked its head back to avoid the blow, but that also bought Gortch time to ready himself for the next attack.

To the left and right, Head Thumpers fought the other two dog heads, using sword strikes and axe swipes to keep the massive jaws at bay.

When the middle head snapped at Rax, forcing him to dodge the attack, Gortch burst forward. His mace came around and struck the monster's neck. The creature flinched, jerked its head away, and another head attacked from the side. Massive jaws opened and clamped onto Gortch's left shoulder. Sharp teeth pierced his plate armor and lifted him off his feet. He cried out in pain.

WHILE THE OTHER dwarves fought against the three monstrous dog heads, Arangoli crept to the cavern wall and eased along it, keeping to the shadows. The fight was frantic, shouts, grunts, and growls echoing in the close confines. When he was beyond the monster, he raced in, wound back, and swung, targeting its hind leg. The hammer struck the side of its knee with incredible force and the enchantment activated, releasing a thump of energy that echoed through the cavern. The leg folded sideways, causing the creature to collapse on its hip. A terrible, ear-piercing yelp came from the beast. It spun toward Arangoli and snapped with its nearest head. He scrambled backward but his heel struck a rock jutting up from the ground, and he fell on his backside. The monster tried to rise, but its leg folded, so it dragged its body around and came for him.

PAZACAR ESCARN STOOD outside the cavern mouth, held his staff ready, and stared out into the night. To his left was Fesgar with a short sword in one hand and a burning torch in the other. The bat colony twisted and spun like a tornado come to life just beyond the alcove where he stood. On the right, Orvatz gripped his flail handle with both hands while a spiked metal ball dangled from its chain. They stood spaced before the entrance while the massive dire bats darted about. Shouts, growls, howls, and the clatter of battle rang out behind them, but they dared not turn around, lest they leave themselves open for attack.

A bat burst from the colony. It raced toward Pazacar, who spun his staff in reaction. The bat darted in with its mouth open, white teeth flashing in the torchlight. Pazacar dropped to one knee, bringing his staff down in an overhead blow. The end of the weapon, made of wood and reinforced with dwarven steel, struck true. A crack resounded as the staff collided with the monster's head. The bat sailed past Pazacar's shoulder and crashed to the ground inside the cave.

Before Pazacar could rise, another monster flew in. Orvatz swung his flail, the spiked ball at the end of the chain coming around hard. But the bat altered its angle, banking toward Pazacar. The flail missed. Desperate, Paz thrust his staff toward the oncoming creature. It crashed into the butt of the staff, the force of the impact bowling him over. The bat landed on top of him and they both tumbled into the cave.

THE CERBERUS JERKED AND YELPED, the jaw gripping Gortch suddenly opening. He landed on his feet then fell to his knees to look up and find the monster spinning away. At the rear of the cave, Arangoli fell to the ground. He was in trouble. Although Gortch's shoulder throbbed and his left arm dangled at his side, he had to act quickly.

Gortch stood, hefted his mace, and shouted, "Attack!"

The other dwarves rushed in with sword and axe strikes targeting the monster's flank. When Gortch spied one of the hind legs dragging limply on the ground, he understood Arangoli's plan.

He charged ahead, wound back, and swung his mace with every ounce of effort he could muster. The mace drove into the back of the beast's other hind knee. The leg folded, and the creature's back end dropped to the ground while it released a mighty howl.

PAZACAR, bruised and scraped but well enough to fight, pushed the dead bat off his legs. He hurried back to his feet to find Fesgar and Orvatz out in front of the cave, slashing and swiping as bats dove at them. The latter struck true when his flail hit a bat in the wing, causing the creature to crash into the cliffside. However, the attack left his back exposed. Paz rushed out, but a bat swooped in from behind Orvatz and landed on his back. The creature's momentum sent the dwarf stumbling to fall on his stomach, his helmet rolling away. The bat bit and tore at Orvatz, who thrashed and shrieked in horror. Pazacar wound back and swung his weapon as he drew near. The staff smashed into the bat's head and sent it flipping off Orvatz. The creature landed on its back and flopped as it tried to right itself. Paz followed with an angry overhead blow, the staff smashing the bat's face in. It fell still.

When he turned to check on Orvatz, another dire bat attacked, forcing him to spin his staff and dodge away.

Arangoli lay on his back as the Cerberus came at him. As the Head Thumpers rushed in and attacked, the three-headed dog turned two of its heads back and fight. The distraction created just enough hesitation to allow Arangoli to roll to the side and avoid the massive jaws of the third head. He rolled again, came to his feet, and faced the monster. The dog head came at him with another snap, teeth the size of daggers flashing while spittle sprayed out. Arangoli dodged to the side, wound back, and swung when the next bite came at him. Tremor smashed into the dog head, the pulse releasing with a thump. The monster's jaw shattered with teeth and drops of blood spraying out to the side. At the same moment, its hind end dropped to the ground.

Gortch and his fellow dwarves swung and stabbed at the massive, three-headed dog. Crimson drops stained the cavern floor. One of the creature's heads hung limply while one hind leg appeared unusable, the other with its flesh torn open and bloody When the creature tried to stand, Gortch launched another attack at the same rear leg. His mace struck the monster's lower leg from behind. The spikes tore into and through the tendon, and the monster crashed to the ground.

Fighting back-to-back, Pazacar and Fesgar fended off dire bat attacks. On the ground beside them, Orvatz bled from his wounds, his body unmoving.

Pazacar's staff whirled faster than the eye could follow as he struck bat after bat. But he was beginning to tire. If he slowed at all, he was certain to suffer the same fate as Orvatz. Fesgar grunted with each sword stroke, a sign that he was also beginning to flag.

A bat broke from the swirling colony and flew straight toward them. When the bat was just strides away, it lurched and spun, sailed wide of Pazacar and crashed into the cliff wall. *What caused that?* An arrow through the bat's head revealed the answer while bringing another question. *Who loosed that arrow?*

Dark silhouettes burst from the night and attacked the bats. Blades flashed in a flurry. The steady snap of bows loosing arrows joined the squeals of the dire bats. Mere breaths later, the remaining bats flew off into the night.

THE HEAD with the broken jaw drooped and swayed limply with the motions of the beast. When the creature's hind end again fell to the cavern floor, Arangoli took the opening and raced in from the side, targeting the middle head as it snapped at Rax. The hammer crashed into the skull, and a thump shook the tunnel. The Cerberus collapsed and ceased moving.

Across the cave, Artgan stood with a torch in one hand, his bloody short sword in the other. Five other dwarves surrounded him. They panted for air, their shoulders slumped, their visible flesh covered in cuts and scrapes, but nobody seemed mortally wounded.

Arangoli circled the dead monster and shoved his hammer into it. When the creature did not react, he turned toward the cavern entrance. "Let's see how the others fare." He passed the other dwarves and stepped outside.

Just strides outside the cavern, Orvatz lay on the ground with

Pazacar and Fesgar standing over him. When Arangoli saw the blood, he knew it was not good. Yet, no bats were attacking.

"Where did the bats..." he stopped mid-sentence when a cluster of humanoid silhouettes emerged from the darkness.

Warriors dressed in black leather stepped into the torchlight. They stood tall and had lean, lithe frames. Each was armed with either a naginata or a bow. Their body type and pale skin made their race unmistakable.

"Drow." Arangoli muttered.

The dark elf in the lead stopped a few strides away. "What could a squad of dwarf warriors be doing in Drow lands?"

CHAPTER 9
THE DROW

Two dozen dark elves stood in a wedge formation outside the cavern entrance. Those near the rear corners held nocked bows, the others gripping the black lacquered shafts of naginatas. All weapons were aimed at the dwarves.

Even if Arangoli and his companions had not been weary from a hectic battle, taking on such a force would have been daunting and foolhardy. Dwarves might be renowned for their raw strength, stout defense, and resilience, but dark elves held an edge in speed and agility. Aware of the situation and wishing to avoid conflict, Arangoli flipped his hammer over, raised it over his shoulder, and slid it into the harness on his back.

"By Vandasal," Arangoli purposely mentioned their shared god, "I am glad to see you."

The Drow at the front of the wedge frowned. "You did not answer my question. What are you doing in Drow territory?"

"In truth, looking for you. We traveled to Talastar by ship, and when we found it abandoned, we made for Domus Ra pass. In the process, we came across these blazing things." Arangoli kicked a dead bat, causing its body to roll over. "We made for the cave and stumbled upon something even worse."

"Worse?" His brow furrowed as the dark elf asked, "What could be worse than a colony of dire bats?"

"That." Arangoli stepped aside and pointed into the cavern.

Artgan, still holding the torch, walked back into the cave. Amber, flickering light advanced around him and illuminated a massive corpse.

"Cerberus!" The Drow hissed. He walked past Arangoli and stopped inside the cavern mouth while staring at the dead monster. "This must be what killed our scouts."

"Your scouts?"

The Drow turned toward Arangoli. "Three pairs of letalis warriors were killed of late, the last pair taken the night before last. My squad and I were sent out to hunt down who or whatever was responsible."

"In that case, it seems you owe us a favor for slaying the beast."

"I'd say you owe us a favor for dealing with the dire bats."

Arangoli grunted. "Good point." He turned to Pazacar, who knelt beside Orvatz. "How is he, Paz?"

The lean dwarf stood and shook his head. "I am sorry."

A mixture of emotions ranging from sorrow to frustration resulted in Arangoli covering his eyes and taking a deep breath. *Two honest, loyal friends have died under my command.* Both deaths had occurred in short order, after years of emerging from fights unscathed.

A hand clapped on Arangoli's shoulder. He uncovered his eyes to find the Drow standing a stride away.

"A good squad leader experiences pain when losing those under his command. A great one forges on and does all he can to ensure the rest of his squad survive."

Arangoli acknowledged the dark elf's point. "Well said."

"My name is Gryzaal, captain among the Letalis. You have a familiar look. What is your name?"

"Arangoli."

Gryzaal dropped his hand and scowled. "You led the skirmish in Ra'Tahal last autumn."

"That's right." Arangoli frowned. "You were there, weren't you?"

"Unfortunately, I was." Gryzaal walked past Arangoli to join his squad. "You said you were searching for us. You have found us, but we shall see how well you like it." He whistled, barked a command in Elvish, and pointed. Guards broke from the wedge and formed an arc around the cavern entrance, where they stood with their weapons ready. "You are under arrest. Give up your weapons. Resist, and you will die."

Arangoli growled, "What warrants this ill treatment?"

"Consider this cautionary," Gryzaal said. "Cooperate and all will likely be well."

"Likely?"

"That is up to Queen Liloth."

Disgruntled, Arangoli looked over his squad. While the dwarves stood ready, he noted slumped shoulders, heavy arms, cuts, bruises, and other signs that they would not be at their best if they were forced to fight. His gaze then settled on Orvatz, lying dead just strides away. *I cannot lose another. Not tonight.*

He reached over his shoulder and drew his weapon. Dark elves standing near him tensed.

"Easy," Arangoli held the hammer out. "Take it. We will come with you peacefully. Betray us, and you will wish you had never crossed me."

Gryzaal nodded. "Based on the stories I have heard, I would be surprised if you agreed to comply without issuing a threat."

"Hmm." Arangoli grunted. "Now that we have come to an understanding, I request that you allow us to bury and honor our fallen comrade before we depart."

The Drow looked down at Orvatz. "I am sorry for your loss. Bury him if you must but be quick about it."

THE SKY STEADILY GREW BRIGHTER, the stars fading as daylight spread across the heavens. Arangoli and his squad walked along a gravel road bordered by a steep hillside. Twenty-five dark elves trailed in their wake in a silent procession. They came to a bridge spanning the river, but rather than cross it and continue down the road toward the pass, they turned and entered a canyon bordered by steep walls of brown rock. The farther they traveled, the more the gap between the canyon walls narrowed until they were only a few hundred feet apart.

A stream ran down the center of the gorge, its waters bubbling over exposed rocks. Leaf trees and shrubs occupied the canyon floor to create a field of green amid the brown rock. A quarter mile into the ravine, they came to a bend. The gap between the walls narrowed further until it was no more than a hundred feet across. The rush of heavy water flow arose above the whispering breeze and bubbling stream. The trees parted to reveal a towering waterfall pouring down a cliff wall that blocked the route. Ladders and steep stairs carved into the cliff face ran parallel to the falls. Hundreds of feet up, at the top of that drop, was a wall made of stone and mortar. The silhouettes of Drow guards standing atop the wall were visible against the early morning sky.

"Are we going up there?" Gortch asked.

"Yes," Gryzaal replied from behind him.

Gortch groaned. "Why are there always so many stairs?"

Arangoli clapped Gortch on the shoulder. "I suspect the entire world conspired to make it so, just to spite you."

"Aye. The world hates dwarves like me. It is not my fault that food loves me so."

"And ale, Gortch. Don't forget how much ale loves you."

Gortch grinned. "I could never forget that. He turned his bad shoulder toward Arangoli. "However, climbing is going to be even more difficult this time."

"That's why you have us. We will get you to the top."

The path narrowed until the river's edge was no more than three feet from the cliff wall. They followed that narrow route and came to a ladder. With Arangoli in the lead, the dwarves climbed up to a shelf thirty feet up. Upon reaching the shelf, they took a staircase carved into the rock. Those stairs led them to a short tunnel, which emerged to another ladder. This process continued with a steady climb until they reached the top, where a narrow ledge separated the wall from a daunting drop. The dwarves and their Drow escort walked along the ledge until they reached the top of the waterfall, where water flowing from the mouth of a cavern fed the stream. Ther ledge ended at another cliff wall rising hundreds of feet up. To the right, just before the dead end, a barred opening in a heavy wooden door allowed the first glimpse of what lurked behind the wall.

"A city?" Arangoli exclaimed as he stood before the door. "I studied the map before we left Ra'Tahal. I don't recall a city located here."

Gryzaal approached. "Maps do not reveal all there is to know about the world."

"Where are we?"

The Drow stopped beside the door and knocked. "You will soon find out."

A dark elf peered through the opening and spoke in Elvish. Gryzaal replied in kind. The door opened and the Drow squad leader led the dwarves inside.

They stepped into a village square, complete with a fountain along one wall. Buildings waited across the square while narrow streets led deeper into the city. Other than the guard inside the door and those posted along the top of the city wall, there was nobody in sight. Yet, noises came from further in, somewhere beyond view, indicating that they were not alone.

Ten strides in, Gryzaal stopped and turned to face the dwarves. "Listen closely. You are to follow and to avoid touching anything."

"What is this place?" Arangoli peered toward the guards stationed on the wall facing the canyon.

"Long ago, it was a city but now it is a place of death."

Allowing that ominous statement to hang in the air, Gryzaal crossed the square, heading away from the canyon and toward the towering wall of rock. Before reaching the wall, he turned and entered a narrow lane with buildings on one side, and a cliff face on the other. Although the sky above was a bright blue, shadows still clung to the alley, as if night had refused to relent. The buildings they passed were quiet, yet when Arangoli peered through a window, he found someone standing over a table. The person wore a simple dress, her black hair dangling down her back. She stood still as if frozen solid. A few buildings later, he spotted someone through an open doorway. The person was on one knee and gripping a shoe with one hand, a needle with the other. Again, the person appeared frozen in time.

"What's wrong with these people?" Arangoli whispered.

Gryzaal looked back with a smirk. "No need to whisper. They cannot hear you."

As much as anything about the eerie city, that statement sent chills down Arangoli's spine.

When they reached the midpoint between the square and the far cliff wall, Gryzaal stopped outside the mouth of a tunnel.

Arangoli glanced through an open window across from the tunnel. Inside, a family of three sat around a table. Two were adult sized while the third was a child. Although the lighting inside was dim, He suddenly became aware of something startlingly wrong. "Where are their faces?"

Gryzaal grunted. "I was wondering when you might notice that. They are made of stone."

"Drow do not have such skill with stone. Only a dwarf could craft statues of such quality."

"True." Gryzaal headed into the tunnel. "Come along."

They followed a corridor broad enough for three people to walk astride without being cramped. The tunnel was long with over a dozen torches visible at the onset. Where it led, Arangoli could only guess, so he chose not to try. Thus far, the strange city had been anything but predictable.

Daylight waited at the tunnel's far end. When they drew near, the hum of chatter arose. They emerged and found themselves in a camp thick with dark elves. Males, females, and even children milled among tents and huts that created a village of sorts. A full third of the people were dressed in the black leather of Drow warriors.

Canyon walls loomed a quarter mile away in both directions. The dark peaks of the Argent Mountains peered over those walls. Water flowed down the heart of the camp before passing beneath two bridges made of logs, one bridge near each end of camp.

"Come." Gryzaal set off toward the water with Arangoli and the others in tow.

They approached the nearest bridge, climbed up, and crossed it. Below them, crystal blue water flowed past before disappearing into a tunnel with a low ceiling. Once across the stream, they came to a wall made of sharpened logs, the pointed end of each log rising up at an angle, the gaps between them roughly a foot apart. There, a dozen Drow warriors stood firm, their backs to the cave lurking beyond the fortifications. None of the guards moved when Gryzaal approached, nor did their expressions change. Their dark eyes glared hard at Arangoli.

Gryzaal spoke with the guards in Elvish. Their response was brief and sharp, which he countered with a barking order. Despite their scowls, they stepped aside. After flashing a sneer, Gryzaal passed through a four-foot-wide gap in the logs with the dwarves following. They crossed the open area, entered the cave, and stopped inside its shadowy confines.

Torches sticking out from walls a dozen feet to either side illuminated the cavern's interior. A strip of purple carpet ran down the middle of the cave floor, leading to a throne made of black obsidian. On the throne sat a female dark elf. A crown of blackened wood rested upon her head, torchlight reflecting off the polished, triangular facets of an onyx mounted at its fore. Her white hair and pale flesh provided a stark contrast to both the crown and her even darker eyes.

Arangoli leaned toward Gortch, who stood on his right. "It is Queen Liloth. Do not say or do anything to anger her." The queen's easily sparked temper was infamous.

"Why are you telling me? You are the one who needs to talk to her."

"Sometimes, I say things aloud so I don't forget to listen to myself."

"You should do that more often. Perhaps we would end up in fewer brawls."

Arangoli chuckled. "Could be."

The moment Gortch chuckled, he winced and slid a hand beneath his armored torso. The metal plate on his chest and shoulder were both dented. His fingers came away bloody.

"You are injured," Arangoli said.

"It was that blazing dog. If not for the plate, I'd be dead."

Arangoli tapped Gryzaal on the shoulder, drawing his attention. "This warrior is injured. Do you have a healer?"

"Our last healer died during the trek from Talastar. However, we do have some nurses who can clean and bandage his wounds."

"That'll do."

Gryzaal turned to one of the guards. They spoke briefly in Elvish before the guard nodded and gestured for Gortch to follow. As they walked off, Arangoli turned his attention toward the throne and the female elf seated upon it.

The queen wore a black dress that starkly offset skin so pale it was almost white. The dress hung loosely on her thin, willowy build. Her hand flowed through the air while she chatted with a male Drow dressed in purple robes. The way she moved, with long black nails at the end of elegant fingers, was mesmerizing. The male dark elf, his black hair tied back in a tail, glanced back toward the cavern entrance. His rat-like face pinched and his eyes narrowed as he stared at Arangoli. Hatred tainted that dark glare. He then turned back toward Liloth and continued speaking in a hushed tone.

Three strides to the other side of the throne stood a single female warrior. With black leather armor strapped to her lithe frame, the threat she posed was clear even discounting the hilts jutting out from her bracers and boots. She held a daunting double-ended sword at an angle across her body, her hands gripping the shaft connecting the weapon's two blades.

Feeling helpless and out of his element, Arangoli stood still and silent while wondering what would become of him and his companions. He longed to hold his hammer, for when it was in his grip, he was invincible. Without it, he felt naked, exposed, and vulnerable.

CHAPTER 10

LILOTH

Gryzaal relied on his well-honed patience as he waited for Queen Liloth to finish speaking with her adviser, Arieldar. A decade as captain of Liloth's elite fighting force had taught Gryzaal much about her and the endless intrigue surrounding her court. Even now, far from Castle Umbra, drama followed. Oftentimes, the male dark elf at her side was the source of that drama.

Arieldar shared no love for Gryzaal, something he had made clear on many occasions. As the queen's advisor, he occupied a position of considerable influence, which he used against Gryzaal at every opportunity. To make matters worse, Arieldar blamed Gryzaal for Rysildar's failed gambit the previous autumn. As a fellow singer, Arieldar also claimed that Rysildar's death was Gryzaal's fault. It often seemed like the advisor spent all his time scheming how to rid himself of perceived competition.

Then, there was the female warrior standing beside the throne, for she was another source of contention.

Nitara had been selected as Liloth's personal guard, a coveted position among the letalis warriors. While Gryzaal and Nitara had often been at odds, he respected her skill in battle and conceded the queen's choice as a wise one. When Nitara met Gryzaal's gaze, the brief connection was an odd blend of tension and mutual respect.

After minutes that seemed like hours, Arieldar turned from Liloth and took position beside her throne. The queen lifted a finger and bent it twice, beckoning Gryzaal to advance.

Gryzaal spoke over his shoulder. "Arangoli will approach the throne with me. The others are to remain here." He then took a deep breath and began down the carpet with Arangoli at his side.

When they were halfway to the throne, Gryzaal whispered, "She is unlikely to address you, but if she does, I suggest you behave in a respectful manner if you wish to live."

The dwarf replied, "I had already planned as much."

"Good, because if you anger her, she is likely to take it out on me as well. I'd hate to die after only recently regaining her favor."

They drew near the throne and stopped two strides away. When Gryzaal dropped to one knee, Arangoli hurriedly did the same.

Gryzaal spoke in Elvish. "Greetings, my Queen. My squad and I have returned. During our outing, we encountered a squad of dwarves and brought them here for dispositioning."

"Welcome back, Captain. Who is the dwarf beside you?"

"This is Arangoli Handshaw. He leads a crew known as the Head Thumpers."

She frowned. "Are they not the same dwarves who infiltrated Ra'Ta-hal, slayed Rysildar, and thwarted our plans to obtain weapons made of Dwarven steel?"

He had feared she would recall their names and involvement, but better to ensure he shared the information up front. "They are the same dwarves, indeed."

Her lips turned up in a smirk. "So, you have brought them as gifts for me?"

"That was not my intention."

"Then, what?" The queen's finger repeatedly tapped on the arm of her throne.

"I am here to confirm my mission as complete. The creature that killed our scouts is dead."

"May I know what creature caused us such aggravation?"

"It was a Cerberus."

Her eyes narrowed. "A creature from the underworld?"

"Yes."

She scowled. "What is a creature from the underworld doing out here, so far from Talastar?"

"I do not know, Your Majesty."

"Well, at least you have dealt with it."

Gryzaal could have accepted the credit and nobody would have known, but something inside him railed against the idea. "In truth, that is how we happened upon the dwarves. You see, they were cornered in a cave by a colony of dire bats. We intercepted the bats, killing most of the colony before the last few fled. When we approached the cave, we found the dwarves inside, standing over the corpse of a three-headed dog the size of three horses combined."

Liloth glanced toward Arangoli. "This dwarf and his companions killed the creature?"

"Yes, My Queen."

She inhaled and flattened her lips. "What do you suggest we do with them, Captain?"

"You seek my opinion?"

The queen snapped. "I just said as much, didn't I?"

Gryzaal considered the situation, and while a grudge remained for what occurred in Ra'Tahal, he suspected the dwarves would be of more use alive than dead. *They have proven their skill more than once. Every able warrior would be required for what he feared would soon come.*

"I need more time to decide. Leave them in my custody for a day or two."

The queen arched a painted brow. "You will take full responsibility for their actions?"

Turning to Arangoli, Gryzaal spoke Dwarvish in a quiet tone. "Can I trust you?"

"What is happening?" The dwarf shrugged. "I didn't understand a word you said."

"You are to be held in my care."

"Do I have another choice?"

"Execution."

"Hmm. Not much of a choice." Arangoli stroked his beard. "You can trust my squad. We will not betray you."

Turning back to his queen, Gryzaal nodded, choosing to place his faith in the dwarves infamous and unreasonable sense of honor. "I will take full responsibility for the dwarves."

Arieldar, who had been silent to that point, interjected. "My Queen. How can you allow these filthy dwarves to live? They killed Rysildar and destroyed our plans. It is their fault that we were forced to flee Talastar."

Liloth glared at him. "You are here to advise, but you do not make the decisions, singer. As for fleeing Talastar, the fault lies with those who pushed our people to delve deep into the bowels of the earth."

The singer clenched his jaw shut, his eyes flaring. He opened his mouth and froze when the tip of Nitara's twin-bladed sword pressed against his neck.

A smirk turned up on Liloth's black lips. "Did you think to use your magic against me, Arieldar? Even if you could best my own abilities, which I think is unlikely, Nitara's blade would drain you of your blood before you could finish the first note."

Arieldar closed his mouth, backed away from the throne and stomped off. Nobody spoke until he was beyond earshot.

"Captain Gryzaal," Liloth broke the silence. "Why don't you give our captives a tour of our little settlement? See if they have any ideas to add to our plans."

Gryzaal glanced at Nitara as she reclaimed her position beside the throne. Sensing he was being dismissed, he nudged the dwarf beside him and rose to his feet. "As you wish, My Queen."

He and Arangoli tread along the carpet. When they walked outside, the other dwarves and letalis warriors followed.

Arangoli asked, "What was that all about?"

Arching a brow, Gryzaal gave him a sidelong look. "You don't speak Elvish?"

"Not a lick."

"Well, rather than see you beheaded, I convinced her to leave you and your companions in my care."

The dwarf narrowed his eyes. "While I appreciate keeping my head, why would you do that?"

As they passed through the camp, Gryzaal then remembered something that had struck him just prior to the dwarves' arrest. "Earlier, you mentioned that you came from Talastar."

"That's right."

"When you reached the city, what did you find?"

Arangoli grunted before replying, "It was empty. Abandoned."

"And why did you go there in the first place?"

"I was sent by Korrigan, King of Clan Tahal. When Rysildar betrayed King Arangar, the agreement between them was declared void. We were to retrieve our people and escort them back to Ra'Tahal."

"Ah. I see." Gryzaal crossed the bridge and made for the far side of camp. "I cannot blame Korrigan. I would've done the same."

Arangoli gripped Gryzaal's arm, stopping him. "I need to know something."

Brow arched, Gryzaal chose not to overreact. "Very well."

"My crew and I were the reason you and your people were ousted from Ra'Tahal. Even though you survived, it cannot sit well with you.

Based on Liloth's reputation, you were likely also punished for your failure."

Gryzaal allowed his grimace to convey his feelings on the subject.

Arangoli continued, "Yet you stood up for us rather than allowing us to be executed. Why?"

As a warrior, Gryzaal was trained to expect the unexpected and to not underestimate the enemy. Despite this, he found himself surprised that the seemingly headstrong and boisterous dwarf was intelligent enough to come to that conclusion so quickly.

"Why do you think we left Talastar?"

The dwarf stroked his beard while eyeing Gryzaal. He gazed left and right before leaning in and speaking in a soft voice. "It was because of the orcs."

Gryzaal blinked. "How do you know that?"

"We visited Castle Umbra and found a way beneath the ruins. When searching the dungeon, we came across a hole in the ground, a hole that led to trouble. An orc killed one of my team before we could react. Then, thousands more appeared. My squad and I raced back to the surface and fought off a few before we were able to collapse a wall and seal the way."

Gryzaal pressed a palm to his forehead. "I had hoped we might have buried them for good."

"It gets worse."

"How so?"

"An unnatural and extremely black cloud appeared above the city, big enough to see from a hundred miles away."

"When did this happen?"

"We saw it late yesterday, right before we resumed our journey."

"Come with me." At a deliberate pace, Gryzaal headed across camp, toward the canyon wall.

The moment any Drow citizen saw the determined look on his face, they hastily moved aside, making way for Gryzaal, his squad, and the dwarves. Bystanders stared as the mismatched entourage of warriors marched past. They advanced beyond the last of the tents and huts and approached the canyon wall.

Stopping, Gryzaal turned to his squad and spoke in Elvish. "Remain here and ensure the dwarves do as well. The dwarf captain and I are going up."

Silent salutes confirmed their compliance.

He beckoned Arangoli, "Follow me."

A vertical strip of openings marked the face of the rock, creating a makeshift ladder. Gryzaal reached up, gripped an opening above him with one hand, and placed a foot in a lower hole as he began his ascent. The top of the bluff loomed eighty feet above. While not of a terrifying height, a fall from there would be deadly, but a lifetime of dancing with death had hardened him and fear rarely found way into his heart. The climb required both strength and endurance, but then again, the life of a warrior demanded both, so the effort was not onerous for Gryzaal. He suspected the dwarf would similarly endure the minor challenge. At the top of the bluff, he stood back as Arangoli joined him.

The dwarf rose to his feet and dusted off his hands while looking around. "What is this about? I assume you didn't drag me up here for the view."

"Actually, the view is precisely why we are here. Come along."

Gryzaal headed down a dirt trail running between leaf trees and bordered by brush. The path ran along a gentle upslope, the hillside and trees masking the view. Voices rose above the crunch of footsteps and the whisper of the leaves swishing in the breeze. Just ahead, four Drow warriors sat among a cluster of rocks, engaged in conversation. Not far from their position was a steep drop below which stood an ancient city overlooking a waterfall.

One of the Drow, a young letalis warrior named Feschall, glanced toward Gryzaal, his eyes widening. He nudged the warrior beside him and stood at attention. As Gryzaal drew near, all four Drow stood tall.

"Captain Gryzaal," Feschall said in Elvish. "We weren't expecting you today."

Arms crossed, Gryzaal scowled, allowing his expression and silence to convey his feelings.

Feschall glanced toward his companions. "What can we do for you, sir?"

"Your post requires you to watch for any trouble, so you can warn the tribe in advance."

"We, um, have full view of the canyon, sir. We saw you and the dwarves coming this way from the start and monitored the group while you passed through the city and entered the tunnel leading to camp."

"Yes, but what of watching the Haghetti?"

The four Drow glanced toward each other before Feschall replied, "There is nothing to see there but endless grass-covered hills, scattered trees, and a river cutting through it all."

Gryzaal tensed, ready to snap before he closed his eyes and took a deep breath. In an even voice, he said, "You are to fully survey the Haghetti once an hour. Should you forego this duty, you will find yourself taking a short walk straight in that direction." He pointed toward the drop into the canyon, just strides to the east.

Feschall flinched. "Yes, Captain."

"Now, this dwarf and I are going to go and inspect the Haghetti. Perhaps two of you should join us."

With an elbow, Feschall nudged the warrior beside him. "We would be honored, Captain."

"Good. Now, lead the way."

The two warriors scooped up their bows and quivers before setting off on a trail leading north.

"What was that about?" Arangoli asked.

Gryzaal slipped back to speaking Dwarvish. "Duty...or lack of it."

"Heh," the dwarf grunted. "It's not easy being in charge, is it?"

"It is not what I expected back when I was a young and eager warrior seeking to advance. Oftentimes, I miss the simplicity of obeying orders and worrying about little other than my own survival."

Gryzaal set off along the uphill trail, following the two warriors in black. He glanced to the side, where the sun hovered above the mountains to the east. The day was young, the daylight more than sufficient to allow for a distant view, assuming no rain fell on the Haghetti. The ground leveled, the trees parted, and the view expanded to reveal the sprawling grasslands to the north.

As the warriors described, the Haghetti was empty without a threat in sight...until Gryzaal peered to the distant northwest, where a gloom as black as night created a striking contrast to the pale blue sky.

The two warriors gasped with Feschall asking. "Is it a fire?"

"That is no fire."

Arangoli said, "That cloud is moving and is closer to us now than it was before nightfall."

"I believe your story, Arangoli." The reality of the situation settled into Gryzaal's stomach like a lump of red-hot coal. "The truth cannot be denied, regardless of how much we might wish otherwise, the orcs have broken through. Their insatiable hunger drives them. They come this way, seeking to destroy us and any living thing that lies in their path." He turned toward Arangoli. "I believe it is time I told you my story."

The dwarf arched his brow. "I am listening."

"Let's head back to camp. I need to pass the news on to the other officers, so we can accelerate our preparations."

As they set off, Gryzaal considered where to begin before sharing his tale. "As you are likely aware, our people are secretive by nature."

The dwarf shrugged. "We all have our secrets."

"Well, ours are plentiful and few were more closely guarded than the entrance to our mines. In fact, to prevent suspicion and others attempting to access the mines, we built the city of Talastar around them and positioned a fortress above the entrance. My people took steps to make the city walls dark and bleak. They designed the stronghold at the heart of the city doubly so. In two thousand years, few outsiders have visited Castle Umbra, and even those who had were unlikely to guess at what hides beneath the palace."

Gryzaal paused his telling while he and Arangoli passed the warriors stationed on the bluff. When they were beyond earshot, the dwarf prodded for more information.

"I don't find it all that strange," Arangoli said. "You have mines hidden under a castle. We dwarves have them below our citadels. However, our tunnels are not filled with monsters seeking to bite our heads off."

"Until recent times, we were not plagued by deepspawn either. The monsters first appeared early last year. After fifteen centuries of mining for vartanium in the depths below Umbra Palace, our miners came to a massive open gallery extending into the depths. Vartanium veins lined this cavern but reaching them was difficult. So, we dug more tunnels and delved deeper and deeper until reaching a flat landing a thousand feet down. Even that was not the bottom of the pit. A chasm ran along one end of the landing, its depths unknowable. That is where we first heard noises warning us that we were not alone."

They reached the cliff wall overlooking the Drow encampment.

"Let us return to camp. After I brief my squad and send a messenger to alert Queen Liloth, we will break our fast while I share the rest of my story." Gryzaal slid over the edge of the bluff, found a foothold, and began descending. As he made his way down the sheer cliff face, he reflected on the plan he had put in motion two seasons earlier. Death was coming, and it may find him, but not until he made the orcs pay a mighty price.

CHAPTER II
THE PREVIOUS WINTER

A squad of forty letalis warriors traversed a dark tunnel. At the lead, Gryzaal gripped his naginata while marching at a steady but not hurried pace. He and the others would need their energy, and rushing at this point would only hasten them toward death.

The party walked in silence, guided by the light of glowing crystals mounted to the top of four staffs dispersed throughout the group. The nearest such crystal was carried by the warrior walking behind Gryzaal, its light casting his own shadow forward.

The tunnel opened to a gallery two dozen strides across and twice the length. Crystals mounted to poles along the rock walls provided enough light to see across the chamber, yet the ceiling proved to be too high for the light of the crystals to reach. Drow warriors stood in three rows evenly spaced across the flat cavern floor, all facing away from the tunnel opening. Beyond the front row, darkness loomed.

A lone female warrior standing at the side of the cavern walked over to intercept Gryzaal. "Welcome, Captain." She held her naginata in her left hand while the other fist pressed against her chest. "We have been expecting you."

"Squad Leader Avarci." Gryzaal looked over the group, quickly counting. Each row included a dozen warriors. "Three dead?"

"Yes, Captain. The monsters have been quiet today."

The statement stirred concern. In the Deep, the quiet moments always preceded those that were most deadly.

"Since we are here, let's initiate the shift change."

"The city?"

"You'll find it empty. The last caravan departed less than an hour ago."

"Then, only we remain."

"And soon, Talastar will belong solely to the creatures of the underworld."

She turned toward her squad and shouted, "Replacements incoming! Prepare for shift change!"

The Drow did not turn but bows and naginatas were raised in salute.

Gryzaal, raised his own weapon and made a forward gesture. His squad of thirty-nine warriors trotted out and separated into three lines, each led by a warrior holding a glowing crystal. The lights and the staffs they were mounted on were passed to members of Avarci's squad. As Gryzaal's team marched in from one side of the chamber, the squad members finishing their shift turned and marched out.

In moments, the shift change was complete, and of the prior squad, only the leader remained.

"May Vandasal watch over you, Captain," Avarci said.

"I fear our god abandoned us long ago, or we would not be forced to resort to such measures." Practical at heart, Gryzaal preferred to place his faith in his own skill and the plan he had so carefully crafted. "Take care to follow the escape route when you pass though the castle. Straying off it would likely be the end of us all."

"My squad and I will follow the plan. We will be away from the city within the hour." Avarci ducked into the tunnel, leaving Gryzaal alone with his squad.

He set his jaw and strode across the ledge, splitting the gaps between warriors as he crossed each line. Beyond the front row, the chasm loomed. He eased toward it and peered over the edge. A wall of vertical rock, three stories deep, was visible below before fading to the blackest of shadows. Distant noises came from the pit. How deep it ran, Gryzaal could only guess. *I wish the Drow miners had never found this chamber.*

Turning from the chasm, he shifted position to the side of the cavern, planted the butt of his weapon on the stone floor, and lifted his gaze.

Somewhere in the shadows high above him, numerous tunnels connected to the gallery. Those tunnels were far larger than the one he and his squad had taken to reach the lowest level of the mine. A powerful desire for vartanium had led his people to the dire situation that eventually forced them to flee Talastar. If only his people would have anticipated the consequences of delving into the Deep.

He imagined Avarci's squad making their way back to Castle Umbra, gauging the time that would yet need to pass before he could begin his retreat. As Liloth demanded, Gryzaal would be the last to leave Talastar. Those in his squad had volunteered for the honor of acting as the rear guard. They understood the risks and had been steadfast in displaying loyalty toward their captain.

A noise came from the chasm, disturbing the stillness.

His heart thumping, his grip tightening on his weapon, Gryzaal tensed. Despite years of fighting in the deep, he had never grown used to the experience. "Binaal. What do you see?"

The archer drew an arrow, knocked his bow, and leaned over the edge. "Something moves down there. It hovers near the edge of the light."

"Call out the moment you get a clear view."

A distant scraping sound rising from the depths caused Gryzaal's hair to stand on end. An eeriness always preceded an attack.

"Red eyes pierce the darkness," Binaal shouted.

"Archers take position."

The six archers in the squad pulled away from the ranks and lined up along the edge of the drop. Half were male, half female. All were skilled and battle trained.

"Ready yourselves."

As one, the archers drew an arrow from the quivers on their backs and nocked their bow. "Take aim and loose at will."

In rapid succession, the bows loosed. As one, the archers drew an arrow from the quivers on their backs and nocked their bow. Again and again, they loosed, their hands moving faster than the eye could track. In the passing of a single minute, the initial quiver of each archer was empty. The archers spun from the chasm and reclaimed their positions in each row. They tossed the empty quivers toward the rear of the room and picked up the full quiver waiting for them.

The first orc burst from the chasm, moving with startling quickness, its black talons flashing as it reached out, prepared to slaughter with a mere scratch. A warrior armed with a naginata reacted with a lunge and slash. The blade sliced through the stomach of the monster, eviscerating it. The orc landed on its side, between the first and second rank. Another thrust ended the beast.

Orcs by the dozens emerged from the darkness, leaping and attacking with fury. The letalis warriors reacted as trained. Naginatas whirled, warriors slashing, dodging, and fighting for their lives. When orcs burst through gaps created by the fracas, the second rank intercepted them. Watching letalis warriors in battle was akin to witnessing a masterful dance with death.

Wave after wave of monsters came at them. When a warrior in the front rank fell, one in the second rank rushed forward to fill the gap. In turn, a warrior from the rear moved forward to join the second rank. Blades flashed, blood sprayed across the ground, and bodies began to pile up.

Suddenly, orcs ceased to emerge from the chasm.

As the last creature was slayed, Gryzaal called out, "First rank, watch the edge. Ranks two and three, discard the bodies."

The warriors in the front moved to the edge of the drop and stood ready. Those behind set weapons aside and began dragging the dead over to the chasm. Bodies dropped out of sight, both those of the dead orcs and of the two Drow who fell victim to their poisonous talons. Screams came from below as monsters attempting to ascend were knocked loose.

When the dead were cleared, Gryzaal issued the next command. "Second rank to the fore. First rank to the rear."

The surviving warriors shifted position and stood with weapons ready.

Gryzaal measured the time that had passed since Avarci's departure. *We only need to hold them back for a short while longer.* Noises coming from the pit warned him that the fight was not over. Squeals and howls echoed in the chasm, a sign that the orcs had stirred into a frenzy.

"Eyes in the darkness," the lookout shouted.

"Archers, take position!" Gryzaal commanded.

When the archers were at the bluff's edge, he gave them leave to loose.

Bows snapped. Arrows loosed. The cries of inhuman beasts came from the pit.

The archers scrambled back just before a wave of orcs crested the edge. Weapons flashed as the Drow warriors attacked. Yet, monsters continued to emerge from the pit, quickly overwhelming the first rank. The second rank engaged, as did the third. Warriors began to fall to the furious onslaught, and with all three ranks already fighting, it was up to Gryzaal to fill the gaps.

He darted forward and slashed, his blade tearing across a monster's throat. He leapt and flipped over the talon strike of another. Twisting as he rotated through the air, he swept his blade beneath him and severed the hand off the next orc. As he landed, Gryzaal swung a backstroke, his blade slicing the enemy orc across its midriff.

In a flurry of fast, efficient motions, he continued down the gap between the second and third rank, his naginata spinning, slashing, and dispatching monster after monster. Then, as suddenly as the fight began, the last orc fell and the fracas was over.

Over four dozen orc corpses littered the cavern floor, but among the dead were eight Drow warriors. With ten already fallen in his shift, Gryzaal counted the loss among the worst he had suffered since the orcs first appeared and slaughtered all but three of the sixty Drow miners working in those tunnels.

Gryzaal issued orders for the dead to be dropped into the pit. The warriors responded with practiced efficiency as they rolled monsters and fallen comrades off the edge. The falling bodies would knock loose any others attempting to scale the wall. He prayed it would buy them the time they needed.

When the last body slid into the pit, he issued the order they had been waiting for. "Ranks ready. Third rank, retreat to the surface."

The line of warriors turned and trotted along the cavern wall. The lead swordsman snatched a crystal from its mounting and headed into the tunnel, raising the light in her hand as a guide for those trailing.

Again, Gryzaal issued the order to retreat, and when the second rank was gone, he released the first rank from their position. The warrior at each end of the rank collected a crystal as letalis warriors headed out of the gallery. Gryzaal cast one last glance back toward the pit and set off in a jog. They had far to go to reach the surface, and should the orcs come after him, the monsters were likely to climb to the top of the gallery and take one of the old mining tunnels. Precautions had been taken should that occur, but if the orcs somehow bypassed the traps set, Gryzaal and his squad would be caught and it could get ugly.

Regardless, at least one of his squad members had to reach the surface, or the plan was doomed. He had guaranteed Liloth success. The entire world relied on it.

TRAILING his squad and chased by shadows, Gryzaal jogged along a gentle incline. The tunnel gradually curved as it took them toward the surface. They came to a branching tunnel, that led to the upper reaches of the same gallery they had departed from fifteen minutes earlier. There, he listened, praying for silence but, instead, hearing distant howls and barks. He burst into a run, chasing after the fading light of the warrior carrying the last crystal.

"They come!" Gryzaal called out. "Go faster!"

Warriors ahead of him relayed the command. The line of warriors quickened their pace. Anxious minutes passed before they came to the massive cavern that was once the heart of Drow mining. Centuries of digging through rock in search of Vartanium had created a multi-tiered chamber hundreds of feet high and thousands of feet square. Columns of rock ran from the floor to the ceiling, evenly spaced across the chamber to ensure the cavern ceiling and the castle above it did not collapse.

The squad raced across the chamber floor, passing columns as they headed toward the nearest staircase. With the walls too distant to see in the dim light of the crystals, time seemed to slow. Darkness loomed in all directions beyond the glow of the light they carried. The noises of angry orcs rose above the thunder of footsteps and rasping of labored breaths.

The far wall came into view, revealing a long, straight stairwell cut into the rock and running alongside the wall. The lead warrior reached the stairs and held her crystal high while ascending. Warriors gathered at the bottom, waiting for those ahead to advance. Gryzaal reached the stairs last and gazed back across the massive chamber. Barking and howls grew louder. Glowing, red eyes appeared in the darkness. When the last surviving squad member began climbing the staircase, Gryzaal followed.

The climb involved three hundred sixty stairs, a strenuous ascent under any conditions. After a wicked battle and a three-mile uphill run, to call it daunting would be an understatement. Gryzaal was only a quarter of the way up when the first orc emerged from the darkness. The creature was not alone.

Dozens of monsters raced in. Rather than angling toward the foot of the stairwell, the beasts leapt, caught a grip on the wall below the stairs, and began scrambling up.

Gryzaal stopped and shouted. "Incoming! Stand and fight!"

When the orc below him was eight feet from the stairs, it leapt. Gryzaal thrust the butt of his weapon, striking the creature in the chest. The orc reached out, attempting to grab the weapon shaft but its hand slipped. It plummeted and struck the stone floor, some fifty feet below. Before it even landed, Gryzaal slashed, taking the head off another monster.

The fight was brief and furious. In the passing of seconds, dozens of deepspawn lay dead at the bottom of the wall, offering another reprieve.

"Go!" Gryzaal bellowed. "Meet in the dungeon's central chamber!"

They resumed their ascent, taking two stairs at a time. All the while, howls and shrieks echoed across the massive chamber. The squad consisted of battle trained warriors, their bodies fit and honed like a sharpened blade. Despite this, their breaths grew labored as they raced up the towering staircase. The light from the crystals moved with them, and soon, the chambers depths were cloaked in darkness. Gryzaal glanced back to find hundreds of red dots rushing in amid the gloom, the glow of the orc eyes giving him a rough count of the enemy force. In the process, he stumbled on a stair, caught himself, and ran to catch the others.

The warriors in the lead reached the door at the top of the stairs and faded from view. The others raced through the doorway with Gryzaal bringing up the rear. The deepspawn chased after them, scaling walls and stairs alike, the creatures moving with impossible speed, their howls steadily growing louder as they drew nearer.

When he reached the top, Gryzaal positioned himself behind the thick, stone door. Three other warriors joined him, and they pushed the heavy door closed. The hinges groaned, resisting their efforts yet slowly giving in. The monsters came into view, rushing in like rabid beasts eager for blood. The door slammed closed. Orcs piled against the other side, shoving mightily as they tried to open it.

Over his shoulder, Gryzaal shouted, "Bring the beam!"

Moments later, four Drow came in with a wooden beam thicker than Gryzaal's waist. He and the others holding the door closed squatted. The beam was lifted over them and dropped into place, both ends wedging into the grooves hewed into the stone walls outside the door. Only then did Gryzaal relax. Resting his forehead against the door, he caught his breath in a brief respite that was interrupted by a thump coming from the other side.

The Drow warriors stood in a spacious chamber carved from solid stone. Wooden posts and heavy beams supported the ceiling. Across the chamber was a broad set of stairs rising one story to an open doorway. Although the dim daylight seeping through that opening promised refuge, the stairs remained vacant. Gryzaal's squad, as well as the one that had left before, had been instructed to avoid that way out.

"The door should hold them for a time. Eventually, they will break through. When they do, they will find the surprises we left them. Now, follow me and take care not to stray off the escape route. One wrong step will be the end of us."

At a trot, he set off through the castle's dungeon level. The first chamber fell behind as he entered a torchlit corridor lined by closed doors. They emerged in another chamber occupied only by a desk, a chair, and an empty rack along one wall. Beside the rack, a staircase ascended into darkness.

Gryzaal hurried up the stairs, turned at the landing, and continued to the top. There, he opened the door and stepped into a corridor illuminated by sunlight coming through narrow windows. The hallway took him and his crew to a dining room. A wrought iron chandelier dangled above a table lacquered in black. A dozen ebony chairs surrounded the table and a huge stone fireplace dominated the wall at the far end of the room. Rather than cross the room and head toward the next corridor, he rounded the table, approached the fireplace, and ducked into the arched opening. There, he reached up into the chimney, pulled a brass lever, and the blackened rear wall swung open. He pushed the hidden door aside and stepped into a narrow passage bordered by walls made of dark stone bricks.

The hidden passageway ran in both directions, one leading deeper into the castle, the other toward the rear entrance. He led his squad down the latter, turned at an intersection, and turned again. When he came to a dead end, he pulled another lever. The wall swung outward and sunlight streamed in. It was a welcome sight. He stepped outside and took a deep breath, enjoying the cool, crisp winter morning air.

Gryzaal stood in a gravel yard with the central keep to his left, the castle's outer wall to his right, and the open drawbridge leading into the castle looming a few dozen strides ahead. There, he waited until his squad vacated the building. The female warrior who exited last pushed the stone door closed, sealing the secret entrance. Only then did he address them.

"You did well today, although it was not easy. It seemed as if the monsters knew we were leaving and they sought to exact a steep cost before our departure. Castel Umbra no longer belongs to the Drow. It is now our gift to the creatures of the underworld. However, I doubt it will be a gift they enjoy."

The dark eyes of his squad members reflected their resilience.

"However, today's efforts have only just begun. We must run to catch our people. Tonight, we will camp twenty miles east of here. In a few days, we will settle in our new home beside Domus Ra Pass. There, we will resume our preparations. One day, the orcs will find their way beyond the walls of Talastar. When that happens, we must be ready."

Without waiting for a response, for none was expected, Gryzaal set off at a jog. He and his squad ran out of the castle, across the open square outside her walls, and down the empty streets of the only city they had ever called home. In his heart, he knew that his people would never return.

He lifted his eyes to the blue morning sky. "Vandasal, if you can hear me, answer me one thing. Will any of us even survive what is to come?"

The lack of an answer was as disturbing as the question itself.

CHAPTER 12
PAISU

Arangoli stood in the shadow of a tent awning, listening as Gryzaal recited his story. The dark elf finished the tale and fell silent.

Stroking his beard while mulling over what had been revealed, Arangoli focused on the aspects of the tale alluding to things unsaid. "I assume the surprises you left for the orcs resulted in the castle's collapse."

Gryzaal nodded. "We plotted out possible routes they might take. With each, we created a trap that when triggered would bring down the ceiling in that section of the castle. We hoped that design would not only prevent them from reaching the surface but would also kill a fair amount of the monsters in the process. Based on what you found, it sounds like the orcs sprung every trap."

"Oh, the building was destroyed with only a few walls still standing when we got there. Two of those, we knocked down to close the opening to the dungeon and buy us time to escape. Too bad it only slowed them down for a few days."

The dark elf narrowed his eyes. "They will come for you."

"Me?" Arangoli blinked. "Why would they come for me?"

"They are like dogs. Once they have a scent, they are relentless."

"Scent?" Arangoli lifted his arm and sniffed. The odor caused him to wince. "I do smell a bit ripe. That's what I get for wearing armor for two weeks without bathing." He admitted, "It might be difficult for them to miss us at this point."

The Drow warrior's lip turned up in a rare display of emotion. "I was going to suggest you and your squad consider bathing."

"Does that mean you intend to let us live?"

"Like I said, the orcs are coming this way."

"Are you certain they won't simply head for the pass and go by us?"

"We will ensure they don't attempt the pass."

Arangoli narrowed his eyes. "You have something planned."

"I have much planned, but I could use a few more stout warriors."

"You wish us to join you?"

"A war has begun. It is not a conflict between races, but one between good and evil. If we were to fight these monsters alone, I fear it would be the end of our people. Yours could be next."

"Have dwarves and dark elves ever fought side by side?"

"Not that I can recall."

Arangoli glanced around the camp, thick with dark elves. Besides himself, eight of his squad had survived, yet they had agreed to a mission to rescue their people, not fight a war. "I need to speak with my team before I respond to your offer."

"Understandable."

"However, If we agree to this, I ask something of you."

"What?"

"The dwarves we sent to you last summer are to be freed, so they can return home."

"I must hold them for another day or two, then they can leave."

"Hold them? Why?"

"Come. I will show you." The dark elf set off across camp, heading north.

Arangoli stood there for a beat and sighed. He was hungry and tired, but rest and food would have to wait.

"When is this blazing Drow going to stop dragging me from place to place?" Grumbling beneath his breath, he set off, intent on catching up to Gryzaal.

Surprisingly, they returned to the tunnel used to enter the camp, the dark confines bringing them back to the abandoned city.

"Why are we back here?" Arangoli asked.

"Follow and I will show you." Gryzaal held up a finger. "However, do not stray and touch nothing."

The Drow headed down the street and stopped outside the first house. Inside was the same faceless person Arangoli had spotted on his way in.

With a nod toward the open doorway, Gryzaal said, "That statue wears a dress and a wig for a reason."

"I figured you didn't do it on a lark."

"How droll." Gryzaal explained, "After battling the orcs for a year, we have learned that they are not intelligent creatures. They act on instinct and attack on sight. The statues arranged throughout the city are bait. Buildings such as this are the traps, designed to spring the moment someone draws near a statue." He gestured. "Come. I will show you more."

They continued down the narrow street, turned left, and followed an even narrower alley. The sounds of workers came from ahead. They crossed a sunlit street and entered another alley, and all the while, the noises grew increasingly louder.

When they reached the next sunlit intersection, Gryzaal turned left. Ahead, working in the shade of a tent awning were dwarves and dark elves.

"My people!" Arangoli blurted.

"Yes."

Two dwarves stood before two separate blocks of stone. Each was moving his hands along the stone while chunks, shards, and dust burst from the points their fingers touched. Even for someone like Arangoli, who had witnessed his people shape stone dozens of times over, it was an amazing sight. He stopped a few strides from the tent while the stone shapers focused on their craft. Guided by hands blessed by a magical touch, the stone transformed from raw, rough blocks to the likenesses of people, one male, the other female.

At the same time, female dark elves measured, cut, and sewed fabric. Swaths of raw material covered one table while a finished dress and tunic lay upon another. Despite all of this activity, the noises Arangoli had first heard came from a nearby building. Curious, he approached the open door and found two dwarves and eight dark elves working inside. The dwarves stood in a waist-deep pit dug into the floor while the Drow hauled small barrels over to the pit and placed them near the interior supporting walls. Lines of thin rope, strikers, flint, and tools lay strewn across the intact portion of the floor.

Arangoli nodded. "You are building more traps."

From behind him, Gryzaal said, "This entire city is a trap."

Turning toward the Drow, Arangoli furrowed his brow. "Nobody lives here?"

"Not for many, many years."

"Why not?"

"In truth, we do not know." Gryzaal ran his hand along the building's outer wall. "Long ago, this was a home for my people. They called the city Paisu. It was said to be a beautiful place filled with life until one day, a caravan traveling from Talastar visited only to find the city empty. No bodies or damage were found to make one believe there was an attack. The populace, a full third of my race, simply vanished. In fear and superstition, the Drow have avoided the city ever since...until now."

"So, this place was empty, lifeless ruins for hundreds of years?"

"Yes."

"Yet, you came back."

"Note that we do not live in the city." Gryzaal shook his head. "My people could not abide doing so. It would be akin to moving into a haunted mausoleum occupied by the troubled ghosts of our ancestors."

"So, you are using the city as a decoy?"

"For the past six months, we have labored to craft a massive death-trap, intent on killing as many of the vermin deepspawn as possible. Should they invade, which I believe they will, rather than finding innocents to feed on, they will be greeted by sculptures dressed as real people and surrounded by death traps. The more monsters fall to this trap, the fewer we will be forced to fight when the time comes."

Arangoli nodded. "I can see that. Where do we come in?"

"These mountains are largely impassible. Even before you led them in this direction, we anticipated them making for Domus Ra Pass, but we will instead draw them to this city, where we will treat them to a nasty surprise. Those that survive will then take the tunnel to our camp, where we will resume the fight. Even if things go as planned, I fear we will be vastly outnumbered. My people have learned much from fighting these creatures over the past year. The most daunting aspect of this enemy, even worse than a scratch of their talons leading to instant death, is that their numbers are countless." He gave a firm nod. "We need you to fight at our side."

Arangoli blinked. "You are asking for dwarves and Drow to band together?"

"It must happen if we hope to survive."

"But my squad is small. The orcs might be mindless, but they are fast and appear relentless. Their superior numbers will wear us down. Despite our skill, we will still lose if the horde is countless as you say."

"That is why I need you to appeal to your fellow dwarves. Clan argent must join the battle. If we fail here, their holds will be next." Gryzaal pointed south. "Domus Ra lies twenty miles south of here. It is a well-protected fortress, but that means little to deepspawn. The citadel will fall, and every dwarf within will be slaughtered. The orcs will then advance to the next settlement and will continue until they are defeated or all life is extinguished. There can be no middle ground."

At some point during the discussion, the workers had stopped one by one until all were staring at Arangoli. Dwarves and Drow alike stood in silence, waiting for him to respond.

The sting of betrayal connected to the coup led by Rysildar remained like a bloody wound yet to scab over. Dwarves and elves had never been close, not as far as Arangoli knew, and the dark elves were viewed in an even harsher light after recent events. Despite all of this, he sensed the weight of the decision before him. *If I side with Gryzaal, will Korrigan support me or will he demand my head for treason? If I deny Gryzaal's request, do I doom my people, or are we doomed regardless?* In the end, Arangoli was a warrior, born to fight. Anything less would be denying that one, certain truth.

"We will do it."

Gryzaal gave a firm nod and clapped a hand on Arangoli's shoulder. "Together, we might give the world hope."

Arangoli dropped his meaty paw on the dark elf's shoulder. "We will fight with all of our hearts. Should we die, it will only be after we have slaughtered ten times our number."

"Agreed."

Dropping his hand, Arangoli stepped back. "Now, let me discuss this with my squad over a meal. You do have food, don't you?"

Gryzaal grinned. "Food we have. Let us return to your warriors. We will dine together, and I will share the details of our plan."

CHAPTER 13

AN APPEAL

"Look at me, Goli," Gortch argued. "I am big, fat, and slow. I should be your last choice."

He and Arangoli stood alone at the edge of the Drow encampment. Their discussion had persisted since finishing their midday meal. Despite his best efforts, Gortch had yet to get Arangoli to concede.

Again, his captain and squad leader shook his head. "You are the only Head Thumper who is injured. I need able warriors here."

"Bah!" Gortch pulled his mace off his belt and held it in front of Arangoli's face. "I can whomp those dirty orcs with one hand tied behind my back." Since the Drow lacked healing magic, his other arm was bound in a sling, his shoulder bandaged. With his armor discarded and badly in need of repair, he had been given a clean tunic, stretched tight by his girth and thick arms.

Arangoli's eyes softened, as did his tone. "I know you prefer to fight beside your squad mates. We will be hard pressed to make up for your absence, but this is important. Besides my name, yours is known the best among the clans. More importantly, the dwarf you must convince owes you."

Gortch arched his brow. "Basteric is holdmaster?"

"He is."

The realization brought a grimace to Gorch's face. "Dwarves hold no love for the Drow, but Basteric has more reason than most to hate them."

"Aye. That is why you must convince him to join the fight and to send a messenger to Domus Skrai. King Fandaric cannot be unaware of the Drow presence here. If given reason to send warriors, he will act."

Gortch frowned. "What are you saying?"

"You must ensure as many Clan Argent warriors head this direction as possible, regardless of the means."

The inference stirred an approach Gortch had not considered. "You're determined for me to do this, aren't you?"

"We need your help, Gortch. Go. Bring back warriors. Maybe you can even visit a healer and have your shoulder mended. If so, we would eagerly welcome you joining the fight."

Shoulders slumping in defeat, Gortch sighed. "Very well."

Arangoli grinned. "I knew we could count on you."

"How far is this walk?"

"Twenty miles." Arangoli pointed toward the narrow canyon connected to the camp. "That direction."

"Twenty?" The number was double what Gortch feared he might say. He shook his head. "There is no way I can make it there by nightfall."

"And, considering the uneven, mountain terrain, you will be forced to camp somewhere in the pass and wait until sunup to resume your journey."

With the sun beyond its apex, that left less than half a day.

"I don't suppose we have a horse to make this go faster?"

"Sorry. You will have to go on foot and sleep in the wild."

Gortch scowled. "This mission is becoming less appealing by the minute."

"I suspect that will continue throughout the day."

"You are going to make me do this."

"We need you to do it." Arangoli shoved a full pack into Gortch's stomach. "You'll find trail rations and two full water skins inside."

"What if I get lost?"

"The canyon walls leave you without choices. Follow them into the pass. When you reach the gravel trail, turn south. The road passes right below Domus Ra, at the southern edge of these mountains."

Gortch shoved his mace back into the loop on his hip, lifted the pack, and slid it over his good shoulder. "I will be back. Don't die without me."

"It'll take more than a horde of ugly arse monsters to do me in."

Despite Arangoli's smile, Gortch heard a tightness in his voice. *He is scared.* The great Arangoli Handshaw being afraid was something Gortch thought he would never see. The realization struck hard and sapped the last of his resistance.

"Very well. I'll go to Domus Ra, speak with Basteric, and see a healer. The moment I am healed, I am racing back here, even if I must do it alone." He thrust a finger into Arangoli's chest. "Do not die until I get back."

"I don't intend to."

"Good. If all goes well, I will see you soon." Rather than wait for a response, Gortch turned and headed down the trail leading to the pass.

The shade of the canyon wall fell behind as ground rose. Even in the shade, the air was hot and stifling. In the sun, it was doubly so. In moments, beads of sweat dotted his brow and left his tunic damp. Without a cloud in the sky and most of the afternoon yet to pass, it would only grow hotter. To make matters worse, Gortch had been awake since the previous afternoon, most of that time spent either walking or fighting. Weary and drenched with perspiration, he focused on his determination to return with a dwarven army.

~

RAGGED AND WORN, Gortch descended the downslope on the south side of the pass. While the north side of the mountain range was covered in rolling grasslands called the Haghetti, the southern side of the mountain was a mixture of brown hills dotted in scattered green scrub and open plains of yellowed grass. The region was termed Domusi, the land of Clan Argent.

The downhill road ran along a rocky wall with a drop exceeding a hundred feet to the other side. Gortch followed it around a gentle bend and the fortress city of Domus Ra came into view, tucked against a towering wall of red-tinted rock that provided shade from the afternoon sun. Walls of reddish stone divided the city from a canyon filled with narrow, rocky spires. After twenty miles of travel sandwiched around a night of fitful sleep on rocky, uncomfortable ground, Gortch's journey neared its end.

Invigorated by the sight of his destination, he tracked along the downhill road until he came to an intersection. One path continued south, toward a barren landscape. The other wound through a forest of stone spires and faded into the shade below the steep cliffside. He took the later route, passed beneath an eighty-foot-tall arch, and continued on.

Shadows lurked among the stone towers to his left and right. Those narrow recesses might be considered places of refuge from the sun or from projectiles launched from the citadel walls, but Gortch knew better. It was whispered among his people that deadly traps lurked among those rock formations. So, he continued across the valley of spires, entered the shade of the cliff wall on its western boundary, and came to a massive set of doors at the base of the mountain. There, he lifted his gaze. A hundred feet above him, the citadel wall stood at the edge of a drop. Armored dwarves posted on the wall peered down at him. Rather than approach the doors and knock, he waited.

A gong resounded. The doors shook and swung open to reveal a chamber twenty feet wide and just as deep. A squad of sixteen dwarves in phalanx formation stared back at Gortch. All wore helmets, armor, and shields while gripping pikes in their right hand. At the rear of the chamber, beyond the dwarven warriors, stood the biggest lift platform Gortch had ever seen.

A dwarf with his helmet tucked under his arm stepped out from the shadows and took position at the fore of the squad. He lifted his chin and looked down his nose at Gortch.

"My name is Landaric, Captain of the Domus Ra guard." He said in a haughty tone. "State your name and clan."

"I am Gortch Onerslate of Clan Tahal."

A murmur ran through the guards, many of them exchanging whispers.

Landaric turned and snapped. "Quiet!" Once the guards fell silent, he turned back toward Gortch. "I have heard of you...if that is really your name. Based on the stories, I thought you'd be larger."

Gortch grimaced and strode forward before stopping in the open doorway. He outweighed the other dwarf by a fair margin. "Perhaps you'd like to test me."

Landaric arched a brow. "You wear no armor and your arm is in a sling."

Grinning, Gortch patted the weapon on his hip. "I could best any three of your squad with this one arm, and from my experience, armor is only needed if you get yourself poked."

The captain scowled, his eyes narrowing at Gortch. He then burst out laughing. "By Vandasal's beard, I believe you are a Head Thumper as you say."

"Good." Gortch smiled. "Now that is settled, I need to speak with Basteric."

"I hope you understand that I need to ask why."

"Are you aware of the Drow camp up the road?"

Landaric's grimace returned. "We are."

"I just came from there, sent by my captain, Arangoli Handshaw."

"What is this about?"

"It is about war. Anything beyond that, I will share only with Basteric."

Landaric stroked his beard in contemplation before nodding. "Come along. I will escort you to the holdmaster."

The squad parted to create an aisle down the center of the chamber. Gortch and his escort walked past the warriors and stepped onto the lift. A quartet of guards approached the doors and pushed them closed as Landaric pressed a palm to the control panel. The lift hummed and began to rise, the entrance chamber fading from view.

Walls of solid rock surrounded the lift while dim daylight beckoned ten stories above.

Landaric turned to face the rear of the lift. "You were at the battle of Talastar."

Gortch faced the dwarf with a frown. He recalled the battle well. It had been a bloody affair. "I was there."

"I hear your squad turned the tide of that fight."

"It could have turned ugly for us if things had gone differently. Even then, Gahagar died and the campaign came to an end."

Landaric sighed. "I wish I could have met him."

"Who?"

"Gahagar."

"If you had met him, you'd never forget it."

"Was he as amazing as they say?"

"He was stubborn and arrogant, but I can't blame him. If my flesh had turned to metal and I had lived for five hundred years, I'd believe I was invincible as well."

The light brightened as the lift rose into a stone building with an open doorway at the rear of the platform. Like the lift itself, the door was easily large enough to drive a wagon through. When the platform stopped, they stepped off and strode outside and into a square occupied by a few dozen dwarves. Many were women, filling brown jugs from a fountain. Beyond the square was the dark opening of a tunnel leading into the mountain. Buildings carved from red-tinted stone bordered narrow streets to the left and right. Directly behind the lift, the city's outer wall loomed, stretching off in both directions. A wagon driven by a bald dwarf with a red beard rolled across the square, turned, and headed for the dark cave at the rear of the city.

When Landaric headed down a street to the right, walking parallel to the city wall, Gortch followed. Citizens paused to stare at Gortch as he walked past. The sling cradling his left arm made him feel self-conscious. The lack of armor made him feel naked and vulnerable. His free hand strayed to the mace on his hip without intent.

The street opened to a keep carved into the mountainside. Square towers stood on both ends of the façade while darkness lurked behind narrow windows in the four-story-tall building.

They approached the quartet of guards posted outside the closed front door. Landaric spoke with the guards, mentioning Gortch by name before opening the door and stepping aside. The guards stared wide-eyed at Gortch as he walked past, but he paid them no heed, for his thoughts had turned to the urgency of his mission.

A receiving hall occupied by wooden furniture with auburn pillows welcomed them. The cool confines of the stone, shaded building allowed the sweat on Gortch's forehead to cool. For the first time since arriving at the Drow encampment, the air felt comfortable. They climbed a staircase to the second story and entered a dining hall illuminated by indirect sunlight. A solitary dwarf was seated at the far end of a long, dark table, his attention on a missive gripped in his left hand. Notably, his other arm ended in a stump below his shoulder.

Landaric stopped shy of the table and cleared his throat. "Pardon the interruption, Holdmaster."

Without looking up, the other dwarf said, "What is it, Captain?"

"You've a guest who wishes to speak with you."

The dwarf lowered the missive and lifted his gaze. When eyes met Gortch's, his scowl slid away. "Gortch Onerslate?"

"Hi, Bast. Sorry that your arm never grew back."

The holdmaster stood and used his remaining hand to caress the opposite shoulder. "You know, there are times when it feels like it is still there."

"Memories. Some are good. Some are bad. All can affect us, I suppose."

Basteric laughed. "Well said. Speaking of arms, what happened to yours?"

Gortch approached the table. "Injured in a fight with a three-headed dog."

"Like Cerberus?"

"Exactly like that."

The holdmaster furrowed his brow. "I thought beasts like that were pure myth."

"So did I until one bit me. I don't suppose you have a healer in your hold."

Basteric looked at Landaric. "Go and fetch Ocilar. Tell him someone important needs his assistance and return here."

"Yes, Holdmaster." The captain of the guard thumped his chest, turned, and ducked into the stairwell.

Alone with the holdmaster, Gortch decided it was time to share the news. "I come from the Drow camp on the other side of the pass."

Basteric grimaced. "Those blazing dark elves have no business there. If they attempt to march through the pass, they will find that Clan Argent does not forget.

"If you recall, it was Gahagar who attacked Talastar. His command started that battle, and while we got the best of the Drow, they were only defending their land. Even I cannot fault them for that."

The holdmaster thumped a fist against his chest. "Those dirty bastards killed my father, my brother, and left me a cripple!"

"We all lost something that day. You'd have died as well if I hadn't acted."

The not-so-subtle reminder worked. Basteric's expression softened. "And I am thankful for it."

"As you said, your father is dead. You are holdmaster, now. It is your job to do what is best for your people."

Basteric frowned. "I am aware of my responsibility."

"Then, I beg you to listen to what I tell you next."

"Go on."

"Have you asked the Drow why they left Talastar?"

"In early spring, I sent an envoy but was ignored. Liloth merely said that as long as she remains on that side of the pass, she is on Drow lands and her actions are none of my business."

"Since then, the situation has changed."

"How so?"

"War is coming."

The holdmaster blanched. "Please don't tell me that they seek revenge for what happened outside Talastar's walls."

Gortch considered doing just that, as Arangoli suggested. He knew he could use Basteric's hatred to his advantage and force the holdmaster to act. Regardless of intent, if Basteric were to send warriors through the pass, they would be forced to fight when faced with the orcs. However, something inside him resisted. He imagined himself as one of the warriors being surprised by the horde of monsters when believing the enemy was something more civilized. They would not be prepared for what they faced, and it was likely to cost far more lives.

He shook his head. "It's nothing like that."

"What, then?"

"I've a tale to share, one you may be hard pressed to believe. However, I swear on the blood of my ancestors that it is true."

"Go on."

"The monster that chewed on my shoulder is not the only one from the underworld. We Head Thumpers just came from Talastar. We found the city abandoned and were chased out by mindless, bloodthirsty creatures called orcs. That horde of monsters is heading in this direction. The Drow have taken up home outside the ruins of the abandoned city of Paisu. There, they intend to make a stand against this evil army. I was sent here to request help from Clan Argent."

Basteric laughed but then stopped when Gortch scowled back at him. "You can't be serious."

"I am deadly serious." Gorch leaned forward. "You owe me your life, Bast. Arangoli needs you. I need you. I intend to leave as soon as my shoulder is healed. Send as many warriors as you can and also send a missive to Domus Skrai. Fandaric needs to know what is coming, so he can prepare as well."

"If I send a missive like that to the king, he will have my head if he discovers it is untrue."

"I know."

"You are putting me in a difficult position."

"I am trying to save your arse. If these monsters get through the pass, Domus Ra is doomed. Your other holds could soon follow."

Basteric snorted. "Domus Ra is impregnable. We will raise the lift. Even if they breach the doors below, we are one hundred eighty feet above ground. How could they get to us?"

"These creatures can scale rock walls as easily as you or I cross this room. Their talons are laced with poison. A scratch can kill in seconds."

Gortch shook his head. "I realize this is a lot, but you have to trust me. This is a warning you cannot ignore."

The holdmaster leaned back in his chair with a frown. "After the Drow betrayed your clan a year ago, you now ask me to trust them and to fight at their side?"

Too exhausted to argue, Gortch raked his hand down his face in exasperation. He pulled out a chair and plopped into it with a heavy sigh. "Listen to me, Bast. You must set aside any past wrongdoings. I am from Clan Tahal. I was among those who freed Ra'Tahal from the clutches of those backstabbing dark elves. If I am willing to fight at their side, despite their wrongdoings, then the threat we face must be dire. Wouldn't you agree?"

"Yeah. I guess."

Tired of the verbal sparring, Gortch pounded his fist on the table. The thump echoed throughout the dining hall, the quake it sent across the table toppling over the candelabra in its center. The suddenness of the act caused Basteric to flinch.

Leaning forward, Gortch growled. "Fight with us or die here, as a coward. It is your choice. I don't care, so long as you get me a healer and a horse, so I can return to my squad before that blazing army of blood thirsty monsters reaches the pass."

Basteric stared across the table, unmoving. It was not anger, Gortch saw in his eyes. It was fear.

In a softer tone, Gortch said, "Send as many warriors with me as you can spare, while you remain here to prepare your defenses. You must alert Fandaric, so he can mobilize the rest of the clan. There is little time, and any delay will cost lives." He pleaded, "Act, Bast. It is your duty."

After a long, weighty moment of consideration, the holdmaster shook his head. "I am sorry, Gortch. I cannot spare any warriors."

"What?" Gortch blurted.

The holdmaster continued, "Tomorrow, I will send a scout north through the pass. If there truly is another enemy approaching, I will then send a messenger to Domus Skrai. In the duration, my warriors will remain here and prepare our defenses, be it against these monsters you speak of or against the conniving dark elves." Before Gortch could argue the point, Basteric held his palm out. "My decision is made. Argue any further, and I will have you locked up."

Gortch fumed, his fist clenching in frustration. He opened his mouth to issue a harsh retort when he was interrupted by someone behind him clearing his throat. Turning, he found Landaric in the doorway. A bald dwarf with a long, thin beard stood beside him.

"Sorry to interrupt, Holdmaster," Landaric said. "The healer is here as requested."

"Thank you, Captain." He lowered his gaze to stare at Gortch. "You are dismissed." When Gortch stood and turned from the table, he added, "If anyone else had come here and spoken to me like that, they would be in a dungeon cell. I'll never forget how you saved my life, but if you do anything to abuse my hospitality, including creating a panic amid my people with your wild tales of monsters from the underworld, I will put you in shackles."

Gortch closed his eyes and clenched his jaw as he held back a heated retort. He headed toward the door, intent on leaving the room without stirring more trouble but only made it two steps before he stopped. Turning with a scowl, he spoke in an even tone. "Whether it is fear, pride, or hatred that has made you so stubborn, I worry that your emotions may be the death of you, Bast. I hope it does not mean the end of the citizens who rely on your leadership."

Thick, palpable tension electrified the air. Basteric glared across the room as Gortch turned and headed out the door.

CHAPTER 14

SUBVERSION

Warmth came from the thick dwarf hands resting on Gortch's shoulder. He sat in a padded chair with an older dwarf named Ocilar standing over him. Minutes passed as the healer's magic tingled along his skin and caused the flesh beneath to mend. More than a day had passed since Gortch had last eaten a full meal. After a twenty-mile journey through the mountains and a night of fitful sleep beneath the stars, he was hungry. Now, with his body fueling Ocilar's magic, his stomach rumbled in anger, demanding sustenance. Seated in the quiet confines of Ocilar's modest home, the noise was akin to thunder, impossible to ignore.

"Sorry," Gortch said.

Ocilar shook his head. "No need to be sorry. Healing absorbs energy, and I hear you came through the pass today on foot."

"Aye."

"You had food?"

"Some rations that ran out this morning."

"So, you've hunger on top of hunger."

"You could say that."

Ocilar smirked. "I am surprised you haven't bitten me. Based on experience, dwarves get ornery when they are hungry. Dwarves your size, doubly so."

"There are few dwarves my size."

"True as well."

Gortch grinned "However, I'd be lying if I didn't admit that your fingers remind me of sausages right now. I have been hard pressed to not take a bite."

Ocilar chuckled and lowered his hands. "Thank you for your restraint. I am rather fond of my fingers." He stepped in front of Gortch and gave a firm nod. "Go on and test it."

Tentatively, Gortch raised his arm and found it pain free. He worked it, testing its motion. Surprisingly, it felt better than ever. "It feels great."

The healer leaned in and began unwinding the blood-soaked bandages. Beneath was pink flesh with no trace of the puncture wounds remaining. When finished, he stepped back. "You are all set."

"Thanks, Ocilar."

"It was an honor to heal a war hero such as yourself."

Gortch stood. "I don't know if I am a hero..."

"Nonsense. Stories about you, Arangoli, and the other Head Thumpers frequent the streets and taverns in Domus Ra. Six years may have passed since Gahagar died, but tales of his campaign continue. Your squad might have been latecomers, but the battle of Talastar was the culmination of that effort. The heroes from that battle hold a special place in the hearts of dwarves from here to Dis Aeldor."

Gortch had spent much of the previous five years away from his own people and had not visited a dwarven settlement other than the ones run by his own clan in that duration. "I had no idea."

"Domus Ra is a small hold. I am willing to bet that word has spread since your arrival. Watch how others react when they see you. I will be shocked if their admiration is not immediately apparent."

Rising to his feet, Gortch picked up his tunic and pulled it over his head. He slid his arms in and stretched it over his paunch. "This tunic is terrible," he said with a frown.

"I expected you to be wearing armor."

"Mine was damaged in the battle that wounded my shoulder."

"In that case, perhaps you should stop by the armory."

Hunger demanded Gortch find food as soon as possible, but he wished to be away at first light and he was unlikely to get assistance from an armorer so early in the morning. He glanced toward the window. Daylight still illuminated the sky but thick shadows clung to the citadel streets.

"Where can I find the armorer?"

"The guard barracks." Ocilar pointed toward the window. "It is the big building beside the keep. Circle round it and enter through the rear entrance."

Gortch gripped the healer's forearm. "Thank you, Ocilar. You are a good, honest dwarf. Your actions may have saved lives."

Ocilar's brow furrowed. "You behave as if something dire approaches."

"Something dire, indeed. Be well, Ocilar. I fear your talents will be in high demand very soon."

Gortch strolled over to the door and slipped out into a quiet, narrow street. He glanced west, where thin clouds left streaks across the sky. The pink tint of sunset provided a stark contrast against the blue. *How many more sunsets will I see?* It was the kind of question warriors were supposed to avoid. Nobody knew the answer, so there was little point in dwelling on when the end might come. He sighed, turned around, and headed back toward the keep.

As he navigated the narrow alleys of Domus Ra, he reflected on his conversation with Basteric. It had not gone well and left him reconsidering Arangoli's inference that he use Basteric's hatred for the Drow to get him to commit soldiers to the cause. The idea of twisting the truth in that manner turned Gortch's stomach, but Arangoli had placed his faith in him and he had failed, which made him want to vomit.

He reached the square outside the keep and spied a two-story building beside it. While the structure was only half the height of the keep, its footprint appeared twice the size. "That must be the barracks."

As he crossed the square, the citizens of Domus Ra stopped and watched. He felt their stares and wondered if they were judging him. A voice inside screamed for him to approach those dwarves and to tell them to flee but doing so would only raise Basteric's ire.

A dark alley beside the barracks took him to the rear of the building. There, he found an even darker passage sandwiched between the cliff-side and the barracks. An open doorway waited halfway down the alley. Warm light glowed beyond the doorway, welcoming him as he stepped inside.

Iron bars ran from floor to ceiling to Gortch's left and right, dividing the entrance from the rest of the room. Beyond the bars, racks filled with weapons stood on one side. To the other, pieces of armor rested upon shelving. Straight ahead was a desk. A dwarf leaning back in a chair, his arms over his chest, his feet up on the desk, dozed with his head drooped to one side. The whistle of a snore came from the sleeping dwarf. He had an auburn beard with a gray streak down the middle, the mark notable and one Gortch recognized.

"Walzar!" Gortch boomed.

The dwarf's eyes flashed open, his arms flung out, and the chair toppled backward. It struck hard, eliciting a crack as the dwarf yelped and rolled onto his side.

Gortch rounded the desk. "Are you alright?" He squatted. "I didn't mean for you to tumble."

The dwarf rolled to his hands and knees and blinked. "Gortch?"

"It's me." Gortch slipped a hand beneath the elder dwarf's arm and lifted him to his feet. He glanced down at the chair and found the wood cracked. "I think you'll need a new chair."

"What are you doing here?"

"I came here on a mission for Arangoli. Why are you working in the armory?"

Walzar dusted himself off. "Basteric decided I was too old for sparring and night watch. He left me in charge of the armory."

"A desk job."

"Yeah. It is often boring, but caring for the weapons and armor gives me something constructive to do." He shrugged. "At least, that is what I tell myself."

"It is hard for me to imagine you giving up your axe."

"In truth, I never thought I'd grow old."

Gortch patted the elder dwarf on the shoulder. "Age might be the warrior's true curse."

"Too true." Walzar chuckled. "What brings you to my armory?"

"I need new armor. My last set fell victim to a massively overfed, three-headed dog."

Walzar blinked. "Cerberus?"

"Aye." Gortch shook his head. "I didn't even think the beasts existed until one bit me."

"That'll do it." Walzar lifted a ring of keys off his belt. "Come on. Let's get you outfitted."

DRESSED IN NEW ARMOR, Gortch stepped through the doorway in the wall of bars and turned as Walzar pulled the door closed. The armorer locked the cell door and hung his key ring on his belt.

"It is funny how naked I felt in that tunic," Gortch said.

"Well, the plate and mail set you now wear was crafted of dwarven steel. Should an oversized dog attempt to bite you, I suspect it is likely to break a tooth."

"Let's hope I don't need to put it to the test." Both dwarves laughed.

As the laughter settled, Gortch said, "Thank you again, Walzar. I wish you well in your retirement."

"Where do you go, now?"

"First, I need food. I am starved. Then, I'll need to find a place to stay the night. In the morning, I ride north."

"North? You intend to face the Drow?"

"Honestly, I intend to fight at their side."

Walzar's brow furrowed. "What of the other Head Thumpers?"

"They are already there, preparing for war."

"Against whom?"

"I...am not allowed to say."

The elder dwarf frowned and stroked his beard. "Interesting."

Gortch considered telling him and going against Basteric's wishes, but Walzar spoke before he could do so.

"It is time for me to lock up. I'll join you for dinner, and you can spend the night in my apartment. It's not much, but I've a spare bed."

"After spending most of the past week sleeping on the ground, a bed is a luxury. I accept."

"Wonderful." Walzar clapped him on his recently mended shoulder. "Let's visit the barracks. Dinner should be waiting."

Not bothered by the idea of eating with the city guards, Gortch nodded. "Let's go."

They walked outside and the armorer pulled the door closed. He used a key to secure the bolt and headed down the dark passageway with Gortch a step behind. They turned down a wider road and walked side by side. Despite his hunger, Gortch felt better than he had since before his injury. His new armor gave him added confidence that caused him to puff his chest out and hold his chin up. They rounded the building and made for the front entrance. Walzar opened the door. Warm light and the buzz of conversation poured through the opening. They stepped inside, and Gortch paused to survey the room.

Twenty tables, each long enough to seat a dozen warriors, filled the room. The benches alongside the tables were full with only a handful of open spots visible. Along the wall to the right was a long counter behind which stood six female dwarves. An open door behind them led to a large kitchen.

Warriors seated at the tables glanced at the two dwarves standing inside the doorway. Many of them jerked with a start and then began nudging the guards seated beside them. The conversation quieted, and soon, everyone was staring in Gortch's direction. Suddenly self-conscious, Gortch removed his new helmet and tucked it under his arm.

Walzar whispered. "It seems word of your presence has spread."

"Seems so."

"Well, staring back at a room full of onlookers won't fill your stomach. Let's get some food."

With Walzar in the lead, Gortch approached the counter and nodded. "Greetings."

The female across from him picked up a tray and put a plate on it. "We've chicken and pork. Which do you prefer?"

"Both would be great."

She arched her brow and then shrugged. "Why not. Just about everyone has eaten already anyway." With tongs, she pulled a pile of shredded pork from a heavy pan and then grabbed a chicken leg and breast from the neighboring tray. Thus, Gortch worked his way down the line, adding potatoes, beans, and hard rolls to the plate before the last server handed him a tankard filled with white liquid.

"What is this?" he asked.

"Milk," she replied.

"You don't have ale?"

"Only when Captain Landaric orders us to tap a keg."

"Fine."

Gortch turned and found half of the seated warriors staring at him. He then spied Walzar halfway across the room, approaching a table with a bench that stood half open. Eager to eat, Gortch followed.

When he reached the table, he sat on the end of the bench and nodded to the eight guards seated with him. Without another word, he began to eat.

Starved as he was, his plate emptied quickly. Nobody at the table said a word during the process. As Gortch used half a hard roll to slurp up some gravy and the last bit of potatoes, a young dwarf seated across from him broke the silence.

"Are you truly Gortch the Grinder?"

It was not the first time Gortch had heard the name. It was one he had earned but did not particularly embrace. "I suppose."

Another young dwarf leaned in. "What is Captain Arangoli like?"

A third dwarf asked. "How many enemies have you killed?"

The last was a question Gortch didn't care to dwell on. Soldiers throughout the room stood and began gathering around his table. He glanced up at them before turning back to the guards seated across the table. "Why are you asking so many questions?"

The dwarves glanced at each other. "Most of us were ordered to remain here with Landaric when Gahagar and Holdmaster Bastilon took the rest of the warriors north, toward Talastar."

"Ah. You have not had your chance to prove yourself on the battlefield."

"No. Not yet."

Gortch found their eagerness to fight ironic considering how Basteric rebuked his request for warriors. "Alright. Let's try this one question at a time. What would you like to know?"

They looked at each other and then one asked, "Did you truly save the life of Holdmaster Basteric?"

"Yes."

"What happened?"

Suddenly, dozens of dwarves were demanding to hear the story.

Landaric pushed his way through the crowd. "That's enough!" The room quieted. "Gortch Onerslate is our guest. Show him some respect."

He turned to Gortch. "Sorry about that. This lot is green, and they have yet to test their mettle. It leaves them eager to hear tales of heroics."

Gortch stood. "I don't mind. In fact, I would be happy to share a story or two...provided you offer me some ale to sooth my parched throat."

Laughter burst out from Landaric "Right you are!" He turned toward a pair of guards. "Gadaric, Kilvan. Go and fetch us two barrels. We've a guest. Tonight, we drink!"

The room erupted in cheers. Landaric then fired off a list of orders, directing the warriors to rearrange the room. In moments, the tables were pushed together along the back of the room while the benches were assembled into six rows. Finally, one table was placed at the fore of the room.

Two barrels were placed on the table, and both were tapped. Mugs were lined up along the serving counter. Warriors began grabbing tankards and stopping by the barrels to fill them. When everyone had filled a mug and was seated, Landaric approached Gortch.

"The room is yours." The captain of the guard handed Gortch a mug. "Drink up and share whatever stories you wish to tell."

"Oh, I have some stories." Gortch grinned.

He turned to the table, filled up his mug, and then sat between the two barrels. The room quieted with all eyes on him.

"Let's begin with the battle of Talastar. As you know, Gahagar's campaign dragged on for decades with him claiming city after city, until he ruled half of the world. My squad, eleven Clan Tahal warriors who call themselves the Head Thumpers, joined his army as they marched north, through the pass outside these halls. We were young and eager to prove ourselves, none more so than our captain, Arangoli Handshaw."

The crowd listened intently, every ear peeled and every eye focused on Gortch. As the night wore on, he recited tale after tale. The barrels were emptied. Two fresh ones were tapped. Eventually, the tales of his adventures concluded with recent events, including his fight against a massive three-headed dog.

"It was difficult to bury Orvatz only days after we lost Brannigan." He frowned in sadness and then downed the last of his mug. How many drinks he had consumed, he was uncertain, but his head buzzed.

A young warrior seated in the second row raised his hand.

"Yeah?" Gortch pointed toward him.

"I am sorry that you lost two squad mates, but does that mean that the Head Thumpers are seeking recruits?"

Gortch grunted. The last words Arangoli said before he left the Drow camp ran though his head. *You must ensure you get as many Clan Argent warriors heading this direction as possible, regardless of the means.* To Gortch, Arangoli's command gave him the power to make a critical decision.

"Yes." He strode forward and looked over the room. Eager expressions marked the faces of the dwarves seated before him. "In fact, I was sent here to recruit as many capable warriors as possible. In the past, Arangoli led a team of ten. He is ready to expand the Head Thumpers far beyond that number. Anyone who wishes to join the fight need merely meet me at the citadel gate as sunrise, armed and ready. We march north to meet my squad mates." He considered doing so before adding, "A new war has begun. This is not a war between races. This is a war between good and evil. The entire world might depend on our decisions and actions. Sleep well. It may be your last night to do so."

CHAPTER 15
SOUL BOUND

I an opened his eyes to sunlight streaming through his childhood bedroom window. He sat up and stretched, working out the kinks and stiffness from a night of solid sleep. The other bed in the room was empty, so he assumed Vic had already left for the day. He approached the window and peered outside. Long green grass covered the hillside leading down to Lake Shillings, its placid waters reflecting the mountains to the north. The cloudless sky spoke of a gorgeous summer day, the kind of day that was filled with possibility.

A shadow circled in the sky. It glided lower, rounded a large oak, and came toward Ian, who hastily opened the window. Lionel flew in and settled on Ian's arm. The drake lifted its nose and licked Ian's face, the warmth of adoration coming through their connection. He stepped back from the window and stroked the back of Lionel's neck.

Noise coming from inside the house pulled his attention from the drake. He padded across the room and opened the door. The salty, distinct scent of bacon greeted him. Hungry, he walked down the hallway and emerged in the common room.

His mother stood over the oven with a fork in her hand. A pan full of bacon sizzled and popped. With brown hair and hazel eyes, Zora Carpenter was a pretty, petite woman who stood no taller than Ian's chin. Beneath a stained apron, she wore her favorite yellow dress, a dress she reserved for special occasions. She lifted her gaze, her eyes meeting his. A smile bloomed on her face, warming his heart and eliciting a smile of his own.

"Good morning, dear."

"Hi, Mother," he replied.

"I made your favorite."

"Pancakes?"

Zora slipped a leather mitt on her hand, bent, and opened the oven. From it, she removed a pan with a stack of pancakes the size of Ian's head. Turning, she set the pan on a mat in the center of the kitchen table. Three plates lay on the table, along with forks, knives, syrup, a jug, and three cups.

"Eat up. You'll need it to regain your strength."

Famished and tantalized by the thought of his favorite breakfast meal, Ian eagerly sat. Lionel hopped onto the table and eyed the stack of pancakes.

"No," Ian waggled a finger. "I will share, but you had better behave."

The drake sat back and waited while Ian speared four pancakes with one jab and slid them onto his plate. The syrup came next, followed by him pouring himself a tall glass of milk. His mother appeared at his side and dropped four strips of bacon onto his plate. He lifted one and handed it to Lionel, who scarfed it down with vigor. Ian took his own bite, the taste of his mother's pancakes just as he remembered, warm and buttery with a hint of vanilla.

He ate with fervor, and soon, his plate was empty. Not satisfied, he reloaded and cleared his plate again, after which, he sat back and sighed. With the morning sun streaming in and his mother happily humming to herself in the kitchen, Ian thought it was just about the perfect way to start his day.

The door opened. He turned toward it, expecting Vic. The man who entered resembled Vic and carried himself with the same, easy confidence, but this man was older, wiser, more solemn. He walked over to Zora, gave her a kiss and then smiled as he stared into her eyes. She beamed back while cupping his cheek.

"I have missed you," Zora said.

"And I, you," he replied.

Ian frowned in confusion. "Father?"

Perry turned and frowned back. "Ian? You aren't supposed to be here. Not yet."

"This is my home."

His father shook his head. "It is your home no longer. If it is to be your home again, it will not be for some time yet."

Seeing his father felt strange, or even wrong, but Ian could not identify why.

Sadness framed his father's eyes. "You must go, Ian."

Ian stood. "But why? I want to be here with you, with mother."

"You must wait until your time. There is much for you to do yet before you can join us."

Zora stood beside Perry, who slid his arm around her back. "Look at him, Perry. He has grown into a man, yet his vast responsibilities weigh upon him and leave him longing to return to his youth, when life was simple."

"We all find moments that leave us longing to go back, but going back is not possible, not when it means you abandon those who need you."

She furrowed her brow. "If we are to send him back, perhaps I can join him."

"It is impossible."

"No. I feel something. A connection to Ian."

Perry gripped her shoulders, turning her toward him. "You belong here. With me."

"We will have eternity. For our son, for both of our sons, allow me to do this for a time."

He stared into her eyes, lifted his hand, and pulled a stray strand of hair from her face. "You are my sun, my moon, my everything, but if I was able to wait this long for you to come to me. I can wait a while longer."

Zora absolutely glowed as she smiled back at him.

Perry turned to Ian. "You must go, son."

The conversation had Ian bewildered. "I still don't understand. This is my home. You are my family. I belong with you."

"You belong with your brother."

Ian glanced toward the door. "Is he out cutting wood?"

"Vic is not here, not yet. He has much to do with his life, as do you."

Zora stood at Ian's side and slid her hand along his back. "I feel your pain, Ian. I know you could not say goodbye to me. You gave me the energy to speak to your brother before I passed. For that, I am thankful, but you cannot allow that gift to end your own life. Not yet. The world needs you."

Images of his mother lying in bed, burned and bandaged, flashed before his eyes. He gasped. "The fire."

"Yes." She peered into his eyes. "I know you tried to save me, but there was nothing you could have done. It was my time. I only held on long enough so you and Vic could say goodbye. Never did I think I would be able to say it as well. Now, you must return to your body."

Ian shook his head. "I don't know how I got here, so how can I go back?"

"I will take you."

She wrapped her arms around him and drove him backward. A powerful force yanked him through the wall. His surroundings blurred, and he felt as if he were plummeting a vast distance. A weariness came over him, forcing his eyes shut.

WARMTH SURROUNDED IAN, soothing him, comforting him. Soft voices called in the distance. Amid the murmurs, he heard his own name. As the realization came to him, a heavy current buffeted him and began to drive him toward darkness. Rather than succumb to it, Ian scraped and clawed through thick muck that threatened to pull him deeper. As he neared its surface, his eyes flicked open.

He lay in a bed with an old dwarf at his side, seated in a chair. Puffy bags drooped beneath the dwarf's eyes while heavy lids threatened to close them altogether. Beyond the foot of his bed, Vic was engaged in quiet conversation with Revita. Vic's face was unshaven, his hair tousled as if he had just woken. Revita's gaze was locked on Vic, her eyes reflecting uncharacteristic concern.

Ian turned his head, sensing a presence. Lying in the bed beside his was Lionel. The drake's eyes were closed, his small chest rising and falling the only signs of life. Tentatively, Ian mentally reached for Lionel. *Wake up. Come to me.*

The drake stirred as Ian had hoped. However, the other response was entirely unexpected.

I am awake, Ian. The voice was familiar and distinctly female. *I am always with you.*

With a gasp, Ian shot to a sitting position. "Mother?"

Vic, Revita, and the dwarf all reacted, the first two turning toward him, the third flinching as if pinched. All three stared at Ian with startled expressions.

"You are awake!" Revita blurted.

The dwarf shook his head. "It is not possible."

Vic rushed to Ian's bedside and dropped to one knee while taking his hand. "Thank the good spirits." His eyes were red and he looked like he had not slept in days.

Lionel popped up in the other bed and shook like a wet dog trying to shed water. The drake climbed across the dwarf's lap and hopped onto Ian's, who then began stroking the back of its neck. Through their connection, Ian sensed Lionel's adoration. Ian then turned toward the neighboring bed. It was empty.

"Where is mother?"

Vic's gaze lowered in an obvious attempt to avoid looking Ian in the eye. "She...is dead."

Ian's mother and father had both been in his dream, but it was a dream unlike any other. It had felt so real. With it, he had experienced a sense of contentment unlike anything he could recall. "But I gave her my magic just as I gave it to Lionel after the willow attacked him. She spoke to you. I heard it."

"Yes. At least I was able to hear those final words before..." Vic raked a hand down his face, obviously still upset. "Then, when you fainted, I thought I had lost you as well."

The dwarf shook his head. "Your body was fading and your mind was gone. There was nothing I could do. Right after I informed your brother that you would soon pass, you woke instead. I don't understand it."

Ian heard none of it. He could focus on only one thing – the loss of his mother and the vacuum it would create in his life. *Why did this happen, Mother?*

Her voice echoed in his head. *It was my time.*

He gasped. "Did you hear that?"

Vic glanced at Revita. "Did we hear what?"

They cannot hear me, Ian. I am with you and you alone.

How can this be?

How is irrelevant. His mother chided. *Now, be a good brother and ease Vic's pain. Tell him of your dream, but do not mention me being with you now. This must be kept between us. He will not understand.*

The momentary loss Ian had experienced was gone. Even then, the memory of that pain of loss was fresh, giving him insight into how his brother must feel. He needed to do what he could to help Vic.

"Something happened." Ian said, drawing their attention. "When I was unconscious, I was back at home in Shillings. Mother and Father were there. They were happy to be together and both told me they were at peace. They said it was not my time, and they did something to me, forcing me to wake."

The dwarf's eyes widened. "We have stories among my people of such experiences. You visited the spirit realm."

Vic blinked. "Is it true?"

"It felt as real as anything I know," Ian said. "I swear it."

The pain in Vic's eyes lessened.

Zora's voice crooned, *That's a good boy, Ian.*

I am not a boy any longer.

You will always be a boy to me.

Ian frowned. *Why are you here, Mother?*

Silence.

Mother?

I heard you.

Are you going to answer me?

Something is very wrong. A darkness infects the land.

I know.

It is worse than you believe. A being from the underworld seeks to dominate the world of the living. Should that occur, even the spirits of those who have passed are at risk, for this...this demon consumes body and soul alike, and anyone subject to such consumption is doomed to an eternity of torment.

Ian slid his legs off the bed and stood. The room tilted, causing him to stumble.

Vic grabbed Ian by the arm, stabilizing him. "What are you doing?"

The dizziness passed and Ian regained his balance. "I am heading to the privy before my bladder bursts, unless you prefer I relieve myself here."

"No." Vic let go and stepped back. "Go ahead."

"Good. After that, I need to eat. I am starved."

Ian walked off, pretending all was well despite his mother's ominous warning. Time pressed against him like a foot on his throat while he gasped for air.

CHAPTER 16
LOST SPIRIT

A gateway opened, the air around its edges sizzling with energy. Ian waited while Vic, Revita, and Lint stepped through before following. He dismissed the gateway and crossed the Hall of Testing in his underground home beneath Mount Tiadd. Troubled thoughts consumed his attention as he led them to the study, where he found Parsigar bent over a table with a quill in his hand. At the same moment, Truhan walked in through the doorway across the room.

"Ah. Ian. I am glad you have returned," said his master.

Parsigar lifted his head and blinked. "When did you four arrive? I didn't even hear you."

"Only just now," Vic replied.

Lint rushed over to the dwarf, hopped onto a chair, and then onto the table. "What are you drawing? It looks like a magical circle. What does it do? What are you going to craft it from?"

The old dwarf pulled the parchment away from the brownie. "Stay away. The ink is wet."

Fists on his hips, Lint scowled. "I only wanted to know what it is."

"It is something I am designing."

"What does it do?"

"I'll not reveal my secret until it is time."

"Why not? What are you hiding? Is it dangerous?"

Parsigar lifted his gaze. "Is he always this annoying?"

Revita laughed. "Most of the time, he is worse."

Truhan scooped the brownie up with one hand.

"Hey!" Lint squirmed. "Let me go!"

"You are to cause no trouble here. What takes place is too important, and I'll not allow a mischievous brownie to ruin it."

Ian noted his master's serious demeanor. The man's flippant, carefree manner during much of Ian's stay was rarely seen of late. It left Ian worried and wondering if Truhan was hiding some dire news. The thought rekindled his own concern for his mother's warning. Ian had yet to share the details with anyone. He decided it would be best to discuss it with his mentor first.

"Hello, Master. May I speak to you, alone?"

"Of course, Ian. Come."

The man led him to the dark tunnel and along it before stopping outside the only physical door in the complex. He pressed his palm to the door while his other hand gripped and turned the knob. The man stepped inside, but Ian did not move. The doorway led to his master's private chambers, the only place in the underground warren Ian had yet to visit. His reluctance to enter sparred with his curiosity. All the while, Truhan's warning echoed in Ian's head. *Your skills are mighty, but you are not prepared for the wards that protect the dangerous secrets this chamber contains. Any attempt to enter without my assistance will be a dance with death.*

His master's voice cut through Ian's musings. "Are you coming in?"

"Is it safe?"

"So long as you touch nothing, all will be well."

Ian stepped inside, his gaze sweeping the room as Truhan closed the door.

A warm, pulsing glow gave shape to the shadowy interior, the light coming from a golden-hued pyramid resting on a stone pedestal at the room's far end. Seven additional pedestals stood in the room, all placed at the tips of an eight-pointed star drawn on the floor. Each pedestal displayed a strange and unique object. A dark doorway stood to one side, sandwiched between two sets of shelving. Thick books and various artifacts filled the shelving. On the wall opposite the doorway was a massive tapestry depicting an ornate scene that grabbed his attention. He approached the tapestry, light reflecting off golden strands amid darker colors.

The scene showed two beings hovering above a vast field filled with various humanoid races, magical creatures, and mundane animals.

"What is this?" Ian asked.

"This tapestry is very old. The two beings in the air represent Vandasal and Urvadan."

"The Dark Lord?"

"He was not always called that. In fact, there was a time when he was revered as a kind and benevolent god."

Ian frowned. He had heard harrowing tales of the Dark Lord but had always dismissed them as rubbish, preferring to believe no such deity could exist. Considering everything he had witnessed over the past year, his doubt had greatly waned. "How could that be?

Truhan appeared at Ian's side while staring at the tapestry. "Legend says that Urvadan and Vandasal once were connected by an unbreakable bond. Together, they created the beings that populate this world. All was well and the world reveled in peace and harmony, or so it was thought. Even gods can be plagued by the ugliness of greed, envy, and betrayal, and when such emotions bloomed in the heart of one brother, they spilled and drowned the other."

"What happened?"

"I cannot say exactly, but stories claim that the strife plaguing our world began with a spat between gods. It is why the races of magic seek to enslave your people. Your gift gives hope to humanity that the balance might shift in their favor."

"But what of the prophecy?"

"The orcs?"

"Yes." Ian pushed past his reluctance. "In fact, that is what I wanted to discuss with you."

"Go on."

"What if these monsters are merely pawns?"

Truhan flinched. "What makes you say that?"

"What if something drives them?"

"Something?" His lips flattened. "Ian, you will have to be more specific. What do you think drives them?"

"A demon."

"Hmm. I see." Truhan narrowed his eyes. "Where did you hear this?"

His mother's voice echoed in his head. *You cannot let him know about me.*

What do I tell him?

No response

"I...saw it in a vision."

"Prophecy?"

"Um. Yeah."

The man turned and strolled across the room with his hands clasped behind his back. With a hard and intense glare, he turned toward Ian. "What did you see in this vision? Describe it to me. Leave nothing out."

Trapped in his lie, Ian stammered. "Well, I...um...It was like the other vision, but this time, there was something in the darkness besides the orcs."

"Something?"

"Yeah. This demon."

"How do you know it was a demon? What did it look like?"

Help, mother!

Relax, Ian. Reach toward me.

How?

With your mind.

Ian took a deep breath, closed his eyes, and extended himself out, toward his mother. His spirit form stepped out of his body and she was there, appearing as solid and beautiful as ever. Truhan stood in the chamber, his body semitransparent and glowing with a red aura. He stared at Ian's physical form, neither of them moving.

"Can he see me?" Ian asked in a soft voice.

"No. Nor can he hear you."

"What is wrong with him? What is that glow?"

"I don't know," she admitted. "Forget him for now. We have little time." His mother took his hand. "Think about the coming darkness."

He did as she asked.

"Concentrate and will yourself there."

Ian pictured orcs as he had seen them, angry, rabid, and blood-thirsty. His surroundings shifted to a rocky mountain pass covered by sand, rocks, and scrub. A swirling darkness flowed down the hillside, coming straight toward Ian. Horrible hoots and howls came from the darkness, the sound sending chills down Ian's spine. As he was about to flee, his mother spoke in a soft, comforting tone.

"Hold still, Ian. They cannot hurt you." She squeezed his hand, reminding him she was there.

The darkness enveloped them, and with it came the same hairless, grotesque monsters he saw in his vision weeks earlier. Blind rage burned in their red eyes while spittle sprayed from mouths filled with sharp teeth. Monsters raced past in rapid succession, some of them passing right through Ian and his mother. The flow of orcs seemed endless with wave after wave trampling the surrounding scrub as they charged along the canyon floor. Their sheer numbers overwhelmed Ian. Even if every army in the world banded together, he did not know if they could match this evil horde on a battlefield. Then, something else emerged from the black cloud. Ian intuitively knew it was the demon.

The being stood thirty feet tall. Horns jutted out from the creature's forehead and curled around its ears. Its long nose was hooked, its chin distended. Beneath a heavy, protruded brow, the yellow of hatred burned in its determined eyes. Reddish skin covered its muscular body, and while no genitals were visible, it was distinctly male. The thing walked with a firm, deliberate stride. Its heavy feet pounded the ground and left footprints many times the size of a normal man. It drew even with Ian and stopped. Slowly, the demon turned its head and looked down at Ian.

The demon spoke in a guttural voice. "Did you think you could spy on me human? Did you believe I would not know you were here? I rule the spirit realm, and soon, I will rule the world of the living." It reached for Ian.

Massive fingers capped by sharp, black talons came at him, but rather than react as he should, terror clutched Ian's throat and held him fast. The demon gripped his arm, its touch like ice.

Ian's mother suddenly yanked Ian backward, but the demon held fast. She screamed his name, but Ian could do nothing but stare at the creature in horror. As the demon reached for her with his other hand, Zora slapped Ian, the force of the blow snapping Ian's face to the side. The world lurched, his surroundings shifting back to Truhan's chambers.

Pain from the slap caused Ian's eyes to tear. He lifted his hand to his cheek and found it warm and sore to the touch.

Truhan's eyes widened. "What did you do?"

"I...I had a vision. I saw the demon again." Ian went on to describe the monster's appearance, omitting how he had frozen in terror.

Truhan gripped the lapel of Ian's robes, pulled him close, and stared into his eyes.

"What is it, Master?" Ian asked.

"You *did* see it, didn't you?"

"Yes."

The man pushed Ian away, his gaze intense as he turned and ran a hand through his hair. "This changes everything." He walked to the door, threw it open, and stomped off.

Ian exhaled, his shoulders slumping. *That was close. Thank you for saving me, Mother.*

Silence.

Mother?

There was no answer.

Mother!!! Ian screamed in his head.

Realizing that she was gone, he recalled the last thing he saw before leaving the shadow realm – the demon gripping her by the hair as she slapped Ian.

CHAPTER 17
SCROLLS OF THE PAST

Numb and feeling as if he had lost a limb, Ian sat on the floor of a dark tunnel while staring into space. The loss of his mother's presence affected him far more than he would have thought. His near-death experience had given him a unique chance to visit loved ones who had died. Even more startling was when his mother returned with him, if only in spirit. Now, she was gone and the silence following her loss was deafening.

Approaching footsteps pulled him from his trance. He looked up as the faint light of the globe down the corridor framed a familiar face.

His brother stopped and looked down at him with obvious concern before squatting and resting a hand on Ian's shoulder. "Why are you sitting in the dark all alone?"

How do I tell him? He recalled his mother warning him not to tell anyone of her presence. Now that she was gone, would that matter? Finally, he gave a simple, honest answer. "I miss mother."

"I do as well. But, as you told me, we can find solace in the fact that her spirit is now with pa."

Rather than easing Ian's pain, Vic's statement made Ian feel worse. *Something has happened to her soul, and it is my fault.*

Vic said, "I was sent to find you."

"Sent?"

"Truhan said he needs you in the library." Vic's brow furrowed. "Something has him upset." He stood and extended his hand.

Ian pushed his own feelings aside and allowed his brother to help him to his feet. He then followed Vic down the corridor. When they reached the study, one of the bookshelves stood open and light seeped through the gap behind it.

"A secret chamber?" Ian said, in shock.

Revita, her arms crossed as she leaned against the table, said, "Mister Secrets insists that nobody go in there except you."

Lint, standing beside her on the tabletop, also had his arms crossed, his face darkened by a deep scowl. "It is so unfair. I want to know what is in there. He does not realize how difficult it is for me to remain here while he pokes around in that hidden room."

Still seated in his chair at the other end of the table, Parsigar looked up from his drawing. "Careful my tiny friend, or your curiosity will be the end of you one day."

Lionel, meanwhile, stood on the back of Parsigar's chair, preening himself.

Revita snorted. "Like when the pipsqueak poked that stone bear in the Tower of Solitude."

The brownie shrugged. "I wanted to prove I was not afraid of it."

"And the rest of us almost got killed for your bravery."

"Almost does not count."

She turned to Vic and gave him a pleading look.

"Sorry," Vic said. "You are the one who saved him during the willow attack."

She overtly sighed. "Even I make bad decisions from time to time."

"Hey," Lint chided. "Would you rather have me dead?"

Revita covered her smirk. "I suppose things would be less interesting without you around."

The brownie gave a firm nod. "Now, you are making sense."

"Ian," Truhan called from the neighboring room. "Come here."

As bidden, Ian approached the narrow opening, eased through, and found himself in a small cavern carved from rock. A small bookshelf stood along one wall, but rather than books, scrolls wrapped around wooden dowels rested on the shelves. A table and a single chair sat in the middle of the room, the lantern on the table providing an island of light. A scroll with tattered edges lay on the table, spread out before Ian's master, who sat with one hand gripping each of the dowels attached to the scroll.

Clearing his throat, Ian stood across the table from Truhan. "You sent for me?"

Truhan stood and tapped the scroll. "I found the passage I was searching for."

"Passage?" Ian stared down at the yellowed material covered with flowing script. "What about?"

"This scroll is quite old, even older than the book of prophecy that mentioned the death speaker."

"What does it say?"

The man pushed the book across the table. "Read it for yourself."

Ian reached for the scroll.

"Take care!" Truhan warned. "Rather than parchment, this is made of tanned treated hide. The hide is thick but it has become brittle."

Gripping the scroll, Ian turned it toward himself, leaned over, and began to read.

WHEN THE VEIL *between worlds is rendered, creatures of the underworld shall walk among the living.*

This marks the end of days.

A mindless, blood thirsty horde shall sweep across the land. These monsters bend to the will of an entity of pure evil, a demon from the land of the damned. This dark host shall devour everything in its path, and demon's might shall swell as it feeds upon the souls of its victims. Left unchecked, it will consume the world of the living, leaving only an empty, lifeless land. The races who succumb to this evil will find themselves trapped in endless torment.

Such an end, forever dooming our world and the souls who occupy it, can only be avoided when armed with knowledge hidden from the world of the living. This knowledge lies in the gilded city, under the protection of the keepers.

High in the world, where the jungle meets the mountains, stands a stone giant that sings tears. Follow those tears should you seek out the gilded city. The keepers reside where the ground meets the sky, where the rocks weep, where the tears tumble to feed the rainforest. There, the keepers watch. There, they listen. There, they remember. The keepers protect knowledge that our world will one day require.

As WRITTEN *on the sixth day of the fourteenth week in the year three hundred seventy-two*

    Eidolon, High Priest of Vandasal

IAN GASPED, recognizing the name of the author. He looked up from the scroll. "Where did you get this?"

"I...cannot say."

"Can't or won't?"

"Some of both, I am afraid. There are some things in my collection I do not recall acquiring. This is among those rare items. However, given its unique and dire message, along with its brittle condition, I stored it in here, where it was safest." He patted the long wooden box resting upon the far end of his desk.

Ian considered mentioning his encounter with Eidolon in the shadow realm, but decided it could not be the same being, not when the scroll was written well over two thousand years earlier. He then considered the message in the prophecy, noting another name, one he had never heard before.

"The text mentions the keepers."

"It does."

"Who or what are they?"

Truhan shrugged. "I cannot say. However, if there truly is a demon involved in what we face, this is the only passage among any work I have read that details such a creature. I fear we must rely upon it if we are to succeed. That means you must locate the gilded city. There, you may discover an answer to our dilemma."

Ian looked back down at the scroll and reread the last paragraph, his finger softly tracing below the words as he attempted to make sense of them. "This place high in the sky, it mentions the dark lord's desolate city. What city?"

"Murvaran."

A chill climbed Ian's spine. It was a place mentioned in tales told to frighten children. "Does such a place truly exist."

"I believe it does."

"How could that be? Wouldn't people have found it?"

"Not if it's location is too difficult to reach." Truhan reached for the same box from which the scroll had come. Removing the lid, he pulled out another, larger tube of yellowed material, which he carefully unrolled across the table.

"A map?"

"A rare and ancient map. Like the prophecy, it was drawn on animal hide thousands of years ago."

Ian leaned over the desk and examined the map. A mountainous region dominated much of the northern half of the map while the lower portion appeared to be thick forest surrounding a lake. A strange dark

143

line ran along the eastern side of the forest with only blank space to the right of the line. The words *Inculti Infinitus* were scrawled in the blank space.

Tapping on the words, Ian said, "This means endless desert in Elvish."

"Very good." Truhan tapped a small star drawn in the northern area of that desert, east of where the mountains met the forest. "Read this."

Tiny text, so small Ian first thought it was merely a scribbled line, spelled out a word he said aloud. "Murvaran."

"Aye."

Ian frowned. "What is this dark line between the desert and the trees?"

"That is a cliff marking where the highlands of the desert drop to the lowlands of the jungle. It is believed that the world was once split down the middle in that very spot, and when the two sections of land melded back together, they were misaligned, leaving the desert thousands of feet above the lowlands."

"Jungles are wet."

"True."

"Deserts are dry."

"Again, your logic is astounding."

Irritated, Ian shook his head. "How could they exist beside one another?"

"Perhaps something causes the clouds to empty upon the jungle and when they reach the desert, they are spent."

"You don't know?"

"I do not know everything, Ian."

Frowning, Ian focused on the map, trying to get his bearings. "If these trees are jungle, this area around the lake could be swampland."

"That is my thought as well."

Ian tapped on the lake. "This is the Stagnum."

"I arrived at the very same conclusion."

Ian traced his finger along a winding river, heading northeast from the lake. That river ran right to a mountain overlooking Murvaran. "This is our route. If what the text says is true, this city of gold is located somewhere in these mountains. There, we will find the keepers."

"If they still exist. Remember, a very, very long time has passed since the scroll was recorded."

Doubt circled, causing Ian to hesitate. "This seems awfully...nebulous."

"What do you mean?"

"You claim that we need to follow a small passage that was written over two thousand years ago and set off to find a lost city and seek out people who may no longer even exist."

"Do you have any better ideas?"

Ian frowned. "No."

"Then, I suggest you prepare yourself for a journey. It is summer, and the Stagnum is likely to be terribly hot and twice as humid." He pointed toward the door. "Now, go. I have tasks of my own to pursue."

CHAPTER 18
THE CRUMI

Raw energy flowed in, heightening Ian's senses. His head buzzed with power as he crafted a construct and opened a gateway. He recalled his first uses of that spell and the effort required to do so. It surprised him how much easier it had become. *My abilities continue to grow more powerful.* The realization inspired him to continue training.

Parsigar stepped through the tear in space, returning to his tower in the ice fields to the distant south. The old dwarf turned back toward Ian. "Be well. I now grasp your magic. The materials and tools I require to craft my gift to you await in my workshop."

"How long do you need?"

The old dwarf stroked his white beard. "I require only a few days to craft the object and to complete its enchantment."

"What are you creating, anyway?" While Ian had other concerns, he remained curious.

The old dwarf cackled and waggled a finger. "Oh, no. You'll not get me to reveal my creation before it is time." He turned away. "Go on. Return here in five days and not before."

As the old dwarf stepped onto the lift, Ian dismissed the gateway. It snapped shut with a pop, leaving him alone in the Hall of Testing. He crossed the floor, his footsteps echoing in the massive chamber. Before he reached the far side, Lint scurried out of the tunnel entrance. Vic, Revita, and Truhan trailed the brownie.

"Can we leave, now?" Lint hopped in excitement. "Can we? Can we?"

Ian arched a brow at Truhan, who nodded. "If everyone is ready, I'll open a gateway."

"Where to?" Vic asked.

"Our destination is in a region I have never visited, so the best I can do is get us closer for now."

"Closer?" Revita crossed her arms. "That is awfully vague. Across this chamber could be considered closer."

"Well, after looking over maps of the region north of here, the Stagnum is the best I can do."

She pinched her face. "A stinkin' swamp?"

"There is a village in that swamp."

"Oh, no," Vic muttered. "They tried to burn us at the stake last time we were there."

Revita's brows shot up. "Someone tried to set you on fire?"

"Yeah," Vic gestured toward Truhan. "Until *he* showed up and scared them off."

She looked Truhan up and down. "I find that doubtful."

"Oh, I can be far more scary than you suspect." The man held his hands high, bulged his eyes, and tilted from side to side. "Rawr," he growled. In truth, Ian found it more comical than frightening. Dropping his hands, the man smiled. "However, in this case, I merely presented myself in the guise of their god, interrupting the ritual that would have sacrificed these two and a pair of dwarves."

Ian recalled the moment well, for it was among the most terrifying experiences in his life. It was also why he could perfectly picture the temple in which he had been bound.

"Who are these people?" Revita asked.

"The Crumi," Truhan said. "They are a tribal people. Their home is called Sacrumi, a village located in the heart of the Stagnum."

"Huh," Revita grunted. "I recall hearing tales of the Crumi while I lived in Greavesport. They are reputed to stalk the night in search of victims who are abducted and never seen again."

Vic nodded. "That is exactly what happened to us, only we survived to tell our tale while the others were likely sacrificed due to the Crumi and their ridiculous beliefs."

"What beliefs?"

"They thought our deaths would bring back the moon."

She frowned. "Bring it back from where?"

"You know how it waxes and wanes each month?"

"Of course. Everyone knows that."

"They believed that their actions were the cause of it returning to a full moon."

Revita burst out laughing, and Lint echoed with his own high-pitched cackle. Neither Vic nor Ian even broke a smile. It was not a laughing matter for anyone who had been tied up and destined to become kindling.

Truhan smirked. "The Crumi might be impressively loyal to their god, but their beliefs range from odd to inaccurate."

Revita asked, "Who is their god anyway?"

Vic said, "Urvadan."

Her eyes widened. "The Dark Lord?"

Truhan grimaced. "Dark Lord or not, don't all gods deserve to have worshipers?"

"What?" She sounded incredulous.

"I am simply saying that you should not judge the Crumi or their god until you know them better."

She shot Vic a look of confusion. The conversation was taking a strange turn that left Ian uncomfortable. Hoping to change the subject and avoid any complications, he cleared his throat to draw everyone's attention.

"Now that Revita is aware of the situation, I will craft a gateway." Ian extended his hand. "The one place in that village I firmly recall is the temple, so that is where we are going. Be ready in case we are met with an unwelcome reception."

Channeling his magic while picturing the temple in his head, Ian opened a gateway. It expanded to reveal a floor of gray stone tiles, each three feet square. Vic pulled his mattock off his back and jumped through. Revita stepped over the rim, looked left and right, and continued forward. The brownie hopped through the opening and was quickly out of view. Ian, with a pack hanging from one shoulder and Lionel perched on the other, crossed over and turned to look back. Yet, Truhan stood firm.

"Aren't you coming, Master?" Ian asked.

"No."

"But you said..."

"I know what I said. Use the map I gave you, keep your wits about yourself, and I am certain you will fare well. I have much to do, and I cannot afford to waste my time tromping through swampland." Truhan turned and walked off.

Although Ian was irritated by the man's constant surprises, he could not afford to dwell on the issue, so he dismissed the gateway and looked around.

They stood inside a pyramidal-shaped, open chamber with two open doorways, each positioned two stories above them. Tiered seating cascaded down from all four sides of the chamber. Dormant, stone braziers stood in the four corners of the temple floor with an eight-sided crystal altar at its center. Morning sunlight shone through a glass window in the ceiling's highest tier and illuminated the temple interior. Thankfully, the building was empty.

"What are these?" Revita asked while squatting over one of eight holes in the floor.

The memory of his abduction and near death remained sharply affixed in Ian's head. Rather than allow the emotion of that event to control him, he pushed it down and spoke in a matter-of-fact tone.

"The Crumi tie the wrists and ankles of their captives to poles, carry them in, and insert the poles into the holes. They then wait for nightfall, which is when they conduct their ritual." Ian peered up toward the window. "Judging by the angle of the light, it is still early. We should go and deal with the villagers, so we can resume our journey."

A tickle of fear pierced Ian's mental shield, causing him to turn and cast one last wary glance at the altar. A frightful and traumatic memory resurfaced, and he relived it in his mind.

HE WAS TIED to a pole and facing the altar as it flared with a magical light that turned to red flames. The heat was so intense, Ian turned away, but there was no escape. He was going to die...until the heat suddenly receded. The light dimmed to reveal a hooded man in black robes standing upon the altar. The unexpected appearance left Ian and everyone else in the temple in shock.

The dark figure then spoke in a booming voice "Crumi people, hear me! I am your god, Urvadan!" He raised his arms high. "Bow before me!"

Gasps came from the crowd. Beginning with the priest on the temple floor, everyone in the chamber fell to their knees and bowed their heads.

The robed figure announced, "The practice of immolation, as you have long performed it, shall end tonight. No longer will you sacrifice others in my name. If you persist, not only will the moon never return, but I will cast a curse upon your people." He lowered his arms. "Praise Urvadan that it be so."

The audience repeated the phrase, many with tears in their eyes and hands wringing in worry.

"These four innocents are now my chosen. You will treat them with respect, and when they leave the Stagnum, you are never to interfere with their lives again. Now, go! Leave my temple while I anoint my chosen and give them private instruction."

The crowd fled the temple with people pushing, shoving, and many falling down, as they scrambled to escape the wrath of their god. In moments, the building was empty. A beat later, laughter came from the robed figure. He lowered his hood and revealed a familiar face. Truhan.

A NUDGE to the ear from Lionel pulled Ian from his reverie. "Vic." Ian's brother stopped a third of the way up the stairs and turned toward him. "How do you think Truhan knows so much about the Crumi?"

"What do you mean?" Vic asked.

Approaching the staircase, Ian said, "When he interrupted their ritual, he knew how they would respond. He knew that they worshiped Urvadan and how to convince them that he was their god."

Vic shrugged. "Didn't you say that Truhan has read many books and traveled to strange places?"

"I suppose, but I have never seen any mention of the Crumi in the histories, and who would purposely travel to the heart of a hot, humid swampland?"

"Well, I'll admit that the man is strange. He might even be the oddest person I have ever met, but until you get answers from him, I would consider this a pointless discussion." Vic turned and continued up the staircase, catching up with Revita while Lint hopped up, passing them.

With a sigh of resignation, knowing he would not get answers to his questions, Ian began his ascent, his feet moving fast to catch up to the others.

When Ian reached Vic, his brother patted his shoulder. "Set thoughts of Truhan aside, Ian. His quirks and penchant for secrecy will drive you crazy if you let it. Instead, you should focus on our journey."

Ian nodded, continued past Vic and Revita, and passed through the doorway. Stepping out into the sunlight, he stopped beside Lint, who was standing at the top of the external staircase.

The village of Sacrumi, consisting of hundreds of huts made of clay and thatch, stretched out below them. An open field of dirt ran through the middle of the village, toward a massive lake bordered by long grass. There was no activity amid the huts, for the dark-skinned villagers filled the central area from the foot of the temple to the fountain at the far end. Every single Crumi stood staring up at Ian and his companions. While most villagers wore little more than strips of brown or green cloth covering their private parts, two villagers standing at the base of the stairs stood out.

The first was a tall man dressed in garishly bright colors of orange, red, blue, and green. He wore a headdress made of colorful feathers and ivory horns on his head. Rings of feathers encircled his ankles while red, green, blue, and orange lines streaked his dark-skinned face. Ian recognized him as the priest who had led the sacrificial ritual they had barely escaped.

The other was a scowling, middle-aged woman, her black and silver hair held back by a headdress made of gold and an array of gaudy gems. She stood with her arms crossed and a thin, iridescent cape draped over her shoulders. The cloak shimmered in the sunlight while her dark eyes glared at Ian, reflecting doubt and distrust.

The tribal priest raised his arms to the sky. "As was foretold,

Urvadan has sent heroes to deliver us salvation. Oh, great heroes..." He dropped to his knees and pressed his forehead against the ground. "We are your humble servants."

The entire village bent knee and dipped their heads, all save for the woman at the front. She barked a brief, harsh order and stomped off. A cluster of twenty Crumi warriors stood and advanced through the crowd. With spears extended before them, they ascended the stairs. Ian recognized one of them as the escort who took them out of the Stagnum and dropped them off near Greavesport.

When the warriors stopped a few stairs below, Ian said, "Hello, Ahni."

She narrowed her eyes. "It is you."

"Yes."

"I am sorry. Chieftess Orahna has ordered us to escort you to the Sacrumont."

He frowned. "The what?"

"Come. Do not resist. You will soon find out."

While Ian could use his magic against them, Ahni had shown him and his brother kindness during their last visit. He viewed the Crumi as misguided rather than evil and hoped he might yet find a way to make peace with them.

He nodded. "Lead the way."

CHAPTER 19
THE SACRED SPEAR

T he Sacrumont was the second biggest structure in the village, surpassed only by the pyramid they had just vacated. With a stone block foundation, walls made of wooden poles bonded together by mud, and a peaked roof made of thick thatch, the Sacrumont was built upon a hilltop behind the temple and was large enough to house the entire village in case of disaster.

Ian tried to imagine the Crumi packed inside it, their sleeping bodies covering every inch of the wooden floor while they slept. It was a strange idea but should the swamp waters ever rise and flood the village, it gave them higher ground to wait it out. He considered asking why the pyramid itself couldn't be used in such matters but held back, still uncertain of the situation. An arc of Crumi warriors gripping spears also stood behind him and his companions. Should things turn ugly, he was prepared to use his magic, but rather than act rashly, he preferred to wait and see why they had been sequestered.

At the far end of the room, a throne made of bamboo stood upon a raised dais. The shoots forming the back of the throne were unevenly cut. Most notably and morbidly, the tallest poles were capped by human skulls. The chieftess sat on the throne, her expression unreadable, the only sign of emotion the tapping of her long fingernails on the wooden chair arm.

The door behind Ian opened, and a pair of men walked in carrying a long, narrow table. A line of men and women followed, each carrying a wicker stool. They circled around Ian and his companions, the men with the table setting it down just strides before the throne. The stools were placed along one side of the table. The villagers then flowed out of the building, leaving only Ian, his companions, a dozen warriors, and the stern female on the throne.

Ahni, who stood to the right of Ian and his companions, frowned. "Why is there a tiny dragon on your shoulder?"

Ian reached up and rested a hand on Lionel. "This is a fire drake. He is a pet of sorts."

"Please," Orahna spoke in Dwarvish and gestured toward the table. "Sit."

Vic shrugged at Ian and then led him across the room, where he casually sat on a stool. Revita, sat at the end of the table, bent and scooped Lint up.

"Hey!" The brownie squirmed. "Let me go!"

"Calm yourself, pipsqueak." She set him on the table. "I don't want anyone to step on you."

"Nobody handles Lint without asking first." He backed from her and waggled a finger. "Because you are the goddess, I will let it pass this one time."

Revita rolled her eyes. "You are more dramatic than a teenage girl."

Orahna leaned forward in her throne. "Where did you get such a strange little man?"

Lint waved his fist in her direction. "I am no man! I am a brownie!"

"I do not know this term, brown eye."

Vic and Revita both burst out laughing. Ian covered his mouth to hide his own chuckling while Ahni shot him a stern glare.

Forcing his laughter down, Ian said, "*Brownie*, not brown eye."

"Why is that so funny?" Ahni asked.

Ian did his best to explain without being vulgar. "We used to say that when someone flashes their, um, bare bottom at you." He sat and pulled Lionel down to his lap.

"Why would someone flash their arse at someone else?"

"It is meant as a slight, or to taunt someone."

Lint shook his head. "You humans are strange."

Orahna sat back. "Some stranger than others. Tell me, brownie. From where do you come?"

"I call Fae Gulch my home."

"Fake what?"

"Fae Gulch. It is a magical, secret village hidden in the wilds of the Vale."

"Ah," the chieftess nodded. "Your home is like Sacrumi."

"No. It resides in a lush forest filled with wonders and dangers in equal measure."

"A forest. A swamp. Both are homes to wonders and danger."

Lint made fists at his sides, his lips tightening. "They are nothing alike."

"Bah. What do you know? I eat meals bigger than you."

When the brownie stomped across the table, toward the throne, Revita pinched the back of his clothing, stopping him. "We are guests, pipsqueak. Sit and be quiet."

The brownie crossed his arms and sat in a huff. Thankfully, he remained silent.

Ian gathered his courage and asked, "Excuse me, Chieftess. Why are we here?"

"That is the precise question I had for you."

"What do you mean?"

She frowned. "How do you know Chutakka?"

"Chew who?" Revita asked.

"Don't play coy with me," Orahna snapped.

Ian glanced at his companions before interceding. "We apologize, Chieftess, but we have never heard that name before."

"You claim you do not know our high priest?"

"Oh." Ian nodded. "So, that's his name."

Orahna thrust a finger at Ian. "You do know him!"

"I guess." He shrugged. "I mean, we have never spoken to him, and he just about burned my brother and I alive, but I recall..."

"Wait." Orahna leaned forward. "You were to be sacrificed?"

"Yes. Last summer. It would have happened, too, if not for..." Ian recalled Truhan's instructions and desire to keep his interference a secret. *He doesn't want me to tell her what happened. Now what do I say?* "Um," Ian stammered. "You see..."

"Hold on." She narrowed her eyes. "You were the ones to be sacrificed when our god supposedly appeared and demanded that the ritual cease?"

Thankful for not having to explain the situation, Ian merely nodded.

She turned her head. "Ahni. Is this true?"

"Yes, Chieftess," Ahni nodded. "I recognize the robed one and the handsome man."

Orahna pointed toward the door. "Crumi! Leave us. Post outside the door. Nobody enters."

Ahni glanced at Ian. "Are you certain it is safe?"

"Do you think they are at threat?" The chieftess arched her brow in challenge.

"No." Ahni admitted.

"Then go. Enter only if I send for you or if you hear trouble from inside."

The warriors turned and marched out the door. When it closed, the room fell silent for a beat, only for the quiet to be interrupted by Orahna's chuckling.

Ian glanced at his companions. Their expressions mirrored his own confusion.

Orahna shook her head. "Your charade, however you executed it, greatly upset Chutakka."

"Charade?"

"You don't truly expect me to believe that Urvadan presented himself to us?"

Choosing to avoid revealing Truhan's involvement, Ian asked a question leading in a different direction. "What makes you think Chutakka is upset?"

"The man has been moping and attempting to come up with another spectacular ritual ever since."

Ian frowned. "I don't understand."

"You are not Crumi."

"No."

"Even if you were, most Crumi are unaware of the friction between me and Chutakka. When High Priest Katechu died three years ago, Chutakka rose to replace him and has been seeking additional means to influence our people ever since. Many of his actions are subtle, but his use of fear and the threat of losing Urvadan's favor have changed how my people behave."

"What about the moon cycle and the sacrifices?"

She laughed. "All a ploy to manipulate my people, but a ploy that has been used for a very, very long time."

"So, you didn't believe those deaths changed anything." Ian frowned. "If you were against the immolation ritual, why didn't you say anything?"

"You are not Crumi. You do not understand our ways. I am the tribal leader in all things other than religion. In that, Chutakka's power is absolute. Should I do anything to usurp or subvert that power, I risk civil war within the tribe." She toyed with the exotic wooden charm on her necklace. "Since you know so little of Chutakka, tell me, how did he know you would emerge from the temple this morning?"

Ian glanced at the others. His brother, Revita, and Lint all merely stared at the queen, their faces unreadable.

"I have no idea." Ian admitted.

She frowned and her fingers resumed tapping the arm of her throne. After a few seconds of silence, she said, "This is disturbing."

"Why?"

"Like his predecessor, and likely all high priests before him, Chutakka uses theatrics to convince his people that he is blessed with arcane arts as gift from the god he worships."

Ian recalled the burning altar threatening to consume him. "His magic seemed real enough to me."

"If you speak of the burning altar, that magic is real. You see, the altar holds an enchantment. Simply drip blood on it and it bursts into flames – any blood, any time, regardless of whose blood or who applies it."

Ian reassessed Orahna against his preconceptions. Unlike the rest of the Crumi, she was well spoken, intelligent, and did not prescribe to the same superstitions as her people. "You are not...what I expected."

She smirked. "I do not blindly follow the words of others. I think for myself. I also understand people and how to deal with them. These skills helped me rise to chieftess when Chieftess Pegasi fell ill."

"Given the isolation of your village, I find that quite curious." Having grown up in Shillings, Ian had come to realize how his views of the world had been limited by his isolation. He acknowledged that he had grown in many ways since leaving his boyhood home.

"Sacrumi may be the home of my people, but as you said, it is quite isolated. I found it too restrictive, so in my youth, I left my people and traveled to Greavesport. There, I learned much about the world and even more about people. Five years later, I returned to Sacrumi with a different perspective, one that allowed me to see the truth."

Vic spoke for the first time. "Please. Tell us. What is the truth?"

"The ambitious seek power and wealth and will do anything to get it. Manipulating others is a valuable weapon to those people, one that is wielded with great frequency and intent."

"Interesting. What other weapons do such people utilize?"

"Fear. Force. Goods. Gold. Whatever is required to get what they want."

"And what is it you want?"

She laughed. "I want my people to flourish."

"Yet, you have admitted conflict with your own priest."

"Chutakka would have my people never advance, never experience anything new, never unearth discoveries that might improve their lives."

"And you wish these things?"

"I do."

"What of Urvadan?"

"Our god? I have yet to see any proof that anything we do makes him happy, nor have I seen anything he has provided to make our lives better."

"You sound as if you do not believe."

"Oh, I believe. I believe that Urvadan is nothing more than the sharpened point of the spear the priests use to manipulate us."

Her lack of faith in her god gave him the courage to ask another question. "Have you heard of the Dark Lord?"

"It is a name the elves and dwarves use when referring to Urvadan."

Ian arched his brow in surprise. "If you know he is evil, why do you worship him?"

"Who claims he is evil?

"I don't know. Everyone I guess."

The chieftess cocked her head to the side. "With what proof?"

Ian had none to give.

"Let me ask you a question," Orahna posed. "What god do the elves and dwarves worship?"

"That's easy. Vandasal."

"And humans outside of the Crumi?"

"We don't honor a god. We pray to the spirits of our ancestors."

Orahna made a flippant gesture with her hand. "That is because you have forgotten your past."

"What past?"

"As I learned from my time in Greavesport, most humans hold little regard for tradition. The Crumi, however, hold fast to it, perhaps to a fault. From generation to generation for centuries on end, we have repeated stories honoring Urvadan as our creator."

"Your creator?"

She pointed toward Ian. "Yours as well."

Ian's jaw dropped at the implication. "That cannot be true."

"True or not, I cannot say. All I know is what has been passed down from our predecessors."

Vic said, "Please share. I am curious."

"Very well." She frowned in thought. "I guess it begins with Vandasal and Urvadan being brothers. They came into being together, with Vandasal a child of the sun and Urvadan son of the moon. These gods and their celestial bodies hovered in a void lacking life. So, together, they willed our world into creation. The gods then gifted the world with life. Vandasal chose to create creatures and races born with a spark of magic while Urvadan took a different approach. His animals and humans lacked magic but were gifted with enhanced fertility, allowing their numbers to quickly multiply.

"But Vandasal was unsatisfied and jealous of his brother, for as the human population swelled, the prayers feeding his power did as well. Thus, Vandasal schemed and schemed until he discovered a way to shift the balance in his favor. He used his might to destroy something precious to Urvadan – the moon's light. This action greatly affected Urvadan, making him weak, ill, and vulnerable. Vandasal, perceiving the moment as his opportunity, smote his brother, striking him down and taking much of his power.

"With the moon darkened, our priesthood proclaimed that Urvadan's favor would be lost forever unless a sacrifice was made. This is when the first immolation ritual took place. The next night, the moon appeared as a sliver in the sky. Days later, that sliver had quadrupled. Soon, the moon had returned in full, but it would not last. As it faded, the fears of the Crumi rose, and when all was dark, they repeated the ritual, which continued ever since...until last year, thanks to you."

Ian blinked. "How long ago did the ritual begin?"

"Centuries upon centuries have passed since the moon began its shifting phases."

The sheer number of people killed for nothing more than a superstition was unthinkable. Ian's stomach turned at the thought of so many innocents having their lives taken away for nothing.

Revita asked, "Why are you telling us this?"

The chieftess nodded. "You wish to get to the point."

"I do."

"Chutakka likely intends to use your presence to his advantage. The fact that he gathered the entire village this morning, and you appeared as he predicted places him in a position of control. I seek to intervene before that can happen, which is why I ordered a private discussion. I have been forthcoming with you. My hope is that you will do the same for me." Her face hardened. "Why are you here?" She held up a finger. "Do not lie. If I sense falsehoods, it will go very badly for you."

"We are armed and outnumber you," Revita said. "Are you certain you are in position to issue threats?"

"Look at the floor below you."

Ian looked down at the floorboards and spotted a seam he had missed before. It ran a few feet beyond the table he sat at and clearly encircled them.

"A trap door," Revita scowled. "How did I miss it?"

Orahna reached toward the spear to her right. "If I pull this free, the trap door opens and you fall. Sharpened spikes line the floor of the pit below you. The landing would be quite bloody and leave each of you with far more holes in your body than you might prefer, so I suggest you remain still and answer my question." She bit off each word, "Why are you here?"

Revita arched a brow at Ian, who in turn glanced toward his brother. When Vic nodded, Ian turned back toward the chieftess and answered for them.

Ian recalled the lines from the prophecy and said the critical line aloud. "High in the world, where the jungle meets the mountains, stands a stone giant that sings tears. Follow those tears should you seek out the gilded city. The keepers reside where the ground meets the sky, where the rocks weep, where the tears tumble to feed the rainforest."

Orahna frowned. "What does that mean?"

Vic's brow furrowed. "Is that a line from the prophecy?"

"Yes. It offers the only clues to locate the city of gold." Ian turned toward the chieftess. "Do you know this place?"

"I do not." Her eyes narrowed. "You speak of a prophecy. What does it foretell?"

"A great evil threatens our world, an army of monsters from the underworld seeking to destroy all life. We believe they are led by a demon. We are traveling to the mountains to the north in search of information that might help us combat this evil."

The chieftess stared at Ian while a heavy quiet settled over the room, lingering until she said, "You truly believe that don't you?"

"I...we do."

"This evil you mention. It will come here?"

"If the visions I have seen are true, this horde seeks to consume all life until our world is nothing more than a desolate graveyard."

"I see." She stood, rounded the throne, and reached up for the spear mounted above it. A click resounded as the spear came free. Lowering it, she turned toward her audience and shouted. "Ahni!"

The front door opened. Led by Ahni, the Crumi warriors rushed in and took position behind the table. Chutakka walked through the door, circled the warriors, and stopped at the far end of the table while staring toward the dais.

"What is this about, Orahna?" the priest demanded. "These heroes have come as I have foreseen, they belong..."

Orahna lifted the spear and blurted, "I have made my judgement!"

She cocked back, the spear tip pointed directly toward Ian. With a thrust, she launched the spear before Ian could react, It sailed toward him and stopped with the shaft above his shoulder. His eyes wide and heart thumping, Ian slowly turned his head. Ahni stood behind him, her hand gripping the spear shaft while the tip hovered in the air between her and another warrior. Her eyes, rather than meeting Ian's, stared toward the throne.

The chieftess said, "In accordance with Chutakka's vision," she flashed the high priest a humorless smile. "These heroes have appeared in a time of great need. A darkness threatens the land and will soon come for the Crumi. These brave strangers are on a quest to stave off this evil. They cannot do it alone. The Crumi will support their purpose by sending our greatest warrior to join them." She nodded. "Ahni, you now hold the Sacred Spear. Take it. Defend these heroes with your life. Save our people."

Ahni shifted to Ian's side, dropped to one knee, and tapped the spear shaft to her forehead. "You honor me, Chieftess. I will give my life if needed. I shall not fail you or my people."

"Rise, my child. Rise and lead these warriors to the lake. Prepare a skiff. Food and supplies will be along shortly."

Ahni stood and gestured toward Ian, who pushed his stool back, lifted Lionel from his lap, and placed the drake on his shoulder. The warriors split and stood to each side of the center aisle while Chutakka directed a hateful glare toward Orahna. Surrounded by silent tension, Ian, Vic, Revita, and Lint followed Ahni outside.

CHAPTER 20
DANGEROUS WATERS

T he afternoon sun heated the thick, humid air of the Stagnum until it threatened to choke the breath out of its inhabitants. Ian, along with Revita and Lint, sat in the middle of a long, narrow watercraft called a skiff. In front of them, Ahni sat on her knees and paddled while Vic, seated in the rear, did the same, the two of them driving the skiff forward with each stroke. Their oars kept time with each other, the rhythmic splash from each stroke like the slow beat of a drum.

The skiff's hull was just wide enough for one person and long enough to hold their entire party and their gear. Two wooden poles branched off to one side of the skiff, connecting it to a log that created a second hull and significantly improved its stability as it cut through the calm waters of Lake Stagnum. Frequently, reeds were visible below the water's surface, reminding the party that the lake was shallow, at least near the western coast where their craft steadily headed north.

With nothing else to do, Ian slid into meditation, his mind relaxing. He opened himself to his magic while numbly staring at Ahni, her lithe, dark arms and shoulders coated in sweat. Again and again, she raised the paddle, drove it into the lake, and pulled it through the water. That act of physical exertion, applying force against another object, spoke to Ian, and soon, a construct formed before him.

The construct was unique. Unlike the others he had discovered, this one was a single, solid circle filled with intertwined, bowed lines wrapped around a solid core. It was shockingly simple, especially when compared to the one used for translocation, yet it was new and spoke of untold possibilities. Ian set his mind to memorizing the pattern, intent on testing it at the first opportunity.

WITH HIS BARE torso coated in sweat, Vic thrust his paddle into the water and pulled, dragging the oar backward and propelling the skiff forward. From the rear of the craft, he watched Ahni, who sat in the fore. The female warrior's dark skin glistened as she rowed, seemingly without effort. He had been instructed to stay in sync with her, and over the hours since they had departed from Sacrumi, he had fallen into the rhythm she set. The repeated rowing, despite its wear on his body, eventually began to happen without applied thought.

Ian, seated between Revita and Ahni, shook his head and looked around as if waking from sleep. He twisted and looked back at Vic. "Are you certain you don't want me to row for a bit?"

"No." Vic's paddle again plunged into the water before he pulled it toward him. "This is good work, like cutting down trees. It is hard but soothing at the same time."

Revita snorted. "Your perspective about work is bizarre."

"How so?"

"Most people prefer to put in as little effort as possible."

"The more effort you put in, the greater the reward received."

She looked over her shoulder. "You are not even getting paid for this, you know."

He shrugged. "Not everything is about getting coin, goods, or something else in return."

"Now, you are being ridiculous."

"What about last night?" Vic and Revita had taken advantage of their private quarters in Truhan's underground home. It might be a while before another such opportunity would arise.

"I certainly got something out of last night." Over her shoulder, she flashed a naughty smirk. "I'd say you did as well."

"Is that why we are together?"

Her smirk slid away. "You know why we are together."

"Perhaps I would like you to clarify."

"Don't make me say it."

He sighed. "Fine."

Her eyes slid down his torso and she smiled.

"Why are you smiling?" he asked.

"This look suits you."

He glanced down at his bare torso, his muscles rippling beneath his pale skin. "What look?"

"You should go without a shirt more often." She bit her lip. "In fact, you should go about without breeches as well."

Vic's cheeks, already warm, grew even more heated. "Vita!"

Her laughter echoed over the still waters of the lake.

"Hush," Ahni spoke over her shoulder. "You outlanders are too loud. It is better to be quiet, like the Crumi."

Revita looked around. "Why be quiet? It's not like there is anyone near."

Miles of water stretched out to the north, east, and south while the long reeds along the western shore were no more than a quarter mile away. Again and again, they passed waterways cutting through the trees, vines and long grass covering the surrounding swampland. Yet, the only signs of life they had seen since departing from Sacrumi were alabaster cranes standing near the shore or flying overhead.

"Hush, I said," Ahni hissed. "There are dangers in the Stagnum. Just because you do not see them does not mean they are not there."

As the Crumi warrior returned to rowing, the skiff passengers fell silent until Ian suddenly jerked and turned his gaze toward the sky.

Vic, still stroking with his paddle, furrowed his brow. "Is something wrong, Ian?"

"It's Lionel." Ian stared up at the fire drake, who circled hundreds of feet above them. "He is warning me. Something comes toward us – a dark shadow beneath the water's surface."

Ahni stopped, turned, and raised up on her knees. One hand shadowed the sun from her face as she peered across the water. Her eyes suddenly widened. "Toward shore!" She spun, thrust her paddle in the water, and stroked with urgency.

Concerned, Vic looked over his shoulder but he saw nothing but open water, so he resumed paddling.

"What's wrong?" Revita asked.

"Quelzarn," Ahni replied.

"What the blazes is a quelzarn?"

"You don't want to know." Over her shoulder, Ahni said. "I am trying to turn, Vic. Stop fighting me."

"Which side do I stroke?" Vic asked.

"The same side as me."

After being told to paddle on the opposite side as Ahni, he suddenly had to shift position, swing the oar over Revita's head, and drive it down into the water on the right side of the craft.

While Vic and Ahni paddled, the skiff continued forward while gently arcing toward the western shore. He glanced back again and this time saw roiling water a few hundred feet away. Something huge was beneath the surface and it was coming fast.

Alarmed, Vic stroked harder, his muscles straining with each pull of the paddle. His pulse raced, his breath coming in gasps as sweat beaded on his brow. In his haste, any thought of keeping time with Ahni was lost.

The craft slid down an open waterway bordered by reeds. Trees a few hundred feet ahead marked land, but when he looked back to find the roiling water no more than fifty feet behind them, he knew they would not make it in time. He lifted his paddle from the water, slid it into the hull, and pulled his mattock from the sheath lying beside him. Fighting while seated would be impossible, so he turned and slid his knees beneath him.

A dark shape rose from the roiling water to reveal a dragon-like head with massive, pointed gills flaring out from the sides. The monster opened a maw filled with jagged, massive teeth. It belted a tremendous roar as a serpentlike tongue snapped out, thrashed, and withdrew. All the while, the gap between it and the skiff closed.

Readying himself, Vic knew he would have only one chance. The creature reared up, revealing a long, sinuous body. The monster then thrust forward, its jaw open and intent on engulfing Vic. He swung an overhead strike. The pick end of his mattock struck a tooth. Sparks shot from the weapon while shards of yellowed tooth sprayed in all directions. The quelzarn yanked its head back and released an angry roar, the deep timbre loud enough to rattle Vic's teeth.

The monster fell away, shook its head, and dove back beneath the water. It turned, its long snakelike body arching above the surface as it swam in a circle. The quelzarn came back around and charged forward. Vic had hoped he might drive it off, but now, he feared he had merely angered it. The monster came in fast, burst from the water, and opened its maw. Again, Vic wound back, preparing to meet the attack with force.

The skiff suddenly lurched forward. With Vic on his knees, facing backward, he lost balance and flipped over the stern. Cool water enveloped him, bubbles rising past as his body spun in a submerged somersault. Fear clawed at his throat while panic set in. He was in the quelzarn's realm, and fighting back while trying to swim would be nearly impossible.

THE GIANT MONSTER reminded Ian of an oversized eel, its jaw big enough to bite a man in half. With the first attack, he readied his magic, but the thing was too fast and Vic was in the way. When it rounded and came in for another attack, he prepared a different spell. Rather than fight back and risk harming or killing his brother, he chose defense.

Ian cast a shield, forming a half circle between the skiff and the monster. When the beast struck, its face collided with the shield and thrust the skiff forward. Vic, who had been on his knees, ready to fight, lost his balance, flipped over the back of the skiff, and plunged into the water.

"Vic!" Ian cried.

The monster bent its long neck back, lifting its head fifteen feet above the water as Vic surfaced. Still gripping his weapon in one hand, he swam on his back and stroked with the other arm while looking up at the quelzarn.

Desperate to save his brother, Ian crafted another shield and then thrust his hands forward, launching it toward the monster with all the force his will could muster. The creature's head snapped back sharply, lolled, and then shook. Meanwhile, Vic stroked furiously toward the skiff. He reached it, raised his weapon over the edge, and dropped it into the hull.

The monster blasted a terrible roar, dove down into the water, and disappeared. As Revita helped to pull Vic back inside the skiff, Ian leaned over the edge and peered into the lake. A dark shape came into view. The quelzarn burst from the water, right below the skiff, lifting the craft and its occupants up and launching them into the air. Screams and shouts of alarm echoed across the lake.

Ian urgently crafted another spell as the skiff fell toward a broad cluster of reeds. A massive blast of air burst upward, powerful enough to send the skiff toward the sky even as its forward momentum continued. They reached the top of their arc, three stories up and, again, began descending. Ian waited until the craft neared the water and launched another spell of lesser strength. Air thrust against the skiff's hull, again slowing it. The skiff crashed down, snapping reeds as it slammed into the water. The impact sent a massive jolt from Ian's backside, right up his spine. Ahni gripped the rails at the fore of the skiff and Revita did the same at the rear while Vic lay in the hull between them. A small scream came from overhead, causing Ian to look up.

Lint plummeted from the sky, his tiny arms and legs flailing frantically. In a prone position, he sped toward the water and was certain to hit it with significant force until Revita's hand darted out and snatched him.

She pulled him in and set him down.

Lint stood in the hull and stared up at her. "You saved me. Again... Goddess."

Revita rolled her eyes.

Ahni hissed. "Hush!"

The brownie spun toward her, planted his fists on his hips, and stuck out his tongue. The Crumi warrior glared back, raised a finger and waved it from side to side. Thankfully, Lint remained quiet, as did the others. Surrounded by reeds standing six feet above the water, they sat still and listened.

Beyond the rustling reeds came the sound of sloshing of water and the heavy breathing of something very large. Reeds bent and snapped as the head of the quelzarn appeared above them. With its head fifteen feet above the water, the snakelike creature slithered through the reeds and turned. Its glassy-eyed gaze swept back and forth as it swam past, no more than twenty feet from the skiff. The creature stopped and turned its head, its gaze sweeping right past the skiff and her occupants. The monster huffed, turned away, and dove into the water. Its long body followed, its tail whipping across the reeds before it also plunged beneath the surface. A tense silence followed.

Closing his eyes, Ian reached out to Lionel, who still circled above them. Through the drake's eyes, he saw the shadow of the quelzarn swim off, toward the middle of the lake. As the drake came around, Ian spied the skiff amid a grove of reeds. Beyond the reeds were trees, indicating that they were near land. *Good boy,* Ian sent to Lionel before opening his eyes.

Ian announced, "Lionel tells me that it is gone."

Ahni sighed, "We were lucky."

Lint threw his hands in the air. "That thing nearly killed us. How is that lucky?"

"The Crumi have long feared the quelzarn. Noise attracts it, so we Crumi know to be quiet. In my life, I have only seen it a handful of times, all from a distance. None who have seen the monster up close have lived to tell the story. This is why we were lucky to survive."

The skiff rocked as Vic shifted to a sitting position. He gripped his mattock in one hand while searching the hull around him. "I'm afraid I lost my oar." He lifted his wet tunic and jerkin from the hull. "I lost my waterskin as well."

Worried, Ian looked down and found his waterskin gone. His pack as well. Worse, water pooled between his legs. A dark line ran down the middle of the hull. When he tested it with his finger, he felt the rough edge of a crack. "We have bigger problems. The skiff is damaged and taking on water."

Ahni grimaced. "We cannot make it across the lake."

"I saw trees just ahead." Ian pointed northwest.

"I see nothing."

Revita agreed. "Me neither."

"I mean to say that Lionel tells me there are trees nearby."

"Fine." Ahni dug her oar back out of the hull. "I will head for the trees. Perhaps we are far enough north to walk." She began to row.

"If we aren't?" Ian asked.

"Let me guess," Lint chimed. "We will get wet."

"We already are wet."

"We will get wetter."

After the splashing and the water filling the craft, there was little of Ian that was not wet. "I am already wetter than I want to be."

Lint shrugged. "More wetter then."

Turning toward the brownie, Ian frowned. "You can't say more wetter."

"I just did."

A sigh of frustration slipped out. "I mean that you can't talk that way."

"What way?"

"Using both the words *more* and *wetter*."

"Maybe you can't, but I have no problem doing it."

Exasperated, Ian looked toward Revita and found her smirking. "Can't you do something about him?"

"I like having him around. He makes me laugh."

"But he is driving me crazy."

"That's what I mean." Her lip remained curled up as she shot him a challenging look.

Giving up, Ian turned forward and peered past Ahni as she slid her oar into the water. The skiff eased ahead, the bow forcing the reeds aside while the poles connected to the log caused them to bend low before snapping upright. All the while, water continued to collect in the skiff's hull.

The green of leaf trees soon appeared above the reeds, which then fell away to reveal a landmass covered in foliage. By the time the reeds parted and the skiff's bow slid onto shore, the water covered half of Ian's legs and left the lower third of his robes drenched. Considering the heat and humidity, the cool water was not unpleasant. Ahni climbed out into waist-high water, gripped the front cross bar, and dragged the skiff farther onto shore. She then retrieved her spear from the skiff before climbing up the bank.

Ian carefully stood, shuffled along the boat while holding the rails, and stepped out. The dark, damp earth beneath his feet squished, his boots leaving a footprint with each step as he continued farther from the water. He stopped at the top of the rise, fifteen strides from the water, and surveyed his surroundings.

Leaf trees with long, bare trunks extended ahead of him, obscuring his view. The tree beside him, like many others, was wrapped in vines attempting to choke the life from it. The tails of vines dangled from its branches. In fact, everywhere Ian looked, vines ran from the forest floor to the tree's upper reaches. The ground was so dark, it appeared black where visible amid thick patches of fuzzy moss.

Lint's nasal voice came from beside Ian. "What is this stuff?" The brownie stomped through the mud raising his knees high with each step. "It sticks to my feet."

Ahni said, "We are standing in peat moss. This is a bog. The Stagnum is thick with them."

Revita pinched her face. "It stinks."

"Yes, but it makes our gardens grow fast and keeps them healthy." Ahni gestured. "Come."

Ian closed his eyes and extended himself toward Lionel. Through the drake's eyes, he could see the lines and clusters of trees were surrounded by patches of water, making a maze of sorts. He pointed southwest. "That way."

Ahni frowned. "We must go north."

"Yes, but if we don't go this direction for a bit first, we will be forced to swim."

Ahni grimaced. "That is unwise. There are many crocodiles amid the bogs."

Lint asked, "What is a crocodile?"

"Something that can swallow your little body in a single bite."

"Maybe we should go Ian's way, then."

The Crumi warrior narrowed her eyes at Ian. "How do you know this?"

"I have a connection with the fire drake. We communicate. He tells me that we must go this way."

Ahni nodded. "Very well. Let's go."

With her in the lead, they left the broken skiff behind. The ground squished beneath Ian's boots with each step, be it on the damp, black soil or the lush, green moss. He pushed vines aside, stepped over fallen trees covered in moss, and swatted at the circling mosquitoes. After walking a few hundred feet, they emerged into sunlight shining at an angle over a long pool of water. With the pool on their right, they picked their way along the bank. When halfway around the pool, a shadow fell over Ian, causing him to look up and notice a dark cloud beyond the trees on the opposite side of the water. A distant rumble came from the west.

"Oh, no," Ian moaned.

"Yes." Ahni ducked past a vine. "It will soon rain. We must find higher ground."

"We are already on land."

"No, we are on a bog." She glanced backward. "It could be out in the middle of the lake by the time the storm is through."

Lint stopped dead still. "What is this?"

"Bogs float. They move."

The brownie looked down and all around, his eyes wide. "That is terrifying..." He smiled. "Yet, it is something I would love to see. I have never heard of such a thing as moving land."

They continued along the water and as they neared the far end of the pool, the reality of the situation became clear.

The bog they stood upon was surrounded by water. A lagoon connecting to the lake waited to their left, the pool to their right, and a narrow strip of water connected the two.

"Do we swim?" Ian asked.

Ahni pointed to her left. "See those?"

Following her gesture, Ian nodded. "Yeah. There are two logs in the water."

"Those aren't logs." She bent, scooped up a handful of the dark, smelly peat moss and threw it. The clump splashed in the water, beyond the logs. In a flash, the two dark things in the water turned and snapped their long, flat jaws. Their bodies were fifteen feet long and as broad as a powerful man. Their tails swished back and forth as they swam away.

"Crocodile," Ahni said.

"They look dangerous," Ian noted.

"The beasts are quite deadly. Encountering one on land is bad. In the water, it is fatal."

Lint asked, "How do we cross?"

She reached out, grabbed ahold of a vine dangling into the water, and pulled it with her as she backed from the water's edge. With her free arm held high, she wrapped the vine around her wrist and gripped it. She burst forward and leapt, kicking her legs out. Her momentum carried her across the water, where she let go, sailed through the air, and landed on the far shore in a crouch, using her spear held level before her for balance.

"See." She turned toward them. "This is how you get across."

Ian embraced his magic and created an invisible platform. "I have another way." He gestured. "Revita. Step on."

The thief arched her brow. "Like when we were in the Vale?"

"Yes."

Shrugging, she bent, grabbed Lint around the waist, and stepped up. Ian set the platform into motion, taking her across the water. At the far side, she calmly stepped off and then set Lint down.

Ahni's eyes widened. "You truly do have magic."

"How do you think I kept the skiff and the rest of us from breaking into a hundred pieces after that monster attacked us?"

She shrugged. "I thought that Urvadan was watching over us."

Ian formed another disk and gestured toward his brother, who stepped on it. "I doubt gods care that much about our problems. In fact, I wonder what they do care about. I have yet to see any hand of god saving or condemning anyone around me." With a push and force of his will, Ian sent the disk and Vic across the water.

"Among my people, we believe differently," Ahni said. "We know that the ways of Urvadan are subtle. There are no coincidences. Events or outcomes that seem random are not. They are tilted for or against us by Urvadan or his treacherous brother. Only our choices and actions are within our control. The consequences of those actions are ours to own as well."

With the others across, Ian considered how to move himself to the other side and wondered if the new spell he had discovered would be helpful. He altered the construct before him, the lines shifting until it recreated what he had seen while Ahni was paddling. When magic channeled through it, a tendril of sinuous light flowed out the other side. Amazed, he watched it snake out across the water.

"Do you see that?" Ian asked.

"See what?" Vic looked from side to side, oblivious, although the rope of magic was winding past him.

"Huh," Ian grunted. "Maybe only I can see it."

When he willed the rope winding around the tree above Vic, the thread of magic responded, snaking around the trunk and then around the thick branches. "It responds to my thoughts," Ian said aloud.

Revita looked left and right, appearing as confused as Vic. "What in the blazes are you talking about?"

Ian ignored her, instead focusing on the tendril of light. He commanded the near end to wrap around his chest, snaking under his arms in the process, pressure coming from it as it gently constricted. The next mental command had the rope lifting him off the ground and then carrying him across. When his feet settled on the far bank, Ian dismissed his magic, and the rope of light faded away.

He grinned. "Incredible."

His brother shook his head. "I still don't understand."

"I discovered a new type of spell. It allows me to physically manipulate objects. It lifted me across."

Vic furrowed his brow. "Why didn't you just create a gateway for us?"

"One gateway consumes more of my strength than a dozen of these smaller spells, and it seemed a waste to use it for such a short distance."

Thunder rumbled, causing everyone to look up through the thick trees, toward the dark horizon.

"Rain comes soon. We must find solid ground." Ahni pulled a dangling vine aside and headed into the foliage.

OVER THE NEXT HOUR, the wind picked up with powerful gusts that tousled Ian's straw-colored hair and whipped his robes. Branches overhead wavered, leaves rustled, and the dangling vines swung wildly. With Ahni in the lead, the party continued across another bog. The strange landmasses ranged in size from a few hundred feet long to thousands. Some water spans were a simple hop to cross while others required Ian's magic.

They eventually came to a landmass that stood higher than the others. After sending his companions over to the island, Ian brought himself across the thirty-foot waterway. They then ascended the upslope, the ground giving with each step. Just as on the other bogs, the ground was made of black, moist earth and thick green moss and leaf trees dotted the island, many strangled by vines. However, the ground had, for some reason, formed into thousands of rolling humps which made Ian think of it as a giant, green and black orange.

He gripped vines as he ascended, to keep from falling in the soft, slippery footing. Halfway up the slope, his boot sank deeper than before and held fast. He tried to lift his leg but found the boot wedged.

"Wait." Ian called out and waited until the others stopped and looked back toward him. "I am stuck."

Vic's brow furrowed. He shared a glance toward Revita and then tromped back toward Ian. "You can't pull it out?"

Only the top few inches of the boot were visible above the soft black soil. "No."

Vic knelt and thrust his fingers into the ground. He began digging chunks of it away, and when he was ten inches down, his scrapes revealed a dark gray rock. Another minute of digging proved that the rock was far bigger than Ian had first guessed. Vic then dug on the other side of Ian's foot and soon exposed another, similar rock.

Using the back of his sleeve, Vic wiped the sweat from his brow. "Your boot is wedged between the rocks."

Ian tried to lift his leg again, but it held fast. "I could have told you as much."

Rising, Vic reached over his shoulder and pulled his mattock from its harness. "Don't move."

"What are you doing?" Ian didn't hide the apprehension from his voice.

"I intend to break the rock."

"Don't hit me."

"I won't miss so long as you remain still."

As Vic wound back, Ian tensed. The mattock came down and struck the rock. Sparks sizzled and shards split off. Ian could not be certain, but it felt as if the ground beneath him vibrated faintly from the impact. Again, Vic struck the rock, this time creating a crack. The third blow struck true, the pick end of the mattock plunging deep into the crack. Sparks sizzled and the chunk of rock broke away.

Ian pulled his boot free and stumbled back. "Thanks."

The ground beneath their feet shook. They staggered as the earth shifted. The ground began to tilt, the upslope steepening. The sensation was disorienting and caused Ian to fall to one knee.

"What is happening?" Lint cried.

The surrounding islands began to sink, at least that is what Ian thought until he realized that the one they were on was rising. The slope tilted further. He tried to grab ahold of something but only found loose, soft earth that quickly tore away. With a cry, Ian fell backward, tumbled along the slope and fell over the edge.

"Ian!" Vic's cry came out as Ian plunged into the lake.

Bubbles swirled around him in the murky water. He stroked and spun until he saw dim sunlight and then swam for it. His head burst above the surface. Gasping, he blinked and looked up to find the island thirty feet above him and still rising. While dark earth and moss covered the portion that had been above the water, the area emerging from the lake appeared as a wall of large, gray rocks, rounded with dips between each. In that moment, Ian realized that such a pattern could not be a natural formation. He was looking at something else. Alarmed, he swam away while watching the strange monstrosity rise from the water.

An edge emerged, thick and dramatic. Beneath the edge was a recess reaching far beneath the island. Water poured over the edge and then something else broke through the surface.

A long, thick cylinder rose beside Ian, covered in gray-green leathery flesh. A head bigger than a carriage emerged from the water, the waves created by it washing over Ian and driving him farther away. Eyes akin to black, glossy cauldrons opened as the head loomed above Ian. Recognition suddenly struck. Ian found himself staring at a turtle the size of his home village of Shillings.

The creature looked down at him and opened a dark and horrifying maw large enough to swallow an entire wagon. Despite himself, Ian screamed in terror.

CHAPTER 21
THE ARCHELA

T he behemoth turtle pinched its eyes closed and turned its head in a wince. The action sent water spraying and pelting Ian.

A deep and slowly spoken monotone voice boomed, "Please do not scream. It hurts my ears."

Ian blinked. "What?"

The turtle looked down at him. "I only just woke and am still drowsy. Besides, I abhor loud noises. I beg you to refrain from making such awful sounds." Each word dragged, the syllables lazily lingering.

"I... um, promise to not scream again." In the air above the turtle head, Lionel circled and squawked. *Quiet*, Ian sent. *Do not anger it.*

"Thank you." The creature tilted its head while peering down at Ian. "You are a human?"

"Yes."

"Ah." The head moved in a slow nod. "I met two humans before my nap. They were much darker than you."

Although it was bizarre to be engaged in conversation with a creature the size of an island, Ian preferred it to being eaten. "They must have been Crumi. They live by this lake."

"Ah. Yes. I recall that name. They were nice fellows."

"When was this?"

"Who is to say?" The turtle's head swayed slowly as it spoke. "Time means little to my kind, and I am the last of us."

From high above the turtle's head, Vic peered down from the edge of the shell while holding tight to a vine. "Ian! Are you alright?"

Ian called up, "Yes. I believe so."

Ahni appeared beside Vic, her face lighting up as she exclaimed, "The archela!"

"Please," the turtle boomed. "Do not shout."

Ian said, "I am sorry. My friends are worried about me."

"Worried? Why?"

"They don't want you to kill me, or eat me, or...do something else bad to me."

"Why would I do those things?" The turtle lowered its head, cocking it as it eyed Ian. "You are not evil, are you?"

"No. Of course not."

"That is good." The turtle nodded. "I cannot abide evil."

Still treading water, dressed and wearing boots, Ian began to tire. "I need to join my friends. Can you lower them down to me?"

"Why are you in such a hurry? We only just met."

Ian considered how to respond. *He cannot abide evil.* "A dark and evil force has invaded our realm. My friends and I are on a quest to stop this evil before it destroys our world."

The turtle's eyes bulged. "What is this evil?" The turtle lowered its head and peered at Ian with its massive, dark eyes. "What is its nature?"

With the massive head so close, Ian found his fear returning. He swallowed hard and replied, "A horde of monsters have crossed over from the underworld. They seek to destroy and consume life. We believe that they are led by a demon."

The turtle's eyes narrowed. "Is this true?"

Ian nodded. "I swear it."

The area around the turtle's eyes tightened. Its voice turned angry, fueled by a rumbling growl. "My kind despise the creatures of the netherworld. They must be destroyed, for destruction is all they know."

"So, you will let us go on our way?"

"Your way? Where do you go?"

Ian pointed past the turtle. "We journey to the mountains north of the lake."

The turtle narrowed its eyes and fell silent. A long quiet moment passed before it nodded. "I will take you there."

Like a rocky shelf slowly breaking off, certain to crush anything below it, the turtle lowered its head. When its chin dipped into the water, the displacement sent waves in all directions, the water crashing over Ian's head and causing him to splutter.

The giant creature rumbled, "Climb up. Join your companions."

The turtle's head sank into the lake until only the eyes and the bridge of its nose were above the surface. The behemoth's eyes were like black, bulbous pools big enough for Ian to swim in. Those eyes watched as Ian drew near, yet the edge of the turtle's shell remained two stories above the water. Despite his misgivings, Ian crawled onto its exposed nose. The creature's skin felt like tree bark, cracked yet supple. Its nose was as wide as a road, making it easy for Ian to gain his footing. As he reached the bridge of the turtle's nose, the head began to rise. Ian stumbled and fell to his knee as the world around him seemed to sink. Up and up, he went until he was above the turtle's shell. He tumbled and slid along the turtle's wet head and down its neck. Just before he was about to slip under the edge of its shell, a hand swept down and latched onto his wrist. He looked up to find Vic standing above him with a vine in his other hand.

"Climb up," Vic said.

Ian scrambled up the neck and, with his brother's help, climbed onto the shell. The two of them ascended the rounded slope, with the help of vines and shrubs growing on the shell. The turtle sank down into the water until only the shell and its eyes were visible above the surface. It then began to swim. The bogs fell away as the turtle swam into the lake and then turned north. Soon, the world was slipping past as if Ian were riding upon a galloping steed.

He and his companions were climbing toward the apex of the domed shell when the sky opened and rain began to fall. They found a log lying beneath the umbrella of a tree with leaves the size of Ian's hand. Already soaked to the bone, Ian did not mind the rain. He settled on the log, cast his thoughts out to Lionel and waited for the fire drake to return.

THE RAIN ENDED SHORTLY after it began, the air seeming somehow even more humid than before. The sun set and the archela, as the Crumi called the giant turtle, continued north despite the dark of the night. When it reached the northern edge of the lake, it began stomping through the swampland, crushing shrubs and bowling over trees as if they did not exist. Beneath a star-filled sky, Ian lay on his side with Lionel curled up against his chest. In his exhaustion, he fell into a deep, dreamless sleep.

CHAPTER 22

PREPARATIONS

Beneath the mid-day sun, Arangoli stood upon a bluff overlooking the rolling plains of the Haghetti. Miles to the north, an impenetrable gloom darkened the land. Vile, blood-thirsty monsters undoubtedly lurked in the black cloud. How many, he could only guess.

He glanced over at the dark elf standing beside him. "What do you think?"

Gryzaal narrowed his dark eyes. "They will reach the pass before nightfall."

"I could have told you that much. What else?"

"Whatever magic created that cloud, it is unlike anything I have ever seen. It is as if a piece of the underworld itself follows those vile monsters."

The cloud extended for miles and miles, its tail end stretching all the way to Talastar. "What if it does?"

The Drow arched a brow. "What do you mean?"

"What if the underworld comes with them? What if that cloud kills anything it touches?"

"Then, we are in deep trouble." He turned from the cliff. "Come. Let's see about the final preparations."

They crossed twenty strides of open ground and stopped before a quartet of dark elf warriors. Gryzaal spoke with them, issuing orders before heading down the path leading to the rock ladder that would take them back down the bluff.

HIS FEET TOUCHING down on the canyon floor, Arangoli turned from the ladder and dusted his hands clean.

Gryzaal gestured toward the nearby tunnel. "Go and see how things look in the city. Notify Axactus and your squad that it is time to wind down construction. I will report to Liloth and then will ready my troops."

"Aye."

Standing in the shadow of the cliffside, Arangoli watched Gryzaal cross the canyon floor. While the wooden structures remained, the tents, wagons, animals, and the Drow citizens were gone. The trampled grass throughout the area was the only reminder of the recently vacated populace.

Halfway across the space, Gryzaal stopped outside a building made of logs. There, he spoke with a quartet of guards before continuing toward the cavern Liloth had turned into her throne room.

With a sigh, resigning himself for the task ahead, Arangoli headed toward the tunnel. He clung to the shaded cliffside until he reached the entrance. Within its dark confines, his thoughts turned toward the plan Gryzaal had so carefully crafted.

As a dwarf, Arangoli preferred a direct approach to most things. As a warrior, he was trained to face an enemy head on. The plan the dark elves had concocted went against such notions. Yet, the approaching enemy was unlike any other. It was not a single monster they could distract and attack from the flank. It was not human, elf, or dwarf fighting for land, gold, or to protect their people. This enemy was plentiful, quick, and driven by an insatiable desire to kill. One could not reason with these monsters. One could not use fear or other emotions against them. The orcs would fight to the last, regardless of the odds. But in this case, he feared that the dark elves were vastly outnumbered.

By nightfall, death would come. The Head Thumpers would add their skills to the fight, but against superior numbers, would it make any difference at all? He was not certain, but he also knew he had to try. The advantageous nature of the Drow's plan demanded it. If nothing else, they would reduce the enemy numbers and slow down their advance.

His thoughts then turned to Gortch visiting Domus Ra. He prayed that Basteric responded better than he feared. Six years had passed since the Battle of Talastar, but dwarves were a stubborn lot, and Arangoli was certain that the holdmaster's hatred for the Drow remained as strong as ever.

At the end of the tunnel, he was met by the pounding of hammers, whacks of axes, and other sounds of active construction. In the street outside the tunnel, dozens of dark elves, along with members of Arangoli's squad, busily cut logs and nailed them together. Each platform was three feet wide and fifteen feet in length. When the section was complete, a team of Drow hauled it over to a nearby building and hoisted it up in the air. Rax and Artgan, both stationed on the rooftop, gripped one end of the wooden platform and lifted it onto the rooftop before turning and fading from view.

Arangoli spied Axactus and relayed Gryzaal's message. Construction was to be wound down, and the city would soon be evacuated. Axactus walked off, leaving Arangoli with nothing to do for a brief time. Curious about the progress made, he approached a ladder leaning against the building and climbed up.

Two stories up, Arangoli crawled off the ladder and rose to his feet.

Flat, stone rooftops stretched out across the small, ancient city. In numerous places along each street, wooden bridges spanned the gap from one row to the next. Ahead of him, Rax and Artgan crossed a bridge two streets over. They then turned and headed along the rooftops while passed by Pazacar and Fesgar, who were heading back toward the scaffold. Arangoli stopped and waited until they were one street away.

"How are things looking, Paz?"

The two dwarves reached the last bridge and crossed to the rooftop where Arangoli stood.

Pazacar stopped and wiped sweat from his brow. "We are connecting the last row of buildings now."

"Well, that is something at least."

Pazacar frowned. "Why do you say that?"

"The enemy approaches."

Fesgar's brow furrowed. "How soon?"

"An hour. Two at most."

"How many?" Pazacar asked.

Arangoli shrugged. "It is impossible to say. That cloud, or whatever it is, darkens the land beneath it as if it were the deep of night. The fore of the army is likely no more than ten miles away, yet even from the top of the bluff, nothing can be seen within the darkness."

Fesgar stared into space. "Then, there is no avoiding this fight."

Whenever Arangoli imagined himself frantically fighting the horde of orcs, he felt fear clawing at his confidence. Fesgar's eyes reflected that same emotion.

Arangoli clapped a hand on Fesgar's shoulder. "Have faith, Fes. Together, we will face this evil and see it vanquished."

"Do you truly think we can win?"

"I think that we must try. If we follow the plan, we will at least reduce their numbers before we are forced to flee."

"How will we know when it's time to begin the retreat?"

"I don't know," Arangoli admitted. "Gryzaal and his letalis warriors are skilled, and they have experience fighting these monsters. I guess I will leave it up to him to decide when things have gotten out of hand."

Fesgar grimaced. "I can't say I am thrilled with placing my fate in the hands of the Drow."

"Me, neither."

Pazacar said, "I'd say our fate has been in their hands since they swept in and dealt with those dire bats."

"Fair point." As Arangoli said it, the front edge of the black cloud moved beyond the cliff wall of the canyon. "Look." He pointed. "The darkness comes."

When Pazacar spun to look, he sighed. "I thought you said we had hours."

"It looks like I underestimated their speed."

The hammer of footsteps came from below, causing all three dwarves to turn and look down. Two dozen Drow warriors ran past, led by Gryzaal. They continued down the narrow street, all the way to the city gate. In moments, the squad of letalis warriors funneled out the opening and were gone.

"There goes the bait," Arangoli said.

"I'm glad you didn't volunteer us for that job," Fesgar said.

Arangoli grunted at the comment. "Running is an elvish thing. Let them do it while we save our energy for the fight." He spied Rax and Artgan two streets over and heading in his direction, their hands empty with the bridge in place. "Let's go see what else needs to be done before the darkness reaches us. When that happens, our preparations will cease, and it will be time to fight."

GRYZAAL RAN along the canyon floor, trailed by two dozen of his most athletic warriors – twenty-four male and female dark elves who wielded the signature weapon of the letalis. Like him, each gripped their naginata in one hand, holding the shaft at the balance point, ready should any trouble arise.

The trail wound past rocks, gradually taking them downhill, toward the Haghetti. The stream that flowed through their camp tumbled down into the canyon and ran along its floor, heading in the same direction as them. In his mind, Gryzaal raced those waters. It gave him something to think about, other than the ominous wall of blackness ahead.

The squad ran past the cavern where they had encountered Arangoli and his crew. They continued until passing the point where the canyon wall turned away. The view opened, and Gryzaal slowed to a stop. His warriors gathered to his left and right while all stared northwest.

A mile out, an impenetrable wall of murk dominated the plains. The black cloud towered a thousand feet into the air and stretched off into the distance, darkening miles of land. Gryzaal found himself mesmerized by the unnatural phenomenon, the sight of it stirring fear and awe in equal measure.

Somehow, he pulled himself out of his trance. "Spread out."

The line of warriors extended until eight to ten feet of open space stood between each of them.

"Crane form." Gryzaal stepped forward with his left foot, cocked his right elbow back, and held his weapon even with his shoulder, blade forward. He barked another command. "Flying lotus."

In perfect synchronization, the entire squad leapt and spun in a choreographed dance with death. Flashes of sunlight gleamed off their blades as they twirled, slashed, and thrust. The forms came without thought, for any letalis warrior trained with the naginata knew them by heart. Time seemed to stop as Gryzaal flowed from attack to attack. He was one with his weapon, and in that perfect union, he found solace.

The dance proceeded for a few minutes before drawing to a conclusion. With the final, spinning leap, they landed at a crouch with weapons extended. The warriors held the pose for a few breaths and then stood with the butts of their weapons planted on the ground beside them.

The warrior to Gryzaal's right asked, "Do you think they have spotted us?"

The cloud front shifted, the billowing edge of it turning south, directly toward Gryzaal and his team. The same howls and shrieks that had haunted his dreams for the prior year echoed across the plains. Hundreds of dark silhouettes occupied the front edge of the storm, their wiry bodies partially masked by the gloom.

"Hold fast," Gryzaal said firmly when the enemy was a half mile away.

His squad members, each tested in dozens of battles, stood their ground while the enemy, their numbers unknowable, closed the gap. The howls grew louder, the monsters sounding frantic and eager for blood.

At a quarter mile out, the glow of red eyes pierced the darkness. Hundreds of them. Only then, did Gryzaal give the command.

"Run!"

They spun and raced off with Gryzaal in the lead. Long, rapid strides carried them along the canyon floor. The incline may have slowed them if not for their trained bodies, honed like sharpened blades. The howling horde chasing them made the two-mile run back seem like ten. They finally rounded a soft bend, and the waterfall came into view. Above the sheer cliff beside the falls, hundreds of warriors stood upon the city wall. Waiting. They would not have to wait long.

Gryzaal ran to the first ladder, slid his weapon over his shoulder and into the harness across his back. He got a foothold and began scaling. The climb, involving ladders and stairs carved into the rock, consumed no more than a minute. By the time he crested the upper edge, the black cloud was only a few hundred feet away.

He took position between the wall and the cliff edge while the first of his squad members completed the daunting ascent.

"Go!" Gryzaal shouted. "Into the city!"

As the warriors regained their footing, they raced off. The cloud-bank crossed over the sun, casting the canyon in shadow. That shadow turned to night when swirling black fog extended toward Gryzaal, wrapped around him, and engulfed the ancient city.

Hooting, howling, and growling orcs bounded toward the base of the cliff, leapt, and began to climb. The lead monster scrambled over to the upper ladder, closing in on members of Gryzaal's squad who were still in mid climb. When it became clear that the last warrior would not reach the top in time, Gryzaal readied himself and jumped.

He plummeted past the three still climbing warriors. His feet smashed into the face of the lead orc, the force of the impact knocking the monster loose. Urgently reaching out, he grabbed ahold of the ladder and caught himself while his lower body slammed against the cliff wall. The falling orc struck another and then a third, knocking them loose, all three tumbling eighty feet before smashing into the ground. Other monsters raced in, trampled over their fallen brethren, and began scaling the wall.

Gryzaal climbed with renewed urgency and reached the top just after the last of his crew. He regained his footing, ran alongside the narrow path between the wall and the stream, and darted through the open door, into the city.

The warriors from his squad stood just inside the entrance. Amber, flickering light illuminated the area, fighting off the murk. It was an odd sensation to realize it was mid-afternoon, the sun hidden somewhere beyond the unnatural cloud.

"Close and bar the doors!" he shouted as he ran past the soldiers stationed at the entrance. Although he longed to rest, there was no time.

He rushed over to the ladder leaning against the city wall, gripped the rungs, and began a three-story climb that brought him to the top of the wall. Torches spaced every fifty feet ran from one end of the wall to the other. Amid the torchlight stood hundreds of warriors, ready to face death.

Gryzaal leaned between two merlons and peered down into the canyon.

Thousands of monsters rushed along the canyon floor and began to scale the cliffside.

"Ready the barrels!" Gryzaal shouted.

In pairs, soldiers along the wall lifted one of two dozen barrels, each holding ten gallons of naphtha, and set them on the wall between the merlons. When the orcs reached the top of the cliff and began up the city wall, Gryzaal shouted the next order.

"Drop the barrels!"

Each barrel was pushed over the edge. Many fell onto unsuspecting orcs, knocking them from the wall before crashing to the ground. The barrels alongside the eastern facing wall struck the top of the plateau and burst with a crack. Dark liquid sprayed out, drenching the rock and running down the cliff face. The barrels along the north facing wall plummeted all the way to the canyon floor, scraping dozens of orcs from the cliffside. The barrels shattered and splashed their contents across the ground.

"Ready the flaming arrows!"

Archers along the wall pulled arrows from buckets, each with a damp cloth wrapped around the tip. Those arrows were held to the torches illuminating the wall and caught fire.

"Loose at will!"

Flaming arrows shot down into the darkness. Arrows struck monsters in a splash of flames, sending shrieking orcs flailing into the depths. When the burning missiles touched the liquid from the barrels, wild flames erupted. In seconds, infernos raged at the base of the wall and along the nearest end of the canyon floor. Hundreds of orcs were caught in the blaze while the fire provided light within the gloom, exposing more of the dark, twisted army.

Thousands upon thousands of orcs filled the canyon from the stream's edge to the canyon wall and extending off into the darkness. The swarming mob pushed forward, forcing unwilling orcs into the fire while others raced beyond the edge of the flames and scrambled up the cliffside. Although the fires did not stop the orcs' advance, it slowed them down. Still hundreds of monsters scaled the cliffside, navigated past the fires at the top, and climbed up the city wall.

"They come!" Gryzaal drew his naginata. "Ready yourselves!"

A pair of orcs crested the wall before him, and he lashed out. The blade end of his weapon sliced across the chest of one monster before cleaving through the wrist of another. Both monsters shrieked and fell, only to be replaced by two more. In moments, Gryzaal found himself fighting for his life.

CHAPTER 23
A DARK DAY

Arangoli and his crew stood on a rooftop overlooking the square inside the outer walls of Paisu. Across the square, dark elves fought off orcs cresting the wall, their silhouettes outlined by the glow of flames. The monsters and the city defenders appeared as nothing more than silhouettes against the amber glow of flames from outside the city. The fight was frantic and soon, bodies began to fall from the wall to land inside the square. Orcs poured through gaps in the defense and descended upon the Drow warriors waiting in the square below the wall.

A second battle took place, just as frantic as the first. Drow blades flashed, severing limbs and slicing across torsos. Yet, the dark elves were quickly outnumbered and only a scrape of the monsters' talons was enough to kill. The tide soon turned in the monster's' favor. Sensing that it was time, Arangoli lifted the horn, took a deep breath, and sounded the alarm.

～

GRYZAAL SPUN AND SLASHED, his blade raking across the back of an orc facing away from him. He came around while ducking low as another orc's talons swiped just above him. Following through with the spin, his blade sliced through the creature's lower legs. It squealed as it fell from the wall.

The horn sounded and none too soon. He thrust and his blade plunged into the neck of an orc attempting to crest the wall. The monster fell, taking two others with it on its way down. Gryzaal spun, searching for another enemy. The bodies of Drow and orc alike lay strewn across the length of the ramparts. Only a handful of the dark elves stationed on the wall remained upright. As the other survivors turned and rushed toward the scaffold, he burst into a run after them.

Gryzaal slashed at an orc coming between two merlons and kicked another off, sending it flailing toward the square inside the city. A pair of monsters blocking the way turned toward him and snarled. Rather than slowing, he leapt, flipped over them, and slashed, his blade tearing through the shoulder of the first monster, severing its arm. Gryzaal landed beyond the two at a crouch. The second monster lashed out, its talons nearly grazing Gryzaal before striking a merlon to his left. He thrust upward and drove his weapon through its midriff as he burst upward, lifting the orc into the air. Turning, he lowered his blade and the skewered monster slid off to fall into the city.

A glance behind him revealed dozens of orcs cresting the wall. Spurred by urgency, Gryzaal ran toward the scaffold, taking care to place each leaping step between corpses.

"Light it, Hashaal!" he shouted to the only other Drow remaining on the wall.

Hashaal tossed the torch in his hand and then leapt onto the scaffold beside him. The torch landed on the top of the wall and rolled into the pool of naphtha, which ignited on contact. Six-foot-tall flames shot along the top of the wall, spreading all the way to the bluff to the west. Orcs climbing over the wall in that area squealed as they caught fire.

When Gryzaal drew near the scaffold, he leapt onto it and then down onto the wooden bridge connecting it to the first row of buildings. He reached the gong stationed on the first rooftop, wound back, and drove the butt of his staff into it. The gong resounded above the noise of the fight. From behind a line of sharpened logs sticking up at an angle from the stone rooftop, Gryzaal looked down into the bloody, chaotic melee occupying the city square.

In response to the clanging gong, the warriors fighting the attacking monsters issued final strikes, turned, and darted down the three open streets leading toward the heart of the city. The monsters gave chase, but Gryzaal stood ready. The moment the last warrior headed down the street below him, he sliced through a rope tied to the rooftop. The gate hanging above the street, a ten-foot-tall panel made of sharpened logs, crashed down, the points at the bottom of the gate crushing a pair of orcs as it slammed into the ground to block the street.

THE MOMENT the last dark elf raced down the street below Arangoli, he shouted. "Artgan, Fesgar! Cut the ropes!"

The dwarves, stationed on opposite sides of the rooftop, chopped down at the ropes beside them. The panels on both sides of the building plummeted with a boom, trapping orcs beneath them while blocking the routes. With all streets blocked off, the attackers pounded against the wooden gates and began to climb them. Dozens filled the square while more monsters poured over the city wall.

Stationed across the rooftops between the two middle streets, Arangoli and his crew stood with weapons ready, knowing the enemy would seek to go over the buildings once they realized the difficulty of scaling the greased gates.

Orcs began to scale the building walls. When the one below Arangoli neared the eave, he raised his hammer and slammed it down, crushing its skull. The monster fell and another replaced it. Again, Arangoli wound back. His hammer came down on its hand, crushing it and breaking off a chunk of stone from the rooftop. A creature burst up to his right, between him and Fesgar. Before it could swipe at the other dwarf's unprotected backside, Arangoli yanked his hammer backward. The hammerhead crashed into the orc's back and released a magically charged thump, launching the orc forward to fall sprawling on its stomach, its spine crushed.

The monsters came in a relentless rush. The Head Thumpers hacked, chopped, sliced, and stabbed at the creatures. The fight was fast and furious, and rapidly had the dwarves drenched in sweat. Bodies began to pile up at the base of the buildings, and while the dwarves stood two stories above the street, soon the mound of corpses stretched beyond the first floor.

Arangoli swung his hammer into the chest of an orc, launching it out toward the heart of the square, which was filled with monsters. Yet, more continued to spill over the top of the city wall. Even dwarves, known for their endurance and grit, would exhaust themselves against such unbelievable odds.

He grabbed the horn dangling from the chain around his neck, lifted it to his lips, and blew a solid, resounding note, sounding the next phase of their retreat. Two enemies came at Arangoli, forcing him to drop the horn and launch a sweeping attack. His hammer crashed through the head of one orc and slammed into the shoulder of another. Both fell as the other head thumpers turned and ran. Only when the last of his crew had abandoned their posts did Arangoli deal one last strike and turned his back on the bloodthirsty horde.

With a string of seven dwarves ahead of him, Arangoli ran for all he was worth. He glanced back to find enemies pouring onto the rooftop and giving chase.

When the lead dwarves reached the last rooftop, they turned and raced across the wooden bridge spanning the gap to the next row of buildings. Arangoli came in last, stopped short of the bridge, and spun around as an orc leapt at him with its arms extended. A desperate swing of his hammer struck the attacker in the ribs and altered its path, causing its talons to barely miss. The monster flew past and sailed beyond the eave to fall face-first onto the street. With dozens of other monsters now rushing down the rooftops, Arangoli franticly turned and darted across the catwalk.

As he reached the next roof, a trio of orcs rushed onto the bridge. An underhand swing of his hammer struck the wooden walkway, knocking it aside. Two of the orcs lost balance and fell. The third orc was joined by two more as Arangoli swung again. This time, the bridge skittered off the rooftop and dropped out of sight, dumping the three monsters with it. The orcs on the opposite rooftop began to scale down. In moments, they would fill the streets and rooftops alike.

The dwarves ran along the top of the buildings and onto a catwalk spanning the next street. They hurried across to where Gryzaal and a dozen of his warriors waited. The moment Arangoli was across, two Drow lifted that end of the catwalk and tossed it over the edge. Elf warriors armed with bows began to loose arrows, felling enemies in rapid succession.

Orcs ran across rooftops across the city while others spilled down otherwise empty streets in search of victims. The monsters faded into doorways and alleys. An explosion shook the city as a building three blocks away crumbled. Smoke rose from the structure, lit up by the amber of flames.

Gryzaal patted Arangoli on the shoulder. "Well done. Let's move on to the bowl before they realize that the city is empty."

Another explosion came from the direction of the square. "It looks like they found another of your surprises."

Gryzaal hopped down the scaffold. "We've plenty more surprises waiting."

The elven warriors followed their leader down to the ground and then into the tunnel leading to the bowl. Arangoli cast one backward glance and followed his team down the scaffold. Howls, growls, shrieks, and cries rang throughout the ancient city while the fires and torches fought against the blackest of nights.

"How many monsters have we killed thus far?" Arangoli mused as he ran into the dark tunnel. The question went unanswered, but the more pressing question went unvoiced. *How many monsters remain?*

DAYLIGHT at the far end of the tunnel beckoned, drawing Gryzaal toward it. He ran out, crossed the abandoned camp, and headed for the nearest bridge. The bulk of his warriors stood along the opposite side of the stream that split the field in half. The area on the near side of the stream was nothing but open fields dotted by scattered buildings made of logs. The nearest portion of the bowl was darkened in shadow while daylight held tight to the rest.

Once past the nearest bridge, he slowed and turned to the squad escorting him. "Light the torches." Another explosion echoed in the distance. "They will soon find the tunnel, and when they do, the monsters and the darkness will come."

The hammer of footsteps came from the bridge as Arangoli and his squad ran across. The dwarves stopped beside Gryzaal and gasped for air while resting their hands on their knees.

Barking and howls came from inside the tunnel. The wall of darkness masking the cliffside rolled across the field as the noises of the rabid monsters grew louder. Enemies burst from the tunnel and raced out into the open bowl. Some monsters went straight for the empty buildings while others sprinted toward Gryzaal and his warriors. Every soldier remained fixed in place as the monsters came at them. By the time the first reached the stream, the cloud had extended over the entire bowl, blotting out the sky while torches lining the near bank of the stream created a strip of light across the bowl. Gryzaal knew that the monsters were drawn toward fire. They would come for him and his warriors, viewing them as targets. He only prayed that the enemy did not know how to swim.

Orcs emerged from the darkness in a full charge. The first ran down the riverbank and stumbled into the water. It flailed, gasped, and bobbed as the current swept it away. Other monsters made the same mistake, and each was carried under the north bridge while heading toward the cavern where the stream passed out of the bowl. Any monster that had not escaped the stream by that point was doomed, for the drop of the waterfall outside of Paisu was nigh impossible to survive.

As expected, the monsters realized the folly of rushing into the stream and, instead, began crossing via the two bridges.

"To the bridges!" Gryzaal bellowed.

The line of Drow warriors burst into motion, a contingent heading north, and another heading south, while a hundred archers rushed up to the shoreline in the middle. Those in the last group raised their bows and began to loose. The other squads formed a grid of warriors before both bridges. With forty warriors in a line and eight lines deep, they held their weapons ready.

Orcs began spilling out from the north bridge. The monsters were met with swift action. The Drow at the fore slashed, sliced, and cut down enemy after enemy. Here and there, orc poison claimed warriors, creating breaks in the front line. When half of the warriors at the fore had fallen and deepspawn bodies littered the ground near the bridge, Gryzaal shouted an order, and the survivors from the first line turned and ran. The orcs gave chase and were met by the second line of warriors. Another frantic battle ensued.

The seemingly endless flow of monsters poured over the two bridges while Gryzaal looked on and issued commands. A spreading mound of corpses littered the ground, expanding each time he called for the lead line of warriors to abandon their post. By the time the last line of Drow were fighting, the area across the stream teemed with deepspawn by the thousands. Gryzaal issued one last command, calling for the retreat.

The warriors turned and ran toward the narrow canyon to the southeast, which eventually connected to the mountain pass. They had been instructed to form a wall before the canyon and hold the monsters at bay. Knowing he could trust them to fight to the death if needed, Gryzaal broke from the group and headed toward the barricade along the eastern wall of the bowl. As he drew near the dark opening to the cavern, he slowed and carefully rounded past the sharpened stakes jutting up from the ground.

A lilting female voice came from within the cavern. "You've done well, Gryzaal."

He stepped into the darkness and bowed to the silhouette before him. "Thank you, my queen."

"Now," she said. "We shall embrace death, and in that embrace, we shall either find salvation or damnation."

CHAPTER 24
THE GLOOM THICKENS

P anting from the exertion, Arangoli climbed the last twenty feet of a steep, hundred-foot rise overlooking the narrow canyon connecting the bowl to Domas Ra Pass. Although blackness obscured the sky directly above him, afternoon sunlight still shone to his left, providing just enough light for him to see the knobs, edges, and cracks along the cliffside. He reached the top, crawled onto the ledge, and rose to his feet. His squad climbed the cliff wall below him with Rax reaching the top first. Soon, all would join him.

"Pull out the wax, Rax."

The dwarf grinned. "That rhymes, you know."

"Perhaps I am a poet, and I don't know it."

Rax laughed as he lowered his pack. While he dug inside, Arangoli peered out over the bowl.

A line of torches ran along the stream splitting the field. In that light, a battle was waged. Monsters clustered along the western bank while Drow fought for their lives on the east side. The monsters poured across the two bridges while additional monsters clustered behind them, eager for blood. Then, the Drow warriors suddenly turned and fled straight toward the canyon mouth below the ledge where Arangoli stood.

"It is almost time." He turned to find Rax holding a ball of pale wax. "Give me some of that."

Rax pinched off a chunk and handed it over.

"Thanks." Arangoli turned to the other Head Thumpers as the last of them reached the top. They looked a bit ragged, their breaths coming in gasps, yet there was no fear in their eyes. "Everyone take a chunk of wax. Shove a good-sized pinch in each ear. Make sure you can't hear anything. From here on, we use hand signals."

Like the others, Arangoli broke his chunk of wax into two, squeezed and rolled both pieces, so they softened, and then shoved them into his ears. The noises of the angry horde slipped away, replaced by silence. With his hearing deadened, Arangoli watched the scene below him unfold.

Orcs by the thousands stormed across the bridges and filled the near side of the bowl. When the monsters reached the Drow warriors blocking the canyon mouth, another battle raged. Flashes of blades, talons, and blood highlighted the fracas. Bodies soon piled up, but neither side appeared ready to relent.

GRYZAAL TOOK position near the rear of the cavern. He slid his hand into his leather jerkin battle coat, found the inside pocket, and pulled out a glob of wax. Anyone who was to remain required such protection. Even then, it was unsafe for him to stand anywhere but in an alcove, as far from the queen as possible.

In the cavern's center stood Queen Liloth. Arieldar, the last male singer, was positioned to her left. Realyth, the only remaining female singer other than the queen, stood to her right. Beyond them, deepspawn stormed across the field, their obscene noises falling silent when Gryzaal shoved the wax into his ears.

The monsters ran toward the cave with mindless fury, straight into the sharpened stakes sticking up from the ground. Even with their impaled brethren dangling from the stakes, they swarmed the area, driven by some unknown, insatiable thirst. Such behavior, despite how bizarre it might seem, had become expected. Knowing the enemy lay at the core of the entire strategy the Drow had employed, but the plan involved more than simply reducing their numbers. The final, desperate element of the counterattack was yet to come. When Liloth opened her mouth and the crystal mounted to the staff in her hand began to glow, the daring war song the Drow had planned was about to come to an epic crescendo.

The two singers bracketing the queen joined in, their wordless song causing the crystal to glow brighter and brighter until Gryzaal was forced to shield his eyes.

A CONE of bright light burst out from the eastern side of the bowl, cutting through the black mist and illuminating the entire field.

"By Vandasal's beard," Arangoli muttered, his voice sounding strangely distant due to his plugged ears.

He and his team stared in shock and awe. Tens of thousands of enemies filled the bowl, packing the area so tightly, there was nary a spot where the ground was visible.

The monsters flinched, cowered, and shielded their faces in the bright light. Those fighting at the canyon mouth, far from the light's center, turned in distraction. The elven warriors stationed in the canyon reacted in a completely different manner.

The Drow made a final attack, turned, and fled down along the narrow canyon heading toward the mountain pass. As they raced below the rocky point where Arangoli stood, he pulled his hammer free from the harness on his back and glanced backward.

His crew stood with their eyes gaping, feet unmoving. To get their attention, he made a gesture with his hammer and pointed with the other hand. When they backed away, he turned his focus on the ground near his feet. A crack in the rock ran parallel to the canyon with only a three-foot break in the center. He strolled over to the space between the two ends of the fissure, planted his feet shoulder width apart, and took a deep breath. A glance into the canyon revealed the last of the surviving Drow racing away from him while orcs gave chase.

Arangoli lifted his hammer before his face, closed his eyes, and touched his forehead against it. *Vandasal, if you can hear me, give me strength. Allow my hammer to strike true.* With the prayer said, he opened his eyes, wound back, and swung a tremendous overhead strike. The hammer head crashed down into the stone. The thump of its enchantment released a pulse that shook the ground beneath his feet. The rock connecting one fissure to the other split. The area shuddered, and another crack resounded. Arangoli frantically backed away as the cliffside broke free and crashed down.

The roar of the rockslide rumbled beneath Arangoli's feet and reverberated in his chest. Millions of pounds of rock tumbled to the canyon floor, crushing hundreds, if not thousands of monsters in seconds. A massive cloud of dust burst up into the air, swirling before settling to reveal a rockpile fifty feet tall and twice the depth, blocking the canyon off from the bowl.

"We did it!" The words came out with a sense of relief that lasted only seconds.

The light shining in the bowl turned dark purple and then chaos erupted.

In a small alcove in the corner of an otherwise perfectly rounded cavern, Gryzaal shielded his eyes and waited while the three singers bellowed notes targeted at the crystal. When the light darkened from white to purple, he lowered his arm.

Something dark and terrible swirled within the crystal. It then shot out like an explosion. Despite his plugged ears, a terrible scream passed over him, sending chills down his spine. A wave of purple-tinted death raced across the bowl. Every monster it touched clamped its hands against its ears, twisted and writhed, and then collapsed. For ten long seconds, the grim, brutal wave washed over the area. The crystal turned back to white, and then faded to black. Liloth's shoulders slumped and her chin dropped to her chest. Arieldar sank to one knee, his head bent over one arm. The other female singer collapsed on her side and lay there, breathing heavily as if she had just climbed a mountain.

The black mist darkening the area began to waver, break apart, and disperse. Night gradually turned to day until the afternoon sun shone down upon the bowl.

Stunned, Gryzaal crossed the cavern, passing the exhausted magic users. Dozens of orc corpses dangled on the stakes across the entrance. Beyond them, thousands of monsters lay strewn across a space a half mile in diameter. He absently dug into one ear and pulled out the wax before moving on to the other. They had done it. They had defeated an enemy fifty times their number.

Motion from the tunnel connecting the bowl to Paisu drew his attention. A creature unlike anything he had ever seen emerged.

Arangoli pulled the wax from his ears as his crew gathered around him. Their elevated location gave them a good view of the bowl and the massacre that had taken place.

Rax whistled. "I am glad we didn't have to face all of those ugly arse things."

Pazacar added, "There must be fifty thousand orcs down there."

"Hold on." Rax pointed. "What is that?"

A humanoid being standing eight feet tall emerged from the tunnel on the north end of the bowl. Thick muscles bulged beneath its dark red flesh. Horns jutted out from its forehead and curled to each side, much like a ram. The creature strolled out into the bowl, its oversized feet stepping over and often right on top of the dead orcs. Ten strides out, it stopped and surveyed the area with its arms crossed. The creature shook its head, dropped its arms to the side, and headed toward the nearest bridge.

"I have a bad feeling about this," Arangoli said.

"What are we going to do?" Rax asked.

A voice inside screamed for Arangoli to turn and run away, but his sense of honor rebelled at the idea. Gryzaal and his people had held their own during the battle. Arangoli and his squad had played a key role, but it was one that inherently had placed them at less risk while hundreds of warriors sacrificed their lives to see it through. Should this ugly creature present a threat, he was obligated to help fight it.

He leaned over the cliff edge, noting jagged edges and ledges that offered an easy way down. "Let's climb down to the rockpile blocking the canyon. If Gryzaal and Liloth appear to be in trouble, we will be able to react much more quickly. Should things go really bad, it will take us less time to get the blazes out of here."

TALES OF CREATURES from the underworld had been deeply ingrained in Drow culture before the orcs had even appeared. The most notable creatures mentioned in those tales were demons. Gryzaal had often worried that one might rise from the deep, yet during a year of fighting in those depths, never had there been a sign of such a creature. This had led him to believe that the stories of demons had just been based on orcs. He now realized that the supposition was pure folly. The tall, muscular figure crossing the south bridge and wading through the sea of corpses could be nothing else.

The demon headed toward the cavern where Gryzaal stood, its pace casual and its mood relaxed. If the sight of an ugly monster from legend had not frightened him, the calm determination it exuded would have.

Liloth appeared at Gryzaal's side. In her hand, she gripped her staff, the crystal atop it dull. When Gryzaal glanced back to see what had become of the other two singers, he found Arieldar helping Realyth to her feet. The two of them then traversed the length of the rug to join their queen.

Gryzaal turned his attention back on the approaching demon, now fewer than fifty strides away. Up close, the horrific fiend was even uglier than anticipated. Yellow, hate-filled eyes stared out from beneath a protruded brow. Its jaw and nose were distended, both coming to a point. Long, black talons bent out from its fingers and toes. Reddish, wrinkled scales covered its ten-foot-tall frame.

The demon strode right up to the stakes, stopped and crossed its muscular arms over its chest. It spoke in a guttural, thick language unknown to Gryzaal. A beat later, it spoke again, its deep voice speaking in another tongue that was also strange to the ear. Finally, it spoke in a language Gryzaal understood.

In Dwarvish, the incubus boomed, "Who are you?"

Liloth replied in the same language. "I am Liloth, Queen of the Drow."

The demon glanced around him. "It was your magic that destroyed my pets."

She nodded. "Yes, demon."

"I am no mere demon. I am Az'Ianzar, demon lord of the Fourth Realm."

"Why are you here?"

"When the portal between worlds first opened, I sent my pets to test the way but they found it blocked again and again. Now that the way is open, I have come to quench my thirst. I will feast upon this world, sating my hunger with the sweet juice of warm blood and fuel my might with the souls of my victims."

"Your pets are dead and no longer serve you." Despite the horror standing before her, Liloth spoke in a defiant tone. "Go back from where you came and never return, or you will suffer the same fate."

The demon lifted its head and laughed. It then bent, gripped two stakes right before it, and tore them from the ground, lifting the impaled orc corpses and making it seem as if it required no effort at all. The creature then tossed the stakes and bodies aside, strode forward, and tore the next pair of stakes free.

In response, Liloth, Arieldar, and Realyth all opened their mouths in song. The crystal flared with magic. The demon shielded its face with one hand but it did not retreat. The warbling aria from the trio of singers grew louder and higher in pitch. A beam of purple light burst from the crystal and engulfed the demon, blotting it from view. Gryzaal had witnessed Liloth use the same spell to deal with traitors. With each occurrence, their bodies had melted to a puddle of blood and goo, their bones turned to jelly. He imagined the same occurring with the demon, but reality delivered a vastly different outcome.

The demon strode out of the light, approached Liloth, and tore the staff from her hand. With a flick, the monster tossed the staff thirty feet away. The crystal struck the cavern wall and shattered. Stunned, the singers fell quiet. A tense, terrifying silence hung in the air as the demon towered over the three magic users. Az'Ianzar then grinned to reveal a mouth full of sharp, jagged teeth. The demon snatched Arieldar by the throat, lifted him off the ground, and opened its mouth far wider than what should be possible. The demon chomped down and bit the male singer's head right off before tossing his body aside. A thick lump slid down the demon's throat and into its body. Then, something bizarre occurred.

A ripple passed over the demon and it began to stretch. Its arms grew longer and thicker. Its head swelled. The rest of its body followed, and in moments, it suddenly stood fifteen feet tall.

Fear clutched at Gryzaal's throat, choking off the air supply. He took a step back as Realyth turned and ran. The demon took three long strides, reached out, and caught the lean female singer by the waist. He lifted her off the ground as if she weighed nothing and bit her head off as well.

Horrified, Gryzaal darted through the opening the demon had created and raced toward the rockpile blocking the canyon that connected the bowl to the pass.

ARANGOLI STEPPED DOWN and planted his feet on a boulder that lay atop the pile of fallen rock. He turned to look over the fields of dead. From his position, he could not see the demon or anyone else alive. His squad mates began to gather around him on the massive boulder.

A high-pitched, warbling song echoed across the distance. *The singers are still alive.* The aria abruptly ended. A scream rang out. The familiar form of Gryzaal came into view as the Drow warrior ran in Arangoli's direction. His eyes appeared haunted, the determined confidence he had displayed earlier now replaced by obvious fear.

Pazacar said, "Something is wrong."

"Aye." Arangoli nodded but kept his attention fixed on Gryzaal.

Fesgar wiped sweat from his brow. "Where is the demon?"

"The cavern, I think."

Another scream rang out and was cut off. In reaction, Gryzaal slowed and glanced backward before immediately sprinting toward the rockpile.

"Go!" The dark elf shouted.

"Go where?" Arangoli called back.

"Run!"

"What is happening?"

The demon strolled back into view.

"By the gods..." Arangoli muttered.

"It's almost as big as a rock troll!" Rax exclaimed.

It was true. The demon had somehow inflated and now stood thirty feet tall. It turned its glare on the dwarves. In that evil gaze, even from a quarter mile away, Arangoli saw a hunger that chilled him to the bone.

The demon raised its head and opened its mouth toward the sky. A dark mist billowed out, swirling around it as it expanded. The mist thickened and expanded until it blocked the sun. The orcs it touched began to move, their cuts healing, their severed limbs regrowing. All the while, the elves stared in horror, locked in a state of shock.

The revived monsters climbed to their feet as the dark cloud spread. It seemed to cling to their bodies as if the orcs were putrid flowers and the mist a swarm of demented bees.

Gryzaal scrambled up the rockpile. "Why are you standing there?"

Arangoli pointed. "Look."

Stopping below the dwarves' position, Gryzaal looked over his shoulder.

Hundreds of orcs stood amid the swirling darkness. The demon at the heart of it all gestured and barked some wordless command. The orcs turned and ran across the field of corpses, coming straight for Arangoli and his companions.

"Oh, blazes."

Arangoli did not enjoy running. In fact, he often despised doing so. It was a very undwarflike thing to do. There were tales of elves running through the forest simply for the joy of it. The Head Thumpers, often with mugs of ale in their paws, joked and scoffed at such bizarre notions. Who would run for no reason at all? It was ludicrous.

Running for urgency was another thing all together.

It was easy to imagine charging into a fight with weapons ready and hearts pounding with the thrill of battle. In contrast, no self-respecting dwarf would run away from a fight, not unless the odds were absolutely, impossibly against them. Despite this admittedly lopsided propensity, Arangoli found himself fleeing an enemy for the second time in a week, and he hated every second of it.

He and the other Head Thumpers ran for their lives. With steep walls of rock on both sides of the narrow canyon, there was only one way to go and nowhere to hide, so they ran and ran. Soon after their flight began, Gryzaal appeared at Arangoli's side and then passed him, the dark elf's long legs carrying him forward at a faster pace but with noticeably less effort. Dwarves rarely envied elves, for who would want to be a member of such an aloof, stuffy race? In this instance, it was difficult not to feel jealous.

Casting a glance over his shoulder, Arangoli found his dwarven companions hot on his heels with Fesgar taking up the rear. In the distance, hundreds of feet away, orcs shrouded by darkness spilled over the rockpile. Having seen how fast the creatures moved, Arangoli knew they could not outrun the horde, not for more than a mile or two. That backward glance proved unwise considering the uneven ground. He stubbed his toe on a rock, stumbled, and fell forward in a somersault. Dust swirled around him as he skidded on his side and came to a stop. With a banged-up shoulder, scraped elbow, and bruised pride, he bound to his feet and set off again, chasing after the rest of his squad.

The ground rose to an incline, and Arangoli's thighs began to burn. Still, he and his crew ran after Gryzaal. At the top of the rise, he chanced another backward glance and then wished he had not. The orcs had cut their lead in half. The swirling darkness and the orcs connected to it would soon reach them. There would be no escape.

He ran even faster, catching up to the others and passing them while pointing toward an outcropping of boulders ahead of them. "Climb those rocks. From there, we fight."

Rax glanced over. "Are you crazy?"

"We can't outrun them. Better to die fighting then fleeing."

While it was a grim statement, nobody argued. They were all dwarves to the core, and dying in such a cowardly way was beyond them.

Arangoli reached the rocks first. He scrambled up, rising some fifteen feet above the ground before he stood on the flat top of the tallest boulder. The surface was ten feet deep and twice the length. The swirling, unnatural cloud and the monsters that hid within were now less than two hundred feet away. He drew his hammer while his squad joined him. There, the Head Thumpers would make their final stand.

CHAPTER 25
THE FINAL STAND

Gortch slogged his way uphill, following the same switchbacks he had taken a day earlier. Of course, going down did not require as much exertion. To make matters worse, it was hot and the garments underneath his new armor were soaked with sweat. Thankfully, the sun had dropped low enough in the sky to cast the mountain pass in shadow. It had been a long day with far too much uphill trekking for his liking, but he also knew that this was the last rise, which offered a semblance of solace.

The ground leveled and then turned to a downslope, his view opening to reveal that he was not alone. Somone was coming toward him. In fact, it was a lot of someones.

Dark elves, all dressed in the black leather of their warriors, jogged along the trail. Their weapons were coated in crimson, all save for those gripping bows. As they drew near, the elves came to a stop.

Hands cupped to his mouth, Gortch called out, "We have come to help fight."

The Drow warrior at the fore, a tall, lean female with platinum hair, called back. "We? Who is we?"

Gortch glanced backward as the first of the dwarves following him crested the rise. "Only me and my new friends from Domus Ra."

"Who are you?"

"My name is Gortch. I am a member of Arangoli's squad."

"The Head Thumpers?"

"Yes. In fact, our numbers have swelled. "I bring one hundred fifty newly recruited Head Thumpers with me."

The clanking of armor drew near as the other dwarves crested the ridge and gathered around Gortch.

The elf said, "You are too late. The battle is over by now."

"Over?"

"Yes. The singers' magic was to destroy the rest of the deepspawn army."

"Where are my squad mates?"

The elf pointed north, deeper into the pass. "They remained behind to close off the canyon, so we could escape and catch up to our people. I suspect the dwarves will be along soon...assuming things went well."

Walzar, standing to Gortch's right said, "The fight is over?"

A younger dwarf added, "You said we would get to face monsters, that we could be heroes."

Gortch gestured for them to quiet. "Until we find Arangoli, let's assume that these monsters are still a threat. Even then, he will welcome you as Head Thumpers. Have faith. It is the Head Thumper way." He resumed his trek, heading downhill. "Just remember, the Drow are not the enemy." Not now, at least, he added in his head.

The two squads, roughly equal in number, passed each other while exchanging wary glances. The Drow appeared tired, so Gortch had no worries about them starting a fight. His crew, however, was filled with young dwarves eager to prove themselves. He suspected they would get a chance. Soon.

No more than five minutes later, another dark elf came into view. Dressed in black leather and carrying a bloodstained naginata, the warrior appeared much like the others, but this one Gortch knew by name.

"Gryzaal!" He called out.

The Drow looked up, but did not reply, instead continuing to run along the zig zagging upslope.

Gortch tried again, "Where is Arangoli?"

Gryzaal slowed and looked back down the pass. "That way, I fear."

When Gortch followed the gesture, he noticed a black cloud jutting above the hillside to the northwest. "The orcs?"

"Yes. Hundreds of them." Gryzaal shook his head. "We had won. It was over. But now..."

Gortch did not wait for the rest of the sentence. Instead, he burst into a run, racing along the downslope with his new recruits giving chase.

A WAVE of monsters washed over the land and converged on the rockpile where Arangoli and his crew were to make their last stand. The orc in the lead scrambled up the rockpile with a string of drool dangling from its open jaw. Mindless bloodthirst filled its red eyes. As it drew near, Arangoli made an underhand swipe. His hammer struck the enemy in the forehead with a crack, launching it backward, into the horde.

To his left, Artgan fought with fury, his sword swiping left and right, hacking anything that dared to draw near. Beside him, Rax loosed arrows as rapidly as possible and did not bother to pause and aim. There was no need. The mass of monsters was so thick, he could not miss if he tried.

To his right, Fesgar hacked and slashed with his sword, taking off the hand of one orc and slicing across the face of another. At one end of the boulder, Pazacar's staff spun like a whirlwind, striking any creature that dared draw near.

The remaining Head Thumpers stood behind Arangoli while fending off monsters that attempted to climb up from the rear of the rockpile.

Arangoli fell into the rhythm of the battle, his hammer felling foe after foe. Crushed skulls, cracked bones, and splattered blood became commonplace. He swung and swung, killing monster after monster as the dead stacked up around the rockpile. Among other things, dwarves were known for their constitution, and Arangoli prided himself as one of the greatest warriors among his people, but even dwarves tired eventually. After an earlier fierce battle, a flight from the city, scaling a cliffside, and another desperate flight, weariness began to settle in. His hammer grew heavier with each blow dealt, but the orcs would not stop coming. No matter how many he and his companions killed, more monsters emerged from the darkness and attacked. Hope slid through his fingers like a greased pig, impossible to grasp. This was the end.

GORTCH TURNED from the road and ran into a narrow canyon. One hundred fifty dwarven warriors ran with him, the faster ones passing him. A quarter mile away, a wall of blackness obscured anything within it.

"Beware!" Gortch shouted between breaths. "Wait! Monsters hide in that gloom."

The dwarves ahead of him slowed. "We want to fight."

"And you will, but if you blunder in, you might die before you even land the first blow. A mere scrape of their claws brings death." Fifty feet from the dark cloud, Gortch turned back and waved. "Everyone gather!"

The dwarves from Domus Ra ran in and clustered before Gortch.

"Shields in front. Form a wedge around me, half to either side. Pikes and archers stay behind the wedge and attack through gaps. The rest of you, man the flanks. Don't allow any monsters inside the wedge."

Moving quickly, the dwarves arranged themselves as commanded. At the head of the wedge with twenty-some shield bearers to either side of him, Gortch raised his mace and began to advance. They marched at a purposeful pace. Howls, shrieks, and the clang of weapons rang out as they entered the mist.

Darkness swirled around Gortch, whose eyes flicked from side to side, in search of enemies. He didn't have to search long.

The leathery skinned backs of orcs appeared just strides ahead. The monsters faced away from him, their attention on whatever lay ahead. The opportunity was too great to ignore.

Gortch raised a fist. "Charge!" He burst forward, leading his squad while winding back.

His mace smashed into the head of an orc, felling it instantly. The shield line crashed into the enemy force a beat later. Swords flashed, sliced, and slashed. Pikes thrust through gaps, piercing orc bodies. When the standing monsters turned toward the new attackers, Gortch called for the shield line to duck. The archers launched a volley, pelting monsters with arrows. He then burst forward with another swipe, taking two enemies in a single blow. The shield bearers plowed over another line of monsters and the coordinated fight turned to chaos.

Gortch waded through corpses, hacking and smashing with his mace as if he were death incarnate. To his left and right, dwarves fought while orcs howled, shrieked, and died.

His hammer feeling heavier than ever, Arangoli struck yet another monster in the head. It fell onto the pile of bodies, now approaching the height of the boulders. The hammer dropped to his side, his breath coming in ragged gasps. He doubted he would survive the next wave of attackers.

None came.

Rather than continue to attack Arangoli and his companions, the orcs turned and swarmed farther down the canyon floor.

Rax asked, "Where are they going?"

"I don't know."

The mist began to break up. As it thinned, daylight seeped in, allowing the view to expand.

No more than a hundred feet away, orcs fought against armored dwarves. It was a frantic battle, and despite the ferocity of the creatures from the underworld, the dwarves fended off every attack. Squeals and shrieks rang out as the monsters died. All the while, the darkness faded. The cries and the sounds of battle quieted as sunlight broke through the mist.

Standing over enemy corpses was the heaviest dwarf Arangoli had ever seen. Despite the new, bloody armor, his size, posture, and the weapon in his hand made his identity unmistakable.

"Gortch!" The name came out as a croak rather than a shout.

"Goli!" Bracketed by dozens of dwarven warriors, Gortch strode through the corpses and approached the rockpile. "I am glad I found you."

Stumbling over to stand beside Rax. Arangoli fell to one knee. "What took you so long?"

Gortch scowled. "I ran into some trouble with Bast. He won't be happy with me, but I resorted to recruiting on my own."

"Recruiting?"

"Yeah. Meet the newest Head Thumpers. I hope you don't mind a few more mouths to feed."

Well over a hundred dwarves looked up at Arangoli.

Falling to his backside, Arangoli began to laugh. Soon, other voices joined his own as their laughter echoed off the canyon walls.

Death had come for them, but they had, somehow, evaded its dark hand yet again.

CHAPTER 26
TEARS OF GOLD

L ight pierced the darkness. With that light came warmth that aroused Ian from the depths of his sleep. He blinked his eyes open to sunlight on his face. When he sat up, Lionel stirred, craned his neck, and stretched.

The eastern horizon split the sun and left half of it hidden from view. Jungle surrounded the giant turtle with a canopy of green that blotted out the land beneath the trees in all directions with two exceptions. The first was the two-hundred-foot-wide path of trampled foliage that trailed behind the turtle and stretched south for as far as the eye could see. The other exception lay to the north, where mountains thrust toward the sky like teeth of green and brown.

"Ah. You are awake." Vic stood and brushed himself off, leaves and dirt falling to the ground beside him.

It's not ground, Ian reminded himself. *We ride on a giant turtle.* Despite the reminder, his mind found it difficult to grasp, as if reality had been turned up on its ear. The scale of the turtle was hard to fathom. How such a glorious, behemoth creature could exist without everyone in the world being aware of it seemed incongruous. For it to be unknown beyond fireside stories shared among the Crumi seemed impossible, yet Ian had discovered that just about anything was possible when it came to magic. He knew very little about the archela, but he had no doubt that the creature was anything but natural.

A cluster of shrubs beyond Vic and Revita rustled, moved, and Ahni emerged. "A new day begins, and we find ourselves far beyond the Stagnum."

Ian peered north. "How long until we reach the mountains?"

"I do not know. I have never traveled this far." She leaned against her spear. "I swear, Ian, you are truly blessed by Urvadan himself."

The mention of the dark lord caused Ian to tense. Blessing or no, the idea of being involved with the infamous god rubbed him the wrong way. "Why would you say that?"

"Surviving the quelzarn attack was beyond fortunate, even if our skiff was destroyed. Such a setback should have cost us a day or more. Then, you discovered the archela, a creature of legend from tales that were old when my grandmother's grandmother's hair was gray and her body wilting. To awaken a creature that is as old as time itself is one thing. For you to convince it to take us to the land beyond the Stagnum and the surrounding jungles, well that is a story that will become legend to my people. Because of this, we travel far faster than expected. We should reach the mountains before the day is out, saving us two or three days of difficult travel." She shook her head. "I would not believe it if I were not a witness to it. As I said, Urvadan himself must have a hand in your quest."

Ian glanced toward his companions. Both Vic and Revita stared at Ahni, him with a worried look in his eyes, her with a smirk on her lips. "Where is Lint?"

"The little one?" Ahni peered into the trees. "He was off exploring most of the night. I suspect he is out there somewhere, provided he did not stray too far and fell off the archela." She gave a firm nod and hefted her spear. "I will go find him. It gives me something to do while we wait to reach our destination."

The Crumi warrior ducked back into the foliage and quickly faded from view.

A beat later, Revita muttered, "I don't trust her."

Vic snorted. "You don't trust anyone."

"True."

Ian frowned. "Isn't it exhausting?"

"What?" She arched a brow.

"Going through life not trusting anyone else."

"I trust Vic."

"Finally," Vic said.

"What does that mean?"

"You finally admit it."

She put a hand on her hip. "Maybe I didn't admit it before because you still hadn't earned it."

"After all we've been through. Why now?"

Chin thrust up, she simply said, "I am a woman."

"What is that supposed to mean?"

"It means that I don't have to explain myself."

"Why not?"

"Women are supposed to be mysterious. It makes men more eager."

"That is simply not true," Vic scoffed.

"Really?" She stepped close to him and gripped his jaw. "You have been awfully eager since the day we met."

His cheeks turned red, his eyes flicking to Ian, who quickly looked away. "That has nothing to do with you being mysterious."

In a throaty voice that oozed sensuality, she asked, "What is it, then?"

"I...um...you..."

Laughter burst from Revita as she shook her head and patted his cheek. "Oh, you are so fun."

Vic's face darkened. "I told you before…"

"I know. Don't make fun of you."

"Then, why do you do it?"

"In truth, you make it impossible for me not to." She leaned in and kissed him. When his grimace remained, she took his hand. "Come. I will make it up to you."

Vic arched a brow and followed as they ducked into the trees.

Suddenly, Ian was alone, or thought he was until he felt a thump on his shin. He looked down to find Lionel peering up at him expectantly. The drake's wishes would have been obvious even without their connection. So, Ian scooped Lionel up and held him to his chest while stroking his neck. The warmth of satisfaction came through their bond. Cradling the drake, Ian wandered over to the log and sat. His stomach rumbled, reminding him of his hunger. Their food had been lost during the ordeal with the quelzarn. They had also lost half of their waterskins, from which they were to sip and conserve until a source of fresh water could be found. With that thought in mind, he peered into the distance.

The sun, now an eighth of the way into the sky, shone down on the thick jungle. Leaves, branches, and vines were everywhere. Then, amid the shadows in a gap between the trees, he spied a river. The water would likely not be fresh and would lead to sickness if they tried to drink from it, at least that far downstream. However, the dark stripe winding through the jungle appeared to come from the mountains. He lifted Lionel and looked the drake in the eyes. *Go. Fly north. Follow the river to its source.* With the words, he sent images. The drake spread its wings, readying itself while Ian did the same. With an upward swing, Ian launched Lionel into the air. Wings flapping rapidly, Lionel rose above Ian, turned into the wind, and flew out over the jungle.

Ian sat back down, closed his eyes, and extended his awareness.

Through Lionel's eyes, Ian soared through the blue sky, free and alive. Although not his first time doing so, it was the first where he was not in a rush, allowing him to bask in the experience. Locked into his connection with the drake, Ian dipped, banked, and banked again, the air pushing against his wings, supporting him while driving him forward. He now knew what it was like to fly.

A broad river came into view. Trees covered in vines lined the riverbanks, their branches bending over it as if attempting to reach the far side. At Ian's command, Lionel turned and flew over the river, following it north. Time seemed to slip away as the two of them became one with the wind. The land below slipped past in a blur, the river snaking north until it met a lake. The drake dove down toward the body of water and leveled. Cool air rose from the lake, with trees, mountains, and clouds in the reflection of its still surface. The drake lifted its gaze and Ian realized that they had reached the jungle's end.

Trees with smaller leaves bordered the lake and covered the lower slopes of the mountains. Rock shelves and steep slopes rose up from the trees. A towering waterfall split those rocks and spilled down into a pool a thousand feet below. A stream flowed from the pool, connecting it to the lake's north shore. Ian gasped at the sight of the waterfall – not for its beauty, but for what it meant.

Something shook him, yanking him back to his body.

He opened his eyes to find Vic on one knee, his face level with Ian's, concern reflected in his eyes.

"Can you hear me now?" Vic asked.

"Of course I can hear you." Ian glanced up at Revita, who stood beside his brother. A frown had replaced her usual smirk. "When you left, I thought you two were going to be alone for a while."

"That was over two hours ago, Ian."

"Two hours?" Ian blinked. "Time passes so quickly..."

"We left you alone for a while, thinking you were doing some sort of magic...thingy."

"Thingy?" On cue, Revita's smirk returned.

Vic looked up at her. "You know what I mean."

"Well," Ian ran his hand through his hair, damp with sweat. The sun had grown hot and the humidity remained as thick as ever. "I was with Lionel." He pointed north, toward the twisting waterway cutting through the jungle. "A lake awaits at the far end of that river. A waterfall feeds the lake."

Ahni emerged from the trees. "A waterfall is good. We need fresh water, and we need it soon." In one hand, she gripped her spear. In the other was a small, writhing person.

Lint flailed. "Let me go!"

Ahni looked at the brownie in her hand. "After it took me so long to find you?"

"I was exploring."

"That is no place to explore."

"Where was he?" Revita asked.

Ahni squatted and set Lint down. "He climbed out from under the arshela's tail."

"What is under..." Ian stopped when he realized her inference.

The brownie scrambled away. "I wanted to see what it was like inside."

"Which is why you desperately need a bath." The Crumi sniffed her hand and pinched her face. "And I need to wash my hands. Yuck."

Revita burst out laughing. Vic and even Ian joined her.

Lint crossed his arms. "I don't see what is so funny."

Despite her laughter, Revita somehow found the words. "You crawled up a turtle's arse!"

The brownie thumbed his chest. "I am the world's greatest explorer. I will go anywhere."

"That much is clear."

Ian's laughter settled as he recalled what he needed to tell them. "In my vision, I saw something above the waterfall."

Ahni asked, "What did you see, Ian?"

"A giant stone in the shape of a skull looms above the falls. Water spills from its eyes, filling the pool connected to its mouth before flowing over the cliff edge."

Vic's eyes widened. "High it the world, where the jungle meets the mountains, stands a stone giant that sings tears. Follow those tears and we will find this city of gold."

CHAPTER 27
WHAT LIES HIDDEN

Beneath the afternoon sun, Revita stood upon the shell of an oversized turtle. Of course, oversized was an understatement, but thinking in those terms added to her amusement. The things she had seen and experienced since meeting Vic were beyond bizarre. She didn't know how their adventures would end, but as someone who had constantly sought trouble simply because it amused her, the exotic quests provided a new and unexpected source of entertainment. The giant turtle was merely the latest in a series of startling revelations.

The turtle swam across a lake at the foot of two mountains. Green leaf trees surrounded the lake while a wall of pale brown rock loomed miles to the east, reminding her of the escarpment that divided Havenfall from the Vale. What lay beyond that wall, she had no idea and considered it another discovery awaiting her and her companions should they end up heading in that direction.

The archela sped across the small lake, toward a stream inlet along its northeastern shore. A quarter mile from the lake loomed a towering waterfall that poured down a daunting, sheer cliffside. According to

Ian, their destination waited at the top of that cliff, over a thousand feet up.

She glanced over at Ian, who stared resolutely into the distance. While his steadily increasing mastery of magic was astounding, it came with a cost she was happy to avoid. It had become obvious that responsibility weighed on him, somehow aging him. He had been little more than a boy when they met, and now when she looked at him, there were times he seemed decades older. No. Preferring a carefree life, she did not envy his magical abilities.

Following Ian's gaze, Revita looked up and spied the small, dark silhouette of Lionel circling in the sky. "What is it like?" She asked.

Without turning toward her, Ian asked, "What do you mean?"

"The fire drake. What is it like to, um, talk to him?"

"He is always with me, regardless of the distance. It is sort of like a warmth in the back of my head. I can ignore it, but if I choose to, I can also reach out to him and see things through his eyes."

"That is how you knew about the waterfall?"

"Yes, and what awaits above it."

She looked up. "Please tell me we don't have to climb that. It looks even worse than the escarpment below Havenfall."

A smile touched his lips. "That climb was a challenge, but in this case, I think we can forego such an ordeal and save our energy for other things."

The turtle ceased swimming and drifted across the water, its momentum expending just shy of reaching shore. It lowered down until the waterline reached the shell.

A deep voice rumbled. "We have reached the northern edge of the jungle. The desolate land looms beyond this range, a land I cannot abide."

The turtle tilted slightly to the right and extended its foreleg until its claws dug into the grassy bank. "Climb down."

Eager to do something, anything, after a day with little activity,

Revita scrambled down the curve of the shell and jumped. Six feet down, she landed on a foreleg that was thrice the width of a road. Although wet, the cracked, leather-like hide provided solid footing. She easily strolled down the length of the leg, toward shore.

Bellowing a high-pitched whoop of excitement, Lint sped past Revita and disappeared into the long, green grass surrounding the turtle's giant claws. She reached a claw as thick as a log and tested her footing on it. The wet claw proved quite slippery, so she jumped down between two of them and climbed up the hillside, where she turned and waited.

Ahni reached her first, the Crumi warrior passing by with her spear in one hand, her dark eyes scanning the surrounding trees. Next came Vic, who flashed a smile and settled in beside her. Last came Ian, who stepped down onto land and then walked along the shoreline until he was below the turtle's head.

Ian looked up at the turtle as he spoke. "Thank you. We are grateful for your assistance."

"Be well, young human. May you find success in your quest. Creatures from the underworld do not belong here." The turtle slid back into the lake, its head and forelegs dipping below the surface. The huge shell floated out toward the heart of the water and sank down until little more than half the tree-covered shell was visible, appearing like nothing more than an island.

Revita shook her head. "I don't think anyone is going to believe this story."

Vic snorted. "Which of the recent events make a believable story?"

"Fair point."

Ian came back along the shore while staring into the sky. A shadow passed over him and then Lionel flew into view. The drake circled, fluttered above Ian, then settled down on his forearm.

With a glance toward the western sky, Ian said, "It looks like we have another two hours of daylight. Unless anyone objects, I'd like to see if we can find this lost city before it gets dark."

"You'll get no argument from me," Revita replied.

Jaw set, Ian extended his arm. A ribbon of light split the air and opened to reveal a flat shelf of rock split by a stream. A stiff wind came through the opening, and although the wind was warm, it was welcome compared to the stifling humidity of the previous two days. Following Vic, Revita stepped through the gateway and surveyed her surroundings.

The rock shelf was a few hundred feet across and just as deep. Scattered, crooked trees sprouted up from cracks in the rock. The drop behind them would be terrifying to anyone afraid of heights, which Revita was not. Opposite from the drop, a wall of rock rose up another sixty feet before melding with the mountain. Water spilled through two openings in the rock, tumbled down the face, and splashed into a small pool at the base. With a dark cavity splitting the pool's surface, the scene elicited the image of a giant stone skull weeping tears, its mouth gaping.

Revita turned toward Ian. "You saw this location through Lionel's eyes?"

"Yes. That's how I was able to transport us here."

"Yet, you waited until we reached this end of the lake."

"I figured it would be rude to leave the archela without thanking it and saying goodbye."

She rolled her eyes. "Now that we are here, what next?"

Ian shook his head. "I don't really know. I guess we need to find an entrance or something. Let's search the area."

They crossed the rock shelf and split up when they came to the pool. Ian, Ahni, and Lint took one side while Vic and Revita hopped across stones jutting above the stream, crossing it to the other side. As Revita neared the rock wall, she discovered that the cavity extended behind the falling water, leaving a narrow path beneath an overhang of rock.

Hoping that the entrance was hidden behind the falling water, she and Vic eased into the recess and stopped where the ground ended and the pool began. Ian and Ahni stood behind the other sheet of falling water while running their hands along the rock wall. Likewise, Revita and Vic searched the wall on their side, but found nothing of note.

Revita sighed and looked the wall up and down. "I don't see any entrance."

Ahni asked, "Are you certain this is where you are to go?"

Ian ran his hand through his hair. "This has to be the right place. It just has to be."

Vic frowned. "It does seem to match the description in the prophecy."

Lint, who stood at Revita's feet, said, "Don't tell me we came all this way for nothing."

She pinched her nose. "You still stink."

He shrugged. "Doesn't bother me." The comment earned him a bath.

Revita slid the toe of her boot behind the brownie, scooped him up with a kicking motion, and launched him into the pool.

Lint plunged into the swirling water and came up thrashing. "Help!"

She squatted, reached out, and scooped him up. "Maybe next time, you'll stay out of the arse of the next giant creature we come across."

As she set him down, she noticed something silver in the water. Ignoring Lint, who swore and threatened to do her harm, she removed her coat and dipped her bare left arm into the water. It was surprisingly cold. Her hand latched onto a metal ring. Tentatively, she tried to lift it, tilt it, and turn it, but it did not budge. Again, she pulled upward, straining, but it held fast.

She looked up over her shoulder. "Come and help me with this, Vic."

He knelt beside her and slid his arm into the water. His hand gripped the ring beside hers. "Ready when you are."

Revita braced herself. "Now."

Together, they pulled, her grunting at the effort while the muscles in his arm bulged. At first, the ring held fast, but then, it began to rise. A section of the pool bottom, little more than a foot in diameter, came up with the ring, tilting upward as it swiveled on a fulcrum point. Water rushed down into the newly revealed opening, and the pool's water level began to drop.

"Now what?" Vic asked.

"I guess we will see." Revita grabbed her coat and stood.

The water level continued to drop, and as the pool depth decreased, a pale, square shape became visible. When the surface had dropped two feet, the ground beneath Revita's feet began to rumble. The square shape in the middle rose up even as the water level sank. Another rumble came from above as the rock overhang tilted downward.

On one side of the water, Revita and Vic backed away while Ian, Ahni, and Lint did the same on the other side. The rock ledge continued to lower until it hit the bottom of the pool. The two struck with a solid thump and the rumbling ceased.

Stairs were hewn into the upper surface of the lowered shelf of rock, leading to a four-foot-wide opening centered between the two weeping eyes.

"We have found a way in." Revita pulled her coat back on, hopped from the pool's edge, and landed on the square stone platform in the middle.

The others jumped over to join her as she began up the stairs. Darkness loomed in the tunnel at the top. She dug into her coat, found her light disk, and held it in her palm. She stopped inside the tunnel and cast one last glance backward.

"Tread with care. This entrance may have been hidden, but that doesn't mean that it will be a friendly welcome. Do as I say, or you may end up dead." Without waiting for a response, she held the glowing disk before her and entered the darkness.

A dozen strides in, a rumble came from behind, causing the entire party to stop and spin around as Lionel flew in through the shrinking opening. The staircase rose back into place, pinching off daylight. Like a mouth sealing shut, the stairs locked into place with a thud, cutting them off from the outside world.

Ahni rushed back to the sealed entrance and placed her palm against the corridor's end. "We are trapped," she said with an edge of panic in her voice.

"It seems we cannot go backward," Vic said.

"Just as well," Ian turned back toward Revita. "Our path is ahead. Lead on."

With a nod, she turned and eased forward.

WITH REVITA LEADING and advancing with caution, they delved deeper and deeper into the underground warren, far beyond the reach of daylight. Cobwebs clung to every corner and covered every recess. From time to time, they came across a web that completely blocked the way. On those occasions, Revita stood aside while Vic, with his weapon held out before him, tore through the web and cleared it away. Twice, on such occasions, a spider the size of Revita's fist scurried off and ducked into a dark recess. As she passed those locations, Revita found herself as far across the tunnel as possible. She wouldn't say so aloud, but spiders made her skin crawl and the thought of having one that size even touch her was enough to make her gag.

The cobwebs were not the only things that gave the impression that centuries had passed since anyone had explored the tunnel. Dust and bits of debris covered the tunnel floor. The only footprints in the dust were those left behind by Revita and her companions. The tunnel also had a dank, musty smell that reminded her of a castle dungeon. She hoped that whatever lay ahead was more welcoming. No sooner had the thought passed through her head than she spied a faint glow down the tunnel. She advanced toward it until the tunnel walls fell away to reveal an open gallery. Roughly cut stone walls stood to the left and right while the high ceiling remained blanketed by shadow. A circular seal consisting of complex runes marked the floor in the middle of the chamber. From that seal emanated a pulsing golden aura.

An ornately carved façade graced the wall beyond the seal, where a pair of stone columns bracketed the grand entrance. Two smaller sets of pillars above the arched doorway supported ornate, stone gables. Closed wooden doors, reinforced with thick steel bands, stood at the top of a short run of stairs. There were no windows nor any other apparent way to pass other than through those doors.

The craftsmanship of the entrance was impressive and worth gazing on in wonder, but something about the chamber irritated Revita like an itch she could not scratch. She stopped and closed her eyes for a beat, listening. Then, she heard it. A faint hum rising and falling in time with the glow of the seal.

She opened her eyes as Lint walked past her. In a flash, she lunged low and snatched the brownie up.

"Argh!" Lint yelped.

Revita glared at him in her hand. "What do you think you are doing?"

He squirmed in her grip. "I was heading toward the door."

"And what would happen if you crossed the seal?"

"How do I know?"

"You didn't consider it might be dangerous?"

Ian noted, "The seal on the floor *is* glowing. It must be magic."

"Which could be deadly," Revita added.

The brownie fell still. "I suppose."

Revita spun around. "We need to go back into the tunnel."

Vic's brow furrowed. "What are you going to do?"

"I intend to do a simple test." She bent and set Lint down. "Go on with the others while I work." She waggled a finger at him. "Stay until I tell you otherwise."

Lint crossed his arms and huffed but did as she instructed, so she let it pass.

Turning back toward the seal, Revita bent and reached into her boot, from where she pulled out a throwing knife. She took aim, wound back, and launched the blade across the room. It spun as it made a flat arc. When it crossed the edge of the seal, the air around it flickered with light. Sparks burst from the blade, sizzling and popping. The knife dropped to the stairs, bounced and smacked into the door with a clatter. The blade was pitch black with smoke rising from it.

"Huh," Lint grunted. "That might've been painful."

Revita arched a brow while looking down at him. "I'd say you'd be one burnt brownie if I hadn't stopped you."

"Do you always have to be right?"

Vic snickered until Revita shot him a stern glare. Even then, he had to cover his mouth to remain quiet.

"Ian," Revita said. "Can you come up to the front?"

The others shuffled aside while Ian moved forward.

He stopped beside her. "Let me guess. You want me to craft a gateway."

"Yes. Place one here and the other side just before that door."

Ian extended his hand, and a portal opened before him as another appeared across the room, inches in front of the door. Sliding past him while digging into her coat, Revita pulled out her pick. She tentatively reached through the gateway while praying she had guessed right. Nothing happened, so she inserted the pick into the lock. The pick glowed, and the lock clicked. The door swung open with a low, resounding groan. Revita pocketed the pick and held her light disk before her as she pushed the door open wider. A creak echoed in the chamber, causing her to bite her lip. She hated making such noise, but the door hadn't been used in decades or longer, and the hinges appeared loathe to cooperate. When the door swung open enough, she stepped over the portal rim and eased through the gap.

The light in her hand gave shape to the immediate area. She stood in a chamber twenty feet across and just as deep, the walls to her left and right curving at the top and joining in a high arch. An open doorway loomed on the opposite wall. Beyond that doorway was a corridor with light at the far end.

She gestured for her companions to follow as she crept toward the corridor. When she neared it, she paused to examine the floor and the opening but found no evidence of possible traps. The light ahead called to her, but she fought the urge to rush forward and, instead, advanced with care. Rustling clothing, the tap of boots on the stone floor, and the whisper of breathing coming from behind informed her that the others were following and doing their best to do so quietly.

As they neared the far end of the corridor, the light grew brighter. Revita emerged from the tunnel and stopped. Her jaw dropped in awe as her companions gathered around her.

They stood near the edge of a massive crater five miles in diameter. Towering walls of dark rock and green plants rose high above the crater floor, encircling the area. The afternoon sun was hidden from view, casting the area in shadow. Foliage ranging from fruit trees to lush crops covered much of the ground, split by a meandering stream that flowed from a lake in the center of the crater and disappeared into a tunnel near where Revita and the others stood. Tall, narrow spires of tan and orange rock jutted up here and there, appearing like towers, the upper portions illuminated by the late afternoon sun. Peaks and rocky cliffs surrounded the valley, forming a gorgeous backdrop. All of this would have been worth the journey on its own, but it was not what captured Revita's attention.

In the heart of it all, along the shores of the tranquil lake, was a city made of white marble trimmed in gold. Tall pillars, arches, golden domes, and gold-tipped, white obelisks filled the space.

"Where are we?" Revita muttered.

A voice she did not recognize replied. "You are in the Valley of Gold."

She turned sharply to find a quartet of armed individuals standing on a rock shelf above the doorway she had just exited. Two of the strangers were male dwarves, another was a female Drow, and the last was a male Sylvan. The dwarves wore grim expressions while holding war hammers before their barrel chests. The Drow planted the butt of her naginata on the ground while her dark eyes glared at Revita.

The male elf nocked his bow, took aim at Revita and spoke again. "Lay down your weapons. You are under arrest."

CHAPTER 28

THE DARK LORD'S JOURNAL

T an gripped Ahni's spear as she tried to raise it. "No. Do not attack."

"They cannot be trusted," she hissed. "One is an elf, another a dark elf. Both are enemies of my people."

"I need you to comply. We came for answers, not to start a fight." He stared into her dark eyes. "Trust me. Should they attempt to harm us, I will handle it."

After a beat, she nodded and lowered her spear.

Relieved, Ian looked up at the dwarves and elves on the ledge above them. "We come here seeking information that might help us stop a great evil that stalks our lands. We mean you no harm."

The elf barked, "This is your last warning. Discard your weapons or suffer the consequences."

Ian sighed and turned to his companions. "Will you do it?"

Ahni shook her head. "I cannot. The Sacred Spear was entrusted to me."

Vic glanced at Revita, who did not appear pleased, and then turned to Ian. "Perhaps we can convince them to let us keep our weapons."

"That's what I thought." Ian moved a few strides away from the others and looked up at the elf archer. "You have our word that we will not attack unless you do so first. If that is not good enough for you, kill me now." Even as he said it, Ian crafted a shield.

The elf grimaced and loosed. The arrow struck Ian's shield and shattered in a spray of splinters.

"What?" The elf exclaimed. "How?"

Ian thrust his hand toward the elf. The shield flew across the gap, struck the elf, and drove him backward against the cliff wall, pinning him in place. Casting another spell, this time beneath his feet, Ian lifted himself into the air, five, ten, fifteen feet, until he was even with the elf and his companions.

In his deepest, most commanding voice, Ian announced, "My name is Barsequa Illian. I wield magic you cannot comprehend." He pointed at the strangers, causing them to flinch. "Should you attempt to attack me or my friends again, I will destroy you."

The two dwarves glanced at each other, lifted their war hammers, and slid them into harnesses strapped across their backs. The dark elf dipped her head in deference. That left only the leader.

The elf, still pinned against the cliff wall, nodded. "We will not attack. I swear it by Vandasal."

Ian released the shield holding the elf and lowered himself until his feet touched the ground.

WITH THE ELVEN archer and the dark elf in the lead and the pair of dwarves trailing, Ian and his companions followed a gravel road that ran parallel to the stream. The air remained warm but was notably less humid than what they had endured much of the day. Green, lush, and full of life – lizards on the riverbank, birds in the trees, fish visible in the water – it felt as if he had entered another world, far from the sweltering swampland to the south.

The party followed a well-worn trail along the stream. The clear water appeared aqua blue against the pale riverbed. A school of orange and black fish lazily swam past. Like everything else in the crater, Ian wondered how the fish came to live there, two thousand feet above the rest of the world. They passed an orchard where a dozen people in gold robes picked fruit from trees and dropped them into baskets. One by one, the people stopped when noticing Ian and his companions. Curious stares followed until the trees obstructed them from view. The party rounded a turn, and the foliage parted to reveal the city they had seen earlier.

Outside the city, a white, stone bridge supported by thick columns connected to an island surrounded by the lake's still waters. A ring of towering stone pillars stuck up from the lush, green island. North of the island, the shoreline trimmed until the lake butted against the cliff. Water ran down the steep rock to become a waterfall, dropping into the far end of the lake.

The leader of their escort, an elf named Draxan, led them past the bridge, under an archway, and into the city itself.

People moved about the city in pairs, two dwarves here, a duo of elves there, all dressed in the same golden robes, whether male or female. The people stopped and stared as Ian and his companions walked past. Such attention made him self-conscious. He smoothed his hair and straightened his robes without realizing it. He then puffed up his chest and raised his chin, hoping to convey a powerful image that demanded respect. Lionel, perched on his shoulder, mimicked his pose.

They came to a tiled square in the heart of the city and then turned from the lake. Across the square, an alabaster palace trimmed in gold backed against the cliff wall. The structure consisted of six tiers made of half circles, each level smaller than the one below, making the building appear like a massive, broad staircase. Windows dominated each floor above the main level, leaving Ian to believe it was intended to allow its occupants to enjoy the spectacular view.

They reached the foot of the building, climbed the stairs outside it, and walked through the open, double doors. A circular entrance hall stood inside the doorway, illuminated by the skylights in the ceiling, twenty feet up. A star pattern graced the center of the black and white marble floor while detailed tapestries lined the walls to either side. With their footsteps echoing off the chamber walls, they crossed the room and passed through an arched doorway.

The next room was ten times the size of the entrance hall with a sunken floor and a rounded dais at the far end. Row upon row of benches filled the shadowy chamber, marking it as some sort of assembly hall.

Their escort turned right and headed toward a curved staircase illuminated by glowing crystals mounted to the wall. The party ascended to a second level corridor and passed a trio of closed doors before entering a spacious chamber illuminated by a wall of windows that ran from floor to ceiling. Like the entryway below, the sky was visible through octagon shaped skylights in the high ceiling.

Plants filled much of the room, some rising from stone planters cut into the floor, others drooping from pots dangling from the ceiling. Winding paths ran throughout the space, all surrounding a bubbling fountain in the center.

A lilting voice came from across the room. "So, the day has finally come."

Amid the foliage near the fountain stood a male elf with his back to Ian and his companions. Dressed in white robes, the elf had a lean build and pointed ears sticking up from his long, white hair. When finished pouring water into a planter, the elf set a metal pitcher down on the lip of the fountain and turned to face Ian, who gasped.

The male elf's face was marred by wrinkles, something Ian had never heard of or seen from the Sylvan. Instantly, he knew this elf was quite old, and for a race that lived for hundreds of years, that was significant. However, his advanced age was not the most notable aspect of the elf's appearance. Shadowy, empty cavities occupied the spaces where his eyes would normally be.

"Thank you, Draxan," the elf said. "You may go."

"Is it safe, Master? These strangers..."

"I place my faith in my gift. You should do the same."

"Yes, Lord Dolon." Draxan, the Drow, and the two dwarves all headed back toward the staircase, leaving Ian and his party alone with the old, blind elf.

Dolon, with his hands clasped at his waist, crossed the room, navigating the winding path without effort. When he drew near, he stopped a few strides from Ian, who could not stop looking into the elf's vacant eye sockets.

"You find my appearance disconcerting," Dolon said. "This is understandable. However, I assure you that I am anything but blind."

"Who are you?"

"Were you not listening?"

"Your name is Dolon."

"It is."

"Are you the leader of this place?"

"I am."

Ian glanced at his companions. "We have come seeking..."

"Information. I am aware. However, that must wait. First, I ask you to follow me." The elf turned and glided across the room and out a door opposite from the one through which Ian and his party had entered.

Revita whispered, "Are we going to follow him?"

"Yes." Ian's brow furrowed. "Why wouldn't we?"

Lint said, "Because that elf is creepy."

"Creepy or not, we didn't come all this way to give up now." Ian set off across the room and entered another corridor.

A window on one side of the hallway offered light while a pair of closed doors loomed on the other. The door at the end of the corridor stood open, and when Ian reached it, he spied Dolon rounding a curved staircase. Ascending, he closed the gap and was only two strides behind the elf when he emerged from the stairwell. The elf then led them up another flight before a corridor took them to an open room at the center of the fourth level. Just like in the atrium on the floor below, a wall of windows along the front of the building allowed daylight to illuminate the room. Rather than being filled with plants, the forward portion of this room was occupied by two sofas positioned perpendicular to the windows. A padded chair and a small round table stood between the sofas. Beyond the sitting area were a desk, a chair, and bookshelves placed along the walls.

Their blind host rounded the furniture and sat in the padded chair, all the while moving without hesitancy or running into anything.

"Please." Dolon gestured toward the furniture surrounding him. "Sit."

Curious, Ian settled on a sofa, took Lionel down from his shoulder, and set him on his lap. He stroked the drake's neck while the others took seats around him. All except Lint.

The brownie marched right up to the round table, squatted, and jumped high in the air. He landed on the table, moved to stand near the edge of it, and began to wave his arms while staring at the elf.

"Are you testing me, little one?" Dolon asked.

"You can see me?" Lint asked.

"Not in any way you know. Now, please sit. I know why you have come. I am here to offer my assistance."

Ian asked, "Why have we come?"

"As foretold long ago, a darkness spreads, seeking to choke the life from our world. Also as foretold long ago, your destiny is to confront this evil, but you cannot do so until you understand its nature. I suspect you have other questions before we address that issue."

Revita blurted, "What is this place?"

"This is the Valley of Gold. This crater has been home to my people for many, many centuries."

"How did you come here?"

"We were guided here by prophecy and have lived here ever since."

"You speak of your vision although you lack eyes." Ian guessed, "You are a prophet."

"I am not just a prophet. I am the most gifted of prophets, my abilities approaching that of a god."

"A god?"

"I see what others cannot. Those visions include possible futures, some of which are so dark and twisted, they cannot be spoken of aloud."

"And you knew we were coming?"

"Your coming was foreseen millennia ago."

"By who?" Lint asked.

"By whom," Dolon corrected. "Your coming was recorded by Dolon the First Prophet."

"I thought you said your name is Dolon."

"So it is, little one. Every prophet is anointed as the leader of my people, each earning the name Dolon in respect of the first."

Ian frowned in thought. "The world is full of possibility. Our lives are our own, shaped by our own decisions. What if we are not who you think we are?"

"So quick to the point." The elderly elf turned his creepy, empty gaze on Ian. "You are creatures of action, aren't you?"

Not knowing how to reply, Ian and the others remained silent.

"My people have lived here in solitude for nearly three thousand years. Never once has any stranger stepped foot in the Valley of Gold... until today. During that span, we have watched, we have recorded, and we have waited for your coming. We knew the day was fast approaching, for millennia of foretold events have led to this moment, yet the future remains unshaped and where it will lead even I have yet to discover."

Ian's brow furrowed. "Are you saying that you cannot see the future any longer?"

"What you term as the future is merely a way to define events that have yet to occur. Some of those events have been visible to us for a very, very long time, but they lead to a small range of outcomes. What occurs beyond that small window of time, we do not know. We only pray that there *is* a future."

Lint snorted. "Of course, there is a future. If not, there would be..."

Dolon nodded. "Nothing."

The brownie's eyes widened. "Nothing?"

"Did you not listen to what I just said? Prophecy has been a means of perceiving events that have yet to occur for as long as my race has existed. It is a gift from the gods, and through that gift, we have been preparing. However, we fear that the world we know will soon cease to exist, for no vision extends beyond a few days from this moment in time. Even now, on the cusp of those tomorrows, I cannot see past them. Instead, I see...nothing."

The hair on Ian's arms stood on end and a chill racked his spine. He swallowed hard to try and wet his suddenly dry mouth and then cleared his throat. "Surely, there must be something we can do."

"Of course there is something you can do. In fact, we pray every day that you will do something. The right something."

"But how do we know what that is?"

"All I can do is arm you with information. The path you choose, regardless of which future it leads us toward, must be of your choosing."

Ian covered his eyes. "I did not ask for this responsibility."

"You may not have chosen to become an instrument of destiny, but destiny chose you."

It was the kind of thing Truhan would say. The thought turned Ian back to the reason for their visit. "What do you know about demons and the Underworld?"

"Ah. There it is." Dolon stood. "Come."

He rounded the chair and headed deeper into the room. Rather than stop at the desk, he continued past it and approached a bookshelf. Reaching up, he ran his fingers along the spines of thick volumes before selecting one. When he tipped it backward, a click resounded. The shelf swung out a few inches. Dolon moved to the edge of the shelf, grabbed ahold, and pulled it open. A dark tunnel lurked behind it.

The elf entered the tunnel and stopped at the edge of the light's reach. Over his shoulder, he said, "Fear not the darkness. There shall be light."

Ian shared a concerned glance with his brother before heading into the tunnel. He placed one hand against the rock wall. It was smooth and cool beneath his palm as he waded through darkness with his other arm extended before him. A creak echoed in the gloom. Warm light bloomed ahead beyond an open door. Thankful for the beacon, Ian walked faster while Lionel bobbed from side to side, feeding off his anxiety. Upon reaching the doorway, Ian stepped through and stopped to look around.

A circular chamber lurked beyond the doorway with only one way out. A table and chair occupied the middle of the room. On the table was a lantern shaped like an hourglass, the upper globe glowing with warm light. Dolon turned from the table and approached the lone bookshelf in the room. He ran his hand along the spines of the books before selecting one, which he carried back to the table. With care, he set the book down, pulled on a ribbon sticking out from the pages, and opened the book.

In as solemn tone, Dolon said, "This ledger was penned by the Dark Lord himself."

"The Dark Lord?" Shadows suddenly seemed to cling to the pages, as if a mere mention of its infamous author aroused some sinister spell.

"Sit. Read these pages. You will understand."

As bidden, Ian rounded the table and eased into the chair. He looked down at pages covered in flowing, elegant script written in Elvish.

"Is it safe?" He asked.

"Do not speak the words aloud and all will be well."

He looked up. "If I speak the words out loud?"

Dolon held up a finger in warning. "The Dark Lord is always listening. Recite words from his own hand, and you are likely to draw his attention."

The ominous statement caused Ian to swallow hard. The hair on his arms stood on end and the script on the page seemed to ripple, as if alive. He steeled himself and began reading, his mind interpreting the words without conscious thought.

As written long ago, *the great dwarf king rose to power. With the sky sword in hand, he was destined to rule the world. Should he achieve his perceived destiny, my worshipers, the few who remain, will be wiped from the world, and my existence will be considered myth until I am forgotten. This cannot be allowed.*

Since my brother smote me and rose to his exalted position, my influence has been limited, particularly over the races of magic. Thus, I was forced to seek another means to guide the hand of fate. My solution came from not our world, but one that resides beside it: The underworld. Vandasal's power is of the sun, but the underworld is a place of forever night. He holds no power there.

Thus, I created an underground structure with a single purpose. This place, a place of magic unlike any other, I named the Temple of Tenebri.

The temple itself is a construct of magic, designed to bridge our world with the underworld. Yet, in doing so, I risked the creatures who roam the darkness invading our realm, so I took steps to secure the temple, the doorway itself bound to a throne that would feed off the life energy of its captive. With the throne ready, I slid through this doorway and entered the realm of the damned. The horrors I found there are beyond description. The greatest among them were the demon lords – beings driven by insatiable hunger and fueled by the souls they consume. Even with my power reduced a fraction of what it once was, my presence alone attracted the monsters that wander the forsaken realm. They swarmed around me like rabid dogs, forcing me to use my abilities to fend them off. This action attracted a demon lord named H'Deesengar. It was then that I faced fear for the first time.

The demon lord's visage was the stuff of nightmares, with horns jutting out from its hairless head, a hooked nose, a distended chin, and teeth like razors. The monster stood nearly twice the height of a man, its muscular body covered in gray, leatherlike skin. When the creature reached for me, I froze. Its hand wrapped around my waist, its sharp talons digging in and causing searing pain. Had I not acted, it would have consumed me, and its power would have risen to unknown heights. It would have crossed over to the realm of the living, and nothing could have stopped it.

When this creature lifted me up, I extended my will back through the tear between worlds and pulled both he and I through. The underworld slid away as I returned to the temple. The demon lord lurched, released its grip, and I fell to the floor. It tried to take a step toward me, but the trap had been sprung. The wards surrounding the throne activated, and H'Deesengar staggered back, fell into the seat, and was held fast. The demon lord screamed and strained against its bonds, but the wards held fast. I had done the unthinkable: Captured a god from another realm and harnessed its power for my own. With this power, I would thwart the great dwarf king's efforts and drag out the campaign for decades. Eventually, driven by their own selfish desires, his own will betray him. The world will slide back to where it once was, and in their complacency, I will act. My return is assured. It is merely a matter of time, something I have in great measure.

· · ·

IAN TURNED the page to find a diagram akin to a spell on one side and that of a structure on the other. The notes on the two pages informed him that they were related to the Temple of Tenebri. He turned to the next page and found it blank. In fact, all subsequent pages were blank.

Dolon said, "As you can see, that entry was the last made in this journal."

Curious, Ian quickly flipped through the earlier pages. A handful of sketches were found amid page after page of graceful handwriting.

"What is the rest?"

"Mostly complaints against Vandasal along with random musings. Other than the last bit you read, there is little of actual import."

Ian glanced toward the other books. "Are those other books..."

"The Dark Lord's journals? Yes." Dolon closed and took the book from Ian. "But none of that matters now, not if the demon the Dark Lord imprisoned has escaped its prison."

Ian's eyes widened. "You believe the demon I saw is the one the Dark Lord captured?"

"How many demon lords do you expect to find within the living realm?"

Pressing his hand against his forehead, Ian considered what he had read. "Where did you get these journals anyway?"

"Brave members from my flock stole them."

Ian blinked. "From the Dark Lord?"

"We have been monitoring Murvaran for thousands of years, beginning long before its denizens disappeared."

"Disappeared?"

"The city lies long abandoned. Even the Dark Lord has not been seen there for centuries. To better understand what happened, we sent a party of warriors to investigate. Those who survived returned with these journals."

"Survived?"

"Yes. The Dark Lord's tower may be vacant, but that does not mean it is not dangerous. And then, there are the warrens beneath the city. Monsters born of evil and hatred roam those tunnels. As a result, they remain unexplored."

Recalling another line he read in the text, Ian said, "The journal said that demons devour souls."

"Demons gain strength by consuming the souls of their victims. The more powerful the soul, the greater it enhances the demon's ability. Souls burning with great magic, even more so."

Ian worried about his mother, his voice coming out as a whisper. "What happens to the soul if it is consumed?"

"The theory is that souls are energy. If that energy is expended, is the soul then lost? Or is it merely trapped within the demon? I cannot say."

On the verge of tears as Ian worried about his mother's soul, he croaked, "What do I do?"

"Ah." Dolon set the book back on the shelf. "You have brought us to the crux of the problem." He turned back toward Ian. "But you ask the wrong question."

"What is the right question."

"Where do you go next?"

Ian wiped his eyes and gave a firm nod. "Please. Tell me."

"I will show you." Dolon walked past Ian and paused while the others moved aside. He then headed back down the dark corridor.

When the others looked back at Ian, he gestured. "Go on. It looks like we are to follow him again."

Revita, Vic, and Lint faded down the corridor but Ahni did not move, instead she stared toward the dark tunnel with a grimace.

"What's wrong?" Ian asked.

Ahni grimaced. "I do not like him."

"Why not?"

"He is an enemy of my god, and therefore, my people."

Ian hadn't considered her perspective, and now that he understood, new worries arose. "Let us follow and listen to what he says. Urvadan or Vandasal, I take no sides. Frankly, I don't care about gods. I need to understand how we can stop this demon and its horde of monsters from destroying our world. Can we agree that is why we are here?"

She nodded. "Very well. Go on. I will take up the rear."

Ian walked past her and headed down the corridor, toward the pale light at its far end.

Troubles and concerns consumed his thoughts and sent his stomach into a frenzy. It felt as if the world was collapsing on him, narrowing his choices and driving him toward something terrible. Possessing unique abilities made him exceptional, something he had always desired. However, he had not anticipated the weight of responsibility that came with such power.

When he emerged from the tunnel, he found everyone gathered at the far end of the room. Their guide then turned and faded down one of the two corridors. The hallway brought them to a pair of staircases, one path ascending, one going down. To Ian's surprise, Dolon descended, leading them back down to the third level, where the elderly elf entered what appeared to be a kitchen. Similar to the other levels, daylight seeping through windows along the front illuminated the space. They headed deeper into the room, passed counters, a table, and a brick oven. At the rear of the chamber, they entered a short corridor that ended at a small chamber where water trickling down the rear wall fell into a marble bowl. The water then spilled from a spout at one side of the bowl and poured into a hole in the floor. A shelf with a dozen metal cups was mounted to the wall to one side of the bowl.

Dolon gestured toward the shelf. "I suspect you are thirsty. Drink. When you are finished, we will proceed."

Eager to quench his thirst, Ian reached for a cup and stopped shy of picking it up. A weird feeling came over him, suddenly making him reluctant. Wary, he asked, "Where does this water come from?"

"A spring feeds this valley, bringing life to what otherwise would be a dead zone. This fountain taps into that same spring, The water spilling from the bowl pours down into the fountain in the arboretum on the second level."

Ian stroked his jaw.

"What is it?" Vic asked.

"I don't know."

Lint walked up to the hole in the floor, reached out with both hands, and caught some of the spilling water in his hands. He scooped the water to his face and drank. "Ah! Refreshing." Again and again, he drank while the others watched.

Ian told himself, *You are allowing Ahni's prejudice against Dolon to affect your thinking.* Aloud, he said, "It's nothing." He reached for a cup and dipped it into the bowl. Lifting the cup to his lips, he drank. The water was cold and soothing to his parched throat.

Vic, Revita, and even Ahni grabbed cups and began to drink while Ian refilled his. He then held the cup to Lionel, who lapped at the water with eager abandon.

Dolon walked to the doorway, paused, and said, "If your thirst is quenched, please set the cups on the table by the door and then follow me." The elf walked off in silence.

Everyone in the party took one last drink, set their empty cups down, and headed back through the kitchen.

The blind elf stood in front of the window at the far end of the room, seemingly staring out over the valley. "The sun will soon set."

Judging by the fading light in the sky, Ian agreed. Still, he wondered how Dolon knew without having eyes. "Where we are going, will we need daylight?"

The elf turned from the window. "Do not worry. I will ensure you are properly cared for."

The comment caused Ian to frown. It seemed a bit odd, but Dolon seemed fond of oddness. As Ian drew closer to the window, the two tiers below became visible, as did the ground outside the building. Hundreds of people in robes stood before the palace entrance.

"What is going on down there?" Ian asked.

"They are waiting to welcome you. We have been expecting you for a very, very long time. Come. It is time for you to make your appearance." The elf walked off, heading back toward the stairs.

Ian cast one last glance outside before following. The idea that some ancient prophecy predicted his coming and that these people had been waiting for him only added to the increasing sense of pressure. Failure came with dire consequences when the fate of the world was in question. It only made it worse to think of the people he would be disappointing. *This was easier when nobody knew what I was trying to do.*

They descended to the ground floor and made straight for the open entrance. When he stepped outside, Ian found hundreds of elves, dwarves, and even humans waiting, all eyes on him. The crowd, all dressed in golden robes, had formed a half circle, leaving the area at the bottom of the stairs clear. With the valley covered in shadow and the clouds painted pink and purple against the deep blue sky, the scene was serene and almost otherworldly.

Dolon stopped at the top of the staircase. The crowd quieted and watched with a sense of expectation.

"Greetings, my children. As recorded over two thousand years ago, the day we have been so keenly anticipating has arrived. For the first time since the gods sentenced us to spend eternity in this valley, visitors have come."

Ian frowned. *Sentenced?*

Dolon turned to Ian. "You will be our salvation. For this, we thank you."

As Ian was about to respond, a strange sensation came through his bond with Lionel. He turned toward the drake perched on his shoulder and found its head lolling. Suddenly, Lionel fell forward. In reaction, Ian's arms formed a basket and caught the drake.

"Something is wrong with him."

Nodding, Dolon said, "Your pet's system is more delicate than your own." Suddenly, the elf turned his gaze across the valley. "The sun has set."

Ian followed Dolon's gaze. A wave of purple light flashed over the valley. The disorientation caused him to stagger. Before his eyes, the golden robes worn by the citizens of the valley darkened to gray. He looked at Dolon as the elf's robes turned from white to black. His face sank in and the flesh on his hands shriveled. Seconds later, Ian was staring at a skeleton with long, white hair. In fact, the entire crowd had turned to skulls and bones.

A chill racked Ian's body. He blinked and tried to concentrate to make sense of what he was seeing, but his thoughts came slowly, as if wading through mud that went to his knees. To clear his vision, he squeezed his eyes shut, but when he opened them, the horrific scene remained in place. "What is happening?"

Dolon laughed. It was a cackling, disconcerting sound. He raised his hood, casting his face in shadow. "Do you not recognize me?'

With the hood up and only skeletal hands visible sticking out from the black robes, recognition struck. He was facing a figure he had met once before, in a place between worlds, where prophetic visions take place. "Eidolon?"

"Very good," Dolon crooned. "When I encountered you in the shadow realm, I had hoped you might be the one. Now that you have come, I will soon be released from this prison. My followers and I will rise. The world will be ours."

The fog in Ian's brain thickened. His eyes grew heavy, regardless of how hard he fought against the sensation. Revita's eyes rolled up, and she collapsed.

"Vitha!" Vic slurred. He bent to help her and instead toppled over to fall beside her.

"Betrayal!" Ahni blurted and cocked her spear back. Rather than launching it, the motion caused her to stumble backward. She overcorrected, dropped to her knees, and fell face first. The spear bounced on the ground, tumbled down the stairs, and settled a dozen strides away.

Alarmed, Ian opened himself to his magic, but his thoughts were jumbled, his eyes heavy. He tried to craft a gateway, but the complex construct was beyond him. He fell to his knees, his free hand holding him up while he cradled Lionel in the other. His hand slid up as he collapsed on his side.

Looking up at the skeletal figure standing over him, he croaked, "Why?"

Eidolon laughed. "Because your soul is the key to breaking this curse."

Fear found its way through the murk in Ian's head. He was in trouble but could not find the strength or alertness required to do anything about it. Through eyes half open, he spied a tiny humanoid figure scurrying along the front of the building before fading into shadows. His eyes drifted closed, and he slipped into oblivion.

CHAPTER 29

RITUAL

"Vita!" A familiar voice called in the distance.

Drawn toward the voice, Revita fought her way toward consciousness. Her eyes flickered open to the pale light of the moon. She tried to sit up but straps across her torso, waist, arms and legs held her in place.

Vic sighed. "Thank the spirits, you are awake."

She turned her head and found him lying on a stone altar, the foot of it a few strides from where she lay. His altar was positioned perpendicular to hers. "What happened?"

"We were drugged."

"Drugged?" Through the haze in her head, she recalled the Valley of Sol, the strange blind elf, and standing outside beneath the darkening sky. *How were we drugged?* She sorted through her memory and recalled drinking water coming out of a wall in the back of the palace. Yet, how could water coming from a spring be drugged? She then realized the truth. "It wasn't the water. It was the cup."

"What?"

"The metal cups. They did something to the cups, so when we filled them with water, the drug mixed with the water."

She turned her head to the other side. Ian lay sleeping on an altar across from Vic's. Likewise, Ahni was strapped to an altar across from Revita's. In the center of the four altars stood a circular stone gazebo surrounded by four ornately carved stone pillars with arched openings between each. A domed top covered the raised floor of the gazebo. Mounted to the top of the dome was a hoop with moonlight reflecting on its metal edge. A ring of stone pillars surrounded the area. Beyond the pillars was the lake. The still water reflected the moon and the city on the opposite shore. Immersed in a gentle silence, the peaceful night was in direct opposition to her rising anxiety.

Straining, she tried to break free, but the straps held fast. She was able to reach her hip but discovered her dagger missing. Worse, the bracer had been removed from her forearm.

"I tried," Vic said. "The straps won't break."

"And we've been disarmed."

"That's why we need to wake Ian, but I don't want to make too much noise and draw any attention." Vic nodded toward her. "You are closer to him. You should try."

When Revita turned toward Ian, she spied motion on the bridge connecting the island to the city. Robed figures walking in a long line flowed over the long span. In their lead was Dolon, dressed in black.

Worried and spurred by urgency, she barked, "Ian!"

When he didn't move, she tried again. "Ian!"

He shifted, turned his head, and responded in a groggy tone. "I can't move. Why is it so dark?"

She then noticed a black strip of cloth wrapped around his head. "You've been blindfolded."

"Revita?'

"Yeah. It's me. Your brother and Ahni are here, too."

"Where are we?'

The members of the order had reached the island, their leader passing through the stone pillars while heading toward Revita and her companions. The others split up into two lines with one rounding the island in one direction, the other going the other way.

"We are in trouble, that's where." Revita said, "Can you use your magic?"

"Not when I can't see."

"I was afraid of that."

Dolon strolled in and paused between Ian's altar and Ahni's. "I see that you are awake. That is good. The ritual will work better when your spirit is full of life and fear."

"Ritual?" Revita had no idea what he was talking about. "What ritual?"

The robed elf gestured with his skeletal hand. "Why the ritual that will return me to life, of course."

"You look a bit underfed but still very much alive."

"I have been trapped here for three thousand years. Every day is the same. I eat, but food has no flavor. There is no joy. There is no pain. This existence is not living. It is torture. For that, the gods must pay. When I am free and the full might of my power has returned, I will claim the worship of the races from men to elves to dwarves. Their prayers will fuel my might and I will rise. Vandasal and Urvadan will fall, and I, alone will be the god of this world."

Revita snorted. "You are delusional."

"You know nothing, puny human!" Dolon snapped. "Your soul will soon be mine, and you will cease to exist." He turned away and raised his voice. "Gather around, my flock. Surround the ring of power and join hands. The heart of night is upon us. It is time for the ritual to begin."

As instructed, the skeletal people in gray robes encircled the ring of pillars and linked hands. Their leader approached the structure in the center of the island, climbed the stairs, and stepped onto the platform.

Reaching out, he wrapped his bony fingers around a metal ring sticking out from each pillar. A soft, haunting aria arose from the ring of robed skeletons. The platform, the pillars, and the arch above it all glowed with a purple aura. The metal hoop mounted to the top of the dome began to spin. Around and around, the hoop went, going faster and faster until it was a blurred globe. Tendrils of white mist and purple light emerged from the globe. The mist and light twisted and mixed together as they rose into the sky. A cloud, thick and angry, began to form and rapidly spread, appearing like a destructive mass eating away at the stars. The cloud billowed and roiled, blotting out the moon as it expanded. In moments, the cloud blanketed the sky, stretching from one rim to the other of the surrounding cliffs. With the moonlight gone, only the glow of the domed platform in the center illuminated the area...until dark purple light bloomed in Dolon's eyes.

Panic struck. Revita strained against her bonds, twisting and writhing, but they held fast. Her breath came in gasps and she was about to scream when a small voice came from nearby.

"Mistress. I am here to free you."

She turned her head to find Lint standing on her altar. Beyond the brownie, she spied Ian, still blindfolded. In a hushed voice, she told the brownie, "Go and remove Ian's blindfold. It is our only hope."

Lint looked over his shoulder, toward Ian. "Are you cert..."

"Yes!" she snapped. "Go. Now!"

The brownie nodded, turned, and jumped off the altar, disappearing from view. Two seconds later, his small shadow reappeared as he raced toward Ian. He jumped, caught ahold of the altar's upper edge and pulled himself up.

Lightning shot across the sky. Thunder boomed. The billowing clouds shifted and extended downward like a giant finger piercing the gloom. Death was coming for Revita, and it was terrifying.

Unable to see or move, Ian lay on a hard stone surface. The wind buffeted him and thunder boomed. Whatever was happening, it was bad. With his eyes covered and his body strapped down, his imagination raged. Despite his power, he was helpless. He was going to die. Worse, his death would unleash some great evil upon the world. He thought he had conquered his fears, but without his magic, he found himself recoiling and wanting to run and hide.

A small voice cut through the ruckus. "Ian."

In response, Ian turned his head slightly and strained to listen, uncertain if it were his imagination.

The voice spoke again, this time slightly louder. "Ian."

"Lint?"

"I am going to remove the cloth covering your eyes. Don't move."

"I won't."

Small hands pulled on his earlobe. A tiny foot slipped into his ear while he felt a tug on his hair. Pressure on his forehead followed as Lint crawled up. His little feet dug in as he tugged. The blindfold held fast at first, so the brownie pulled harder. Bit by bit, the blindfold climbed up Ian's forehead. The tight part slid over his brow and a cry rang out as Lint fell off his head.

Ian opened his eyes and blinked to clear his vision. He lifted his head and saw Eidolon with his hood back, his skeletal face tilted up, his jaw open in extasy. White and purple magic swirled around him while a massive, thick cone of darkness snaked down from the clouds above the crater. Ian had no idea what the blackness was, with certainty, he knew it was bad. Desperate to stop it, he opened himself to his magic.

Bending his wrist to raise his hand, Ian crafted a construct around it. He channeled the magic through the construct. A cone of flames shot out toward Eidolon, but the fire split and bounced off the glowing stone gazebo. He ceased the spell, and the fire evaporated to reveal the skeletal figure beneath the dome unharmed. Crafting a different spell,

Ian tried again. A small shield formed and shot toward Eidolon but dissolved just before reaching him.

The black funnel cloud split into four tentacles, each descending toward Ian and one of his companions. Whatever that was, Ian knew with certainty, he was finished if it reached him.

He then noticed the spinning hoop on top of the dome above Eidolon. His intuition screamed that it was a critical element of the sinister ritual. Desperate, he crafted another spell, bent his wrist upward, and released it. White hot lightning shot out and struck the spinning hoop. Rather than destroying it, as Ian expected, the electricity arced and shot up toward the cloud in dozens of forked bolts. Desperate and out of ideas, Ian pulled in more magic and fed the spell, launching lightning strike after lightning strike at the spinning hoop. Each bolt refracted up into the cloud, where sparks and flashes danced amid the roiling darkness, as if energized. With each strike, the spinning hoop slowed until it suddenly began to turn in the other direction. Still, Ian loosed lightning bolts at the hoop, the electricity fanning as it arced up into the cloud.

A descending tentacle of darkness stretched toward Ian. When it drew close, Ian sensed a frosty chill emanating from it, the cold air turning his gasping breaths into swirling mist. Just before it touched him, the tentacle recoiled, jerked, and yanked backward. The four fingers of black mist shot upward and combined back into one that rapidly withdrew back into the cloud, which churned as if it were about to explode. Lightning crashed in a flurry of white-hot flashes. Bolt after bolt, coming from dozens of locations across the cloud, all converged on the metal hoop.

Eidolon, still gripping the metal rings beneath the dome, shook with a terrible violence as sparks crackled and popped across his skeletal body. His robes burst into flames first, followed by his skull. The fire rapidly became a raging inferno too bright to look upon. Intense heat emanated from the platform, so hot that Ian feared he might be burned as well. Eyes closed, he clenched his fists and winced, but the straps held fast.

The heat dissipated as quickly as it had come on, the cacophony turning to still silence.

Ian opened his eyes and raised his head to find the pillars supporting the dome charred and blackened. A pile of smoking ash lay on the platform. Of Eidolon, nothing else remained. The clouds grew lighter in color and then began to evaporate. The moon appeared through the breaking clouds, its light bathing the valley as stars reemerged. Relieved, Ian lowered his head to the stone altar and released a deep sigh.

Lint walked into Ian's view and stopped near Ian's shoulder, standing on the altar while he peered toward the dusty remains on the platform. "Something tells me that we won't have to worry about that guy anymore."

Revita said, "Maybe not him, but we have other trouble."

Ian lifted his head as the robed people surrounding the island moved toward its center. They wound around the pillars and slowly advanced in the direction of the four altars. Elves, dark elves, dwarves, and humans all stared at the ashes on the platform as they converged. The people stopped shy of the altars, the look on their faces unreadable.

Draxan broke from the others, walked between Ian and Revita, and stopped short of the charred gazebo. He put one foot on the second stair, leaned forward, and drew a deep breath. With a powerful exhale, he blew on the ashes and sent them scattering across and off the platform.

The elf stood and turned toward Ian. "Do you know what you've done?"

Surrounded by hundreds of people and still tied down, Ian doubted he could fight them all off, nor could he protect his brother and the others. Rather than fight, he sought diplomacy. "I was only trying to save myself and my companions. I didn't mean..."

Draxan took three rapid steps toward Ian, to stand at the foot of the altar. "Whether you meant it or not, you've done something we did not think possible. You have freed us."

"I...what?"

"The curse that held us captive. It is gone. For the first time in thousands of years, we are fully alive."

"I don't understand," Ian admitted.

Gesturing toward the crowd, Draxan said, "Free them. This is no way to treat our saviors."

Surprised by the turn of events, a sense of relief washed over Ian as his bonds were cut away.

Once freed, Ian sat up and swung his legs over the edge of the altar. People patted him on the back while others gripped his hand and dropped to one knee while profusely thanking him. This went on for some time before the crowd began to disperse.

As the area cleared, Draxan approached and clapped a hand on Ian's shoulder. "Are you well?"

"In truth, I am tired." Ian recalled Lionel succumbing to the drugs before he blacked out. "Where is my fire drake?"

"The tiny dragon is safe. Come. I will bring you to him."

Ian stood and staggered when his knees gave out, but Vic was there to catch him.

"Are you alright?" His brother asked as he lifted Ian up by one arm.

Numbly, Ian nodded. "I am just tired. Well, exhausted actually." A long day, being drugged, and the extensive use of magic had left Ian shaky and weary.

"Let's bring you to Dolon's quarters, so you can rest," Draxan gripped Ian's arm, helping him toward the bridge. "I will return in the morning and will answer any questions you may have."

While many questions demanded to be asked, Ian was exhausted, mentally and physically. Sleep was a welcome idea and far more important than satisfying his curiosity.

CHAPTER 30

THE CURSED

V ic crossed the bathing room on the palace's fourth floor. With a hand on the doorknob, he stopped at the door and looked back.

Morning sunlight streamed through a high window. A puddle of spilled water surrounded the copper tub in the middle of the room. A dry towel lay over the back of a wooden chair in the corner of the room while another towel was tied around his waist, leaving his bare torso exposed. Vic saw none of this. His attention was on the person in the tub.

With her hands covered in foam as she scrubbed her raven hair, Revita arched a brow back at him. "Why are you staring at me like that?"

He smirked. "I am enjoying the view."

She lowered her hands and gave him a flat lipped look. "You already had your turn."

"Maybe I could use another?"

"I told you before, sometimes a girl needs a moment to herself. Let me enjoy the rest of my bath in peace. Besides, I need to wash the collected odor of the last few days off. I think I sweated a third of my body weight off in that humidity." She pointed toward the door. "Go on. Just save me some breakfast."

With feigned reluctance, Vic opened the door and pulled it closed behind him before heading to the first room on the right. The bed he had shared with Revita the previous night was a mess. Their clothing lay strewn across the floor, adding to the chaotic scene. The clothing could use a washing, but that was one luxury they did not have.

He found his small clothes, dropped the towel, and pulled them on. His breeches, boots, and jerkin followed. He felt a bit naked without his mattock, but Draxan had promised they would be returned, so he hadn't pressed the issue the prior evening.

Vic exited his room and headed down the corridor, slowing to peer into the other bedrooms as he walked past. The bed in Ian's room was unmade and still occupied by the small red and black form of Lionel, who lay curled up amid a nest of blankets. There was no sign of Ian. The next room, used by Ahni the night before, was empty as well. A delicious aroma beckoned him forward, and as he neared the end of the corridor, he was greeted by Ian's voice.

"...and the pastries are delicious, Coralai."

An unfamiliar female voice replied, "Thank you, Ian."

Vic walked into the kitchen to find Ian and Ahni seated at a table, brightly illuminated by morning sunlight coming through the wall of windows beside it. Deeper into the room was a female dwarf wearing an apron. She busily stirred something in a bowl while a half dozen disk-shaped cake patties occupied the baking sheet beside her.

"Good morning, Vic," Ian said. "I was wondering when you would show up."

Vic approached the table and sat across from his brother. "I would have joined you earlier, but Revita demanded a bath and offered for me to join her. Saying no to such an invitation is beyond me." He grinned.

Ian chuckled. "I can imagine." He cut though the food on his plate before scooping a fork full of cake and apple compote into his mouth. "Mmm," he moaned as he chewed and swallowed. "You need to try some of Coralai's apple crisp, Vic. It is delicious. I'm on my second helping."

Ahni nodded. "It is quite good." An empty plate sat on the table before her.

The female dwarf approached the table with a plate in one hand and a bowl in the other. "Greetings young man." She slid the plate in front of Vic. A disk-shaped pastry covered in a cinnamon crumble sat in the center of the plate. "Would you like one or two scoops of apple slices?"

Vic shrugged. "Two, I guess."

The dwarf woman dumped two scoops of apple on top of the pastry. Steam rose from the apples, and with it, a delectable scent that caused Vic's mouth to water. Eagerly, he picked up his fork, cut a piece off, and scooped it into his mouth. The apple was a bit tart, nicely complementing the sweet, crisp layer on top of the pastry, which was warm and moist.

He continued eating without pausing until the plate was clean. Coralai appeared at his side and slid another pastry onto his plate before scooping on more apple slices. As Vic was cutting into the second piece, Revita's voice came from down the corridor.

"Get back here with that!"

The patter of rapid footsteps echoed in the corridor. Lionel burst out, his wings partially extended for balance as he ran. Around his neck was a black corset with one of the cups covering the top of his head. He scurried under the table as Revita came running in. She held the towel over her chest, the rest of it wrapped around her with the bottom of it barely covering her thighs.

"Give me that, you winged rat!" Revita squatted beside Vic and reached under the table.

The drake darted out the other side and raced deeper into the kitchen. Giving chase, Revita went after him. Lionel rounded the counter and rushed toward Coralai.

"Eeek!" The dwarf woman cried as she stumbled backward to avoid the drake. She tripped and fell, launching the bowl in her hand.

The bowl sailed across the room as Ian rose to his feet and struck him straight in the chest. Instinctively, he grabbed it with one arm and staggered backward, falling back onto his chair. The chair toppled over, taking Ian with it. The bowl in his arms flipped, dumping its contents directly onto his face.

Revita jumped over the fallen dwarf woman and lunged to catch Lionel by the tail. The drake squawked and flapped its wings, but she held on fast. She pulled Lionel toward her, released her grip, and snatched the corset off the drake's head.

Lionel scurried away, turned toward her, and puffed his wings out while blasting a sharp hiss.

She climbed to her feet and waggled a finger at Lionel. "Next time you steal my stuff, I am going to feed you to a troll."

Revita stomped past Lionel and out of the room.

Boisterous laughter echoed in the kitchen. Vic turned to find Ahni holding her stomach and tears in her eyes as she chortled heartily. He started to laugh as well, partly because of the comical image of Lionel wearing the corset, partly because of Revita giving chase, and lastly because of Ian, who sat up with apple slices and sauce stuck in his hair and on his face.

Ian frowned at Lionel. "Look what you did."

The drake lowered his head in shame.

"Let's go." Ian stood and walked to the corridor. "I need to clean up, and you need to think about the mess you caused."

Lionel, his head still drooping, waddled into the corridor with Ian following.

Ahni, still laughing, stood and bent to pick up the fallen bowl. She approached the dwarf woman, who was dusting herself off while chuckling and shaking her head. "Thank you for the meal. It was better than I anticipated." She handed Coralai her bowl and walked off.

Vic stood and collected the empty plates. "Is there any left for Revita?"

Coralai frowned. "I have more cakes, but I'll have to cut up and cook more apples."

"Don't worry about it. Two cakes will be fine. In fact, I will bring them to her." Vic set the empty plates on the counter.

"Very well." Coralai put two cakes on a plate and held it to Vic. "I will go tell Draxan you are finished with breakfast. I suspect he will be here for you soon."

Vic headed down the corridor and chuckled again as images of the morning's events replayed in his head.

FOLLOWING CORALAI, Vic descended to the building's ground floor. There, he found Draxan and two male dwarves. The elf held Vic's mattock. One of the dwarves held Revita's knives in one hand and her bracer in the other. The final dwarf gripped Ahni's spear with the butt of the spear resting on the floor.

Draxan held the mattock out. "Your weapons, as promised."

"Thank you," Vic accepted his mattock and slid the strap over his head and shoulder. As he fit it onto his back, Revita and Ahni retrieved their own weapons.

"I trust you slept well," Draxan said.

"Well enough, and breakfast was delicious."

Draxan smiled. "As was mine. In fact, it has been a very, very long time since I enjoyed a meal."

Revita slid a throwing knife into her boot and stood. "Were your past meals so bad, then?"

"You do not understand. We were akin to walking dead. Each day the same, lacking joy or purpose. We ate for nourishment, but every-thing was beyond bland. Our senses of smell, taste, and touch were numbed by our condition. At night, our flesh would shrivel up and leave bodies as little more than bones. For many centuries, I prayed for it to end, but the master would not allow it."

"Eidolon?" Ian asked.

"Yes, although in your presence, he commanded us to call him Master Dolon."

Vic scratched his head. "I don't understand. How could you live for so long? Why did you turn to skeletons at night?"

"Come. Walk with me. I will explain." Draxan headed outside.

They descended the stairs and headed toward the lake, Vic and Revita to one side of Draxan, and Ian, with Lionel on his shoulder, to the other. Ahni and Lint trailed closely behind while the dwarves stood on the front stoop, watching them depart. When they reached the road that ran along the lake, Draxan turned and headed north with Vic and his companions in stride.

The elf began his story. "Many, many years ago, I was a simple warrior in a Sylvan tribe called the Arboranis. Eidolon was two hundred years my senior. He was both the spiritual leader of the tribe, and the tribe's scryer. In fact, his ability to foretell the future led to our tribe becoming the most powerful in the realm. Blessed with the gift of prophecy and able to predict events with startling accuracy and detail, my people won every battle with ease. You see, with his guidance, we knew the enemy's position and battle strategy. Hidden wealth was easily discovered. The weather was always on our side. In less than a decade under his guidance, we rose to become the most powerful people in the world. But Eidolon was unsatisfied, for his unique ability left him believing that he could rise to godhood. Thus, he gathered his most devout followers and set out to create a kingdom led by the mightiest prophet in history.

"We traveled from nation to nation. At each stop, Eidolon would speak before crowds, delivering his message and issuing predictions of the near future. With regularity, those foretellings came to pass and more believers would join his flock. After three years of travel, he had gathered more than ten thousand dedicated followers, be it elves, dark elves, dwarves, or humans. We did not simply follow him. We worshipped him, treating him as a god walking among us. Still, Eidolon's ambition remained unsated.

"At his bidding and guided by his ability to peer into the future, we attacked the human city of Galfhadden." Draxan shook his head. "It was a brutal slaughter. With their warriors dead, we captured the remaining humans and forced them to worship Eidolon. Our leader saw himself as something more than mortal and his worshipers exceeded twenty thousand, but he was no god. This soon became apparent, as did the penalty for seeking to rise above all others.

"Until the capture of Galfhadden, Eidolon's ascendence had gone unnoticed by the gods. Doing so angered the human god, Urvadan. However, Eidolon and many of his followers were children of Vandasal, so Urvadan approached his brother with his grievance. Together, they forged a plot to deal with Eidolon and to teach a harsh lesson to prevent others from seeking to rise beyond other mortals. It turns out that the power to know the future can be a bad thing...if others can manipulate what you see.

"The gods planted an image of Eidolon ruling over a beautiful city made of gold and overlooking a mountain lake. From there, his rule would be absolute and would last for eternity with his people treating him as a god. In the vision, Eidolon and his people climbed a mountain-side to a hidden entrance that led to the city.

"So, we marched south from Galfhadden, across the moors, but as we tracked through mud and swamps, the going was slow. The summer heat combined with the lack of fresh food and clean water cost us dearly. Thousands of people died before we reached the mountains south of the moors. Those mountains were the gateway to the Inculti desert, an even harsher land. I begged the master to turn west rather than cross that desolate land, but he insisted. His destiny waited across that desert, so we continued. It was terrible. Each day, we lost hundreds of people, some succumbing to the heat or dehydration, others fleeing in the night. We finally came to another mountain range and eventually to the mountain we stand upon now. A week of searching, using clues found in Eidolon's visions, eventually led us to a hidden tunnel and a secret door. That door took us to the most beautiful valley we had ever seen." He gestured toward the lake and the falls at the north end. "The city, the orchards, and more were waiting for us to claim them, for all were uninhabited. We had no idea it was a trap. The prophecy that had led us here had been constrained to hide the entire truth.

"When the four hundred and sixty-eight followers who remained with Eidolon entered the valley, a pair of bright lights descended upon the city. From them came a pair of men dressed in regal attire, their skin glowing with power. But they were not men. We discovered we were looking upon the gods themselves.

"Together, Vandasal and Urvadan chastised Eidolon for his ambitions. They then approached him and each placed a hand on the master's shoulders. A darkness twisted around Eidolon as they laid a curse upon him, a curse that extended to his steadfast and remaining followers. They said that if he wished to live forever, like a god, they would grant him that wish. One might perceive their action as a gift, but it came at a terrible cost. Rather than living a life in eternal glory, it turned out to be a curse of endless suffering. A seal was placed outside the entrance to the valley. One that Eidolon would never be able to cross. The curse also turned him into a living corpse, unable to feel or experience any of the joys of life.

"The curse extended to his followers in many ways, but more than anything else, it tied us to him as if he were our god and we could not exist without him. His command and control over us was absolute, and just like his, our lives were empty and lacking joy. We could not reproduce, but we also could not die. If commanded by Eidolon, we could leave the valley, but our absence never lasted long, for there was a powerful internal need to return so we could again receive his blessing.

"Thus, it has been for thousands of years, until last night. You see, by destroying Eidolon, you broke the curse. We are free. Finally. For that, we thank you."

Vic glanced at his companions, gauging their reaction. While Draxan's tale was outlandish, it was difficult to deny the events of the previous evening.

Ian's brow furrowed. "You have lived in this valley for thousands of years?"

"Aye."

"And you never left?"

"While most citizens have not, I was able to go on a quest many years ago."

"A quest?"

"I believe the master showed you the journals."

"Do you mean Urvadan's journals?"

"I do."

Ian shrugged. "He had me look at one of them. That was not long before he drugged us."

"Yes. His intention was to earn your trust, and when your guard was down, ensure you drink from the tainted cups."

Vic scowled as his anger about the betrayal returned. "He paid for his treachery."

"Aye," Draxan said gravely. "I believe he paid a steeper price than you expect."

"Why do you say that?"

"In his quest for power and seeking a means to overcome the curse, Eidolon delved into forbidden magic he learned by studying the Dark Lord's journals."

Ian glanced at Draxan. "How do you know so much about the journals?"

"I was the one who led the quest to retrieve them."

Eyes widening, Ian asked "You visited Murvaran?"

"I did."

"The demon. Did you see it?"

Draxan shook his head. "I did not descend below the city during my visit. Doing so would have been misaligned with the orders given by the master and disobeying him was beyond me."

Vic looked at Ian. As brothers, he had known Ian since he was a babe and found it easy to guess what he was thinking. "You intend to visit Murvaran?"

Ian nodded. "I do." He then turned to the elf. "So, you know where Murvaran is located?"

"Not only do I know, but I can also show you."

"You can. How?"

Draxan pointed toward a staircase zigzagging up the wall of the crater. "We merely need to climb to the top."

Vic peered up. The crater's rim was easily a thousand feet above them. "That's a lot of stairs."

"Aye."

Jaw set, Ian gave a firm nod. "Lead the way."

Draxan clapped Ian on the back and headed down the path leading to the staircase.

CHAPTER 31
AN EXPANSIVE VIEW

T he ascent up the hillside consisted of thousands of stairs and consumed a significant portion of the morning. As he climbed, Ian considered the tale Draxan had told them about his master and how they came to live in the remote yet gorgeous valley. He tried to imagine what it would be like to live for thousands of years without joy, love, taste, adventure, discovery, or any other rewards that motivate people to work toward something they believe in. Worse, Draxan and the other citizens were under Eidolon's control for the entire duration. It was slavery of another sort – slavery that had lasted for a hundred lifetimes. Although Ian was merely trying to save his own life, his actions had destroyed Eidolon and ended the curse. He didn't know if he should feel proud to have done something so monumental for Draxan and his people or if he should feel ashamed that his motives had been so self-serving.

He reached a landing, paused, and looked down while gasping for air. The sun shone down on the Valley of Gold. Rushing water tumbled down the cliff wall across the crater from where he stood. The falls poured into the deep blue waters of the lake. With the green island and ring of gray stone pillars in the center, it made for a majestic view even when discounting the city of gold. Add that in, and Ian could think of no place he had ever visited that was more impactful. Only Havenfall approached its grandeur. *I can see how Eidolon was tricked into coming here. Had I seen this in a vision, I'd have wanted to visit as well.* He turned back to the staircase above him, where his companions were already turning the next switchback alongside Draxan. Not wishing to be left behind, Ian took a deep breath and resumed his climb. Thankfully, he carried no extra weight. He had lost his pack days earlier. As for Lionel, the drake glided high above the crater, turning in broad, lazy circles.

When Ian reached the next turn, he looked up and realized he was only two switchbacks from reaching the top. With his destination in sight, he increased his pace in an effort to catch up to the others. He focused on each stair, pumping his arms while panting in time with his rapid strides. Again, he found himself thankful for his training. Half a year of regularly scaling a mountain, among his other physical training, had improved his strength and endurance and enabled him to function much better than he would have otherwise. Two hours after he had begun his ascent, Ian crested the final stair and climbed up onto a rocky plateau.

Draxan stood a few strides away while Vic, Revita, and Ahni faced him. Ian approached even as Revita squatted and set Lint on the ground.

"Don't cause any trouble, Pipsqueak." Revita pointed a finger of warning at the brownie as she stood upright.

Lint crossed his arms. "I do not ask for trouble. Trouble seeks me out is all."

She frowned. "Is this what it would be like to have a child?"

Vic grinned. "If your child is like the mother, then yes, it is." He then dodged when she tried to punch his arm.

"Careful, Vic," she warned. "You never know what I might do to you while you are sleeping."

His smile melted. "What would you do?"

"Let's just say that you would not like it." Her smirk said as much as anything.

Vic glanced at Ian. "How am I supposed to sleep with that kind of threat hanging over me?"

"Don't ask me. You are the one who fell in love with a thief."

Revita's brow furrowed. "Love?" She looked at Vic. "You love me?"

A wild look appeared on his face, his eyes shifting as if he were searching for a place to hide. "I...um...well..." He ran his hand through his hair. "Yeah. I thought you knew."

"Are you certain?"

"Of course I am certain. Why do you think I have been with you for the past year?"

She smirked. "I thought you enjoyed..."

Before she could finish the sentence, Vic clamped his hand over her mouth. "Yes. I've enjoyed our time together. Let's keep it at that."

She gripped his wrist and removed his hand from her face. "If you wish to keep this hand, I suggest you do not do that again."

Abashed, he stepped back. "Sorry. I was afraid of what you might say."

"You can't control what I say."

Vic winced. "This conversation has taken a bad turn." He looked at Draxan. "I assume we climbed up here for more than the exercise."

"Yes," The elf nodded. "Come. I will show you."

When Draxan turned and headed along a dirt trail, Lint hurried after him.

Easing beside Revita, Vic said, "We can talk more about this later."

She gave him a naughty smile. "You sure you only want to talk?"

He laughed and the two of them headed down the trail while Ian turned his attention to the winged creature in the sky above them.

Ahni shook her head. "I find your people confusing. You say things you don't mean and hide things you wish to say."

"You have no idea." As Lionel floated in, Ian held his forearm up and waited for the drake to land on it. He then lifted Lionel to his shoulder and headed down the trail. "Come. Let's see if this climb was worth the effort."

A warm wind blew Ian's hair as he crossed the uneven surface. The trail turned from dirt to rock and back to dirt repeatedly as they ascended a slight incline. They crested the rise and the view extended to reveal a squat tower made of chunks of stone bonded together by mortar. Beyond the tower, the mountainside fell away to expose an expansive vista.

They followed the trail right up to the tower's door, which Draxan opened before ducking inside. Lint darted after the elf while the others followed. The tower's interior was dark, the only light coming through the open door. Ian paused a beat and waited for his eyes to adjust.

The shadows eased back to reveal a wooden floor, a staircase, and a table with two chairs. They climbed to the second level where another windowless room contained a pair of unoccupied bunk beds. Draxan, at the top of another flight of stairs, opened a trapdoor in the ceiling. A sunbeam streamed in as the elf climbed out, trailed immediately by an excited brownie.

Ian ascended the last flight and emerged onto the tower's rooftop, where a waist-high wall surrounded an area twenty feet across. The only other object on the roof was one of instant curiosity.

A massive tube, only inches in diameter at one end and two feet in diameter at the other, stood facing northeast. Wooden poles banded together formed a frame supporting the tube and held it firmly in place.

Draxan walked up to the wall beside the tube and pointed. "See that?"

Ian took position beside the elf and scanned from horizon to horizon. Empty, desolate land extended to the east of the mountain he stood upon while a towering escarpment lurked to the south. The land below the escarpment was green and filled with life while the area above it was nothing but empty desert. To the distant north was another mountain range with open desert covering the span in between. To the northeast, where Draxan pointed, a city built upon a plateau overlooked the barren desert floor. A dark spire thrust up from the heart of the city.

"What is it?" Ian asked.

"That is Murvaran, home of the Dark Lord."

The statement sent a chill down Ian's spine.

"How far is that?"

"It is a harsh two-day walk."

The thought of climbing down the mountain and crossing the dry, dangerous desert was less than appetizing. *I need to know if the demon is there.*

"Would you like a better view?" Draxan asked.

"Yes, but how?"

"Come." The elf moved to the narrow end of the tube, squatted, and peered into it. "Look through this device."

When Draxan moved out of the way, Ian took his place. As the elf had done, he closed one eye and used the other to peer through the small glass opening at the end of the tube. When doing so, the city appeared as if it were less than a mile away.

Murvaran lacked an outer wall. Its buildings were made of dark stone and were arranged in an odd and quite specific pattern. The outer edge of the city was circular in design while straight streets ran from the outer edge to the center like spokes in a giant wheel. Everything was built around a dark tower rising from the city's core. It then struck Ian that Murvaran had been crafted to resemble a giant construct, turning it into a magical spell of sorts. Toward what ends, he had no idea. While the city's layout was a certain oddity, more striking was the lack of life.

Ian pulled his gaze from the tube and turned to Draxan. "Does anyone live there?"

"It was abandoned when I visited, and that was hundreds of years ago. Nothing lives there. Nothing can survive. You see, that city used to be part of a lush oasis, but something occurred two thousand years ago to turn the land surrounding it into a desolate desert. The humans who lived there fled or died or…" he shrugged. "Just disappeared."

Vic approached the tube and peered through for a look. "What about the Temple of Tenebri?"

Draxan shrugged. "I know nothing of a temple. I only visited Urvadan's tower. That is where we found his journals, which we carried back to Master Eidolon, as we were bidden."

Lint piped up. "I want to look."

Revita sighed and squatted with her palm open. "Jump on." When he did, she lifted the brownie to the glass opening in the tube while Vic moved aside.

"Ooo," Lint said. "It's sort of like Ian's portals, but instead of taking you someplace far away, it allows you to see someplace far away."

Ian ignored the chatter, his mind turning the situation over and arriving at a decision. "We are going to Murvaran. Today."

"Today?" Draxan shook his head. "You have no water. No supplies. You will have to return to the Valley of Gold before you go. Even then, it is a two-day journey to reach the city. A very difficult two days."

Ian looked around the tower rooftop, memorizing the details. Returning here would be easy. He then drew in magic, extended his hand, and cast a gateway.

Draxan jerked back. "By the gods. What is that?'

Through the opening was a dirt path leading up to Eidolon's tiered palace. "This is the best way to travel." Ian stepped through. "Come on. We need provisions before we visit the home of the Dark Lord."

CHAPTER 32

MURVARAN

A trio of female dwarves scurried around the kitchen while Ian, Vic, Revita, Ahni, and Lint looked on. Among the dwarves was Coralai, who removed freshly baked hard rolls from the oven while the others stuffed fruit and nuts into a pair of packs. Coralai approached Ian and his companions with a basket of rolls.

The kind dwarf woman held the basket out. "Take one. Eat. The rest will go into the packs."

As bidden, they each grabbed a roll. It was warm to the touch and steam drifted up from the soft innards when Ian broke it open. The scent was too alluring to deny, so he tore off a smaller piece and popped it into his mouth.

From the room at the back, Draxan emerged with five waterskins draped over one arm. "They are all filled, and before you ask, they contain only fresh water. You needn't fear being drugged again so long as you avoid the metal cups."

Ian swallowed and accepted a waterskin. "Thank you." His brow furrowed. "Why five? Lint doesn't need a waterskin."

"The pipsqueak? The skin is bigger than he is." Revita slid a waterskin over her head and shoulder.

Lint, who stood on the table, planted his fists on his hips. "The waterskin might be bigger, but I am much fiercer and would easily win in a fight."

She frowned. "You want to fight a waterskin?"

"I don't want to. I am just saying that I would win."

"Against an inanimate object." She smirked. "What are you going to fight next? An apple? A pair of breeches?"

The brownie crossed his arms. "I will fight anything I must."

Draxan shook his head. "The fifth waterskin is not for the little man. It is for me."

Lint growled and waved a fist in the air. "I am no human. I am a brownie!"

Having heard the complaint before, Ian ignored Lint and turned to Draxan. "You wish to come with us?"

The elf patted the bow on his shoulder. "I have some skill with the bow. After all, I've been training with it for many centuries. If you will have me, I would like to help any way I can. Besides, I have been to Murvaran before and that may be of use to you."

After brief consideration, Ian nodded. "I would welcome your help."

"Good," Draxan nodded. "In that case, meet me outside when you are ready. I must go and relay instructions to my people."

The elf headed to the stairwell and faded from view.

Ahni frowned and whispered in Ian's ear. "Are you certain that is wise? Can we trust him?"

Ian understood her reluctance given the recent betrayal by Eidolon. However, Draxan had not given Ian any reason to believe he would betray him as well. "We could use some guidance and none of us have been to Murvaran before. If it makes you feel better, I will watch closely for any signs of treachery."

She nodded gravely. "As will I."

The three dwarves finished stuffing the packs, buckled the flaps down and handed one to Vic and one to Ahni.

Coralai approached Ian. "We wish you well in your quest. Thank you again for freeing us from that awful curse."

Surprisingly, she wrapped her arms around Ian and hugged him. Ian froze for a beat before hugging her back. The other dwarves followed, and soon, everyone was hugging everyone else.

"Come on!" Lint said from the corridor. "Let's go. We have an ancient, abandoned city to explore!" With a whoop, he darted toward the stairs and was gone.

Revita said, "You have to admit, he does not lack enthusiasm."

Vic laughed. "No, he does not."

They walked off, followed by Ian and Ahni. A quick descent down two flights brought them to the ground floor. As Ian stepped outside, he reached out to Lionel, sensing the drake somewhere near the south end of the valley, busily eating fruit. When he felt the drake coming toward him, Ian peered expectantly in that direction. Moments later, a dark shape flew over the buildings, dove down beneath an arch, and floated in with wings extended. Ian picked Lionel off his arm and set him on his usual perch before descending the front stairs.

Even as Ian approached his companions, Draxan appeared on the path near the road and came toward them. A bow was slung over one shoulder, a pack, a waterskin, and a quiver over the other.

"What's in the pack?" Ian asked.

"The torches you requested, along with a few other items that might be of use."

Considering that the sun was high overhead, half of the day had already passed.

Wishing to avoid losing any additional time, Ian pictured the tower on top of the crater rim and cast a gateway. "Let's go."

Lint jumped through first, followed by Vic, Revita, Ahni, Draxan, and finally, Ian. The moment he was through, Ian dismissed the portal, approached the tube, and peered through it. He examined the city closely and picked a location at the near edge. With it firmly in his mind, he stepped back and cast another gateway. Beyond the opening was a flat plaza paved in dark and light stone tiles.

Wishing to be first this time, Ian stepped through, the heat increasing significantly as a dry desert wind hit him. He then turned slowly while examining his surroundings.

He stood on a plaza made of tiles, each three-foot square. The buildings began over a hundred feet from the plaza's outer edge. Exposed rock and sand covered the ground outside the city, whether on top of the plateau or on the barren flat ground below. In the distance, a mountain appearing to have a flat top loomed. From where Ian stood, it was impossible to guess that the amazing Valley of Gold lay hidden in a crater at the top of that rise.

The others came through the portal, and when they had gathered around him, Ian dismissed it, turning to Draxan. "The question is how to get to the temple."

The elf shrugged. "As I said, we did not visit the temple. We did not even see a way to go underground."

"What of the buildings?"

"They were in remarkably good condition despite being long abandoned." Draxan peered down the nearest street. "The city looks exactly how I remember it."

Ahni pointed toward the desert. "Look at the sand."

Everyone turned to look.

"Besides there being an awful lot of it, what are we looking at?" Revita asked.

"The wind carries the sand. It falls and forms dunes outside the city."

"I can see that much, but why do I care?"

"Look at these tiles. Do you see even one grain of sand on them?"

Ian suddenly understood. "The city is completely clean of sand. In fact, the elements do not affect it. That is how the buildings are in such pristine condition despite having stood for thousands of years."

Vic asked, "How is such a thing possible?"

Pointing at the tiles, Ian said, "I believe this plaza, and maybe even the buildings, form a spell that protect the city."

"A spell?" Vic frowned while peering toward the dark tower at the heart of the city. "Do we have anything to worry about?"

"I don't think so. The spell seems passive. Remember, Draxan and a few others visited the city years ago."

"True," Draxan nodded. "Other than some difficulties we faced while inside the tower, we came upon nothing nefarious."

Ian lifted Lionel from his shoulder and looked the drake in the eye. "Take flight. Circle above and around the city. Look for a way underground."

He followed by sending images of a tunnel and a descending staircase across their bond. The drake puffed up its chest proudly and coiled its legs, ready. In coordination with his pet, Ian thrust up with his arm. Lionel flapped his wings, turned into the wind, and rose up toward the blue sky.

Draxan peered up as the drake grew more distant. "Will he really do as you ask?"

"More or less," Ian admitted. "He has good intentions but can get distracted. However, Lionel is not the only one with eyes. While he searches from above, let's do the same on foot."

Ahni said, "Maybe we should split up."

"Good idea. Vic, Revita, and Lint can take that street." Ian pointed to the right. "Draxan, Ahni, and I will take the one on the left. When we reach the city center, we will reconvene. If you come across trouble, shout or run. Either way, do something to alert the other party."

Vic frowned. "I'd rather be with you." Before Ian could reply, he added, "But I understand. I'll try to keep these two out of trouble."

The comment earned Vic an elbow to the ribs from Revita before she headed down the street. He grunted and shot Ian a lopsided grin before following. With a hoot, Lint darted off and passed them both. Ian turned and gave his last two companions a nod before heading down the other street.

The buildings on both sides were crafted of charcoal-colored stone, the streets laid with bricks of the same hue. Everything had been constructed with startling precision, each brick fitting perfectly with its neighbors while the ornate elements such as buttresses, arched reliefs, ornamentation, statues, and stained-glass windows combined to create distinct and impressive architecture. It was the type of craftsmanship Ian had come to expect from dwarves, which left him wondering who had constructed the city in the first place. No window or door was broken. In fact, everything appeared perfect, as if it had only existed for days rather than millennia. Randomly, Ian chose a building, approached it, and tested the door. It opened to a room with furnishings.

"Hello?" He called.

There was no answer. There wasn't even any dust on the tables or shelves.

He pulled the door closed and continued.

Draxan shook his head. "Hundreds of years have passed, but everything looks exactly how it did when I was here last. It is as if this city is frozen in time."

"Hmm." Ian considered the idea. "Perhaps that is how the spell functions. It is difficult to say."

They continued, passing beneath an arch spanning the street and connecting the upper stories of buildings on both sides.

As they neared the center, the street widened and buildings grew more imposing. With entrances a flight above the street and columns atop the stairs, each structure had short towers capped by domes of gleaming copper. Ian tried to imagine what the city might have been like when it was filled with life. It must have been majestic.

At the end of the street, they came to a sprawling, circular square paved by colored tiles in the pattern of a giant eye, the tower itself the iris. The tower was hundreds of feet across at the base and it matched the Tower of Solitude in height. It suddenly occurred to him that the two towers were strikingly similar yet in many ways as different as could be. One was located in a frozen, empty landscape, the other in a city above the scorching desert. One tower was so pale, it blended in with its snowy surroundings while the other was so dark, it was almost black. *I wonder if they are each a reflection of the personality of their god...if gods have personalities.* He didn't know if it were odd or expected to think of gods as if they possessed traits similar to mortals.

Ian turned to find Vic, Revita, and Lint crossing the edge of the plaza. "Did you find anything?"

Vic shook his head. "Only empty buildings and none that seemed to be what we are looking for."

The brownie walked past Ian and stared up at the tower. "Can we go inside?"

Go inside the Dark Lord's tower? Despite his determination to find the temple, Ian recoiled at the idea. Aloud, he said, "Only if we must."

Draxan said, "The dangers inside are many, and the lift we found on the first level only went up." He shook his head. "I don't think that is the way to the temple."

Lint threw his arms in the air. "Where are we supposed to go? Do you expect us to search every building in this city?"

"I..." Alarm came through Ian's bond with Lionel, stopping him in mid-sentence. He closed his eyes and extended his awareness until he saw the world through the drake's eyes.

Lionel soared high above the city, which appeared as a massive eight-pointed star with an eye in the center. The image reinforced Ian's belief that it was some sort of construct, toward what ends, he was uncertain. He then lifted his view to the horizon and realized why Lionel had reacted with alarm.

A wall of darkness had swallowed the mountains to the northwest, across the Inculti desert from where the Valley of Sol was located. Lightning flashed, illuminating the cloudbank before it again darkened.

Ian opened his eyes and turned northwest. Through a gap in the buildings, he spied that same darkness and he pointed toward it. "A storm is imminent."

The others turned toward it.

"A monsoon," Draxan said. "It appears to be a bad one. It would be best if we found shelter before it hits."

Ian gave a firm nod. "The storm is still forty or fifty miles away. Let's see if we can find the entrance to the temple before it strikes."

Vic shrugged. "Where do we start?"

"Let's walk along the perimeter of this square and look down the connecting streets. Maybe something will stand out."

Keeping outside the mosaic of the eye, they began along the plaza's outer edge. Each street they passed appeared similar to the last. With the storm coming and lacking clues as to where they should look, doubts crept into Ian's head. *Is there truly a temple? If so, is it located below the city or was that a falsehood intended to mislead people seeking it?*

They reached the north side of the tower and Ian stopped.

A rounded alcove lay nestled between two buildings facing the center square. An obelisk made of polished obsidian thrust up from the alcove. Four stories above, the same height as the tallest buildings other than Urvadan's Tower, the tip of the obelisk pointed toward the darkening sky.

"That looks interesting." Ian approached the obelisk and when he drew close, read the words engraved on the black stone surface. "It is in Elvish."

Vic stopped at Ian's side. "What does it say?"

Translating as he spoke, Ian replied, "The veil between worlds is thinner than the edge of a sharpened blade. Beware lest you incur a mortal wound that bleeds uncontrolled. Should the path be opened, it cannot be closed quickly enough. Heed this warning or thou shall unleash death and destruction upon this world."

Revita crossed her arms. "What the blazes is that supposed to mean?"

"It is a warning, I guess." Ian reached out and touched the word veil. "Prophecies warn of tearing the veil between life and death. If creatures from the underworld stalk our lands, perhaps they can do so because the veil is damaged."

"What is the veil?"

"I don't know," Ian admitted.

Draxan said, "I have seen a landmark like this before."

Ian turned toward him. "You have? Where?"

"In a graveyard in Galfhadden." He frowned. "Only that one marked the entrance to an underground warren where they buried their leaders."

The statement caused Ian to look down at the tiles at his feet. They felt solid beneath him. "Did it move?"

The elf frowned. "Did what move?"

"The obelisk."

"I don't know. All I can tell you is that a steep staircase descended right in front of it."

Ian examined the base of the obelisk, eight feet across and just as deep. Without doubt, the structure weighed many tons. He placed his palms on the front of the smooth, black stone and found it hot from the afternoon sun. With a thrust, he leaned into the obelisk but only succeeded in pushing himself away from it. A sigh slipped out as he stepped back.

Revita snickered. "You didn't really think you could move that, did you?"

"I don't know. I suppose not. It's just..." Unwilling to give up, Ian stepped close to the spire again.

He placed his palms on it and then ran them along the hot, polished surface. Beneath his fingertips, he located faint and imperceptible cracks where stone blocks met each other to form the obelisk. From side to side, he ran his hands before slowly raising them. His hand ran across a stone block that felt cold to the touch and continued onto a neighboring block, which was hot like the others. Curious, he returned to the cold one, placed both hands on it, and pushed. The block sank two inches. A click resounded and the entire obelisk slid away from him. A stair appeared, and then another, until a steep, dark stairwell was revealed. The obelisk stopped with a thud, six feet from its initial position.

Lint walked up to the edge and peered into the darkness. A single word was carved into the top step, a word he said aloud. "Beware." He looked up at Ian. "Are you certain we need to go down there?"

"Yes."

"I have a bad feeling about this."

Ian peered into the sky and sent a command to Lionel. "You are welcome to remain up here if you like."

"By myself?"

Turning to the others, Ian asked. "Are the rest of you coming with me?"

Firm nods and determined expressions made their stance clear and left Ian thankful that he didn't need to go down alone.

Lint puffed up his chest. "If you are going down, I had better go with you to make sure you don't get in trouble. Who knows? I might need to save you like I did last night."

"Who knows?" Ian somehow kept from smiling as he turned toward the tower across the plaza. A dark shape rounded the tower, and dove toward them. Lionel swooped in with wings extended, fluttered for a beat, and landed on Ian's forearm. "Draxan. It looks like we are going to need those torches."

"Right." The elf lowered his pack and removed a leather-wrapped bundle from which he pulled out two torches. "How do you intend to light them since you told me not to bother with a flint?"

"Just hold them up."

When the elf did as requested, Ian held Lionel out toward them. "Ok Lionel. Let's see some fire."

The drake took a deep breath, opened its jaw, and sent a burst of flames out, engulfing the upper end of the torches. The flames sputtered as the drake hacked and coughed. The heads of the two torches crackled as they burned.

Vic stepped forward and grabbed a torch. "Revita and I will take the lead."

Draxan nodded. "I will take the rear."

A shadow fell over them and a cool wind stirred Ian's hair. He looked up as lightning flashed across the cloudbank. Thunder boomed a moment later.

"The storm is nearly upon us." Ian turned to his brother. "Let's go before we get wet."

Vic began down the stairs, the torch eating away at the darkness as he descended. Revita scooped up Lint and entered the stairwell. Ian, with Lionel on his shoulder, followed. Ahni and her spear came next with Draxan at the rear. The stairs were steep, forcing them to advance at a careful pace. Above, thunder boomed again, immediately followed by the hammer of heavy rain. By the time Ian reached the bottom stair, three stories below the surface, water was spilling past his feet and running into a long, dark tunnel with a gentle downslope. They followed the running water, wondering where it would lead them.

CHAPTER 33
FROM THE DEPTHS

F lickering torchlight danced off the tunnel walls. The aura of the torch extended no more than fifteen or twenty feet ahead of Vic. Impenetrable blackness loomed beyond that light. As he advanced, Vic continually scanned the tunnel walls and floor in search of any sign of trouble.

From behind him, Revita asked softly, "Are you watching for traps?"

Over his shoulder, he whispered, "Yes. As you taught me."

"Good. Just don't grow complacent."

"Are you worried about me?"

"If you trigger a trap, I worry about all of us."

She still has trouble admitting how she feels. Nobody was more aware of Revita's aversion toward displays of affection or true intimacy than Vic. There were times when he wished for more, but he also knew that pressing her on the subject would also push her away. He believed she loved him even if she could not say the words. Would that ever change? He was uncertain. Rather than worry about it, he hoped that taking baby steps would ease her in that direction.

Since entering the tunnel, they had descended at a steady rate. Vic estimated they had covered a quarter mile by the time the corridor began to bend. They rounded the gradual turn while still descending. On and on, the curve continued until Vic was certain that they were heading back toward the heart of the city. Shortly after the tunnel straightened, a faint, warm light appeared from ahead. Vic blinked and held his torch back, thinking the light was just his imagination, but as he advanced, it only became more pronounced.

"Do you see that?" He asked over his shoulder.

"I see light," Revita replied.

"Tell the others to remain quiet. Especially Lint. We don't know what that is yet."

He continued along the tunnel while Revita relayed the message, his gaze fixed on the light ahead. Something about it felt wrong. Without conscious thought, he reached over his shoulder and slid his mattock from its harness. Whatever waited ahead, it could not be good, not hundreds of feet below the home of the Dark Lord. The light grew brighter as he spied the tunnel's end. Slowing, he crept toward the light and emerged into a cavern of immense proportions, not stopping until he approached a ledge thirty feet from the tunnel entrance.

A drop of hundreds of feet waited just a stride from where Vic and his companions gathered. The cavern's walls to his left and right were each at least a quarter mile away, perhaps farther. The roof of the cavern stood only eighty feet above the tunnel's mouth while the far end of the cavern was so distant, Vic was uncertain how far it extended. All this he took in at first glance, but what held his attention occupied the heart of the massive space.

A pyramid hundreds of feet tall stood in the heart of the chamber. Made of stone like charcoal, the dark pyramid cast a striking contrast to its crystal peak, which appeared like a giant prism. The peak glowed with red-tinted light bright enough to illuminate the entire cavern, and a beam of that light shone straight up through an opening in the cavern ceiling.

Revita said, "It seems we found the source of the light."

Ian added, "That must be the Temple of Tenebri."

"What are those?" Lint pointed down as hoots and grunts echoed in the chamber.

The sounds bounced off walls, causing Vic to look left and right before following the brownie's gesture. Then, he saw them.

Humanoid creatures with gray skin and wiry builds moved along the cavern's floor. Some huddled around an underground stream that wound its way through rocks while others danced around a brazier filled with glowing coals. A group of the creatures headed toward the entrance at the base of the pyramid. They hopped and loped with their backs hunched and arms flailing. Then, they were gone.

Draxan hissed. "Goblins!"

Vic spun toward him. "You mean like the monsters in fireside stories?"

"They existed long ago but were supposed to have been exterminated. They were a failed experiment by the Dark Lord, one that even he saw as a mistake. I have not seen one since my youth, over two thousand years past."

"Goblins." Ian grimaced. "We will have to..." His eyes widened as he stopped in mid-sentence. "Is that a dragon?"

Vic followed his brother's gaze and spied a large, winged creature flying over the pyramid's peak. The monster released a loud, screeching cry and came straight toward them.

"That's no dragon," Draxan tossed his torch to the ground and slid his bow over his shoulder. "That is a wyvern, another creature thought to be extinct."

"It's coming for us," Vic said.

"Fire." Draxan nocked his arrow. "It is attracted to fire."

Vic glanced at the torch in his hand. "Everyone get back in the tunnel. I'll draw its attention."

As the others backed from the cliff edge, Vic waved the torch, the trailing flames creating streaks of light. The wyvern, while smaller than a dragon, had a body the size of a carriage, its webbed wings thirty feet from tip to tip. Unlike a dragon, it had clawed arms sticking out from the wings rather than having independent forelegs. The creature lacked the spiked crests that ran from a dragon's head to its tail. Its scaled hide was a dark, dull gray, and sharp white teeth filled its open mouth. All of this, Vic absorbed in seconds, for that was all the time he had before the monster struck.

The wyvern dove toward him and brought its hind legs forward, each foot capped by thick black talons and big enough to clamp around Vic's torso with ease. Just before it reached him, Vic tossed the torch into the air and then dropped to his belly. The wyvern soared in, snapped its jaw closed, and the torch was gone. It folded its wings back and beat them urgently to stop itself before it struck the cavern wall.

Positioned a dozen feet back in the tunnel, Ian waited with Draxan on one side of him, Revita on the other, and Lionel clutched against his chest, the drake squirming to break free. The dragon-like wyvern flew in with Vic diving just before it struck. Having learned the hard way that dragons were immune to elemental magic, Ian wondered if the same applied for the monster before him.

The wyvern sailed past Vic and beat its wings as it slowed, creating a furious wind in the tunnel.

Ian opened himself up to his magic and crafted a construct, prepared to shield off the tunnel.

To his left, Draxan loosed. His arrow struck the wyvern in the chest as the creature landed. Quickly, Draxan reloaded and loosed again, the next arrow plunging into the monster's neck. The wyvern released a deafening screech. Rather than come after the elf as Ian expected, the monster spun around, its snake-like tale whipping into the tunnel and striking Ian's legs. He flipped over with a yelp and landed hard on his back, the impact knocking the wind from his lungs. In the process, he lost his grip on Lionel, who broke free and took flight.

Ian rolled onto his side and gasped for air as the drake circled over him, flapped its wings mightily, and shot out of the tunnel.

WHEN THE WYVERN landed between him and the tunnel opening, Vic scrambled to his feet and burst toward the beast, hoping to get a clean strike at it from behind. The monster spun around, its mouth opening in a terrifying shriek while spittle sprayed out from it. The wyvern stomped toward Vic, who dove aside. The monster's jaws snapped closed, barely missing him.

Landing on his hands, Vic rolled to his feet, spun and lashed out. The pick end of his mattock tore through the creature's right wing in a spray of sparks. Faster than one might think possible, the wyvern spun on Vic, a head half the size of his body crashing into him and sending him sprawling. He rolled over as the monster stomped toward him.

PRECIOUS AIR FILLED Ian's lungs as he crawled to his hands and knees. Lionel had flown out of the tunnel, and Ahni chased after him. A hand slid under Ian's arm. He looked up to find Revita standing beside him.

"Can you do something?" She asked as she helped him to his feet.

"I was going to when…"

"Do something! Your brother is out there fighting that thing."

"Right." Ian nodded and walked past Draxan, who stared down a nocked arrow, waiting to strike. "Please don't hit me. I am going in." Drawing his magic, Ian headed toward the chaos outside the tunnel.

VIC HURRIED to his hands and knees and scrambled toward his weapon, which lay ten feet away. The growling, furious wyvern stomped after him, its heavy footsteps rapidly closing in. As Vic reached for the mattock, the wyvern's head came down, forcing him to yank his hand back. The monster's massive jaw smashed into the rock shelf right where Vic's arm had been a second earlier.

The wyvern shook its head and slung a long trail of drool out, which fell right across Vic. The monster turned and snarled as Vic tried to scramble away. Suddenly, one of his hands went over the edge and he fell on his side with his head and half his upper body dangling over the deadly drop. He pulled himself up and turned as a mouth with teeth the size of daggers came at him.

A burst of fire shot overhead and struck the monster in the face. The wyvern pulled back and shook its head. Vic looked back to find Lionel hovering above him. The drake inhaled and blew another burst of flames but they died off as he began to hack and cough. The wyvern lunged for Lionel, snapping its jaws, but the drake flew sideways and then circled around while the wyvern spun in pursuit, its head lunging and jaws snapping closed again and again.

No longer the target of the monster's anger, Vic rolled to his feet and raced over to his weapon.

IAN STOPPED outside the tunnel to take survey of the battle.

Spear held ready, Ahni was stalking toward the wyvern, who stood a few strides away with its back facing her. The monster suddenly turned and swept its tail out, taking her legs out from beneath her. It then stomped off toward the far end of the rock ledge.

Concerned, Ian rushed over to Ahni and helped her up. "Are you well?"

"Well enough." Her eyes were tense, her lips tight as she stood and gripped her spear. "I just need a clean strike and I end this."

"Are you certain?"

"Very."

The spear in her hand seemed far too small to do enough damage to a creature of that size, but she seemed certain, so Ian set his mind on giving her a chance.

A small burst of fire came from beyond the wyvern. Lionel flew into view and rounded the giant monster as it twisted in pursuit. Ian set his jaw and cast a construct. A cone of flames burst out, striking the wyvern in the side. It bawled a mighty shriek and spun toward Ian, who realized he was in trouble. The wyvern stomped toward him with its jaws open wide. Spinning away, Ian raced back into the tunnel.

Vic scooped up his mattock and spun toward the monster to find its back to him. The wyvern raced toward the tunnel as Ian darted inside. Seeing his opening, Vic ran up to the wyvern, raised his weapon, and chopped down. The axe edge of his mattock struck and cleaved clean through the monster's tail, severing off the last six feet.

A horrible shriek came from the wyvern as it spun back toward him. Vic held his weapon ready. It would be dangerous, but he was determined to hit the monster on the head and end the battle. The wyvern came around, teeth flashing as it sought its new target – Vic.

Ahni released a roar and raced in from behind the monster with her spear held over her head. She leapt high and drove the spear down into the creature's exposed back. The spearhead plunged into the wyvern's flesh and the monster froze. An amber glow spread out from the spearpoint and then something shocking happened.

A blast shook the rock shelf as the entire rear third of the wyvern's body blasted apart. Dark blood and chunks of flesh shot out and splattered across the ledge. A pink mist hung in the hair as what remained of the wyvern collapsed in a heap.

~

Ian, Draxan, Revita, and Lint emerged from the tunnel, their jaws slack as they stared down at the giant corpse. A massive, gory cavity was now in place of where the creature's body had once met its tail, which had been blown off as well. Ahni stood a dozen feet to the right, much of her body covered in wet, crimson splotches. The sacred spear lay between her and the dead wyvern, amid chunks of its flesh. She approached the monster, bent, and picked up her weapon.

"I guess you were right," Ian said. "You only needed a chance to get close."

"The sacred spear is quite deadly." She frowned at the blood covering the lower half of the weapon. "It now needs cleaning."

A ruckus of hoots and howls came from below.

Vic swept a chunk of flesh from his cheek. "Yuck." He walked over to the edge of the rock shelf and peered down. "I think we are in trouble."

Ian crossed to join his brother as the others gathered around.

The last of the goblins ran from the cavern floor and climbed a sloping path along the steep rock wall. The creature joined a long train of fellow monsters, their wiry forms like shadows marching up switchbacks. The ones in the lead turned the last switchback and began along a ledge that ran a quarter of the way around the cavern before reaching the ledge upon which Ian and his companions stood.

"They are coming for us," Vic said.

"And there are hundreds of them." Revita glanced toward Draxan. "How many arrows do you have left?"

"Not nearly enough."

"Then I suggest we figure something out quickly."

CHAPTER 34

OUT OF TIME

I an monitored the long line of goblins climbing the path along the cavern wall. He had no more than a minute before the first monsters reached him, yet he waited, one hand stroking Lionel's head while the other cradled him.

Vic gripped Ian's shoulder. "Are you going to do something?"

"Yes."

"What are you waiting for?"

"If the goblins are up here..." Ian pointed toward the temple. "They aren't down there."

Lint snorted. "That much is obvious. What are you going to say next?" He altered his voice, making it even more nasal than usual. "If the goblins are wet, they aren't dry? If the goblins are full, they aren't hungry? If the goblins are asleep, they aren't awake?"

Giving the brownie a flat glare, Ian said, "I intend to make a gateway outside the temple entrance. I want the goblins to be otherwise occupied. The farther they are from the temple, the more time we have."

"Oh." Lint looked down at the pyramid and nodded. "That makes sense."

The hoots and howls grew louder and more frantic as the goblins rounded the cavern.

"Alright, everyone." Ian stared down at the temple entrance and firmly fixed it in his mind just before turning and casting a gateway.

A ribbon of light formed between him and the dead wyvern. It opened to reveal the base of the pyramid with a reddish light emitting from an open doorway. Vic, with his weapon in hand, stepped through first with the others quickly following. The goblins raced along the ledge toward Ian, their red eyes wild with blood lust. He passed through the opening and dropped the spell, causing the portal to snap shut with a pop. Turning, Ian scanned the area in search of trouble.

The cavern floor consisted of numerous, flat tiers, some sloped, others level. Clusters of rock and boulders stood here and there, and an underground stream ran along the far wall. Orange coals burned in a brazier no more than twenty feet from where Ian and his companions stood. The only goblins visible were those along the cliffside path and those gathering on the rock shelf high above. Ignoring their angry howls, Ian turned back toward the pyramid.

Now that he was close to it, the structure appeared even more impressive than before. Its angled face was made of row after row of dark stone blocks four feet across and twice as thick. Ian could not imagine how much those blocks must have weighed, but he marveled at the feat of engineering that must have taken place to construct the temple in the first place.

The doorway was framed by thick pillars supporting a flat sheet of stone two feet thick. Broad enough to easily accommodate a wagon and twice the height, the opening should have appeared inviting. The red aura coming from inside made it anything but.

"I don't know what awaits us inside," Ian said. "Be ready for anything."

Lint, who stood in front of the doorway, kneaded his hands while staring into the building. "This feels wrong."

"What do you mean?"

"There is something inside...something...evil."

A chill wracked Ian's spine. A voice inside him screamed to flee but he ignored the plea. *We have come too far to turn back now.* "Let's go." Somehow, the words came out without his voice cracking.

Together, they advanced past the pillars and into the pyramid.

The warm glow came from the opposite end of a long corridor and from two sets of doors, one to each side of the hallway. Both sets of doors pulsed with a sinister red light.

"Stay away from the doors," Ian warned. He had seen such wards before.

"That means you as well, pipsqueak." Revita said.

Lint looked up with a hurt expression. "Why would you say that?"

"Why? Have you forgotten the mess you created with the moarbear statue in the Tower of Solitude?"

"I told you before..."

"Yes. I know. You wanted to show the bear that you did not fear it. Please don't try that with the doors."

The brownie crossed his arms with a scowl. "Fine."

Vic gestured. "More red light ahead."

Despite his belief that any magic emanating a crimson glow was certain to be nefarious, Ian gave a firm nod. "That is where we go."

They continued along the corridor. Over a hundred feet in, they passed another set of pillars and stepped out into a cavernous open space.

The walls stood hundreds of feet apart, rising to a vaulted ceiling sloped to match the pyramid's exterior. Braziers the size of wagon beds burned in each corner of the temple floor. In the center of the chamber stood a dais eight feet tall and surrounded by stairs. The top of the dais appeared empty beneath the beam of red light streaming down through the pyramid's crystal tip, bathing everything in the color of blood.

"What now?" Vic whispered. "It looks...empty."

Ian didn't need Lint's warning to know that something very, very bad loomed ahead, despite what his eyes told him. Still, he had come for a purpose, and until that purpose was fulfilled, he needed to press on.

"There is no need to endanger all of us. Remain here but be ready in case of trouble." Ian squatted and set Lionel down on the floor. "Stay." Alone Ian lifted his foot and stepped onto the first stair.

The moment his boot touched the stairs, light flashed and a wave of nausea passed over him. He staggered up the next two stairs and caught himself. The dizziness passed, allowing him to stand upright. A backward glance caused him to freeze in panic. His companions stood rock still, but that was not what he found so disconcerting. Lionel had taken flight and was a few feet off the ground with his wings partially extended. The drake did not move. In fact, he appeared frozen.

A deep and gravelly voice came from above him. "You dare to trespass in the Temple of Tenebri?"

With a gasp, Ian spun around and discovered the dais no longer vacant. Upon an obsidian throne sat a creature just as dark in appearance as the evil in its heart.

Black, leathery skin covered the demon's muscular body. Its head was distended and grotesque – with spikes rather than hair, fangs jutting up over the upper lip, and eyes a solid yellow with black slits for pupils. Although the creature sat, its immense size was immediately apparent, for it filled a throne that could have sat three or more men at once.

"Come closer, boy." The demon leaned forward in its throne. "You've come for me, I suspect. I am waiting."

Gathering his courage, Ian climbed the stairs and the top of the dais came into view. Tiles covered the upper surface, black on the outside, white in the middle, all laid out in the pattern of an eight-pointed star with the throne at its center. A beam of red light shone down upon the throne. Somehow, the beam of light held fast to the shape of the star.

Ian stepped onto the dais but stopped short of the light. "What is your name?"

"I am called H'Deesengar."

"What are..."

The creature held up a hand large enough to engulf Ian's head. Black nails curved to a point at the end of each finger. "A question for a question. I've answered yours. Now answer mine."

Ian swallowed. "Very well."

"You have my name. What is yours?"

"I am called..." Ian considered giving his birthname but thought better of it, concerned that it might give the demon some power over him. "Barsequa Illian."

"Barsequa? In what way are you gifted?"

"Oh, no. It is my turn to ask of you."

The demon grinned, revealing a mouth full of pointed teeth. "Go on."

"What are you doing here?"

"I came here on a bargain made with Urvadan, but he is a creature of lies and betrayal." The demon lifted his gaze and held his arms out. "I have been trapped here in this temple ever since. Now, tell me about your gifts."

"I am a wizard. I can wield magic, magic unlike anyone else."

"I see. That is how you made it past my pets."

"Your pets?"

"The goblins. The wyvern. The ogres."

"Ogres?"

"You did not come across them?" The demon stroked its distended chin with a black fingernail. "How strange."

Ian glanced back toward his companions, suddenly concerned. They remained unmoving, the drake still as if about to take flight.

"How come my companions aren't moving?"

"The spell that contains me does so in all dimensions."

Ian turned back toward the demon. "You will need to explain further."

"This spell trapped me in both space and time. I cannot leave this dais, that much I assume you surmised. However, it also holds me slightly in the past, trailing the passage of time just enough where it leaves me out of phase with the rest of your world."

The concept was difficult to fathom and left Ian wondering what spell could do such a thing. He glanced back at his companions again. Something about the situation bothered him, but he could not quite put a finger on it.

Vɪᴄ ʜᴇʟᴅ his breath when Ian lifted his leg and prepared to climb the dais. He was not the only one with the desire to intervene. When Lionel tried to take flight, Vic reached out and snatched the drake by the neck. The next time he looked toward his brother, Ian was gone.

Lionel squawked and flapped, trying to escape.

"Just stop!" Vic growled. "You are to stay here with us, just as Ian said."

The drake thrashed and squawked louder. To rid himself of it, Vic squatted and let go. Lionel landed with wings extended. It righted itself and squawked again, right at Vic. Raising his gaze past the creature, Vic then spied a dark shadow along the far wall, near the brazier. The shadow moved closer and a creature came into view. It stood as tall as the tallest man but with shoulders twice the width. Its arms were overly long with massive hands dangling at its knees. The creature wore only a tattered loin cloth, the rest of its muscular body covered in green-tinted flesh. It was hairless and had a huge jaw with an underbite that left two pointed teeth jutting up over its upper lip.

"What in the blazes is that thing?" Revita blurted.

THE DARK LORD'S DESIGN

Draxan spun toward it and groaned. "Looks like an ogre, another creature not seen for centuries."

Vic glanced back down the tunnel they had taken to reach the temple interior. It remained empty, but the hoots and howls of goblins echoed in the distance. "There is nowhere to run."

"Then we fight." The elf drew an arrow, raised his bow, and loosed. The arrow struck the ogre in the chest and shattered. Quickly, he drew and loosed again. The arrow careened off its shoulder and struck the wall. "As I thought. Definitely an ogre."

"How do you know?" Revita asked.

"Ogres were said to have skin like armor, which makes them difficult to kill. They are reputed to be even stronger than they look but are notoriously known to be as dumb as rocks." He backed away as the monster continued its plodding advance.

When Lionel burst into flight, heading toward the ogre, Vic snatched the drake by the foot. It flapped and squawked angrily as it tried to break free. He glanced toward the dais, and although he could not see Ian, something told him that he needed to buy Ian time.

"Let's back into the corridor. We need to distract this thing, keep it away from Ian."

With a swing, Vic brought the drake around and let go. Lionel flew down the corridor, covered its entire length, and sped out into the open cavern outside the temple. The ogre's eyes followed Lionel, causing it to pause. When the drake was out of sight, the monster looked back toward Vic and his companions and resumed its heavy strides.

The ogre was as big as a bear, and that reminded Vic of what he had been taught about dangerous woodland creatures. Running from them was a trigger and made them react as if you were prey. Calm and caution were best, so that was what Vic and his companions must do. "Slowly, now." With careful steps, he shuffled into the corridor while keeping an eye on the advancing monstrosity.

THE DEMON SMIRKED AT IAN, as if it knew something Ian did not. It was disconcerting, but what about the situation was not?

"The Dark Lord," Ian pressed. "Where is he?"

"Urvadan comes with every cycle of the moon. He stays for a few days, using his power to reinforce my prison and then he leaves. I have not seen him in weeks, so I suspect he will return soon."

Knowing that the Dark Lord was away brought Ian relief. Facing the demon lord was terrifying enough, even with it held captive. To face a god, an immortal being of untold might, was something Ian wished to avoid at any cost.

Forging ahead, Ian decided that his curiosity had been sufficiently sated. It was time to get to the crux of his quest.

"There is another demon who threatens my world."

The smirk fell away from the demon's face. H'Deesengar leaned forward with a scowl. "There can be no other. Not here."

"Oh, there is."

"Prove it."

Ian frowned. "He looks much like you, but reddish flesh and horns that curl at the sides of his head."

A mighty thump shook the dais when the demon pounded a fist against the throne. "Az'Ianzar," he spat. "How did he cross to your plane?"

"I don't know." Ian needed to regain control of the conversation. "This demon consumes souls."

"Souls feed my kind, sustain us, and increase our might."

"How do I free those souls?"

H'Deesengar laughed. "You cannot. Those souls become a part of us." His laughter quelled. "Unless…"

"Unless what?" Ian pressed. "I must know."

Revita backed into the corridor while nervously watching the slowly advancing ogre. The monster did not speak or react. It merely continued to stomp toward them and emit low grunts with each stride.

From behind her, near the entrance, came Lint's voice. "The goblins are coming back down the trail. They will reach the cavern floor soon."

Shadows surrounded them as they backed from the illuminated temple. As it grew darker, the pulsing red glow of the doors on each side of the chamber became more prominent. The corner of the wall momentarily obscured the ogre before it lumbered back into view. It entered the corridor, its massive, hulking body eclipsing the red light.

The monster blasted a terrifying roar. In reaction, Revita held her bracer out in a protective pose while making a fist. Six spiked blades popped up from the bracer, appearing like the crest on a dragon's back. The ogre clenched its hands into fists, its pace increasing. Sensing it was about to charge, Revita flung her arm toward it, launching the spikes. Four blades struck the creature, the tip of each slicing into its leathery flesh while the other two sailed wide, bounced off the corridor walls, and clattered along the floor. The ogre roared, this time as it charged. She backed away, but there was nowhere to run and she had no idea how to kill it.

"There must be a way," Ian insisted, unable to keep the desperation from his voice. "I have to free those souls."

H'Deesengar stroked his long, pointed jaw. "I suppose it is possible if you can overfeed Az'Ianzar."

"Overfeed the demon?"

"Demon *lord*," H'Deesengar corrected. "Nothing has unlimited capacity. Demons consume life. Demon lords even more life. However, if he were to overfeed on life, he would become vulnerable, for his flesh would become stretched too thin."

"Too much life?"

The demon lord leaned forward, its yellow eyes staring at Ian with terrifying intensity. "I suspect you know of something where life itself is concentrated in the form of a living being unlike any other.""

The inference caused Ian to gasp. To sacrifice something as sacred as what H'Deesengar suggested was unthinkable. *You are speaking to a being of evil, Ian told himself. How can you trust anything it says?* Aloud, he asked, "Why should I believe anything you say?"

"Az'Ianzar and I are rivals. Should you find a way to defeat him, his realm would ripen for the taking. One day, I will escape these bonds, and when I do, his dominion would easily fall under my control."

"Power. You seek power."

"We all seek power. I merely choose not to deny it."

Ian rubbed his jaw. "So, if I can overfill this demon lord with life, then what?"

"Then you must seek a means to pierce his flesh." The demon lord sat back. "In this, I will say no more. I do hope you are successful, for Az'Ianzar and I are sworn enemies. Should he no longer exist, I shall claim the fourth realm for myself when I am freed from this prison. Now, go before it is too late. Should Az'Ianzar conquer this realm, he will come for me. Given how this prison limits my abilities, such a confrontation would go quite poorly. Thus, in this, you and I are of one mind. I wish you success."

Ian heard the words but paid them little attention since his brain was working through the problem. When he realized what the demon lord inferred, he found himself in another dilemma. To save the captured souls and the world itself, he would have to bring death and destruction to the most beautiful city he had ever visited.

CHAPTER 35
DOORWAYS

Vic readied himself as he continued backing from the ogre. They came to the middle of the corridor, and when they were between the two pulsing, red doors, Revita loosed her blades. The monster, with numerous metal spikes jutting out from its muscular body, reacted in anger and rushed toward her. When the charging fiend was a dozen feet away and coming fast, Vic attacked.

He burst forward, ducked, and swung with all his might. A fist the size of his head swept over him as his mattock came around. It struck the ogre in the knee. The pick broke the skin and blue sparks sizzled along its leg. The ogre's momentum tore the mattock from Vic's grip. The creature stumbled, bent, and pulled the mattock free before tossing it aside. It roared again and swung its long arms in a broad arc, forcing Ahni and Revita to dive out of the way lest they find their heads crushed.

From her knees, Ahni came around with her spear and thrust. The spear tip stuck the ogre in the hip, but rather than pierce the skin, it bounced off. Vic, expecting another explosion, stood stunned when nothing happened. Thus, he was unprepared when a massive fist came toward him.

WHEN THE OGRE turned on Vic, who was weaponless, Revita had to act. She pressed the gem on her bracer to recall the blades. Those embedded in the ogre's torso tore free, raking and skittering along its armor-like hide before snapping back onto the bracer. The blades that had originally missed the ogre launched from their resting spots at the foot of the dais stairs. They shot down the corridor, straight toward Revita. One struck the ogre's hand, plunged through it, and emerged covered in dark blood. The other sailed wide of the monster, narrowly missing Ahni as it sped toward Revita. Both snapped back onto her bracer. Despite all of this, the ogre's massive mitt continued toward Vic as if nothing had happened.

JUST IN TIME, Vic leapt backward, the wind from the ogre's fist passing by ruffling his hair. The fiend stepped toward him and roared. Lacking a weapon to defend himself, Vic backed from the monster. Pulsing red light shone on the ogre and cast Vic's shadow on the beast. Startled, he glanced backward and found one of the warded doors right behind him. When he turned back toward the creature, he found its massive fist coming at him again. Desperate, Vic ducked and dove aside. The ogre's fist struck the door with a deep thump. A flash of angry light bloomed and enveloped the monster's body. The ogre froze, its eyes bulging as its skin began to crack and pop. Fire burst from the ogre's eyes, mouth, and every other crack along its body. The beast toppled backward and struck the floor with a heavy thud. Flames crackled, their flickering light brightly illuminating the corridor as the hulking corpse burned.

DISTURBED by what he had learned, Ian turned from the demon lord and descended the staircase. As he stepped off the last stair, the world shifted. A wave of nausea passed over him as his surroundings tilted this way and that. He staggered but did not fall. A moment later, the world stabilized and the disconcerting sensation passed.

Alarm struck when he discovered his companions gone from where he had left them. He then spied a fire in the corridor surrounded by familiar silhouettes and headed toward them.

"What happened?" Ian frowned as he tried to make sense of the massive, humanoid shape within the flames.

Vic climbed to his feet and rubbed his elbow. "We ran into some trouble." He took a few steps and bent to pick up his mattock.

Revita snorted. "Some trouble? I'd say about five hundred pounds of trouble."

Ahni eyed her spear tip with a frown. "The sacred spear barely scratched that thing."

Ian looked down at the burning corpse. It was the width of three men. He then recalled the demon lord mentioning his pets – goblins, a wyvern, and... "An ogre?"

Draxan approached with his bow in hand. "How did you know?"

From the far end of the corridor, Lint yelped. "Goblins! Here they come!"

Everyone spun toward the brownie. Beyond the entrance, the gray, wiry bodies of dozens of goblins raced into view. They hooted and howled as they rushed toward the temple entrance.

Lionel! Ian called out through the bond. *Come fast!*

He then turned from the burning ogre and cast a gateway. "Everyone through. Now!"

Ian looked over his shoulder, toward the temple entrance, while the others jumped through the portal. Lint raced along the corridor floor with his eyes reflecting fear. Goblins driven by mindless fury poured into the tunnel corridor, chasing after the fleeing brownie. A dark winged shape dove in and leveled right above the goblin's heads, releasing a puff of fire that caused the creatures to shriek and shy away, slowing them.

As Lionel sped toward him, Ian stepped through the gateway. The drake shot through the portal the moment Lint hopped through. The lead goblin lunged with an outstretched arm, and Ian dismissed his magic. The portal snapped shut. A gray, clawed hand fell to the floor and rolled to rest against Ian's boot.

Draxan lifted his gaze while slowly turning.

Ahni held her spear ready while doing the same. "Where have you brought us this time?"

"We are in the mountain home of my master." Ian held his arm out as Lionel circled and landed on it. "This is the Chamber of Testing. Come. You can meet my master. We will eat, rest, and discuss what comes next."

IAN LAY IN BED, unable to sleep amid a night of tossing and turning. Lionel, who had become irritated by Ian's repeated movements, lay curled up on a padded chair in the corner of the room. The drake was not the only one irritated. His inability to sleep had left Ian frustrated and worried. He would need his rest for what was to come. The battle against his insomnia was one he lost. Conceding, he decided his time was better spent anywhere else than in bed, so he threw his covers aside, got up, and began to dress.

From his wardrobe, he chose midnight blue robes trimmed in silver and tied them with a silver sash. They were meant to be for special occasions, but he decided that saving them for an event that may never happen would be a waste. Besides, what could be a more special occasion than saving the world?

He turned to the mirror and smoothed his robes. The way they shimmered in the light of the orb made him appear regal. His light brown beard had grown in nicely, making him appear older and somehow wiser. Bags shadowed his green eyes, a marker of his restless night. In addition, his brown hair was a mess, so he made for the bowl on the vanity and began splashing water on his head. The comb beside the bowl was then raked through his hair, untangling it, taming it. He then dried his face with a towel and made for the curtain-covered doorway, slowing to grab the orb from the sconce on the wall before ducking into the corridor.

The orb ate away at the gloom as he made his way toward his master's chamber. He stopped outside the door. The rap of his knuckles on the oak echoed in the corridor. He waited for a beat and knocked again.

"Master?" Ian tried.

No answer. In fact, Ian had not been able to find Truhan since his return from Murvaran. Not being able to speak with his master about what he must do was another cause for his insomnia. It also fueled his frustration. He considered opening the door but thought better of it. Instead, he headed along the corridor, passing the chambers where Ahni, Draxan, Vic, and Revita slept. A light came from the end of the corridor, spurring hope that his master had returned.

Ian strolled into the study, stopped, and scanned the room, taking in the bookshelves, the desk, the sofa and chairs, and the column in the center. Of Truhan, there was no sign.

"What are you doing awake already?"

Spinning around, Ian spied Lint standing on a table, surrounded by pieces from a wooden puzzle. "I couldn't sleep."

"Maybe you can help me with this puzzle. I took it apart but can't seem to figure out how to get it back together."

When assembled, the puzzle formed a dodecahedron. It had taken Ian weeks to master the puzzle. "It can be tricky, but I assure you, there is a way to reassemble it."

"You sound as if you don't want to help."

Ian needed something to put his mind toward, but the puzzle would only be a distraction. Time was short, and his energy was finite. He needed to do something constructive, something to prepare him for the daunting task he had set upon himself.

"No. You are on your own in this, Lint. I have other things I need to do."

"Maybe *you* could use *my* help?" There was a hopeful tone to Lint's offer.

"I would accept your help if I could figure out what to do next."

"I don't understand. You say you have things to do, but you don't know what to do?"

Ian sighed and sat on the chair. "I guess not. I am just worried. The world is in danger. There is a demon out there consuming souls, souls that are trapped for eternity unless I can find a way to defeat the demon. I am worried, though. What if my magic is not enough?"

"Isn't that why you went in search of the Paragon in the first place?"

His eyes widening, Ian blurted. "Parsigar!"

"That's the old dwarf's name."

Standing, Ian knew what he must do. "I need go see Parsigar. With everything else going on, I forgot about him."

"Take me with you."

Ian eyed the brownie, who seemed to find his way into mischief on a regular basis. "I don't know..."

"Please, Ian." Lint walked up and tugged on Ian's sleeve. "The nights are so boring with everyone asleep and me having nowhere to explore. Either take me with you or let me venture up the staircase at the end of the back corridor."

The brownie had been forbidden to approach the staircase for good reason. While it led to the source, the path was impossible to tread without Truhan, at least if one wished to survive.

"Fine. You can come with me." Ian held a finger up in warning. "But cause no trouble. Do you hear me?"

"I won't," Lint said in a surprisingly earnest tone.

"Good. Hold on while I cast a gateway." Ian turned toward an open space and conjured a construct. He firmly pictured a room in the Tower of Solitude as he cast a gateway. "Go on." When Lint jumped through, Ian followed and dismissed his magic.

Ian and Lint stood in a chamber a dozen feet wide and just as long. An orb the size of an apple rested on a sconce sticking out from the wall, the purple glow emanating from the orb giving shape to the room. Behind Ian stood the empty shaft of the tower lift. An open door with a padded wooden chair graced the wall opposite the lift. The first time Ian had seen Parsigar, the dwarf had been seated in that chair, waiting to find out who had visited the tower after living there for so long – his first visitors other than the god, Vandasal, of course.

"The lift is gone," Lint said.

"I see that." Ian made for the door. "That makes it unlikely for Parsigar to be on this floor, but let's inspect it anyway since we are here.

With Lint following close behind, Ian entered a curved corridor that brought him to the kitchen. The room was empty, the chairs pushed in to the bare table. Through the frost-coated window, soft moonlight shone across the frozen landscape outside the tower. Curious, Ian approached the oven, held his hand toward it, and found it cold.

He returned to the corridor, passing the bathing room and Parsigar's bedroom. Both appeared unused, as did the next two bedrooms.

"As I thought," Ian said to himself as much as to Lint. "This floor is empty. Let's take the lift to the upper floors."

"Where do you think he is?"

"We will inspect the other floors on our way up, but I expect to find him in his workshop." *I hope he is finished with his creation.* The last part, he kept to himself, afraid to say the words aloud.

The two of them retraced their steps back to the lift chamber, where Ian approached the shaft opening and pressed a palm on the bronze panel beside it. A low hum came from above. It was faint at first but grew increasingly louder as the lift descended.

The platform came into view to reveal a pedestal near the front with a bronze control panel. Ian waited for Lint to climb onto the platform before he lifted the globe from the sconce. The room fell dark other than the island of light around Ian's palm. He stepped onto the platform, pressed his hand to the control panel, and it began to rise.

CHAPTER 36
A GIFT FOR THE GIFTED

As Ian had expected, the elderly dwarf was not found on any of the levels above his living quarters, floors containing wonders that had astounded Ian with his prior visit, some bordering on disbelief. This time, he felt nothing but rising dread. The tower had been named Solitude for good reason, yet it now felt more like a crypt than a home.

The lift climbed toward the last level that Parsigar claimed as his, for the uppermost floors belonged to the tower's owner and were strictly off limits. As Ian waited for the lift to emerge from the shaft, he wondered what he might find in Vandasal's quarters should he dare to attempt venturing into the tower's upper reaches. His curiosity promised unimaginable treasures awaiting, but at what cost? If Parsigar were not found, could Ian risk the wrath of a god?

The shaft opened to reveal a pie-shaped workshop illuminated by orbs evenly spaced along the side walls. Vials, crucibles, open books, and tools covered the six workbenches along the wall to the right. Each table was crafted of dark wood, thick and heavy. An anvil, a hammer, and a forge stood along the far wall, the coals in the forge simmering with a soft glow. To each side of the forge was a window, covered in frost, now with morning light visible through icy crystals. Shelving and racks stood along the wall to the left. Strange contraptions, weapons, and artifacts made of metal, stone, and wood filled the shelves and racks. An arched doorway nestled between sections of shelving led to another chamber in one direction while an arch between two work-benches opened to a neighboring room in the other. Of Parsigar, there was no sign.

Ian stepped off the lift, still holding the orb as he crossed the work-shop. He glanced through the arched opening leading to the raw mate-rial storage room, but it was dimly lit with bins and crates visible amid the shadows. Turning from the storage room, Ian led Lint toward the other archway and stepped into Parsigar's library. Rows of shelving ran along the walls and throughout the space, each ten feet tall and filled with thick tomes. The chamber encompassed half of the floor. Light streamed through the long, frost-coated windows above the shelving. To the left side of the room, near the hub at the center of the tower, was a desk. Parsigar occupied the chair beside the desk while his upper body lay across it, his eyes closed and his spectacles on the floor.

"Parsigar!" Ian gasped and ran over.

He knelt beside the dwarf and shook him gently. "Parsigar? Can you hear me?"

When the dwarf did not move, a lump clogged Ian's throat. Tears blurred his vision. He dropped his forehead to the desk and cried.

Fulfilling his quest and locating the Paragon was supposed to be the answer. Parsigar was to craft a magical object that would help Ian save the world. He had endured so much to get to this point, this was not supposed to happen. The old dwarf was not supposed to die.

A weak groan came from beside him.

Ian lifted his head and blinked. "Parsigar?"

"Water," the old dwarf croaked.

Hope and urgency lifted Ian to his feet. He looked left and right and then spied a table with a cluster of cups resting upon it. A hand pump stuck out from the wall beside the table. Ian raced over and began to pump. Water emerged, and Ian filled a cup, which he then hurried back over to Parsigar. With care, he helped the dwarf sit up and held the cup to his mouth. Parsigar drank while water spilled over the cup's sides, wetting his wispy white beard.

When the cup was empty, Ian lowered it. "I feared you were dead."

The old dwarf closed his eyes, seeming weary. "All things die, Ian. My time nears. I am tired. My body longs for rest."

"But what of my quest?" Ian bent and scooped up the fallen spectacles. "You promised to help me. The world will…"

The dwarf patted Ian's hand. "Easy, my boy." He accepted the spectacles and slid them on.

"I'm sorry."

"Help me up."

Ian slid an arm around the dwarf and lifted, bringing him to his feet.

Parsigar said, "Now, take me back to my workshop. There is something I must show you."

As requested, Ian helped the old dwarf hobble across the room.

The brownie walked alongside Ian. "What's wrong with him?"

"I don't know."

"I tire," the dwarf croaked. "Soon, I will begin the long sleep, where I will rejoin my king." He lifted his eyes toward the ceiling. "Oh, Gahagar. I did not fail you."

Lint frowned. "How could you fail a dwarf who has been dead for years?"

"When he sent me here, it was to protect a secret, which I have done. It was also so I might be ready should the world require my talents one last time. In this, I have achieved my greatest creation."

Ian had to know. "What is it?"

"When we get to my workshop." The dwarf leaned so heavily, he would have collapsed had Ian not been at his side. "I will show you."

As Ian walked the elderly dwarf across the room, Lint circled them like an excited pup. "What is it? I need to know! Please tell me. Is it a magical staff? Or maybe a wand? Oh. Could it be a crown that would make Ian king of all magic?" He yipped, his voice even higher. "Oh! I know. I know. It's magical boots that allow Ian to walk on water."

Ian interjected before the brownie tossed out another idea. "Why would I need to walk on water? How does that help anything?"

"You could then run across the sea."

"And go where?"

"How am I supposed to know? I haven't been anywhere other than the Vale and the places you've taken me."

Choosing not to prolong the pointless conversation, Ian fell silent.

When the trio crossed beneath the archway, Parsigar gestured weakly. "That workbench."

Ian turned and headed toward the workbench with a chest made of dark wood and black metal bands resting upon it. Rather than having a rounded top, as Ian was used to, this chest was flat on top and had sides that rose only a handspan above the workbench surface. It was two feet wide and almost as deep.

With Ian's help, Parsigar slid onto the stool beside the workbench. The old dwarf groaned with his eyes closed.

"Are you well?" Ian asked. "Can I get you anything?"

Parsigar opened his purple eyes and slid his spectacles up to the bridge of his nose. "No. I am merely gathering my strength of will."

"For what?"

"Open the box."

Butterflies swarmed through Ian's stomach while he stared at the chest. As Lint had expressed out loud moments before, his mind raced at the possibilities of what the box might contain. He reached for the clasp, which lacked a lock. His fingers flipped it up as the other hand lifted. The lid creaked as it rose. Light eased into the felt-lined, shadowy interior to reveal something unexpected.

The object was made of silver bands, each about two inches wide and twice the length, all interconnected in a loop less than three feet in circumference. The loop was incomplete, two ends meeting but not connected. Curious, Ian reached for the object, wrapped his hands around it, and lifted it out. It was far lighter than expected, the links clanking together as he turned from the box and toward the daylight coming through the windows.

Gems of various colors were mounted to the object with one in the center of each link. The gems and silver links gleamed in the light, and although Ian now held the old man's creation and admitted that it was a thing of beauty, he had no idea what it was or how to use it.

"What is this thing?"

"I call it the Girdle of the Gifted."

"Girdle?" Ian frowned. "You mean like women's undergarments?"

"I suppose, but you wear it around your waist. It was made for you."

Lint laughed. "You are to wear women's undergarments?"

Ian frowned. "Can we call it a belt instead?"

Parsigar shrugged. "I suppose it doesn't matter what you call it."

"Alright. What does it do?"

"Ah. We have come to the heart of the matter." Parsigar closed his eyes and lowered his head. A long silent moment followed, and for a beat, Ian feared the old dwarf had passed. As he lifted his head, he asked, "What occurs when naphtha is thrown on a fire?"

"The fire burns much hotter."

"Now imagine if a dozen barrels are dumped onto a bonfire."

"It becomes an inferno."

"This is what the girdle will do for your magic."

The idea of having his magic boosted as the dwarf described filled Ian with longing to test it out. "What must I do?"

"You simply replace your sash with the girdle. The end links clasp together in the back."

Excited, Ian set the belt back down in the box and began untying his sash.

"There is one last thing," Parsigar said. "Before the girdle is finished, I must give myself to it."

Ian froze. "What?"

"Dwarf magic comes from within. To perform it, a dwarf must give a small piece of himself. This is true for stone shapers, metal wrights, and healers. For spell wrights, it requires more significant sacrifice, for it places a great strain on our life energy, and my life force wains."

"What are you saying?" Ian dreaded the answer.

"This act is one I will not survive."

His heart sinking, Ian shook his head. "No. You cannot do this."

"I can and I must." Parsigar reached out and put his hand on Ian's. His touch was cold, his hand shaking. "I have lived far longer than my peers. Everyone I knew is gone. I should have passed many years ago. I welcome it. I have been blessed with the opportunity to give this gift to the world, to give you hope. Do not feel sad for me. I do this of my own free will."

Despite the old dwarf's words, a tear tracked down Ian's face. "What will happen?"

"The girdle will be finished, as will I."

Ian cleared the lump from his throat. "What about your body?"

"Perhaps you can return me to Ra'Tahal so I might be buried with my king?"

"Yes. Of course."

"May the gods grant you strength to do what must be done, young man. It was an honor to meet you."

The dam broke and tears streamed down Ian's face. "I will ensure the world knows about your sacrifice."

"No." The dwarf shook his weary head. "My role is intended to

THE DARK LORD'S DESIGN

remain omitted from the history books. In this, I am content, as I was when I helped Gahagar rise to wield his famed sword." He turned toward the belt and stroked it. "It is time to complete my greatest creation. In this, my heart is full."

The dwarf wrapped his hands around the belt and closed his eyes. The gems in each link began to glow. Red, amber, yellow, green, blue, and purple light bloomed around the belt, the aura growing brighter and brighter until Ian was forced to shield his eyes. A hum arose, joined by a vibration, causing the tools, vials and other objects littered across the various workbenches in the chamber to rattle. The hum rose to a crescendo that made Ian's head buzz. Then, the chamber fell silent.

Ian lowered his arm as Parsigar's limp body toppled from the stool to land on the floor with a heavy thump. He did not move.

Lint, who stood beside Ian, whistled. "Now that was something to see."

When Ian knelt beside Parsigar and lifted the old dwarf's wrist, he felt no pulse. Sorrow clung to him like a heavy weight, threatening to drag him down, but in his head, he heard Parsigar chastising him. *Do not spoil my sacrifice. It was my time and my choice. Honor it, as you honor me.*

He wiped tears away with the back of his sleeve, stood, and approached the workbench. Upon it lay the belt, the gems dull and lifeless once again. He removed his sash, his robes falling open as he reached for the belt. With both hands, he wrapped it around himself and connected the clasp. He then spun the belt around so the clasp was in the rear and the largest link, the one with a ruby the size of a healthy strawberry, was centered below his navel. Ian pulled his robes tight beneath the belt and turned to Lint.

"How do I look?"

The brownie frowned while examining Ian from head to toe. "Other than your puffy eyes, you appear as a mighty magic user should."

Ian wiped the last of the tears away and opened himself to his

327

magic. What used to be a simple stream now raged like a massive, roaring waterfall. His breath came in gasps as he staggered, his head buzzing as if he were drunk. The sensation was akin to the first time he had used his magic but ten times as bad. He felt like he was aboard a ship in rough waters, his stomach churning as the room tilted. Overwhelmed, he fell to his knees and began to vomit.

After a minute of retching, the world stabilized and his nausea eased.

Lint patted Ian's hand, which rested on his knee. "Are you well, now?"

"Yes. It is just a bit much."

"I hope you don't do that when it is time to fight. Things might go poorly if you are on your knees and puking while surrounded by enemies."

Ian nodded. "I will have to ensure that doesn't happen." He climbed to his feet and wiped the sweat from his brow. "Time to visit Ra'Tahal. Korrigan will see that Parsigar receives a proper burial."

With the sitting room of his tower in Ra'Tahal firmly envisioned, Ian used a trickle of the magic filling him and crafted a gateway, which was typically a taxing spell. In this case, it consumed an imperceptible amount of his energy and still the portal flared open to twelve feet in diameter – twice the usual size. The lower edge of the portal sliced through the stone floor while the sides cut a workbench in half on one side and split a pedestal in half on the other. The table collapsed and the pedestal pieces toppled in opposite directions.

"Oops," Ian said to himself.

Lint looked up at him. "Are you trying to show off?"

"Actually, I was holding back."

"You might want to be careful next time." Lint walked right through since the bottom rim of the portal was somewhere below the floor.

Ian followed and discovered that the oversized portal had cut into his sitting room floor but had, luckily, avoided destroying any furniture.

Turning back to the gateway, he formed a shield in the shape of a horizontal disk and slid it beneath Parsigar. Under Ian's control, the disk raised the dwarf off the floor and carried him through the opening.

Ian dismissed the gateway, walked over to the curved staircase leading to the tower's upper reaches, and shouted, "Winnie! I am home!"

CHAPTER 37
SHATTERED

A gong resounded, waking Shria-Li. Again, it rang out. She waited, praying it would not ring a third time, for that meant Havenfall was under attack. The gong rang again.

She bolted out of bed and made straight for her balcony, where she tore open the door and stepped outside.

The pale light of dawn illuminated the sky but the sun had yet to crest the horizon. The clanking of armor came from below as a string of guards ran along a path and faded from view. A moment later, a screech came from somewhere above.

A trio of griffins flew over the palace, each with the head, wings and forelegs of an eagle, the rest of their bodies appearing much like an oversized werecat. The creatures were as big as a wagon and notoriously fierce. More worrisome, they were meat eaters and would only attack elves if they were hungry.

The monsters disappeared behind the Tree of Life as they flew toward Havenfall's business center. Shria-Li stared into space while she recalled being the target of a griffin attack a year prior, when Safrina had asked to see the barrier and the Vale beyond it. They had been lucky to survive the attack and would not have if three Valeguard warriors had not been close by at the time.

The chill of morning caused her to shiver, for she was dressed only in her shift. Knowing there was nothing she could do, she headed back inside and made for her bathing room, where she stripped down, and began to wash. The attack, with monsters breaching the barrier, could not be ignored. The incursions had become more and more common, raising concerns among the populace. The citizens of Havenfall would need assurances from their ruler, but with their king gone, that role fell upon the queen. Given how her mother had been behaving, Shria-Li was doubtful that she would respond without assistance. *Mother will need me at her side. I will be there to give her strength.*

Dressed in her finest gown, a circlet of golden leaves nestled in her pale blonde hair, Shria-Li knocked on the door to the royal quarters.

No answer.

She glanced at the guards stationed in the corridor. "You are certain the queen is inside?"

"Yes, Your Highness. She has not left since the king departed."

That statement caused instant concern. "Did she at least eat yesterday?"

"She did not eat breakfast or anything else during my shift. I was told that servants brought dinner last night, but she chased them off immediately."

"Still?" As far as Shria-Li knew, her mother had not eaten since her father departed, three days earlier.

"As of yet, no breakfast has come today."

Concern for her mother caused Shria-Li to push protocol aside. *I have given her time to grieve.* She walked in and looked around but the room was empty.

"Mother?" Her voice echoed off the high ceiling.

After a beat without a response, she descended the short run of stairs and made for the royal bedroom. The rapping of her knuckles echoed in the spacious chamber. Silence. She gathered herself, opened the door, and slipped inside.

The royal bedroom was actually three interconnected rooms, each separated from the neighboring space by a row of marble pillars. The first area consisted of a sitting room with a divan, a sofa, and a pair of lounge chairs, all padded with cushions covered in dark green velvet. The sitting area surrounded a stone fireplace bracketed by stained glass windows, their beauty a footnote to the chaotic mess.

The sofa and chair cushions had been slashed, leaving piles of white feathers everywhere. Shria-Li's passing stirred feathers on the floor as she crossed the sitting area and came to the bathing room.

A sunken pool surrounded by flagstone occupied a windowed alcove to her left and a wall of wardrobes to her right. Positioned at the center of the wardrobes was a vanity, the stool beside it tipped over, the oval mirror above the vanity shattered. A brush, a bowl, and jars of makeup lay scattered across the floor.

Once past the bathing area, Shria-Li came to the final space. To one side was another divan, its cushions shredded even worse than those in the sitting area. On the opposite wall was an oversized bed with twisted wooden posts at its corners, the posts interconnected with a web of vines. Green, sheer cloth panels draped down from the vines, vaguely obscuring the mattress, covers, and the bed's occupant.

Shria-Li approached the bed. "Mother?"

Tora-Li groaned. "Go away."

Stifling a groan, Shria Li said, "There was an attack. Didn't you hear the alarm?"

"I don't care."

Shria-Li's frustration boiled over. She tore the curtain aside and found her mother curled up and hugging a pillow. "Didn't you hear me?

Monsters broke through the barrier and entered the city. You are queen. Your people need you."

Tora-Li began to cry. "How did my life come to this?"

"I don't know, but you must put aside your grief and find a way to move forward."

"People whisper in the corridors and the streets of Havenfall. They laugh behind my back. They blame me for Fastellan breaking his vows."

"Blame you?"

"I should have done more. I should have kept him happy. Had he found what he needed in this bed, he would not have gone seeking another." She bawled, "How could he do this to me with a human?"

Shria-Li frowned. They had reached the crux of the issue. She knew her mother viewed humans as inferior – something far less than an elf. For many years, Shria-Li had felt similar, but Ian and Safrina had both done much to alter that perception.

"I understand that you are hurt and maybe even embarrassed, but you must overcome the pain and put your pride aside. You can mope and cry later, but now, you will get dressed and go out to lead your people."

"I can't do it alone."

"You need not do it alone." Shria-Li bent and slid an arm beneath her mother, helping her sit up. "Come. I will help you. When you are ready, we will go to the throne room together. I will be at your side the entire day."

Tora-Li nodded weakly, turned her lower body, and slid her legs off the bed. It would be a long and trying day, but Shria-Li was determined to see it through. *Get to tomorrow and we will see how she feels.* One question remained. *How many tomorrows will be required of me?*

A PAIR of guards marched down the corridor ahead of Shria-Li and her mother. Another pair trailed them as they stepped outside to a flagstone courtyard. An umbrella of tree branches thick with golden leaves provided shade and left the area cool despite it being early afternoon on a sunny day. A palanquin made of ornately carved wood and white cloth with gilded trim sat waiting, surrounded by four brawny humans and an elf with a stiff posture and a whip on his belt.

The elf stepped forward and bowed. "Greetings Your Majesty, Your Highness. The palanquin is prepared as you requested."

Shria-Li waited a beat, but when it became clear her mother would not reply, she took control. "Thank you, Espertan, Take us to commerce plaza straightaway."

Espertan frowned. "Are you certain that is wise, Your Highness?"

Shria-Li turned toward a female guard with a curled rune on her breastplate. "Lieutenant Phusi-La. Did you not tell me that the monsters have been dealt with?"

"Yes, Your Highness. They are dead."

Shria-Li turned toward Esperatan. "To the square. Now."

Tora-Li walked over to the palanquin, pulled the curtain aside, and sat.

Thankful she did not have to drag her mother, Shria-Li ducked into the seat across from her and allowed the curtain to drop closed. The human porters lifted the palanquin to their shoulders and they were off. As she rode in comfort, Shria-Li reflected on the long, difficult morning, most of it consumed by getting her mother dressed and ready for the day. Thrice, the process was waylaid by her sobbing and her return to wallowing in self-pity.

By the time they arrived in the throne room, a line had formed outside it. Each petitioner asked questions pressing the queen on the same subject. *Has the barrier failed? Are we doomed? Will more monsters attack? Can you keep us safe? My home is destroyed. Where will I live?* Rather than deal with such questions with calm and grace, the queen lost her temper and began to berate the crowd. Shria-Li interjected and demanded the throne room be cleared before things got any worse. A heated conversation had ensued with Tora-Li threatening to retreat into her chambers for the rest of the day. Shria-Li insisted that she must do something to ease the worries of her citizens, and in lieu of reopening the throne room, she suggested that a public appearance might be just the thing. Now that they were on their way to the commerce center, she found herself plagued by doubts.

She looked at her mother and found Tora-Li staring numbly into space. *She is unwell. How did this happen?*

Leaning forward, Shria-Li put her hand on her mother's. "All will be well. Have faith."

"Faith?" Tora-Li shook her head. "Faith in what?"

"In yourself. In your people. In your god."

She laughed. "My god? Where was he when my husband broke his most sacred commandment? Now, the Sylvan have no king. The barrier is failing. Your ability prophesized the end of our people. Well, the end is here, and it is because Vandasal has abandoned us."

The statement caused Shria-Li's jaw to drop. She stammered, trying to figure out how to reply, how to deal with someone in such a dark place. Her mother's words were heresy, and if the high priestess heard them, she would likely have an apoplexy and then faint away dead.

The palanquin ceased jostling, was lowered, and was gently set down on the ground. Without hesitation, the queen pulled the curtain aside and climbed out. Shria-Li followed and straitened her dress. She was completely unprepared for what she saw.

Smashed carts, broken wagons, fruits, vegetables, and spilled grain covered the northern portion of the square. Amid the mess lay the torn and bloody corpses of eight humans and three elves. A griffin lay among them with dozens of arrows sticking out from its head, wings, and torso. Turning from the grizzly scene, Shria-Li found more bodies of both humans and elves scattered across the square. Three corpses lay face down in the fountain in the center of the square, the water turned red. Just strides from the fountain was another griffin, this one with a spear through its throat and a broken one jutting out from its hind quarters. Shocked and numb, Shria-Li crossed the plaza and headed toward the ruins of the apothecary.

The human workers she had seen the day before now lay dead. Vacant eyes stared into space, their clothing and flesh shredded. Blood stained the alabaster stone block around them. The body of a griffin lay on top of a female Valeguard warrior, her armor scratched, her helmet lying beside her bloodied head. When Shria-Li's stomach recoiled, she covered her mouth and stumbled in the opposite direction. She gagged and tears tracked down her face. Dozens had died, turning it into the most violent day in Havenfall in a very, very long time. Then, she lifted her gaze and found people crowded in the streets connecting to the square with armored guards holding them back.

Shouts rang out, calls filled with anger and fear. People questioned their safety. They demanded answers and reassurances that such an event would not happen again. Shria-Li could not blame them. She turned, seeking out her mother. Tora-Li stood over the fountain, her expression unreadable as she stared into the crimson water.

As she approached the fountain, Shria-Li called out. "Mother." There was no reaction. When she reached her mother's side, she touched her arm. "Mother. These people are afraid. You must say something to ease their fears."

"How could this happen?"

"We have known that the barrier was failing for some time, now."

"Why is this happening to me?"

"To you?" Shria-Li frowned. "People died, Mother. Fathers, daughters, brothers, sisters, mothers and others have lost their loved ones."

Tora-Li spun around. "This is your father's fault."

"Father? He is not even here."

"Exactly. He abandoned us."

It became clear that her mother was not going to address the crowd, so Shria-Li turned and crossed the square. She took position a dozen strides from the center street and raised her arms. The crowd quieted.

"The queen wishes you to know that she is greatly saddened by what has occurred here. Good people died today. Her sympathies go out to those who lost their loved ones. She understands that you are afraid. She will meet with the Valeguard and together, come up with a plan to ensure this does not happen again.

"If you wish to volunteer to help in the recovery of this disaster, remain here, because your assistance will be needed and appreciated. The queen urges the rest of you to return to your homes. Embrace your loved ones and show them strength to ally their fears. When there is more information to share with you, the queen will craft a declaration and ensure it is properly disseminated. May Vandasal watch over you. Have a good day."

Shria-Li turned from the crowd and crossed the plaza, ignoring the shouts and questions that chased after her. She made straight for her mother, took her by the arm, and escorted her back to the palanquin.

"Get in," Shria-Li's tone left no room for argument.

Thankfully, Tora-Li did as instructed.

Shria-Li then turned to the palanquin commander. "Espertan. Take us to the Vale overlook."

He blinked. "Are you certain, Princess?"

"Yes. Not only must we meet with Captain Rozenne, but we must also display strength. The confidence of our people is shaken, and a visit to the overlook will show them that the queen is not afraid." In response to the troubled look on his face, she added. "Do not worry. The Valeguard will be there to protect us."

She climbed into the palanquin, again sitting across from her mother. Rather than meeting Shria-Li's gaze, Tora-Li stared at the curtains, her thoughts obviously far more distant. The palanquin shook as it was lifted. A rhythmic jostling followed, indicating that they were off and heading toward the overlook.

"Mother."

No reaction.

"Mother. I need you to listen."

Tora-Li's eyes shifted toward Shria-Li.

"We are going to visit the barrier. You needn't even speak when we get there. However, I need you to get out of the palanquin and show no fear."

"Why would I be afraid?"

"I..." Shria-Li frowned. "You just visited the scene of a massacre. I was worried how that might make you feel."

"I feel...nothing." She resumed staring into space.

The remaining five minutes of their journey consisted of silence so awkward it bordered on torture. The jostling stopped, followed by the sensation of the palanquin being lowered. Once it settled, Shria-Li leaned forward, gripped her mother's hand, and squeezed.

"You can do this, Mother. As I said, you merely need to make an appearance. You are queen. Project a regal image. I will speak with the Valeguard." Without waiting on a response, for she doubted there would be one, Shria-Li stepped out and held the curtain aside as her mother joined her.

A hillside covered in waist-high shrubs stood to one side of the palanquin while bare, open ground ran from the shrubs to the edge of terrifying drop, a good distance away. A line of branchless tree trunks towered over the drop. The base of each was at least a dozen feet in diameter, and the trees thrust up into the sky like spears pointed toward the heavens. The trunks, each hundreds of feet tall and imbued with an ancient enchantment, ran parallel to the cliff edge, covered the width of the island, and continued along the top of the escarpment for as far as the eye could see in both directions.

A trio of Valeguard warriors approached with a male elf in the center leading them. The leader removed his helmet and shook his brown, shoulder-length hair. Damp, dark curls clung to his forehead and temples.

Shria-Li addressed the male elf. "Captain Rozenne."

"My queen," Rozenne dipped his head. "Princess."

Tora-Li only stared back in response.

"Listen, Captain," Shria-Li sought to take control of the situation and draw attention from her mother. "We have just come from the commerce center."

Rozenne grimaced. "It was a grizzly fight. We lost two Valeguard and three city guards before killing those beasts."

"You did not mention two dozen citizens."

"Well, thankfully most were slaves and can more easily be replaced."

It was Shria-Li's turn to grimace. "Slaves or not, they are members of our society. Their lives hold value same as that of anyone else."

"Yes. Well, we did our best, but the griffins flew past our line of defense and reached the city center before us. By the time we got there, it was carnage."

She turned and looked up at the nearest barrier post. "Did the barrier not even slow them?"

"It did not."

"Why?"

"Because, sometime last night, the spell failed completely. I fear it will never return."

She spun toward him. "The barrier is gone?"

"It is."

Her heart sank. "So, we are vulnerable."

"And we have no idea how to revive the enchantment."

"What are we going to do?"

"I fear we must reevaluate our defenses. We may need more guards and should reconsider how we deploy them."

"More guards? From where?" Recruitment had already been low with fewer births in recent generations.

"These are questions the queen must consider."

Shria-Li turned to talk to her mother but discovered she was not there. She then spotted Tora-Li walking along the cliffside and heading toward the southern falls. Cupping her hands to her mouth, Shria-Li shouted. "Mother!"

Tora-Li continued walking as if she had not heard a word.

Considering her mother's troubled state of mind, worry clutched at Shria-Li's chest. "Oh, no." She walked toward the woman and shouted over her shoulder. "Rozenne! Help me!"

Her walk turned into a run, her skirts in her hand as her strides grew broader. Time seemed to slow and she felt as if she were running through knee-deep muck. Her slippered toe then struck a root jutting up from the ground, and she fell forward. Her hands struck first, slid along the ground, and left her palms scraped. Rozenne appeared at her side and helped her to her feet.

"Thank you," she said while bursting back into a run. "Mother!" Her shout rang out, and although Tora-Li was still a few hundred feet away, there was no way she did not hear it. Still, the queen displayed no sign of acknowledgement.

The rush of the falls rose above Shria-Li's own gasps and grunts. The noise grew louder until she slowed to a walk. By then, her mother was standing out on a rock shelf and peering over the Vale. No more than twenty feet from her position, the falls gushed over the edge. A thousand feet below, the water splashed into a lake at the base of the sheer, rocky cliffside. A river flowing from the lake meandered along the floor of a lush, green valley that stretched many miles to the east and west. To the distant north, the inner sea defined the horizon. Despite its beauty, the Vale was a place of great danger, which Shria-Li was aware of as much as anyone.

"Mother," she called out.

Without turning from the view, Tora-Li spoke, her voice barely audible above the roar of the falls. "I was young and unsure of myself when my parents died. Rather than attempt to rule on my own, I agreed to marry your father. He promised to always put the good of our people first, but he refused to promise that he would love me. I thought, given time, we would grow closer and would bond. I hoped your birth would solidify our marriage, but he refused to open himself to the idea of loving me. Perhaps I was to blame as well, for the wall between us hardened over time, rather than eroding. Then, came his dalliances. He remained discreet and pretended those trysts did not exist, so I did the same until that human girl came into our lives." She spun around and shouted. "With a human! How could he?" Her voice echoed over the Vale. Her face turned up toward the sky. "Vandasal! I call upon you to curse my husband, for he has betrayed our marriage, he has abandoned our people, and he has violated the laws of our race, which you gave to us so long ago. Curse him to a life of endless self-hatred! Make him regret his actions and the harm he has caused!" Tora-Li lowered her chin, her eyes meeting Shria-Li's. "Pray for me. Rule well. Guide our people in their time of need."

She took two steps backward and dropped out of sight.

"Mother!" Shria-Li screamed.

The shock holding her frozen lasted only a few seconds. She then rushed over to the rock ledge, slowed, and peered down. Many hundreds of feet below, the mist of the falls swirled in the air. Of her mother, there was no sign.

Her legs gave out, and she fell on her side. The dam burst and tears started flowing. Shria-Li cried and cried. Never had she felt so alone.

CHAPTER 38

JOY

"Mistress!"

Rina opened her eyes to afternoon sunlight streaming through the window. She rubbed the sleep away and called back. "Yes, Harriet?"

Hurried footsteps came from the stairwell. The chambermaid appeared in the doorway to Rina's bedroom. "Mistress," she panted. "I am sorry to wake you."

Sitting up and smoothing her hair, Rina reassured the woman. "It was time for me to wake anyway. I cannot nap the entire afternoon away." Half awake, she stifled a yawn.

Harriet frowned. "You may wish to make yourself more presentable."

"Why?"

"That is what I wanted to tell you. The guards at the gate sent word. Someone comes up the trail."

The fog of sleep instantly evaporated. Rina shot out of bed and rushed to the window.

Her room on the fourth floor of the south tower offered an easy view beyond the castle wall. Beyond the chasm, through a gap in the rocks below the neighboring mountain peak, she spied a horse ridden by a figure in green and gold armor. Her heart leapt for joy.

"It's him!" Rina stared out of the window, unable to remove her gaze.

"His Majesty?" Harriet asked from behind her.

"Fastellan returns." When Rina spun from the window, she noted the woman's frown. "I mean, King Fastellan, of course."

"Yes. Well, in that case, do you have any orders for me, mistress?"

"I assume his room is ready?'

"I cleaned it the day he left. As far as I know, nobody has stepped foot inside since."

"Go and make sure. You may wish to open the window and door as well. This place grows musty quickly."

"Good idea, Mistress."

"Also, stop by the kitchen and let Gus know that the king is here. He has probably been on the road for two and a half days and will be expecting a meal of substance. Tell Ned to hurry down and help the king with his horse and armor."

"As you wish, Mistress." Harriet rushed out of the room and down the stairs.

Rina closed the door and turned to the mirror. Her dress was wrinkled, her long, golden hair untamed. She moved closer and inspected her eyes to ensure they were not puffy. Satisfied, she tore off her dress, made for the wardrobe, and chose a blue one, recalling how Fastellan had commented on how it matched her eyes. Before donning the dress, she wet a washcloth and scrubbed her armpits and other areas that required such attention. She then opened a small vial given to her by Miral. It smelled of Lilac, and when Rina dabbed a bit of the liquid on her wrists and behind her ears, so did she. The dress, once slipped on, was secured by laces in the back. It was tight around her slim waist and rounded hips and a little loose on her modest chest. She then grabbed her brush and stroked through her hair with vigor, tearing through snarls like a powerful wind forcing grasslands to bend to its will.

When finished, Rina set the brush on her vanity, spun toward the mirror, and inspected herself, turning this way and that. Satisfied, she burst from the room and rushed down the curved staircase. Her feet moving as rapidly as she dared, she sped down the stairs and then crossed the common room at a hurried walk. She opened the front door and stepped outside.

A cool breeze balanced the warmth of the afternoon sun. The castle gate was closed, the four guards on duty guarding it as always. A wooden building with a sloped roof hugged the wall to her left. The wide door to the building stood open, the stall inside empty. Outside the building, a chestnut stallion stood with its head in a trough.

Ned, the tall, broad-shouldered castle porter, rose from a kneeling position, his head appearing above the stallion's flank. He set a pair of green shin guards into a cart, the armor clanking against the breast-plate sticking out from the cart. A male with long, platinum hair emerged from behind the horse and rounded the cart. The moment Rina saw his face, her heart leapt and a smile bloomed. He smiled in return and her heart soared. Only through practiced restraint did she remain on the stairs as he approached. She drank in his stunningly handsome appearance – chiseled jaw, golden eyes, broad shoulders with a lean torso – and pinched herself to ensure she was not dreaming.

Fastellan climbed the stairs, stopped before her, and cupped her cheek. He leaned forward, his lips met hers, and her eyes slid closed. The kiss was soft and gentle at first but then he pulled her close, and the passion in their connection exploded. Her head swam in sea of bliss.

When he pulled away, her heart thumped like a drum, her breath coming in gasps. She realized Ned was staring from the stables, as were the guards at the gate. Somehow, she wrangled her jumbled thoughts into line and spoke.

"Others are watching," she whispered. "What of propriety?"

"I will hide my love for you no longer."

"Love?" Hearing the word from him sent her spirits to entirely new heights. "What of your duty?"

"I shed my duty. I do not intend to return to Havenfall."

The gravity of his statement struck her. "You abdicated?"

"I am king no longer. Tora-Li rules alone. The strings she had tied to me have been severed."

Rina mentally sorted through the stunning turn of events and its impact on her. "What about us?"

He smiled, and somehow, her joy doubled. "We will live here. Together. I shall give you my bond, but first, I must eat." His hand slipped around hers. "Come. Dine with me. Let us begin our life together."

Floating on a cloud of unbridled happiness, Rina allowed him to escort her back inside Shadowmar Castle, their new home.

A BEAM of late afternoon sunlight shone through the window at a flat angle, illuminating the castle's common room. Empty plates and bowls and baskets with leftover food littered one end of the long dining table. Rina set her fork down and sat back, her stomach sated, her heart still elevated far above the white mountain peak that overlooked Shadowmar Castle.

Fastellan sat in the chair beside hers and finished the last of his steamed vegetables. He then used his bun to soak up the remaining gravy from his plate before popping it into his mouth. A drink of wine chased the food down. An empty chalice joined the other dishes on the table. His gaze shifted to meet Rina's, and she again felt that flutter in her chest.

"That was much needed," Fastellan said. "I pressed hard during my journey from Havenfall, for I was anxious to see you...to be with you in full." He reached across the table and held her hand. "Rather than assume, I must ask."

"Ask what?"

He slid off his chair and dropped to one knee, her hand still in his as he stared into her eyes. "Safrina Miller. Will you give yourself to me? Will you be my partner in life? Will you accept my bond?"

She wiped away tears of joy. The words burst from her mouth without thought. "I will. With all my heart, I will."

Rising to his feet, he pulled her from her seat. "Come."

They crossed the common room and climbed a curved staircase. Rina found herself caught between the thrill in her chest and the disbelief in her head. After the better part of a year of longing for this moment, it had arrived, something she wondered if it were even possible.

On the third and uppermost floor of the main keep, they followed a corridor deeper into the castle. At first, she wondered where they were going, but as the rooms slid by and only one chamber remained ahead, she realized their destination. Anxiety swirled in her stomach as he drew her through the doorway and into a dark room from which came the sound of flowing water.

Fastellan activated a lantern dangling from a hook near the doorway. Light bloomed to reveal a chamber carved from the mountain itself. Water ran down a rock wall at the rear of the chamber spilling into a pool cut into the rock. A marble column with a metal rod in its core jutted up from the center of the pool. A wooden shelf with towels resting on it stood near the doorway while a row of hooks stood beside it.

Without a word, Fastellan began to undress, beginning with his tunic, which he tossed to the floor. Her eyes slid down his lean, muscular torso as he removed his belt and dropped it onto the pile. His boots came off. His breeches followed. When he removed his small-clothes, Rina blushed and turned away after realizing that she was staring. The sound of water splashing came from the pool. She turned back and found him in the waist-high water.

"Are you going to join me?" he asked.

Despite her beauty, Rina had never been with a man. Yet this was no man. He was an elf. He was a king. *A king no longer*, she told herself before adding, *if this union is to be, you must give yourself to it*. Pushing beyond her anxiety, she reached back and began unlacing her dress. Once done, she slid one shoulder free, and then the other. The dress dropped to the floor. She gathered the skirt of her shift in her grip and raised it up, over her head. Finally, she pulled her small clothes down and kicked them aside. Her gaze lifted to meet his. Rather than judgement, disappointment, or worse, desire filled his eyes. Emboldened, she approached the pool and stepped down into the water. It was cold, but with each step she took toward the center, it grew warmer. By the time she reached him, it could have been considered hot.

He cupped her chin, bent and kissed her. "Fear not, my flower. I will never bring you harm."

"I...don't know what to do."

A smile turned his lips up. "I will guide you. Together, we shall become one."

He took her hand and placed it over his heart. "Do not move this hand."

His hand slid up her torso, the motion giving her a quiver of pleasure. When it was over her heart, he held it in place.

"Close your eyes and open yourself to me," he crooned.

Rina did as instructed, having no idea what to expect. A strange sensation came from his palm, a warmth beginning in her chest and spreading throughout her body. A tingling followed, and then, a presence bloomed in the back of her mind. It was soft at first, but slowly grew more intense. From the presence came raw emotion. Love. In that love was the heat of desire. Her entire body began to shake. She gasped as waves of pleasure washed over her. His lips met hers. She melted into them, and they were one.

CHAPTER 39

APOLOGIES

I an secured the belt Parsigar had created around his waist and tucked his midnight blue robes in so they were smooth on his lean frame. He turned back toward the bed and met Winnie's emerald eyes. "I am sorry. I must go."

"Can't you stay one more night?"

It had been a wonderful night that began with love making, followed by tears about Parsigar's death. Then, Ian had fallen into a deep and peaceful sleep that took him beyond daybreak. Rested and armed with the Girdle of the Gifted, he was as ready as he would ever be. Now was the time to act.

"In truth, I should not have stayed last night." *You must be strong, Ian,* he told himself. *You cannot allow her to lure you back to bed.*

She pushed the covers aside, stood from the bed, and sidled up to him. Her hand began at his stomach and slid up his torso, toward the gap in his robes. "This tower is so lonely when you are away." Leaning in, she kissed him, her lips warm and soft.

Despite his body demanding otherwise, Ian pulled away. "Listen. I would love to do nothing but spend the day and night with you. In fact,

I'd spend night after night in this tower if I could wake each morning with you in my arms."

She grabbed his hand and placed it over her heart, the silk of her shift a thin layer between his palm and her supple flesh. "You can, Ian. Stay."

His pulse thumped in his ears, and his body reacted. It was even more difficult to remove his hand than it had been to end their kiss. "I cannot be so selfish. My abilities make me responsible for those who are more vulnerable. Something is coming. Something very bad. I know what I must do, and I believe I have the power to stop it." He gave her a sad smile. "It would be selfish for me to stay, and in doing so, I would doom us all. I fear there is no hiding from this evil. We must expunge it or we will all perish."

"Why you?"

He sighed. "I have asked myself that question often over the past year and keep coming to the same answer. Destiny, fate, the gods themselves, whatever it is, something chose me." The moment he said it, he realized the truth. "I guess Truhan chose me. Was that choice made so I might fight this evil that plagues our world, or was it for something else?"

She shook her head. "I don't know."

Ian touched her cheek. "I did not expect you to answer. The question is for my master, if I ever see him again."

Winnie frowned. "I don't trust him."

"Why not?"

"He keeps too many secrets. And the way he uses you seems unfair. If he knows so much, how come he sends you to do his bidding?"

Such thoughts had crossed Ian's mind, but he often dismissed them because Truhan promised to help him master his abilities. Yet, hearing the words aloud and spoken by someone else brought him additional clarity.

"Those are questions he must answer." He glanced toward the east-facing window. A narrow beam of sunlight shone through a gap in the curtains and painted a stripe of light along the opposite wall. "The sun has crested the city wall. The day advances, a day filled with tasks for me to complete."

"Where do you go, now?"

"I must return to my brother. He and Revita are likely worried about me. Then, I visit Shria-Li. She must know what I plan before I seek out our enemy."

"This enemy you speak of. Who or what is it?"

Ian considered telling her but he did not wish her to worry any more than she was already bound to do. "I cannot say, exactly. However, I now have the power to deal with this enemy and a plan as to how to get it done. Know that I do this for you, for us, and for the poor souls that this evil preys upon." Silently, he added, *I will save you, Mother. I swear it.*

He leaned in, kissed her one last time, and went for the door. "I am off to find Lint. I will return when I am able."

"I love you."

The words lifted his heart and brought him a smile. Unlike the previous time, he had no trouble replying in kind, "And I, you." He opened the door. "Be well until I see you again."

Ian descended to the kitchen, checked it and continued down when he found it empty. Upon reaching the ground floor, he called out, "Lint! It's time to go!"

A clay jar on the bookshelf wobbled. Curious, Ian approached as the lid popped up, slid aside, and fell onto the shelf.

The brownie's head rose from the opening. "It's about time."

"What are you doing in there?"

"I was bored and thought I would see what it was like to sit in a dark jar."

"Why?"

The brownie climbed out and slid down the round belly of the jar to land on the shelf. "I just told you. I was bored."

Ian considered asking again but thought better of it. He lifted the lid and leaned in to cover the jar. A nasty odor greeted him. "What is that smell?"

Lint shrugged. "I thought the jar would work well as a privy."

"What? Why?"

"I have to go somewhere you know. It's not like this place has a shrub I can use."

"Well, this jar just became unusable." Capping the jar, Ian lifted it from the shelf. He walked it over to the trash bin by the desk and set the jar in it. "I am leaving. I hope you are ready."

"I am always ready but help me down first."

When Ian returned to the shelf and held his open palm out, Lint stepped on.

"Hold still." Ian cracked open his block against magic. Even then, enough flowed into him to cause his head to buzz. He then crafted a small gateway, having learned his lesson from the last one. The minimal effort required to do so made him curious as to the boundaries of his newfound strength.

Ian stepped through and dismissed the gateway before heading across the Chamber of Testing. Before he even made it across the room, Vic and Revita emerged from the connecting tunnel.

"Ian!" Vic exclaimed. His voice quickly shifted from surprise to anger. "Where were you?"

As he continued toward them, Ian explained, "Lint and I made a visit to the Tower of Solitude."

"How dare you?!" Revita thrust her finger in Ian's face.

"I..."

She crossed her arms and scowled while tapping one foot on the floor. "In case you didn't realize it, you left without notice and did not tell anyone where you were going or when you would be back." Her arm thrust out, her finger pointing toward the exit tunnel. "Without you, we have no way of leaving this place other than marching across the Agrosi. Had we given up and left before you returned here, we'd have an entirely different set of problems."

"I..." Ian tried to reply but was sharply cut off by his brother.

"You were gone for almost two days!" Vic covered his eyes, visibly trying to calm himself before dropping his hand. "Do you know how worried I was? You can't do that to me..." He glanced at Revita. "To us."

Ian looked down at Lint, who still stood on his hand.

"Don't look at me," Lint shook his finger at Ian. "I just came along because I was bored."

With a sigh, Ian squatted, set Lint down and stood to meet his brother's stern gaze. "You are right, Vic." He had not fully considered how it must have been for them. "I didn't expect to be gone for so long." He drew a deep breath, trying to steel himself and keep his emotions in check. "Lint and I went to see if Parsigar was finished with the item he was crafting. When we got there, we found him in bad shape. In fact, I feared he was dead at first. When he stirred, he bade me to help him to another room, where he showed me this." Ian tapped on the belt around his waist. "To finish it, he had to give the object energy that would cost him everything. When he did so, he...he died."

"What?" Vic shook his head. "That's horrible."

"Horrible is how I felt about it, but Parsigar insisted. He only asked that I see him buried with his king in the catacombs beneath Ra'Tahal. Of course, by then it was mid-day because time moves so differently in the tower than it does elsewhere."

Revita frowned. "I forgot about that."

"Yes, well, per Parsigar's wish, we visited Ra'Tahal, where I met with King Korrigan, who insisted I stay to participate in the ceremony to honor their Paragon. By the time it was finished and we laid Parsigar to rest in the crypt below the Hall of Ancients, the sun was setting. I considered returning here at that point, but I did not wish to sleep alone, so I spent the night with Winnie." Ian shook his head. "I can see how you not knowing where I was or when I would return would have been worrisome."

"Worrisome?" Vic snorted. "I wish it would have only been worrisome."

A squawk alerted Ian, but not soon enough. A winged creature burst from the tunnel and sped toward him without slowing. Lionel struck Ian in the chest, the impact causing Ian to stumble and fall. He landed on his back and slid a few feet before coming to a stop. The drake folded its wings in and furiously licked Ian's face while a surge of excitement came through their bond.

"Easy," Ian laughed and tried to shield his face with one hand but the drake nosed his hand aside and resumed licking. Thankful for the affection but deciding there was only so much he could take, Ian pushed Lionel back. "Yes. I am happy to see you, too." He sat up and stroked Lionel's back, but the drake was too excited and continued to twist and squirm. "I guess this is what I get for leaving you."

Revita said, "He should have bit you."

Ian cradled Lionel in one arm while rising to his feet. "You sound like you would like to bite me."

"I am considering it."

"As I said, I am sorry. It was not..." Ian stopped as Draxan and Ahni emerged from the tunnel.

Draxan nodded and gestured toward Vic. "I told you your brother would be fine. You need to show patience. All things come with time."

Ahni grunted. "Says the elf who has lived for thousands of years."

The elf frowned. "Yes. I can see how you humans, who live such brief lives, might feel more anxiety about such things."

Ian held Lionel toward his brother. "Take him, so he doesn't try to follow me."

Vic asked, "Where are you going, now?"

"Havenfall. I need to meet with Shria-Li."

Draxan stroked his jaw. "Havenfall was no more than an Elvish settlement on a river island when I last visited."

Revita whistled. "In that case, if you ever visit there, you will be in for a surprise."

Ian braced himself as he prepared to share the rest of his plan. "I think it best if the rest of you remain here."

"What?" Lint exclaimed. "But..."

"No." Ian shook a finger toward him. "This will be a tricky thing. I can't afford for you to cause trouble."

Vic grimaced. "You had better have a good reason for leaving us behind."

"I have many reasons, the first being that you don't speak Elvish well. In addition, this is not a visit for pleasure. I need to warn the elves to prepare for battle."

"You think the army has made it that far south?"

"Not yet, but that will soon change."

His brow furrowed, Vic asked, "How do you know?"

"I...cannot say." That was a lie. In truth, Ian did not want to say it aloud. To anyone. "Unlike the last trip, I intend to see this through and be back before nightfall. I need you five to eat, rest, and be ready. When I return, we begin our search for the demon and his army."

CHAPTER 40

CROWNED

The throne room in Havenfall Palace teemed with energy. Following the abdication of their king and death of their queen, the Sylvan people were eager to see a new queen crowned. At least, that is what High Priestess Valeria told Shria-Li before walking out of the adjoining antechamber and striding out toward the dais. Shria-Li approached the doorway and peered through, careful to remain in the shadows.

Thousands of elves filled the seats that formed the half circle around the dais. More stood along the outer wall, hoping to witness an event that occurred once or twice in a lifetime, even for elves who lived for centuries. Armored palace guards stood at the base of the dais, their expressions grim. There had not been much to smile about as of late.

Valeria followed an aisle along the rear of the chamber, climbed the dais stairs, and stood in its center. The aura of the trees and thrones cast a golden halo around her while sunlight streamed down through windows in the dome above, completing a scene of inspirational right-eousness. Despite her squirming stomach, even Shria-Li was moved by the imagery, for Valeria appeared as if she were touched by the hand of Vandasal himself.

The priestess raised her golden scepter, a two-foot-long rod of twisted branches that formed a globe at one end. The scepter flared with bright, golden light and sent a sparkling burst across the chamber. The crowd quieted even as the light faded.

"People of Sylvanar. Today, we gather not to mourn Queen Tora-Li, but to celebrate her life and the sacrifices she made to ensure our peace and prosperity. Tora-Li now sits at Vandasal's side, and for that, we are thankful.

"However, her death leaves a vacancy that must be filled with one who has been anointed as heir, and it must be done with alacrity. Given the challenges we face, here in Havenfall and elsewhere in Sylvanar, we require a leader of intelligence, courage, and charisma. Today, we crown such a person, for she has been trained to rule since birth. She was lost for a time, stolen away from us until the hand of Vandasal himself led her back to us so she would be able to assume the throne in our time of need. Shria-Li, please approach the dais."

With a breath of courage, Shria-Li smoothed her white gown and strode out. The sensation of having thousands of eyes focused upon her was impossible to ignore as she descended the sloped floor. Upon reaching the dais, she rounded it and stopped before the center aisle, where she climbed the stairs. As instructed, she stopped two stairs below the top.

The high priestess gestured. "Please kneel."

Shria-Li knelt on the top stair.

Valeria smiled down at her. "Do you, Shria-Li, give yourself to the people of Sylvanar? Do you agree to guide them through challenges, regardless of the odds? Do you dedicate yourself to steer them toward prosperity? Do you guarantee them everything in your power to ensure victory? Do you give everything of yourself to Vandasal, so he might imbue you with the wisdom and grace required to ensure a better future?"

In a surprisingly clear, firm voice, Shria-Li replied, "I do."

"By the grace of Vandasal, I hereby crown you, Shria-Li, queen and absolute ruler of Sylvanar."

The high priestess closed her eyes and lowered the scepter. When it touched Shia-Li's head, light flared in a burst of golden sparks. When the light died, a crown of golden leaves rested upon Shria-Li's head.

"Rise!" Valeria commanded. "Rise, Queen of Sylvanar!"

Shria-Li stood, climbed the dais, and continued past Valeria, not stopping until she reached the twisted, golden staff standing between the thrones. She gripped the staff. It bloomed with golden light and sang out to her, begging her to use its power. When she raised the staff above her head, the light brightened like a star awakening. The crowd burst into cheers and they began chanting her name.

After a night filled with sorrow and tears, the moment was shockingly inspiring not only to the crowd, but to Shria-Li herself. Her heart soared, and for the first time in over a year, she experienced the thrill of unbridled hope.

SHRIA-LI CLIMBED into the same palanquin she had ridden in with her mother a day earlier. This time was different. This time, she was alone with the curtains removed, leaving it open at the sides. The title of queen came with responsibility to her people. For them, she was determined to project strength, to inspire confidence in her people.

The porters lifted the palanquin to their shoulders. A call rang out and a column of armored guards armed with spears marched down the road leading from the palace to the rest of the city. The porters followed the armored warriors. Last came the Valeguard, dressed in armor in the warm color of dwarven steel, their winged helmets and shock lances making them distinctly different from the warriors in blue. The train of hundreds marched out, into the city. The moment the palanquin reached the edge of the palace grounds, Shria-Li found elves and humans lined up along the roadside, watching for her. Hoping to inspire them, she smiled and waved. Some smiled back. Some waved. Many did not. Frowning jawlines and fearful eyes were far too common.

The parade continued across the city, reached the western edge, and turned down another street. Again, they crossed the city beneath the mid-morning sun. Shria-Li grew warm, her brow damp with sweat, yet she smiled and waved. Anything she would ask her people to endure, she would endure as well.

Through the city, past homes, shops, gardens, and squares, they marched. The parade entered the commerce center, packed with citizens and full of life, marking a stark contrast to the grizzly scene from Shria-Li's last visit. Despite the bloody, disturbing images haunting her, she maintained her smile and waves. Blessedly, the square was soon behind her, allowing her to concentrate on anything else other than those who had died in the griffin attack.

They wound past buildings, golden trees, and green foliage before passing the fountain that fed the city's aqueducts. The parade then entered a path leading toward the golden tree that towered over all else on the island city. The shrubs bordering the path parted to reveal the palace garden. Per tradition, once introduced to the people of Havenfall, the newly crowned king or queen would visit the palace garden and pray before the Tree of Life, the most sacred symbol of Sylvan culture.

The column stopped with the palanquin positioned beside a short path leading to the pool that surrounded the tree. The porters lowered the palanquin and set it on the ground. Shria-Li climbed out, stood upright, and gave Espertan a nod of thanks. With all eyes on her, she began down the path when a ribbon of light split the air. The ribbon opened until it became a circular window to another place. A person in midnight blue robes stepped through. The portal disappeared with a pop.

"Ian?" Shria-Li muttered in surprise.

The warriors filling the garden, their numbers north of two hundred, reacted with weapons drawn while the Valeguard warriors nearest the palanquin rushed past Shria-Li. In response, Ian thrust a hand toward them. The snap of bows came from further out as dozens of arrows were loosed, every one of them bursting into pieces just before reaching Ian's outstretched hand.

"Stop!" Shria-Li cried.

The Valeguard warriors standing between her and Ian froze rather than attacking.

"Ian," Shria-Li said. "What are you doing here?"

"I came to talk to you. Why are they attacking me?"

She closed her eyes and took a deep breath. "Lay down your weapons. He is a friend." As the warriors before her lifted the tips of their lances toward the sky, she slid between them and approached Ian. "I apologize for their rash behavior. Your timing was poor. They were merely trying to protect their queen."

Ian looked left and right. "Where is your mother? I owe her an apology."

When Shria-Li tried to reply, the words caught in her suddenly dry throat. Ian's image blurred as tears formed. Overwhelmed by the sense of loss she had yet to fully comprehend, she lunged forward, wrapped her arms around him, and wept.

CHAPTER 41
A TROUBLED REUNION

Adozen palace guards escorted Ian and Shria-Li along a palace corridor. Considering how long and hard she had wept, Ian knew that something bad had happened. Rather than press her, he had just held her while enduring the stares from a garden full of elven warriors. Her sobs had tugged on his heartstrings while the quiet audience had created an awkward discomfort. When the tears ceased falling and Shria-Li had regained her composure, she had ordered the Valeguard to return to their barracks before addressing the palace guard.

The guards in the lead stepped out onto a terrace, separated, and took position to the left and right of the entrance. Shria-Li walked between them with Ian a stride behind and still confused as to what was occurring.

The second story terrace overlooked the eastern end of the palace garden, the golden trees overhead casting it in shadows. As Ian crossed the terrace, the memory of his last visit came to him. He recalled sitting with his brother, Revita, and Shria-Li as they shared a nice breakfast with Queen Tora-Li. Then, King Fastellan walked in and Ian had reacted poorly, voicing accusations that would have been better expressed in private rather than in front of servants and palace guards. Those accusations, right or wrong, had been hurtful for the queen and Shria-Li, whom Ian considered a friend. Ashamed of how he had behaved at that moment, Ian told himself to do better. Considering how she had responded upon seeing him, something troubled Shria-Li and she needed his support.

Ian pulled out a chair beside Shria-Li, who settled in at the head of the table.

"Have you eaten yet?" She asked.

"No."

"Are you hungry?"

He considered how best to answer. "I could eat if you wish to."

She gestured toward the door. A guard nodded, turned, and walked off.

Shria-Li turned back to Ian. "I don't know why you are here, but I am happy to see you."

Again, Ian considered his response and tried to focus on her feelings. "It is good to see you as well, although your sorrow pains me. Is there anything I can do?"

Her gaze dropped to the table. "You just being here is enough."

"What happened?"

"Four days ago, my father left Havenfall. He abdicated his throne. He will not return."

"What?" Ian pushed past his shock. "Why?"

"Since…" Her eyes flicked toward him and away again. "Since Safrina, the relationship between him and my mother had soured and seemed to grow worse by the day. My mother was hurt, and she took that out on him until it became too much, so he left her. He left all of us."

The sting of regret left Ian's mouth dry and his stomach churning. *This is my fault.*

She reached out and rested her hand on his arm. "This is not your fault, Ian. The fault lies with my father. It was his choice alone to break his vows."

"Still, if I had not said..."

"The issue would have come up eventually, with or without your involvement."

He appreciated her trying to ease his conscience, but the guilt plaguing him refused to relent.

"There is something else, something worse." Her voice cracked with the last word.

"Worse?"

"The situation did more than hurt my mother. It broke her."

Oh, no.

Shria-Li took a deep breath before she continued, "During the days after my father left, she remained locked in her chamber. I hoped that time alone might allow her to work past her sorrow. Instead, I fear it allowed her to slip into a much darker place.

"The city experienced a griffin attack yesterday morning. I forced my mother to come with me to view the scene. My hope was to reassure the people of Havenfall with a public display of resilience in the face of tragedy. To reinforce that message, we then visited the Vale overlook to inspect the barrier. While there, my mother..." She covered her mouth as her eyes teared up. "She leapt off the cliff."

It took a beat before Ian fully realized what had occurred. He had climbed the escarpment. The drop from the top was terrifying. The image of Tora-Li flailing as she plummeted flashed in his imagination. Surviving such a fall would not be possible.

Shria-Li sobbed, dried her eyes with her fingers, and wiped her nose with her forearm. Seeing her cry like that and having lost his own parents, Ian was overcome with empathy. The guilt at having played a role in such a dark series of events was too much. Tears emerged despite his efforts to avoid them. He covered his eyes with his hand and fought to regain control. After a full minute, his emotions had calmed enough for him to wipe his eyes and look at her.

She stared into space, her red and puffy eyes a contrast to her graceful nature, white gown, and golden crown. It suddenly struck him.

"You are queen."

Shria-Li nodded. "I was crowned earlier today."

He then recalled the griffin attack. "And the barrier?"

"It has failed. Other than the escarpment itself, the city has no protection from the monsters who roam the Vale."

A bell rang in the corridor. A male elf holding the bell emerged, crossed the terrace, and stood a few strides from the table.

"Your meal is ready, my Queen," he said in Elvish.

Shria-Li nodded. "Please, Westalin."

The elf rang the bell again. A trio of human servants, two females and a male, emerged with food, drink, and tableware on platters.

Her composure fully regained, Shria-Li said, "Enough of this troubling talk. Let us eat and you can tell me what has happened since I last saw you."

Ian was thankful to discuss anything else, so he eagerly launched into his tale, giving himself time before he revealed the real reason behind his visit.

THE MEAL and discussion with Shria-Li were cathartic. Not only was Ian able to help her understand what he had gone through since last seeing her, he weaved in numerous side stories that brought her laughter and him smiles. In addition to Lint's antics, he finished off by sharing a recent escape featuring his pet drake.

"...and then, Lionel scurries through the cook's legs. The poor old dwarf woman thought he was attacking. She stumbled, fell backward, and the bowl of apple compote went flying directly at me. I ended up on the floor as well, but with my head and upper body covered in apple slices and sauce."

She chortled. "That must have been a sight!"

"Yeah. Even though I was angry at the time, I'll admit it is quite funny to look back upon now."

Her laughter calmed, she asked, "Speaking of Lionel – where is he? From what I have seen, he usually follows you around like a second shadow."

"I left him with my brother and Revita. He wasn't too happy about it, but I thought it might be best to avoid any possible misunderstandings. Considering the situation I stepped into in the palace garden, I feel good about that decision."

"Yes. It was likely for the best."

Ian picked up his fork and absently pushed the uneaten food across his plate while he gathered his courage. He had shared much of his tale with Shria-Li, all but the most critical aspects. "There is more I must tell you."

"Is this where you share why you came to Havenfall?"

"It is."

She frowned. "Whatever it is, you are afraid of how it will affect me."

"Am I so transparent?"

"You've been here for two hours, yet you haven't touched upon the subject. Your story led you to Murvaran, but you did not reveal what you discovered while you were there. I think I can safely assume your visit was not simply so you could battle an ogre and a wyvern."

"Yes. Well, when I entered the heart of the temple, I met H'Deesengar, the demon lord who was imprisoned there. The same demon lord mentioned in the Dark Lord's journals. I discovered that a rival demon lord is at the root of the evil we face. I also learned that demon lords consume souls, which fuel their magic. Each enemy he faces makes him stronger. In fact, H'Deesengar claims that this new demon lord could soon rival or exceed the power of a god. He is already likely to be immune to my magic, and he drives his horde of orcs, who are reputedly fueled by insatiable hunger."

This statement had Shria-Li fully engaged. "Do you believe this to be true?"

"Based on my visions, I do."

"Is there nothing we can do to stop him?"

"H'Deesengar claims there is one thing. Should a demon lord be filled with too much life, he will become vulnerable.""

"What?" She frowned. "Does he wish to allow this fiend to kill and consume the souls of entire cities? How many deaths would it take to reach such a level?"

"I don't know, but based on the conversation, it might require hundreds of thousands of lives to be lost before reaching that point."

"That is horrible."

"I agree. However, there is an alternative."

"What alternative?"

"There is something else he could consume that is filled with life, something other than human, dwarf, or elf souls."

Her eyes narrowed in thought, widened, and she turned to look at the giant tree across the palace grounds. "You cannot," she gasped. "My people..."

Ian reached out and gripped her hand. "It is the only way. If I don't try, how many will die?"

She looked at him with horror in her eyes. "You are asking me to risk my people and to sacrifice something as sacred as our very existence."

"This is why I came to you before initiating my plan."

Shria-Li shook her head. "You cannot do this."

Ian pressed his lips together and weighed sharing a secret for the first time. "I must do this."

"Why? There must be another..."

Ian blurted something he had feared to voice, "The demon consumed my mother's soul."

She blinked. "What?"

"My mother was badly burned in a fire. I tried to use my magic to save her, but I don't even know if healing is something I can perform. I did the same thing I did with Lionel, only she died in the process. At least, her body died."

"What does that mean?"

"Her spirit remained with me, bonded as Lionel and I are bonded. Only, when I was in a prophetic dream and she was at my side, the demon lord appeared and caught her, but not before she forced me out. I woke, and she was gone. I fear...I know her soul was consumed by this monster. To save the innocents of not only Havenfall, but all of the world's cities, I must defeat him. I only pray that the souls he has consumed are then free to move on to the afterlife."

Shria-Li sat back with her hand pressed against her forehead. "I don't know how to process this."

"It is a lot. I know. Trust me, I wish none of this were true."

"What do you intend to do?"

"I plan to find this dark army and challenge the demon lord. When he comes for me, I will craft a gateway and run."

"To Havenfall."

"Yes. To Havenfall."

She sat back and chewed on her lip while staring into space. "The barrier has failed. My people are no longer safe here. Now, you wish to turn our city into a trap."

"There is no other way. I am sorry."

Her eyes closed for a long, silent beat before opening. "Give me two days."

"Every day I wait, more innocents die."

"That might be true, but my people deserve a chance to survive as well, especially considering the sacrifice you are asking of them."

Ian nodded. "That, they do." He considered the request and realized he had another issue to address in the meantime. "It might take me that long just to locate this monster. Alright. I will return at sunset the day after tomorrow. Do what you must to prepare in the meantime."

"We will prepare as we must. What do you need of my warriors?"

Ian rubbed his bearded jaw in thought. "I suspect monsters will flood the city in the process, and while they may be deadly, they are a distraction from our primary foe. I will bring them to the big square in the middle of the city. When the demon comes through, I will bait him to follow me. Keep your warriors out of my way and have them ready to defend against the orc horde. That is all I ask."

"I will ensure it is as you request."

He stood. "I should leave. I have much to do as well."

Shria-Li stood, approached, and hugged him. In a soft voice, she said, "Thank you for being my friend. Thank you for warning me, so I might save my people."

He hugged her back. "I give my friendship to you freely because you have proven worthy of it. Despite all else, I had no choice but to come and see you before I proceed." When Ian stepped back, she wiped her eyes once again. "Be well, Queen of the Sylvan. I will see you in two days. I only pray this gambit brings us victory against the rising darkness."

Hand extended with the intent to cast a gateway, Ian staggered. The world around him twisted, warped, and darkened. He pressed his palm against his forehead as his surroundings faded to mist. When the fog cleared, he found himself on a castle tower, high above the world. A frantic battle took place in the courtyard below. The world shifted, and the battle was over, the courtyard littered with corpses. That's when his vision turned into a nightmare.

CHAPTER 42

SHOCK

In her new room, which she shared with Fastellan, Rina sat before an oval mirror, humming to herself as she brushed her hair. Late morning light coming through the open balcony doors filled a chamber twice the size of her old room. Despite the sunlight, a soft mountain breeze coming through the open balcony doors kept her cool. In fact, it felt perfect.

She mused about her time with him since their bonding. An evening of passion preceded a most restful night of sleep. Best of all, she reveled in the memory of waking in his arms, the two of them lying together for over an hour before climbing out of bed to break their fast. Talk of their new future together accompanied the meal before Fastellan left to send word to his guards and the castle staff. Now dressed and finished taming her hair, Rina set the brush on her vanity, stood, and stepped outside.

The balcony faced south, the drop below it terrifying. To her left, a sheer cliffside rose up hundreds of feet while the third floor of the castle stretched out in the other direction. The southern wall of the castle yard was visible beyond the tower at the front. These elements were foot-

notes to the main attraction – an expansive view consisting of mountains to the south and forests to the east, the trees broken up by fields
and winding rivers before fading into the fog of distance. While the
view was breathtaking, Rina only had eyes for the other person
standing on the balcony.

Fastellan turned toward her and smiled. "You look ravishing, my
flower."

She beamed. "You flatter me."

"There is no longer need for me to hide from the truth, so it comes
freely."

He stood in a green doublet, tightly fitting his torso with puffy
shoulders and golden leaves sewn down the outside of each sleeve. The
gold matched the color of his eyes.

"You cut a handsome figure yourself, my love."

His hand slid around her lower back while he bent and kissed her.
Their lips brushed against each other once, twice, thrice. He then
looked into her eyes. "It is time. Let us go and address the staff."

A nervous twinge sent her stomach swirling. "I am ready, so long as
you are at my side."

He lifted his gaze past her, his smile turning to a frown. "It looks as
if a storm is coming."

Rina spun toward the dark, ominous cloud above the mountains
south of them. "Strange. I don't know how I missed that when I stepped
outside."

"It will be here soon, which is all the more reason to deal with the
staff straight away.

He took her hand and led her back into their bedroom. They made
straight for the door, followed a corridor toward the front of the building, and descended the stairs below the south tower. At the ground
level, they found nine elves and three humans waiting. Eight of the
elves were guards, while the ninth was Miral, a female cultivator who
had traveled from Havenfall with Rina to take up residence at the castle.

The humans consisted of the chambermaid, cook, and porter. Only the four guards posted outside were required to complete the attendance of the castle staff.

Fastellan spoke in the bold, strong tone of someone used to leading others. "Thank you all for meeting us here. Let us move outside, so the guards on duty may join us. I prefer to address you all as one."

Rina, with her hand still holding Fastellan's, crossed the common room alongside him and stepped outside. The rest of the staff followed as she and the former king descended the stairs and crossed the castle yard, passing a sunken garden while on their way toward the castle gate. As they drew near, Fastellan gestured toward the guards, the ones on the wall making for the stairs, while those standing inside the gate approached. In moments, everyone was together with sixteen pairs of eyes on Rina and her beau.

"Good citizens of Shadowmar, I thank you for joining me in this new mountain home. You agreed to come here under the pretense that this would be a new stronghold for the Sylvan people. More importantly, you did so with me requesting your presence as your king. The situation has changed, and with that change, I wish to offer you the choice to remain or to return to Havenfall." He paused and delivered the news. "I have given up the throne and passed rule to Queen Tora-Li."

Worried looks passed between the guards and staff, but Fastellan forged ahead.

"I am no longer king, and no longer her husband," Fastellan continued. "I have nullified those vows, for our union was under the stipulation that I would enter it simply to guide her and help her rule the Sylvan people. She now has the experience, strength, and wisdom to do so without me. The two of us never bonded, but we did provide our people an heir as was our duty. With my duty fulfilled, I have shed the crown in pursuit of my own life as a free citizen." He lifted Rina's hand to his lips and kissed it. "Now that I am free to follow my heart, I have chosen Safrina to be my partner in life. We have bonded. This castle is our home, where we rule together. However, this is a large estate. We cannot care for it or protect the castle and its inhabitants on our own. If you agree, we would welcome you to remain here and serve us. For your service, you will receive a fair wage. It is a simple life, but it could be a good one without the pressures and hectic lifestyle you find in Havenfall."

Again, the elves and humans exchanged looks. Some of the elves appeared quite troubled while others seemed contemplative.

Fastellan said, "I will give you some time to consider your decision. Whatever it may be, you have my gratitude for all you have done here." He turned to Rina. "Will you escort the staff back to the palace? I will remain and brief the guards before they complete their shift change."

She smiled. "I will see you soon." Turning to the staff. "Come along. If you have any questions, I will be happy to answer them."

Rina headed back toward the castle and cast a glance toward the ominous cloud. The three human staff members followed while Miral sidled up beside Rina.

"Pardon, Mistress," Miral said. "I have a question to ask."

"I will answer the best I can."

The female elf appeared troubled. She glanced at Rina and hesitated before speaking. "This is…awkward."

Rina stopped shy of the stairs leading to the castle entrance. "I have nothing to hide, Miral. Ask your question. As I said, I will answer the best I am able."

The three humans stopped two strides away. Miral cast a glance toward them before asking in a timid voice. "What do you know about Vandasal?"

"He is your god."

"And what do you know about his scripture? The commandments he set down to the elves and dwarves who worship him?"

Rina shrugged. "In truth. I know very little about those things."

Miral kneaded her hands. She was reserved by nature, but this was something beyond her shyness. "According to Vandasal, it is forbidden..." Her eyes flicked side to side, as if she sought a place to run and hide. "It is forbidden for an elf to...to...to be with a human."

Rina frowned. "That doesn't make sense. Humans and elves live together all across Havenfall."

"No. I mean...in bed."

Her inference abruptly became clear. Rina recalled the strange stares of the past day. She thought it was because they believed Fastellan was still married and was betraying his wife. Now, she realized that there was something more, something deeper. By bonding with her, Fastellan had crossed a line drawn by his god.

"I did not know," Rina said. "Is this the first..."

She was cutoff when a lightning bolt crashed down and struck a pillar at the corner of the castle yard garden. The boom of thunder shook the ground, the thump of it reverberating in her chest. Everyone staggered and spun toward the column as it toppled over. The marble column struck the stone tiles and cracked with chunks skittering across the ground. A swirl of smoke came from the location of the lightning strike. The smoke cleared and a figure in white robes stood in its place. A pale blue glow surrounded the male figure, who was facing in the opposite direction. He had long, gray hair and a beard to match, his posture stiff and fists clenched.

"Fastellan!" A male voice boomed.

The former king stood before his guards, stunned and unable to respond.

The robed figure strode toward Fastellan. "You have much to answer for."

Fastellan's jaw worked, but no words came out at first. In a shaky voice, he asked, "Vandasal?"

"Yes!" His voice was like thunder. "I am your god, a god you chose to betray, just as you have betrayed your people and your wife."

"I did not..."

"Do not lie to me!" Vandasal stopped three strides from Fastellan. "You broke your vows. For that alone, you deserve punishment, but when you soiled the purity of Sylvan blood by lying with a human, you have broken your contract with your god. For that, you will suffer for eternity." He pointed toward the castle. "You wish to spur your responsibilities and hide in this remote location? So be it. I curse you to wander Shadowmar until you die. Furthermore, you will never age and your flesh will be impervious to attack. For millennia, you will haunt this place. Alone."

The god raised his arms to the clouds, which began to swirl. Spinning faster and faster, the clouds formed a funnel that shot down and engulfed Fastellan.

Held fast in shock and horror, Rina could not speak or move. She told herself that she was stuck in a dream and demanded that she wake, but the nightmare continued.

Screams came from the funnel, its dark, smoky exterior masking its captive. The screams grew louder and deeper until they became raging growls from something inhuman. The funnel began to dissipate until it was gone. The dark mist faded to reveal a figure on one knee. It rose to stand upright, its height twice that of the nearby castle guards. It was a thing of horror.

The creature's head was that of a bull, as was its body from the waist to its hooves. The torso and arms appeared to be that of a massive, muscular man. The monster that was once Fastellan lifted its face to the sky and roared. *A minotaur.* Rina had heard fireside tales of such a creature, the kind of stories meant to frighten children. Now, the love of her life had become a monster.

The minotaur lowered its gaze to meet that of the god standing before him.

"So, it is done." The anger was gone from Vandasal's voice, now replaced by sorrow. "I wish this tale had ended otherwise." He dropped his head and his form blurred into mist until he was gone.

THE DARK LORD'S DESIGN

The minotaur roared again, turned and burst toward the nearest guard. The monster lifted the elf like he weighed nothing and threw him thirty feet. The elf struck the castle wall with incredible force and fell to the ground. He did not move.

The other guards reacted, those with bows in hand, drew and loosed. The minotaur stood only strides away, yet the arrows careened off its body as if it were made of stone. Six warriors gripping spears charged in at the same time. The spear tips skittered across the monster's flesh, leaving little more than scratches. The minotaur grabbed two spears and lifted, flipping the spear bearers up into the air. They lost grip of their weapons and fell to the ground. With broad, wild strokes, the monster attacked. The spear butts clanged off helmets and dented armor, felling half of the guards in seconds.

Ned ran toward Rina and gripped her arm. "We must get inside."

Miral and the other staff members rushed past and through the front door. Stunned, Rina glanced over her shoulder as Ned dragged her up the stairs.

Across the castle yard, the frantic fight continued but only four of the elven guards remained upright and backed away while watching the minotaur tear an arm off one of their comrades. That was the last scene Rina witnessed before she was dragged inside the castle.

CHAPTER 43
INTO OBLIVION

Rina backed from the closed castle door, unable to think, unable to act. Shouts, roars, and screams came from outside. She did not believe it was real. It could not be real. The love of her life could not be a bloodthirsty monster.

Ned slid the bolt in place, locking the door. He then ran past her, to the sofa. "Gus. Grab that end. We will move this against the door."

The two men lifted the sofa, carried it across the room, and set it down with the back against the doors. They immediately began stacking other pieces of furniture, building a barrier. By the time they finished, the noise outside had stopped.

Miral ran over to the window and drew the curtain aside. She gasped in horror. "Oh, no. Please, Vandasal. Why?"

Harriet cried. "What's wrong?"

"The guards are down. The monster...it is coming this way." The elf woman dropped the curtain and backed away until she collided with the dining table.

A boom shook the door. It held. A second boom followed, joined by the crack of wood as a split appeared near the bolt.

"Weapons!" Ned shouted as he ran toward the storage room. "We need weapons."

Another strike shook the door, the crack broadening, the pile of furniture moving a few inches. The next blow caused the wood to split wide, snapping off a section of the thick, oak door. A gap appeared. Ned ran out of the storage room, carrying an axe and a sledgehammer. He gave the latter to Gus.

"Get ready. If any part of the monster comes through, we attack."

The men – one well over six feet, with broad shoulders, the other six inches shorter but his portly build making him the heavier of the two – took position about ten feet from the door. Harriet grabbed Rina by the arm and pulled her toward the rear of the chamber. The room fell quiet, the silence filled only by their ragged, fearful breaths.

The door blasted open, and the massive, horned bullhead burst through. The momentum sent the pile of furniture flying, striking both Ned and Gus, causing the porter to spin and stumble off to the side while the cook went sprawling and slid across the floor. The minotaur stood inside the doorway, roared, and lifted a fallen chair. It stomped toward Gus, who rolled and tried to get to his feet. The chair came down on his head and drove him face-first to the tile. The monster tossed the splintered remains of the chair aside and turned toward Rina and the other two females.

With a yank, Rina pulled free from Harriet's grip and walked toward what remained of her lover. "Fastellan. It is me. Safrina. Please listen. I know you are in there, somewhere."

The monster's dark eyes stared at her, and for a second, she thought she saw recognition in those eyes.

Ned rushed in from the side with his axe coming around. The axe head struck the minotaur in the torso with enough power to cut through a four-inch-thick tree. Rather than doing significant damage, the blade merely split the skin and bounced off.

The minotaur roared, spun toward Ned, and lunged. Its hand

engulfed Ned's head. The monster picked him up off the ground with one hand, lifting him until his kicking boots were three feet off the ground. Ned screamed in agony. The minotaur launched him across the room. He struck the wall just to the side of the entrance, his head cracking, his body folding and tumbling to the floor.

The monster turned to face Rina, and when its dark eyes connected with hers, the truth became clear. Nothing of Fastellan remained, at least nothing she could reason with. Her shock slid aside, replaced by the urgent need to survive.

"Run!" She spun and bolted toward the north stairs.

Miral ran after Rina while Harriet headed toward the other stairwell. She never made it.

The minotaur raced after Harriet, grabbed the back of her dress, and lifted her off the ground. It was the last thing Rina saw as she raced up the stairs. Although she could not see Harriet, the woman's terrified cries carried up the stairwell, eliciting horrific images even after her screams were abruptly cut off.

On the third floor, Miral caught up to Rina and grabbed her by the arm. "Let me draw him away from you."

"What? You can't."

"I will find a place to hide." She pointed toward the door to the tower. "You go through that room. It leads to the outer wall. Maybe you can get clear of the castle."

"What about you?'

"Don't worry about me."

Miral shouted into the stairwell, taunting the beast before rushing up the stairs, toward the fourth floor. The monster's roar echoed from below and sounded far too close. Rina darted into the tower room and closed the door.

The room had been used by a pair of guards, the beds cleanly made, the chairs neatly pushed under the table in the middle of the room.

Another door waited at the far side, and she raced toward it, opening it. Wind blasted through the doorway.

Rina grabbed a spear from beside the door, went outside, and pulled the door closed by its looped handle. Inspiration struck. She lifted the spear and slid the butt end through the loop, pushing it until the spear shaft was wedged against the outside of the doorframe. If the minotaur had followed her, it should at least slow the monster down.

Turning, Rina emerged from an alcove and stepped onto the castle wall. The cool, storm-driven wind tugged at her hair and dress. To one side, the castle yard waited over twenty feet below. To her other side, beyond a waist-high outer wall, was a terrifying drop into a deep, rocky crevice.

She hurried along the wall and made straight for the stairs leading down to the castle yard. When she reached the stairs and began down them, the sight of the carnage the minotaur had left behind caused her to stop in shock.

The broken bodies of a dozen elf guards lay strewn across the plaza. With heads and limbs twisted in grotesque, unnatural positions and blood splattered everywhere, it was immediately clear that they were all dead. Struck by the horror of the scene, Rina covered her mouth and fought to keep herself from vomiting. She closed her eyes and tried to erase the images, but they would not dispel. *This can't be real. This can't be happening.*

A noise from the direction of the castle caused her to lurch. Her eyes flashed open and she turned to find the monster outside and coming toward her.

A scream burst from her lungs as she spun and scrambled up the stairs. Her foot stepped on the hem of her skirts and she fell, striking her shin hard on the edge of a stair. Intense pain flared from the bruise, but she fought past it and regained her footing. Limping, she climbed up and reached the top of the wall. A backward glance revealed the monster climbing after her. Panicked, Rina hobbled as fast as she could to the door. She gripped the spear and pulled, but it held fast. Again, she pulled, straining, but it was solidly wedged.

The monster reached the top of the wall and stomped toward her. Desperate, Rina again tried to appeal to the love of her life, hoping there was something left of him to hear her.

"Please, Fastellan," she pleaded while easing toward him. "It's me. Safrina."

The monster stopped a few strides from her, appearing to listen.

"Yes. It's me. Your flower," she crooned. "I won't hurt you. I am your friend...and more."

The monster cocked its head.

A spark of hope bloomed in Rina's chest. "We can be together. I will care for you and will find a way to change you back. You can be normal again."

The beast roared, burst toward her, and grabbed her by the arms. It lifted her until her eyes stared evenly with his.

"Please," she cried.

The monster turned, held her over the chasm, and let go.

A shriek of pure terror burst from Rina's lungs as she plummeted with her face toward the sky. The castle shrank into the distance as she fell deeper and deeper into the gap.

At only eighteen summers, her fleeting life had come to a tragic end.

IAN FOUND himself on one knee, his hand on the ground to stabilize himself as the swirling vision faded away. Although the vision had dispelled, the urgency it conveyed remained with him. A hand rested on his shoulder, and he looked up to find Shria-Li looking down at him, her eyes reflecting concern.

"Are you well?" she asked.

Still on the terrace overlooking the palace garden in Havenfall, he rose to his feet. "I must go."

Ian pictured the image from his vision, cast a gateway, and stepped onto a castle wall overlooking a sprawling courtyard. Twenty feet away stood a towering monster with the head and legs of a bull and the body of a muscular man. The minotaur held a woman above his head, her pale blue dress whipping in the wind. The beast tossed her over the edge and turned toward Ian, its eyes filled with fury as it charged.

In reaction, Ian cast a protective spell and thrust his palm toward the minotaur. The shield smashed into the monster and blasted it off the wall. The minotaur flipped backward as it arced through the air. By the time the beast fell to the castle yard, over a hundred feet away, Ian was already bent over the wall, peering into the abyss, past Rina's falling body. He quickly cast a gateway down at the bottom of the chasm while picturing the top of the wall, right where the minotaur had been standing when Ian first arrived.

Rina fell through the portal at the bottom of the gorge and shot out of the one on top of the wall, straight toward Ian. He cast another spell, this time thrusting a blast of air forward to slow Rina's momentum. Even then, she crashed into him with enough force to launch him off his feet. Hugging her and curling his head in, he fell onto his back and rolled, nearly falling off the wall and into the castle yard in the process. Pain shot through his shoulder and hip, causing him to groan as he lay on his side, holding her.

"Rina?" Ian asked.

Panic struck when she did not respond. He rolled her onto her back and hovered over her while on his hands and knees. He held his cheek before her lips and felt the light whisper of her breath.

"Rina?" Ian softly stroked her cheek.

Her eyes flickered open. "Ian?" She furrowed her brow. "Am I dead?"

"I got here just in time."

"I was falling. I thought..."

"I know."

The sky opened and it began to pour. The rain was cold and noisy as it hammered on the stone ramparts.

Ian asked, "Can you stand?"

"I think so."

He gripped her hand and helped her to her feet. She staggered, and he caught her by the arm, steadying her.

A roar came from across the castle yard, drawing their attention. The minotaur stood, turned toward them, and pounded its chest. It then burst into a run toward the stairs.

"Oh, no," Rina covered her mouth, her eyes in pain. "Fastellan."

Ian put his arm around her. "I am sorry, but we should leave."

She nodded, her tears mixing with the rain running down her face.

Ian crafted a gateway, gently turned her toward it, and helped her through.

CHAPTER 44

A DISTANT CALL

Vic emerged from the tunnel and stood on the mountain slope. He climbed onto a boulder and looked over the rolling plains of the Agrosi. Although it was mid-afternoon and the summer sun shone down on his back, the wind balanced the heat and kept him cool. It was a quiet and peaceful moment, allowing self-reflection and clear, uninterrupted thoughts.

Ian had just returned with Rina after an altogether traumatic experience. She was distraught and could barely speak. Concerned for her, Ian took her to his room and allowed her to curl up in his bed while promising to remain with her for the rest of the day but not before relaying their next task to Vic. They had to locate the demon and his army, and they had to do so quickly. With that in mind, Vic wandered Truhan's underground warrens, mulling over the situation before making his way outside.

We must cover a lot of ground and do so faster than the fastest horse. Traveling using Ian's gateways was incredibly fast, but only if he could firmly picture his destination. The best he could do was take them to Greavesport or to the Valley of Gold. From there, any travel would consist of a series of gateways, each leap limited by how far Ian could clearly see. Determined to figure out a better way, Vic breathed in the fresh air, drank in the tranquil scene, and allowed his mind to work on the problem.

A year earlier, he would have never believed he would be in such a situation. Then again, the places he had seen and the things he had experienced in that time would have been beyond his imagination as well. The events and discoveries of the past year passed through his head – from the magical creatures of the Agrosi to terrifying monsters found in the Vale, from the wild and hectic prison break to storming Bard's Castle, from the graceful elven city of Havenfall to the dwarven stronghold of Ra'Tahal, from the deserted city surrounding Mur Tower to the frozen landscape outside of the Tower of Solitude.

Wait.

He then recalled something that had slipped into the recesses of his mind since their encounter with a mighty dragon. Vic had discovered a giant egg in a heated underground cavern. That egg became his obsession, which drove him to visit it and talk to it numerous times a day until the egg hatched and young dragons emerged. His time spent with the egg had formed a bond with the hatchlings, and through that connection Umbracan had spoken inside Vic's mind. *When the time comes for us to battle, call out to me. I will come. I welcome this new purpose.*

At the time, Vic had replied, *I pray it will not be required, but I would feel blessed to have such a glorious warrior on my side.*

Well said. Be well, Champion. Umbracan had stretched its wings out, flapped them, and lifted into the air.

Although Vic had not seen the dragon since, he now hoped he might see it again soon. Eyes closed, he called out. *Umbracan. We need you. The world needs you.* His thoughts stilled as he waited with his breath held.

Then, a voice echoed in his head. *Champion?*

Yes. It is Victus. We prepare to face the orcs and the demon who leads them.

Demon? Creatures of the underworld do not belong in the world of the living.

You will come?

I will.

You will find me and my companions on the eastern slope of the lonely mountain rising above the Agrosi. Vic imagined the mountain surrounded by miles and miles of grassy plains.

The distance is great, but I will be there when the sun rises next.

I thank you. The world thanks you.

Rest well, Champion. Soon, we go to war.

Champion.

Vic opened his eyes to a dark chamber. Dim light seeped in through the gap below the curtain covering the doorway. Revita lay beside him, the soft, rhythmic whisper of her breaths informing him that she was still asleep.

Champion. Said a voice inside his head.

Yes, Umbracan?

I have arrived. I sit atop a lonely peak. The stars fade. Daybreak approaches.

I will be outside soon.

He sat up and blindly felt in the darkness. His fingers found his breeches, which he picked up. As quietly as possible, he began to dress.

With a waterskin and pack over one shoulder, his mattock and harness over the other, Vic marched along a dark tunnel, guided by the soft purple light of the orb in Ian's hand. Daylight appeared ahead. They stepped out of the tunnel and rounded the boulder that blocked it from view.

We are outside on the eastern slope, Vic sent.

I come for you now.

"Where is the dragon?" Ian asked.

"He was waiting on the mountain peak." Vic turned and peered into the sky above the mountain as a massive, winged creature took flight. "There he is."

Ian squinted toward the creature. "Does Umbracan know what you intend?"

"No. Not yet," Vic admitted.

"And you left Revita without sharing your plan."

"She would have wished to come with us."

"I have no doubt." Ian snickered.

"Why are you laughing?"

"She is going to be pissed at you."

Vic sighed. "I left a note so she would not wonder what became of us, but I suspect she will be quite cross with me."

Ian gave him a sidelong look. "I find it ironic how upset you were when I left you guys behind, and now you are doing the same to Revita, Ahni, Lint, and Draxan."

Lint popped up from the pack on Ian's back. "Ha!" The brownie laughed. "Did you think you could leave without me? I'll not spend another boring day wandering those tunnels."

Groaning, Vic said, "I should have expected you would try something like this."

Lint crossed his arms and thrust his chin out. "But you did not, because Lint is too smart for a dumb human like you."

Narrowing his eyes, Vic said, "Sometimes, I'd like to squeeze the snark right out of you."

"If you do, Mistress Revita will be very cross with you."

Vic sighed. "Fine. You can come along." He thrust his finger at the brownie. "But you had best behave, or I will feed you to Umbracan."

A shadow fell over them as a heavy thump shook the ground. A deep, rumbling voice asked, "Did someone say my name?"

They spun to find the dragon standing on a rock shelf no more than a dozen strides away. Despite having met Umbracan little more than a week earlier, Vic had forgotten how imposing the dragon was.

Standing two stories tall with a body twice the length, not including the tail, Umbracan towered over them. Sunlight shimmered off the iridescent purple scales covering its head and neck while a silver sheen seemed to dance along its black wings and body. Amber eyes with black slits for pupils stared down at them, each eye the size of a watermelon. At the end of a snout big enough to sleep on, the dragon's nostrils flared with each breath.

The dragon opened its maw to reveal teeth the size of short swords. It then spoke. "I have come. Where are the monsters of the underworld?"

Vic climbed the hillside, moving closer to the dragon. "That is why I called for you. We must locate the creatures of darkness quickly. It would take far too long to do so on foot."

"You wish me to search for them?"

"Yes, but we would join you."

The dragon narrowed its eyes and it growled, "You seek to saddle me like a beast of burden?"

The angry reply surprised Vic, and he hastily sought to stave off any misunderstanding. "No. Nothing like that. We would only ride with you to find the dark army as allies, if you will allow us."

"Hmm." The dragon cocked its head. "You are tiny, so it would be of little consequence to carry your weight. I suppose you could find seating at the base of my neck." Umbracan nodded. "Very well." Stomp, stomp, stomp, its massive feet thumped on the rock and shook the ground as it turned. The tail came around and stopped short of striking Vic. "Climb up. Once you are in position, we ride."

After a glance toward his brother, Vic approached a tail as thick as a tree trunk.

"You go first," Ian said as he stopped beside Vic.

"Right."

Vic climbed up onto the tail with one foot on each side of the crest running down the dragon's spine. He then scrambled up, using the crests as hand holds. The crests grew larger as Vic scaled up the monster's back. At the same time, so did the gaps between each crest. By the time he reached the base of its neck, he found he could easily sit between two crests. He slid in and glanced back to see how Ian fared.

Rather than climb up as Vic did, Ian floated above the dragon, came toward Vic, and slid down into the gap behind him.

"That doesn't seem fair," Vic said.

Ian shrugged. "Fair or not, I figured I'd be less likely to fall if I did it that way. To tell you the truth, a spell like that used to be difficult and a bit tiring." He patted the belt given to him by Parsigar. "With this, it takes less effort doing things with magic than it would any other way."

Umbracan bent its neck and looked back at Vic. "Where do we search?"

Ian pointed north. "That way is a city by the sea. We begin there."

The dragon arched a brow, his voice echoing in Vic's head. *What do you think, Champion?*

Vic looked over his shoulder and asked Ian. "How do you know where to begin?"

"The visions I experienced showed me a seaside city under attack. If the horde has not yet reached the sea, we may have a chance to save the people who live there."

"And you think it was Greavesport?"

"If not Greavesport, then we move on to Krotal.

Vic nodded. "In that case, we go north, Umbracan."

The dragon seemed to coil itself as it took a few strides and leapt off a rock shelf with its wings spread. They soared out toward the plains as the mountainside dropped away. A few flaps of its mighty wings took them higher. The dragon banked, turning from east to north. It then flapped its wings, gaining speed as the ground slipped past, thousands of feet below. It was a terrifying yet thrilling experience and one unlike any other Vic could recall. *I am flying on a dragon.*

With the upper half of his body sticking up from Ian's pack, Lint whooped and thrust his fist into the air. "We are flying!"

Vic did not blame the brownie, for it was the most glorious moment of his life.

THE RUSH of flying thousands of feet in the air lasted for a while, but the longer they traveled, the more it began to feel normal, as if Vic had numbed to the experience. The wind whipped his hair and buffeted him as if he were standing against the strongest of storms, and the risk of slipping and falling thousands of feet to an instant and ugly death helped to keep him vigilant. He had no idea how fast they were travelling, but it was far faster than a galloping horse. Perhaps as important, they were able to fly in a straight line, not bound by roads or impeded by the landscape.

They flew over rolling hills and tree-covered mountains until the sea came into view. The dragon then banked east, toward the water and upon nearing the shoreline, it turned north again. A bay came into view, a winding river flowing into it. On the north side of the bay, a city hugged the waterline. Ships occupied a trio of piers jutting out into the harbor.

Vic pointed and shouted. "There's Greavesport."

Ian leaned over Vic's shoulder as they approached the skies above the city. "I don't see any signs of trouble."

Having briefly visited Greavesport the prior year, Vic vaguely recalled the details of the city. Yet, seeing workers on the docks and the streets thick with people, all appeared as one might expect. In his head, he sent a message to the dragon. *Umbracan. We need to continue north-west. Follow the shoreline. Seek out the next city.*

As you wish. The dragon turned northwest and sailed out over the sea.

A ship, its sails full, a white wake trailing it, was heading in the same direction. The dragon caught up to the ship and was quickly past it. Minutes later, the ship was too distant to see.

When the shoreline turned west and the dragon approached the seaside beaches, it turned again. With mountains, trees, rivers and fields to the right and nothing but open sea to the left, they flew toward the ever-changing horizon. An hour after reaching Greavesport and just over two hours after taking flight, another seaside city came into view.

"There!" Vic shouted. "That must be Krotal."

Much like Greavesport, Krotal was nestled on the north side of a river where its fresh waters mixed with the salt of the sea. The city's harbor did not appear natural, for two breakwaters extended from the shoreline like a finger and thumb pinching together to create a narrow gap through which a ship sailed even as the dragon approached.

Also like Greavesport, its only city wall ran along the shoreline, protecting it from a sea attack. The inland borders of the city were undefined with buildings spreading out from the center like the points of a star. The outskirts of Krotal consisted of tree-covered hills surrounding farmer's fields, while the center of the city thrust up in a solitary peak capped by a mighty castle. Citizens milled about the city, the streets thick with wagons, carts, and people on foot.

"All looks well," Ian said. "I don't understand. My vision..."

From Ian's pack, Lint exclaimed, "Look to the north!"

Vic turned his attention toward the northern horizon and spied a cloud so dark, it could not be natural. Despite the distance, the sight of the cloud sent a chill down his spine.

"That is what I saw," Ian said. "The monsters who wish to destroy our world lurk in that darkness."

Vic called out. "Toward the cloud, great dragon. Let us see what trouble awaits."

The dragon flapped its wings, passed over Krotal, and flew above the sprawling forest.

Beyond those trees, evil stalked the land.

CHAPTER 45

HUNTED

Sweat beaded on Arangoli's brow, his feet and eyes heavy, his thoughts lost in a mindless haze of exhaustion. He was not alone. Over a hundred dwarven warriors trailed him as he marched along a gravel road. Some of the dwarves were longtime friends, while most were new recruits to the Head Thumpers. Those dwarves looked up to Arangoli – leader, hero, and the most famous dwarf of his generation. Their faith in him was inspiring but it also came with added responsibility. Determined to keep them alive, he kept on walking despite his body and mind demanding he drop to the ground, curl up, and sleep.

Miles and miles of open grasslands bordered the southbound road. The wind whistled across flatlands and whipped Arangoli's beard about like a drunk squirrel, but that breeze provided little relief from the heat of the sun, for the wind was warm as well. It was mid-morning, and in the numbness of Arangoli's brain, he knew the heat would only grow worse as the day advanced.

He glanced over his shoulder, beyond the column of dwarves,

toward what pursued them. A wall of darkness blotted out the horizon. Within that cloud lurked a host of monsters that chased them with relentlessness. Despite the dwarves foregoing sleep and marching throughout the night, the sun had risen to reveal that the cloud had cut their lead in half. Now, three hours later, the gap had been halved once again. Some teammates had suggested that they run to try and outpace it, but Arangoli would not allow it. Running would only drain their reserves, and if forced to fight, their exhaustion would see them slaughtered. Others demanded they turn and fight but doing so in open flatlands against an enemy with superior numbers was even more foolhardy than running.

A mile west of the road, a herd of bison burst into a run. The stampede raced away from the dark cloud, and Arangoli found himself wishing he and his crew could be riding with the bison. While the gap between the herd and the horde of monsters increased, the dwarves seemed to be steadily losing their lead.

He turned his attention to the dark forest to the south as it slowly drew closer. If they were to fight, doing so among trees offered their best hope. When lacking fortifications or an elevated position to sway the battle in their favor, the forest offered a less desirable advantage but an advantage, nonetheless. They would hide and attempt to attack the enemy flanks as the monsters passed by. It would not stop the orcs from reaching and destroying Krotal, but it might slow them and reduce their numbers...so long as the demon lord did not bring their corpses back to life again.

The march continued south, the trees slowly drawing closer, the summer heat rising as the day advanced. Arangoli glanced up and found the sun still to the east. Although likely only three hours had passed since dawn, it felt like thrice that to his mind and body. A dark shape then appeared in the sky, the sight of it causing him to stop.

"Oof," Rax grunted when he ran into him. "Why'd you stop?"

"Look." Arangoli pointed toward the sky above the forest.

A creature as big as a warship flew toward them, each wing the size of a sail, a long, sinuous tail trailing behind it. The creature's silhouette was unmistakable.

"A dragon!" Pazacar blurted from beside Arangoli.

Rax asked, "Do we run?"

"Run where?" Arangoli asked. "The forest is too far to reach before it reaches us. The grass barely comes to our knees and won't offer any cover. We certainly can't turn and run back the way we came."

Dwarves gathered around Arangoli, all eyes staring toward the legendary monster as it flew toward them. With nowhere else to go, the choice became clear.

"Form up!" Arangoli bellowed. "Shields in front. Ranged weapons to the rear."

Pazacar frowned. "You intend to fight a dragon?"

"Only if we have no other choice." Arangoli took two strides forward, drew his hammer, and glanced back over his shoulder. Nobody had moved, all eyes still toward the sky. He drew a deep breath and barked, "I said, form up!"

The dwarves scrambled into their positions with three dozen shield bearers along the front line and the others creating three more rows behind the shields. Those armed with short bows, crossbows, and spears took up the rear.

"Good." Arangoli nodded. "Now, stand ready, but do not attack. Nobody so much as raises a bow toward the monster until I issue the command."

Gortch called out, "What if the dragon attacks and cooks you?"

"If that happens, you give the order." Turning back around, Arangoli gripped his hammer with both hands, planted his feet shoulder width apart, and waited.

For a moment, he thought the dragon would pass over them, but just before it was directly overhead, the creature turned, its wings outstretched as it dove down, circled around, and flew toward Arangoli no more than two stories above the road. He braced himself, ready to dive out of the way should it strike or launch a cone of fire at him. Before that could happen, the dragon reared back, flapped its mighty wings, and settled down on the road. The monster stomped toward Arangoli and his squad, stopped twenty strides away, and turned. Shockingly, two people sat on the dragon's back.

"Goli?" one of them said. "What are you doing out here?"

Gortch's voice came from behind Arangoli, "Am I imagining it, or do I see Ian and Vic riding on a dragon?"

Through the murk of his exhaustion, Arangoli wondered if he had fallen asleep. In case he was not dreaming, he thought it best to act quickly. "Stay here. I will go see what they want."

Rax snorted. "I'd rather go skinny dipping with a moarbear than go near that dragon."

Arangoli strode toward the monster and realized he was still holding his hammer. Deciding it would be best not to pose a threat, if one could even threaten a dragon, he flipped it over and slid it into the harness on his back.

"Vic. Ian." He nodded. "Mister dragon. It is good to see you."

The dragon dipped its head. "Well met, dwarven warrior."

Arangoli stopped short of the dragon and looked up at his friends, seated fifteen feet above him. "It is good to see you two."

"You as well," Vic said.

Ian pointed north. "Do you know that something bad is coming this way?"

Arangoli glanced toward the cloud. It was no more than a few miles away. "Not bad. Worse than anything you can imagine."

"Did you encounter the orcs?"

"I'd say we killed at least twenty thousand of the buggers."

Vic whistled.

Ian frowned. "You have fewer than two hundred dwarves here. How is that possible?"

"We worked with the Drow. It was their plan. Despite everything, the plan went well and would have worked if not for the blazing demon."

His eyes widening, Ian asked, "You saw the demon?"

"Yes, and the blazing thing bit the heads off Queen Liloth and her singers." The deaths, although sickening, were footnotes to other startling details. The memory brought a frown to Arangoli's face. "Doing so seemed to fuel the demon. It tripled in size and then began resurrecting dead orcs. We were lucky to escape alive. That was two days ago, and we have been running ever since."

"What happened to the Drow?"

"I wish I knew. It was night when we emerged from the mountain pass. Rather than chance being trapped in Domus Ra, we continued south and made camp at the edge of the grassland, which allowed us to rest for a few hours. When the sun rose and we found the mountains hidden beneath that blasted, evil cloud, we knew it was time to run. However, we saw nothing of the Drow. It is as if they just disappeared."

Vic asked, "Did Domus Ra fall?"

"In truth, I have no idea. The orcs seem to have our scent, and they refuse to stop chasing after us. For all I know, they ignored Domus Ra completely."

The dragon and its two riders stared north, toward the ominous black cloud. After a moment, Ian spoke. "We need to slow the monsters down."

Arangoli shook his head. "You don't understand. Their numbers have swelled. Tens of thousands, maybe more, orcs are charging south. They behave like rabid animals and fight with mindless abandon. We are spent and are unlikely to be of much use in a fight unless we rest."

Ian narrowed his eyes in thought. "Can you make it to the forest?"

The edge of the wood was no more than two miles away.

"Yes. Then what?"

"Run into the forest. Remain on the road. We will be waiting for you a mile in."

"And?"

"And then, I will get you out. Once you are cleared of the woods, we will strike." Ian patted Vic on the shoulder. "Would Umbracan fly us back to the forest?"

Vic nodded and seemed to concentrate. The dragon coiled, reared back on its hind legs, and flapped its wings. Powerful gusts buffeted Arangoli, forcing him to duck and back away. The dragon rose higher into the sky and flew south.

Arangoli did not know what Ian had planned, but the boy seemed confident. Regardless, it was better than any other option they faced. He turned toward his warriors and spoke as he walked back to join them.

"Head Thumpers!" he said in a loud voice. "The dragon riders are our friends. They have come to help, but they wish to slow down the demon and its spawn. We are to continue south and lead them into the forest. I know we have marched far with little rest, but I ask you to push on for a few more miles." He paused. "Remember, we now have a dragon on our side."

The dwarves cheered in a display of Head Thumper enthusiasm. A shadow fell over them, dousing their enthusiasm as the front edge of the cloud darkened the sun. The gap between the dwarves and the monsters had shrunk to little more than a mile.

"Let's go!" Arangoli turned and broke into a jog.

The column of dwarves ran toward the forest, fueled by determination and little else. They had exhausted their food a day earlier and their water just before nightfall. They had not slept for days, yet they ran and did so without complaint.

The distance to the forest edge gradually closed, the tree line beckoning with the promise of safety. At the lead of his crew, Arangoli reached the forest edge and slowed briefly to look over his shoulder.

The unnatural cloudbank was less than a mile away, the silhouettes of hundreds of monsters now visible through the dark mist. The squeals and howls of the psychotic monsters carried on the wind, reminding the dwarves of what pursued them.

Trees enveloped the road, narrowing the view. The shadows of the forest offered relief from the heat, but there was no time to consider or enjoy such things. They were running for their lives, knowing that a turned ankle or a stop to rest might lead to a gruesome death. Still, Arangoli ran and his crew ran with him.

They rounded a bend and the dragon came into view, waiting in a flowered glade at the side of the road. Ian, his arms crossed over his dark robes, stood on the gravel no more than thirty feet from the dragon. Arangoli ran toward Ian, slowed, and came to a stop a few strides away. He wiped his brow and gasped for air.

"Well done," Ian said.

Arangoli then noticed a tiny little man sticking up from the pack on Ian's back. "Did you use your magic..." He sucked in a breath. "to shrink a man and stick him in your pack?"

The tiny figure shook a fist. "I am no man. I am a brownie!"

Ian rolled his eyes and spoke over his shoulder. "We know, we know. Now be quiet, Lint. We don't have time for your attitude." He turned his attention back to Arangoli. "I am going to send you and your squad to Ra'Tahal. There, you can eat and rest, but not until you warn King Korrigan about what we face here. Tell him to ready every warrior he can spare. I will come at sunset to bring them to Krotal. There, we will face this enemy in a battle unlike any other."

Still panting from the run, Arangoli shook his head. "I don't understand. How are you going to..."

Ian thrust his hand toward the side of the road. A strip of light appeared and stretched until it met the ground, the top of it seven feet up. The light split open to create a rift with a sunlit square on the other side. Ra'Tahal's central keep towered over the far end of the square while a half dozen dwarves passing through stopped and stared in shock.

"Go," Ian commanded. "Remember. We fight at sunset."

Caught between his exhaustion and shock, Arangoli didn't even bother to reply. He staggered through the doorway with his squad following. In moments, the Head Thumpers filled the square. The doorway closed with a pop and was gone.

CHAPTER 46

FIREFIGHT

S eated on the neck of a dragon, Vic waited while his brother sent the Head Thumpers to Ra'Tahal. The last dwarf ran through, the gateway disappeared, and Ian walked back toward Umbracan.

"Are you ready, great dragon?" Ian asked.

Umbracan rumbled, "The spawn of evil will know pain on this day."

From the pack on Ian's back, Lint complained about the plan yet again. "Is there no other way?"

"We have been through this, Lint," Ian said. "Consider it a sacrifice to save our world."

The brownie crossed his arms and thrust out his lower lip. "Fine."

Ian looked up at Vic. "Meet me on the road a few miles south of here when you are finished."

The shrieks of orcs drew closer, stirring Vic's anxiety. "Please take care, Ian. We don't know much about these monsters."

"I will do what must be done."

A dark, murky mist rolled around the bend, all but blotting out the road despite it being mid-morning and sunny elsewhere. Dark-skinned creatures rounded the corner and began squealing in anger or hunger or whatever drove them. Dozens upon dozens of monsters raced down the road, straight toward them. A portal opened before Ian, who stepped through and was gone. Vic looked over his shoulder to find his brother standing on the road a quarter mile away and in the opposite direction of the horde.

The horde charged in with wild fury in their red eyes. When they were just fifty feet away and closing fast, the dragon drew in a deep breath, bent forward, and blasted fire at the creatures. The flames lit up the murk and set orcs ablaze. Those in the center collapsed while the ones near the edges of the road shrieked, flailed and stumbled into the forest, spreading the fire. Charging monsters slammed into those who were burning, in a frantic, chaotic mess.

Umbracan leapt and took to the air. Vic held on tightly as the dragon rose in a twisting spiral while surrounded by swirling, unnatural darkness. It felt like being surrounded by black smoke from a fire but it had no scent and did not trouble Vic's breathing.

High above the forest, the dragon then turned and flew east, toward the sun, which appeared like a green ball of dim light. A mile out, the gloom began to dissipate until the dragon burst from the cloud and soared out into the sunlight.

The forest stretched for many miles to the east and south while the flat, grassy plains waited a mile to the north. The dragon banked left in a broad circle, coming around to face west when above the forest's northern edge. Vic got his first good view of the cloud from the side and gasped. While the forward edge of the darkness thrust a mile or two into the forest, the cloud trailed for miles upon miles, seemingly splitting the plains of Domusi in half. The overwhelming numbers they faced became clear.

The dragon dove down and leveled above the treetops as it entered the cloudbank. Dark mist enveloped Vic and then a cone of flames burst forth as the dragon launched another attack. Rather than targeting orcs, the flames licked the treetops they flew past. Again and again, the dragon ignited the northern edge of the forest.

IAN DISMISSED his gateway and turned as the dragon set the vanguard of the orc army on fire. The dragon then took flight and was lost in the dark mist.

Burning orcs lay on the road and alongside it, the orange of flames cutting through the darkness allowing Ian to see despite him being a quarter mile away. Monsters began to jump over their burning brethren and race down the road while others circled around and ran through the forest. It was just as well and all according to Ian's plan.

He conjured a construct that had almost killed him on its initial use, something that had led him to avoid using it since. It was not only dangerous but was also quite destructive, and that was before Ian's power had been boosted by the girdle of the gifted. When the orcs were no more than fifty strides away, he channeled magic through the construct.

A flurry of twenty-foot-tall cyclones of fire burst forth, the flaming tornadoes dancing along the ground as they spun toward the charging monsters. The blazing funnels wandered and turned in random patterns. Some wove into each other and bounced off while others tore into the forest, igniting any tree or shrub they touched. The charging orcs tried to turn and run, but thousands of monsters were in their way. Chaos reigned as the cyclones of fire smashed into the horde, setting everything in their path ablaze. Shrieks echoed through the forest as the monsters burned and burned.

"Woah!" Lint exclaimed from Ian's pack. "That was amazing. Can you do it again?"

"Yes." Ian raised his arm to shield his face as the flames burned higher and higher.

The intense heat of the inferno forced him to turn and run. When the air cooled, he stopped and channeled the spell again. He repeated this process three more times, the tornadoes of fire turning from dozens to hundreds. All the while, the fire spread wider and wider.

～

Vɪᴄ ʜᴇʟᴅ on tight as the dragon made a sharp turn. It came around and Vic got his first view of the destruction taking place.

Fire raged to the north, all along the forest's edge, the glow of the flames turning the rising smoke and the unnatural cloud a burnt orange. Likewise, spreading fire raged to the south, evidence of Ian's efforts.

The dragon launched another attack, the flames bursting out from its snout to ignite treetops. Again and again, it struck, painting a two-mile wide swath of forest with orange flames. Upon completing the second pass, the dragon burst out from the cloudbank and soared into the sunlight, where it turned south, rounding the plumes of smoke carrying on the wind.

After passing beyond the black cloud and columns of smoke, Umbracan turned west and a gap in the trees came into view, marking the roadway.

～

Iᴀɴ ᴄᴀsᴛ ᴏɴᴇ ʟᴀsᴛ sᴘᴇʟʟ, sending spinning spouts of flames skittering down the road and into the surrounding trees. The monsters were beyond his view, many of them dead or trapped and surrounded by fire. The wind, coming from the west, seemed to feed and spread the blaze as he had hoped. Left unchecked, the fire would burn for days on end and may consume the entire forest, but new trees would eventually replace those that turned to ash. He was glad that Shria-Li was not with him to witness such intentional destruction of nature. More would follow. Of that, he had no doubt.

He ran out from the shadow of the dark cloud, into sunlight, and rounded a bend. Another glade waited ahead, and in that glade was the dragon. Ian made for it and slowed to a walk when he drew near. His breath coming in gasps, he put his hands on his hips while approaching the massive reptilian monster.

Lint shouted from over his shoulder. "Vic! You should have seen it! Ian sent firestorms after those evil monsters."

"And it looks like the plan worked," Vic said. "The fires you started burn heartily and have spread east."

Ian nodded as he drew closer. "The wind. It will keep the enemy from going around in that direction.

"So, you expect them to round the fire's western flank?"

"I do. Hopefully, we significantly reduced their numbers as well."

Vic frowned. "I've no doubt that thousands died, but..." He ran his hand through his hair while staring into the distance. "We saw the scope of the demon's dark cloud. It stretches for miles and miles. Even if we killed ten thousand monsters, ten times that number remain."

The news was not unexpected, but Ian still found himself disappointed. "As we already knew, this would do little more than slow their advance. They are coming for Krotal and we had better be ready."

He cast a spell, lifted himself into the air, and set himself onto the dragon's back. "Take us back to Krotal. It is time to evacuate the citizens and prepare for war."

AT VIC'S DIRECTION, Umbracan soared from the forest, across a series of farmer's fields, and over the seaside city of Krotal. People in the streets stopped to stare, many pointing toward the sky as a creature from legend flew overhead. The dragon approached the hill in the center of the city and climbed higher. It sailed up above the hilltop castle, where it banked in a tight circle.

Vic sent. *Land in the castle yard.*

What of the soldiers?

Warriors in silver and black armor scrambled along the ramparts. Five circular towers thrust up from the castle's fortifications, two of them occupied by ballistae, two others by catapults, leaving only the gate tower undefended by a war machine. A quartet of soldiers raised one of the ballistae to the sky and loosed. The dragon banked in the other direction, causing the four-foot-long bolt to sail wide of its mark.

Ian shouted. "Land. I will shield us."

Vic added, "You heard him."

Umbracan flew out over the city, turned, and came back toward the castle. A flurry of arrows came at them, reminding Vic of a swarm of angry bees. The arrows shattered in a spray of splinters that drifted on the breeze as they fell toward the ground. The dragon sailed above the castle walls, causing the warriors to cower in fear. Wings flapping mightily while rearing its body back, the dragon rapidly slowed and then fluttered down into the castle yard.

Warriors in black and silver rushed in with swords, spears, and halberds thrust out before them. Their weapons struck an invisible wall and slid up toward the sky just before their bodies slammed into the same unseeable obstacle. The soldiers fell to the ground with a terrible clatter of clanking armor.

Ian floated up from the dragon's back and bellowed. "Stop!"

The guards on the walls and in the castle yard froze and stared in shock.

Again, Ian issued a loud command. "Do not attack! If you do, you will regret it. We have not come to fight you."

A soldier strolled out from an alcove and slid his sword into the scabbard on his hip. "My name is Ludwin. I am the captain of the castle guard. State your name. Why have you invaded Krotal Castle?"

Ian floated down to the ground, turned a hard glance around the yard, and approached the man. "My name is Barsequa Illian. My brother Vic and the great dragon, Umbracan, have come to save the people of Krotal. A grave danger approaches, and we have little time to evacuate before the city is under attack."

"Attack? By whom?"

From Ian's pack, Lint shouted, "Orcs! Black hearted, evil orcs!"

The captain blinked. "Is that a tiny little man?'

Before Lint could issue his angry response, Vic intervened, shouting down from the dragon's back, "He is a brownie from the Vale."

"Please ignore the brownie for now," Ian said. "We have little time and can't waste it on unimportant matters. An army of monsters from the underworld come this way. They will be here by nightfall, and when they arrive, they will slaughter anyone in their path."

The captain stared at Ian for a beat before tipping his head back and laughing. "You almost had me." He shook his head. "Monsters from the underworld. Who would believe such a thing?"

Umbracan lifted his head and blasted a cone of fire into the sky. Soldiers around the yard and surrounding walls shielded their faces and shied away from the burst of heat.

The dragon then lowered its head and leaned toward Ian and the captain, who staggered backward with wide eyes.

Umbracan's deep voice rumbled in the confines of the castle yard. "The wizard speaks the truth. Orcs, vile creatures who eat human flesh, come this way. An army of a hundred thousand monsters pours down from the north. To ignore this threat is to sentence your citizens to certain death."

Ludwin pulled his helmet off and wiped his brow with a shaking hand. "Yes. Well, I suppose it would not hurt to take one of you to speak with Duke Gastwick."

Ian nodded. "I will go but only if you command your men to stand down. Should they make the mistake of attacking, I suspect this dragon will cook them without reservations."

The man looked up at Umbracan and called out, "Sheath your weapons! Nobody attacks unless the strangers attack first!" He then turned to Ian. "Follow me."

"Take my pack, Vic. It'll only be a distraction." Ian pulled the pack from his shoulder and used his magic to float it up in the air, with Lint holding on tight.

When the pack was within reach, Vic grabbed the strap and drew it toward him. "I will wait here and try to keep Lint out of trouble."

The captain led Ian across the castle yard and disappeared through a doorway. Vic lifted his gaze from the door to his surroundings. In the castle yard and on the surrounding ramparts, sixty or seventy soldiers in black and silver armor stared at him with apprehension in their eyes. Having so many eyes on him while surrounded by silent tension, he felt self-conscious and exposed. To counter such feelings and hoping to dispel the tension, he began to whistle to himself.

HIS JAW SET IN DETERMINATION, Ian followed Captain Ludwin down a dark corridor, up three flights of stairs, and into an expansive chamber illuminated by indirect sunlight coming through windows overlooking the city and the sea beyond it. A sitting area surrounding a stone fireplace consumed one side of the room while a desk, chairs, and bookshelves stood on the other. A man in a black doublet with silver trim sat at the desk, his quill moving rapidly as he wrote something on a sheet of parchment.

Ludwin cleared his throat and spoke. "Pardon the interruption, my Duke."

The man did not look up as he dipped his quill in the inkwell. "I told you I was to be left alone this morning, Ludwin." Gastwick's tone left no room for argument.

"Yes. I recall my orders well, however, a dragon has landed in the castle yard."

The man's head popped up, his dark eyes alert. His long jaw, covered in a black goatee waxed to a point, turned down in a scowl. "What nonsense is this?"

"A dragon flew in, along with two young men and a tiny little... brownie." Ludwin turned toward Ian. "This is one of the young men. He demanded he speak with..."

"Demanded?" The duke shot to his feet, his volume rising as well. "Who dares to demand anything of me in *my* city?"

Ian instantly did not like the duke. They had little time, and he had even less patience. He strode across the room, got a good view through the window, and decided it would do. With one hand, he cast a gateway directly behind the duke while placing the other end right outside the window. He then cast another spell, wrapped a rope of magic around the duke's waist, and thrust it out, through the gateway.

The duke yelped as he was lifted off his feet and then screamed when he found himself dangling a hundred feet above the hillside.

"Help!" Gastwick cried.

When the distinctive ring of a sword being drawn came from behind Ian, he turned toward Ludwin. "Attack me and I drop him."

The man froze.

"I do this to get the duke's attention and will not harm him so long as he listens." Ian turned back toward the gateway and the duke out in the open air beyond it. "You will listen if you wish to live."

"Yes. I...I will. Please, don't drop me."

"I have come to warn the city. An army of monsters comes this way. These creatures are mindless and cannot be reasoned with. They are driven by bloodlust and a mere scratch of their claws can kill. The dragon your captain mentioned is real, here, and fighting on our side.

The dragon, my brother, and I met this army of monsters this morning at the far edge of the forest that lies north of Krotal. We set fire to that forest in hopes of slowing their advance. Even then, I expect them to arrive by nightfall. We must prepare for this attack and evacuate anyone who cannot fight."

As Ian spoke, the fear appeared to slide from the duke's face. The man looked past Ian, toward his captain. "Ludwin. Is any of this true?"

"There can be no doubt about the dragon being real. In addition, my men reported smoke on the northern horizon less than an hour before the dragon appeared in the sky over the city."

Deciding that the duke's attitude had shifted in his favor, Ian pulled the man back through the gateway, set his feet on the floor, and dismissed both spells.

The duke straightened his doublet and frowned. "How did you do that?"

"I am a wizard. I command magic far greater than you can imagine. The dragon, my brother, and I are here to help fight this evil, but we need to clear the city and form a plan."

The duke stroked his goatee. "If the enemy force is as imposing as you claim, I don't know how we can face them and hope to win. Between the city watch and castle guards, I only have four hundred men."

Ian considered lying but decided against it. "This is a fight we cannot win."

Gastwick threw his hands up. "Then why have you come to me?"

"I told you, we need to evacuate the city and you must begin that evacuation now.

"Then, what?'

"We will reduce their numbers and slow their advance."

"You are asking my men to sacrifice themselves?"

"I am asking them to fight. They will not fight alone. I will bring others and double the size of your force. I also will lend my magic to the fight in addition to the might of a dragon. Here, we will make this enemy pay a steep price. You see, I am not trying to save Krotal. I am trying to save the world."

The duke's anger and fight seemed to drain from his face. He plopped down into his chair and raked his fingers down his face. "Then, it is over. I have ruled for only three years, and it is already over."

"I cannot guess at what might be remaining of your city when this is finished, but this is a chance to make a real difference, a chance to become a legend."

"A legend," the duke stared into space. He then nodded. "A legend."

The man slid his chair up to the desk, pulled out a new parchment, and dipped his quill in the inkwell. With rapid, eager movement, the quill danced along the page. In moments, he had crafted a missive, which he held out toward Ludwin. "Captain. Give this to one of your men and have him ride down to the city watch. They are to begin evacuation now. Every ship in port will take as many people as they can carry. The rest will cross Hatternick Bridge and head toward Greavesport. Anyone who wishes to remain must agree to fight. When the missive is off and on its way, return here. We must discuss a plan."

CHAPTER 47
ASSEMBLE

With only his weapon strapped to his back, Vic strolled into the Chamber of Testing. Ahead of him were Ian, Lint, Draxan, Ahni, and Revita. The group settled in the center of the chamber and formed a circle.

As Ian was about to speak, Lionel, who was seated on his shoulder, blasted a loud squawk of alarm. Everyone turned as another person emerged from the tunnel that led outside. While the person was familiar, his garb was not.

"Master!" Ian said in surprise. "Where have you been?"

Truhan approached wearing a black doublet with gold trim. Runes and twisting lines of gold ran along the border, lapel, and collar, matching the golden buttons that tracked down the center of his torso. Likewise, a belt of gold cinched the doublet around the man's waist while nearly reaching his thighs. Gold stripes ran down the sides of his black breeches, stopping where the breeches were tucked into his tall leather boots. Most striking was the man's cape, cardinal red with gold piping and a collar that stood tall and wrapped around the rear of his head.

"Like you, I have been preparing," Truhan said.

"Preparing for what?"

"Fate has led us to this point and the actions we now take will determine which future awaits us.

It has become clear that the time of great darkness looms. We cannot allow it to come to pass. While I have sat aside and avoided direct interaction up to this point, I no longer have that luxury. If I must act, I must be prepared."

Ian's brow furrowed. "You intend to come with us?"

"My path differs for yours."

"What do you intend?"

"We shall see. The future is unwritten, but rest assured, there will come a point in which my actions will impact this world."

"Don't you think...'

"This is not up for discussion, Ian. Now, tell me what you have planned."

Ian glanced toward Vic. "Give me a moment. My master and I need to talk in private."

"We will be here, waiting." Vic knew more than the others, some of which was to remain a secret. He assumed that is why Ian wanted to speak with Truhan alone.

When Ian and Truhan walked off to the corner of the chamber, Vic risked a glance toward Revita. She glared at him with her arms crossed.

Vic asked, "How long do you intend to be angry with me?"

She shrugged. "I haven't yet decided."

Lint said, "I told you she would be cross for leaving without her."

"Hush, you little imp!" Vic snapped.

Revita said, "Why are you yelling at the pipsqueak? He did nothing wrong."

Frustrated, Vic clenched his fists and then released a sigh. "I told you a dozen times, I am sorry, but I did what I did at Ian's request. Why risk anyone else?"

"But you took Lint with you."

"He hid inside Ian's pack. By the time we figured it out, it was too late." When she gave him a flat-lipped glare, he tried again. "I left you a note, so you wouldn't worry."

"I see. A note." Revita arched a brow. "Does that give you leave to go wherever you wish whenever you wish?"

Ahni snorted. "You two sound as if you are married."

Revita's eyes widened and her jaw dropped before she overcame her shock. "Well, I am only saying..." She thrust a finger at Vic. "You rode a dragon without me."

Vic rolled his eyes. "Is *that* what this is about?"

"Yes and...the rest of what I said as well."

"If it will make you happy, you can ride with me tonight."

A smile tickled the corner of her lips. "I can?"

"It'll be dangerous, but all things considered, I'd rather have you near me than worry about what might be happening to you elsewhere."

She smiled and looked down at Lint. "See. I told you."

Vic frowned. "Told him what?"

"Never mind."

Lint snickered.

Ahni chuckled. "Oh, yes. You two *definitely* sound like you are married."

Married? Considering how Vic had been surrounded by drama and near-death experiences since meeting her, he had not given it much thought. If they somehow survived and the world did not end, what would their life be like together? Before he was able to contemplate the question, Ian walked back over while Truhan crossed the chamber and faded into the tunnel leading to his study.

"If everyone is ready, let's begin." Ian nodded. "Ahni. You are first."

She stepped forward. He cast a gateway into the Temple of Urvadan in her home village of Sacrumi. Without hesitation, she hopped through and ran across the chamber. As she was climbing the stairs toward the open doorway, the portal disappeared.

"Draxan. Your turn." Ian opened another gateway.

Beyond the opening was the Valley of Gold, covered in shadows, the late-day sun hidden behind the bowl of the crater. The elf hurried through and the portal snapped shut.

"Alright," Ian said. "It's time to visit Ra'Tahal."

WHEN THE OTHERS joined him at the ground floor of his tower in Ra'Tahal, Ian dismissed the gateway. He lifted Lionel off his shoulder, set the drake on the back of a chair, and walked over to the staircase.

He called up. "Winnie?"

Footsteps came from above, so Ian climbed the stairs. As he reached the second-floor landing, Winnie rounded the curve of the stairs above him.

"How is Rina?" he asked.

Winnie shook her head. "Much the same as when you brought her here."

That had been at noon, eight hours earlier. "Has she eaten at least?"

"I was able to get her to eat some soup." Winnie glanced up the stairs. "Perhaps another night and she will pull out of it."

"We can only hope." Ian could not claim to understand what Rina was going through. Losing a loved one was difficult. To have that person turn into a psychotic monster that tried to kill you was something else altogether. He took Winnie's hand. "Thank you for taking care of her."

Winnie smiled. "You may know her best, but she is my friend as well. Besides, even in her current state, having her here makes the tower feel less lonely."

Ian leaned in and kissed her. "Thank you anyway." He glanced down the staircase. "The others are waiting for me, so I must go. I simply wanted to see you and find out how Rina was faring."

Winnie gripped his hand. "Be safe, Ian. I can't say I understand what is happening, but I am scared."

"I am as well."

He hurried down the stairs before she said anything that might make him reconsider his plan.

At the bottom, he scooped Lionel off the chair and made straight for the door. "Let's go."

The group stepped outside onto a shaded street. Orange clouds against a deep blue sky informed Ian that sunset was imminent. He led the group along the narrow streets and came to a square filled with armored dwarves lined up in columns and facing the central keep. A familiar dwarf stood on the stairs outside the keep entrance, facing the warriors with his helmet tucked under his arm. Upon seeing Ian enter the square, the dwarf descended the stairs and walked between two columns of warriors.

"Vargan," Ian called out. "Are your warriors ready?"

"Aye," Vargan stopped a stride from Ian. "Arangoli tells us we are in for a fierce battle."

"We shall see. I can promise that your weapons will get bloody. That much is certain."

Vargan slid his helmet on with a grin. "My soldiers and their weapons are prepared."

"Where are Arangoli and the other Head Thumpers?"

As Ian said it, the keep door opened and a heavy-set dwarf emerged. Had his face not been visible, Ian would have known him regardless by his notable frame. "There's Gortch, now."

As the big dwarf crossed the yard, Vargan explained, "Korrigan housed Goli's crew in the keep. In fact, I gave Goli my bed for the day, but only after he took a quick bath."

Ian snorted. "I've no doubt. I caught a whiff of him this morning and it smelled like he hadn't washed up for weeks."

Vargan laughed and turned toward Gortch as the big dwarf drew near. "How did you sleep?"

"Like the dead."

Ian asked, "Where is Goli?"

"He is rousing the rest of the crew. It takes longer now that our numbers have swelled."

"Good," Ian said. "I will come back for them after Vargan and his warriors are in place."

Gortch grimaced. "I am to go with Vargan."

Vargan's brow furrowed. "What is this?"

"Goli thought you could use a second in charge. I tried to talk him out of it, but he insisted."

After a beat, Vargan nodded. "That, I could." He laughed and clapped the big dwarf on the back. "It'll be good to have you along, and you've already earned the respect of every warrior in the clan, so they are certain to follow your command as if it were mine."

Ian turned to Vargan. "Before I bring your men to their post, let's pay a visit to Krotal Castle, so you meet with Captain Ludwin."

"Ludwin?"

"He is in charge of the city's defense. He knows what is at stake."

"Let's do it."

As Vargan turned and ordered his men to wait for him, Ian pictured the yard of a castle a thousand miles away. He cast a gateway to that location and stepped through it.

Vic, Revita, and Lint stood aside as hundreds of armored dwarves poured through the gateway. The portal hovered above a gravel road overlooking a river, its waters dark in the failing light of sunset. The city of Krotal awaited just downstream from their location while a forest loomed in the other direction.

The column of dwarven warriors followed Vargan down the road and headed toward a bridge spanning the river. A steady train of carts, wagons, and people on foot poured across the bridge, all heading toward the east bank of the river. To the west, in the center of the city, Krotal Castle and the hill it stood upon blocked the setting sun.

Gortch stepped through and stopped beside Vic and Revita, all three of them looking back at Ian, who remained on the other side of the gateway.

"Hold the bridge as long as you can," Ian said. "When you retreat, you must ensure that the bridge is destroyed."

Gortch gave a grim nod. "Vargan and I will see it done."

"Good, because many lives depend on it."

Turning, Gortch marched after the other dwarves.

With the dwarf gone, Vic addressed his brother. "Please be careful. If this demon lord shows up..."

"I am fighting a war, Vic. I'll do what I must. I expect you would do the same."

"I suppose I would."

"Be well."

The gateway winked out of existence, but Vic continued to stare into the space where it had been.

Revita put a hand on his arm and turned him toward her. "Your brother will be fine. Goli is there to watch his back."

"I worry that Ian will try to hold the castle longer than he should."

"Rather than worry about what he is doing, let's focus on our task." She looked up into the air. "Where is your dragon friend?"

Lint's voice came from the road below them. "His name is Umbracan."

She looked down at him. "I know that."

"Then, why didn't you say it?"

"Why don't you shut your trap?"

"What trap?" Lint looked around. "Do you think we need to worry about traps out here?"

She rolled her eyes. "Sometimes I'd like to strangle that little runt."

Somehow, the comical banter between Revita and the brownie helped Vic move beyond his concern for his brother. He closed his eyes and cast out a call. *Umbracan. We are waiting beside the river.* He did not have to explain more, for it was the exact same location the dragon had landed at for Vic and Ian to dismount earlier that day.

I waken, the dragon said. *Has the time come to fight?*

Even as the dragon posed the question, a black cloud slid across the sky northwest of Krotal, turning the dimming light of sunset to twilight in moments.

The enemy approaches the city, Vic sent.

The creatures will know pain and destruction on this night. A sensation of anger came through the connection. *I will be there soon.*

ARANGOLI AND HIS CREW, now numbering north of a hundred dwarfs, stood outside Ra'Tahal's central keep. The dwarves were uncharacteristically quiet. Some fidgeted while others stared into space with a resolute glare, as if challenging the air before them to a fight. Two meals, a copious amount of water, and six hours of sleep had done much to revive them, but a grim task awaited. Every one of them knew what it was like to fight those monsters, even if most had only gotten the briefest of tastes before finishing the job.

A circle drawn on the ground stood just strides from Arangoli's position. He stared at that vacant space, torn between willing something to appear there and hoping he and his crew had somehow been forgotten, but such was not to be. The air shimmered as a portal opened to reveal a castle yard in the grip of dusk.

From the other side, Ian waved. "Come through. The enemy is almost here."

With a gut full of determination, Arangoli slid on the helmet given to him by King Korrigan. The wings jutting out from the sides marked him as captain while the gem at the front of the helm held an altogether different significance.

Over his shoulder, he shouted. "Head Thumpers! We go to battle." He spun toward them. "Remember, the castle defenders are not our foes. Save your anger for the monsters who seek to destroy us."

He then hurried through the gateway and moved to the side to allow his crew space. A few strides away stood Ian and a man in black and silver armor.

"Arangoli," Ian gestured toward the man beside him. "This is Captain Ludwin. He is coordinating the defense." He turned toward the man. "Ludwin, this is Arangoli, captain of a fighting force known as the Head Thumpers."

"Well met, Captain," Ludwin said with a nod. He glanced toward the growing cluster of dwarves. "How many soldiers are under your command?"

"I've one hundred thirty-eight with me. Twenty-six wield ranged weapons. The rest prefer to fight face to face."

"Good. We should have enough to completely man the castle walls and the five towers." He pointed toward the doorway beside a broad tunnel. A closed portcullis was visible in the shadows. "Inside the gate tower is a stairwell leading to the top of the wall. Take your soldiers up and have them cover the western wall. My men will take the north, east, and south. Note the rope strung above the wall. It is to be cut before the enemy swarms your warriors."

Arangoli peered up above the wall and noted something dangling from the ropes. "What is in the buckets?"

"Kerosene."

"Ah. Enough said."

Ian turned to Arangoli. "I intend to fight from the top of the gate tower. It is the only one lacking a machine of war. I could use someone there to watch my back if you will agree."

Arangoli stroked his beard and nodded. "That is a good position for me to issue any necessary orders to my squad. Allow me to deploy them, and I will meet you atop the tower."

"I knew I could count on you."

When he had first met Ian, Arangoli had been at his worst, lost in a drunken haze and lacking any sense of life direction. Despite this, knowing that he had Ian's confidence was a boost to Arangoli's pride. He puffed up his chest, turned to his squad and bellowed orders.

"We are to guard the castle's front wall. Pazacar, you are leading a squad on the north side of the gate tower. Rax, you have the south. We will split up so the most experienced fighters are mixed in with those still counting the monsters they kill."

Without waiting for a reply, Arangoli marched over to the open tower door and began ascending. A battle loomed, and he was ready to crack some heads.

Ian waited until the last of the dwarves had cleared the castle yard before turning back to Ludwin. "Have you had any recent updates on the city's evacuation?"

"A caravan of citizens heads toward Greavesport. The soldiers I have out in the city are going door to door to ensure the buildings are vacated and locked. However, a portion of the population refuse to leave their shops or homes. Either they don't believe in the threat or they are hoping it will bypass them."

While unsurprising, Ian had been worried about how many might react that way. He told himself, *You cannot save them all. Focus on what you can control and know that you have done your best.* Moving past the issue, Ian asked, "What of the ships?"

"Just minutes ago, a runner informed me that the last ship is boarding passengers. However, the waterfront continues to fill with those who would rather sail than walk. When that ship sets sail and they are left behind..."

Even as the man said it, the castle yard darkened. The fore of the unnatural cloud eased across the sky above, the sight of it turning Ian's stomach upside down. The moment he had foreseen in his ominous prophecy had come. It was time to face the enemy that would destroy his world.

CHAPTER 48

BESIEGED

From the winch room at the top of the gate tower, four flights above the castle yard, Arangoli waited until the last of the Head Thumpers ran past and out onto the wall. He then turned to find Ian climbing the ladder leading to a trap door ten feet above. When Ian disappeared through the opening, Arangoli gripped a rung and began to climb.

Arangoli poked his head through the trapdoor to a circular tower rooftop surrounded by a wall made of merlons. Between the unnatural cloud over the city and its position on the wrong side of sunset, the only light came from a flickering pair of torches, one placed on each side of the tower roof. He crawled out, climbed to his feet and walked over to join Ian near the outer edge.

The city of Krotal spread out before him, the darkness broken up only by the light of torches illuminating the perimeter of open squares evenly spaced around the castle like spokes in a wagon wheel, each roughly a thousand feet away.

As he sidled up beside Ian, Arangoli asked, "Why are the streets dark?"

"Didn't you say that the monsters are drawn to fire?"

"Yes." Even before he fought the orcs, he had learned as much from the Drow.

"We want them to fill the squares." Ian lifted the drake off his shoulder and tossed it into the air.

"Traps?" Arangoli's eyes followed the drake as it circled, flew higher, and faded into the night.

"You could call it that." High-pitched cries and howls came from the northwest. Ian peered in that direction, his gaze distant. "They come."

The noise of the horde grew louder as they drew near the city. Anticipation and fear pulled Arangoli's mood in opposite directions. As a warrior, he thrived in battle and often ran headlong toward enemies, determined to impose his will upon them, but waiting for a fight to come to him was different. It was often said that waiting was the hardest part of anything one faced, and when expecting an attack, the painful aspect of the wait was boosted tenfold. Spurred by rising anxiety, he reached over his shoulder and drew his hammer. Just holding the weapon calmed him, his nerves settling, his posture resolute.

"Let them come," Arangoli growled. "Tonight, we turn destruction back on those who seek to destroy us."

Darkness dominated as the unnatural cloud extended over and beyond the city, blotting out the stars and leaving the full moon as nothing more than a faint, blurred smear in the night sky. As a thief, Revita often embraced the shadows, for they allowed her to move about unnoticed. But the gloom falling over the city of Krotal was something else, a phenomenon born of nightmares.

She, Vic, and Lint stood near the river, surrounded by darkness. Other than the dim circle of the moon, the only light in view came from the torches at both ends of the bridge, a quarter mile away.

"He comes," Vic said, his face toward the sky.

Revita looked up, searching for movement. A massive shadow appeared, coming straight toward them. Just shy of reaching their position, the dragon flapped its wings to slow itself and sent powerful gusts that caused Revita's raven hair to whip wildly. Lint grabbed ahold of her ankle and held on as the dragon landed a dozen strides away.

"Greetings, Champion." Umbracan rumbled. "I see you brought your mate."

Revita arched a brow at Vic. "Mate?"

"Um...well..." Vic stammered.

Umbracan said, "Climb on. We go to battle."

"Right." Vic strode toward the dragon. "No time to chat, Revita. It's time to fight."

She let the issue slide, bent, and scooped Lint off the ground before setting him on her shoulder. "Hold on to the collar of my coat." Before he could reply, she approached the dragon as Vic climbed up.

With practiced ease, Revita hopped onto the dragon's tail and scrambled up onto the massive creature, using the crests along its spine as handholds. She then settled into the gap behind Vic and held on tight.

"Ready," she said.

The dragon burst forward, opened its wings, and leapt off the riverbank. It flew over the water, flapped mightily, and climbed higher and higher while turning back toward the city. The ground fell away as they rose into the sky, heading toward the castle, its ramparts illuminated by dozens if not hundreds of torches.

The sensation of flight carried an unexpected thrill. *I am flying...on a dragon!*

Lint whooped in delight. To her surprise, Revita whooped with him.

Ian stood atop the gate tower and peered out over the city. The terrifying noises of the approaching enemy thickened, fueling the rising tension surrounding him. Orcs then poured into the first torchlit square. Screams of their victims joined their inhuman shrieks and howls. The monsters spilled from the square into every connecting street. In moments, the orcs occupied two more squares and continued to spread throughout Krotal like a rapidly spreading disease.

Their shrieks and howls grew louder and louder, informing Ian that they were ascending the hillside. The first of the monsters appeared in the light of the torches at the base of the castle. One became ten. Ten became a hundred. And, in moments, thousands of orcs flowed up to the castle wall and began scaling the ramparts like a swarm of ravenous spiders.

Magic flowed into Ian, boosted by the enchantment of the belt around his waist. He cast a spell conceived weeks earlier but never tested for the fear of its potential. The spell combined elements of two attacks, and the result was as devastating as he had feared.

A dozen spirals of electricity burst from the construct, spinning in disks of sparking light. Hundreds of bolts burst out from each lightning storm in white streaks that shot down toward the ground. The bolts split and arced, each of them striking multiple orcs. The spinning funnels of electricity spread across the city. Hundreds of lightning strikes turned to thousands before the storms expelled and the skies fell dark. Burning orc corpses littered the streets, hillsides, and rooftops. Yet, tens of thousands of monsters continued to spill through the city and charge toward the castle.

Vic held tight as Umbracan cut through the dark cloud high above Krotal. Behind him, Revita sat at the base of the dragon's neck with Lint holding fast to her coat.

Amber dots forming a rectangle became visible through the mist far below, informing him that they were above the castle. As planned, Umbracan circled, waiting for the signal. Although Ian had not told Vic exactly what he had planned, he promised it would be impossible to miss while also insisting that they remain far from the ground until it was finished.

He then spied a dozen spirals of white light launch from the castle and fan out over the city. Lightning rained down from the storms in a display of wild, untamed, and dangerous magic. The cyclones of electricity wreaked havoc in a spectacular display of destruction until fading before reaching the city squares, each illuminated by a ring of torches. Without a doubt, Vic knew that the magic attack was the signal and once it was finished, he reached his mind out to Umbracan.

It is time to attack. Make for the first square.

The spawn of evil will know my fury.

The dragon tucked its wings in and dove. Vic's innards tickled and his throat tightened as the dragon broke through the mist and plummeted toward the ground. When they were seconds from impact, Umbracan spread his wings, leveled, and sped over the city, toward the first square. Monsters by the thousands filled the streets below, many of them scrambling across rooftops as they flowed toward the castle where Ian and the city defenders waited.

The first ring of torches came into view, marking the border of a city square. Umbracan sped past the buildings, flew over the square, and Vic gasped at the sight.

Thousands of monsters writhed in a tightly packed throng, leaving not a single inch of ground uncovered other than the fountain in the center of the square. A stack of barrels sat in the center of the fountain, the normally clear water replaced by a dark and dangerous liquid.

The dragon opened its mouth and a cone of fire burst out. The flames licked the crowd of monsters before striking the fountain and its contents. The kerosene in the fountain ignited in a flash of light that shot eighty feet into the air. Umbracan flew past the square only a beat before the barrels in the fountain exploded.

The thump of a massive concussion passed over Vic, immediately followed by a wave of heat, briefly turning the cool night air into the hottest of desert days. He looked back as a plume of flame shot hundreds of feet into the air. Against the bright light of the inferno were hundreds of bodies spinning and flailing through the air. The tower of flame collapsed to a raging fire extending beyond the square in all directions.

"Wow!" Lint shouted. "I didn't know fire could be like that."

Revita said, "That was just the first square. We have four more to blow up."

Vic turned forward. "Let's make the monsters pay, Umbracan!"

The dragon banked and flew toward the next square.

ARANGOLI STOOD at one side of the tower, watching as the Head Thumpers stationed at that section of the wall fought off orcs. The monsters scaled the walls faster than he had thought possible. Their charge had been reduced by Ian's magic attack, but they still came.

He turned, intent on crossing to check on the opposite wall when an enemy burst onto the tower rooftop. Ian thrust a hand toward the orc and some invisible power launched it into the night. Another appeared and another, forcing Ian to respond with haste. Occupied, he didn't see those coming over the wall to his backside.

With a roar, Arangoli charged the new pair of orcs. He wound back and swung as he neared the first. The hammer struck the creature in the side, crushing ribs and sending it tumbling across the rooftop. He kicked at the next while ducking. His heel drove into the monster's knee while its talons swept through the air above Arangoli's head. He came up with his hammer before him, and drove the hammerhead into the orc's chin, shattering its jaw, snapping its head back, and lifting it clean off its feet. The orc crashed into another cresting the wall and took them both over the edge. A trailing shriek followed before cutting off abruptly.

Two more monsters burst over the wall, one to each side of Arangoli. Since his hammer was already above his head, he slammed it down toward the enemy on his right. The fiend moved its head aside to avoid the blow but the hammerhead came down on its hand, crushing it against a stone merlon. A thump of magic released, shattering orc fingers and splitting the merlon from the wall. The merlon broke in half, both pieces and orc tumbling off into the night.

The other monster launched itself at Arangoli with its talons flashing. Desperate to avoid those claws, he urgently dropped backward. The monster struck his helmet, sweeping it right off his head as its dark, leathery body slid past.

Arangoli rolled and made a blind swing. The hammerhead connected with the monster's ankle, crushing bone and causing the creature to spin and fall to its back. Before it could rise, Arangoli burst forward with a massive underhand strike. The hammer connected with the orc's forehead, ending it.

As Ian released another shield spell and knocked three orcs off the wall to his right, a larger group came over the wall to his left. He altered spells, created a wedge of air and blasted it at their lower legs as they landed on the tower rooftop. The wedge swept the feet from beneath the monsters, causing them to flip forward. Before they landed, the tail end of the wedge caught them and blasted upward, launching them into the air and out beyond the castle.

With a break in the action, Ian raced over to the gap between the nearest merlons and peered down to find dozens of monsters scaling the tower. He crafted another spell, this one turning into a cone of flames. Fire engulfed the nearest orcs and caused them to fall, their bodies burning as they slammed into the monsters below them, knocking them from the wall. Again and again, he launched cones of flames, adjusting his aim with each blast until the wall was cleared and burning corpses lined its base.

A distant roar came from across the city. He lifted his gaze to the northwest, in search of its source.

Fires burned in the squares to the east, north, and west, creating bright islands of light amid the smaller fires and heavy gloom surrounding them. Then, he saw motion between two of the squares. Distant booms came from the direction. At first, he thought it was the rumble of explosions. That perception changed when a towering behemoth stepped into the firelight.

The giant stood thirty feet tall with a body covered in red-tinted flesh. The creature was hairless, muscular, and obviously male. Its distended jaw stuck out while sharp, white teeth jutted up over its upper lip. The monster's eyes were yellow, its pupils like slits. Horns curved from its forehead and swept backward in a full circle so their points stuck out even with the creature's eyes. Without a doubt, Ian knew it was the demon lord, and it was coming for him.

CHAPTER 49
DESPERATION

Gortch and two hundred dwarven warriors stood on the road leading toward the waterfront sector of the city. Terrified citizens fleeing Krotal raced past his squad and Vargan's, who was stationed along the road coming from the inland side. Screams and inhuman howls carried from the city, only to be interrupted by periodic explosions.

Then, to Gortch's right, the first orcs appeared on one of the streets leading into the city. More followed, this time rushing along the road leading from the harbor. Within moments, the monsters were coming from all directions, all chasing after fleeing citizens.

"Shields to the fore!" Gorch bellowed.

The sound of hurried footsteps and the clanking of armor came from behind him.

"Archers ready bows. Loose on my command." Again, Gortch issued orders without looking back at the warriors in his charge. Instead, he watched the oncoming monsters and the innocents attempting to flee them. Trailing the other citizens on the street leading from the city was a family, the mother and father each carrying a small child. It soon

THE DARK LORD'S DESIGN

became clear that the orcs would catch the family before they could reach his squad.

Gortch shouted. "Archers aim for the monsters in the street. Do not strike the fleeing humans." A beat later, he called out, "Loose!"

A flurry of arrows sailed overhead. The arrows dropped beyond the family and plunged into the monsters at the front of the mob, their shrieks and cries echoing as they went down. The orcs trailing them did not slow, trampling their brethren while charging forward.

Gortch drew his mace while mentally urging the family to hurry. Monsters drew closer and closer. Just before the family reached Gortch, the father stumbled, fell, and rolled with the child hugged against his chest. Despite his training and knowing that he should take position behind his shield line, Gortch reacted.

He ran past the downed man, wound back, and launched a massive swing as the lead monster closed the gap. The mace struck the creature in the shoulder, took it off its feet, and launched it a dozen feet to the side. The next came at him but Gortch spun aside and its momentum carried it past him. He followed with his arm extended, his mace careening off the creature's skull, taking half its scalp off, and cracking its head open.

The man got to his feet and stumbled toward the dwarves holding the shield line as he chased after his wife. Gortch raced after them. The moment he passed the dwarven warriors at the front, the shield bearers shifted to close the gap.

Monsters slammed into the shields and swiped with their claws, trying to get past them.

"Pikes!" Gortch shouted. "Attack!

The shield bearers dropped to their knees. The dwarves behind them thrust their pikes over their heads, impaling twenty orcs at once. Their bodies fell limp, many with their skewered bodies dangling from the pikes, a few making weak attempts to strike with their talons. Another wave rushed in, eager to replace those dangling from pikes.

"Sheild bearers, strike!"

The dwarves on their knees burst upward and thrust their shields, driving the dead orcs off the pikes and into the monsters behind them. The dwarves then pivoted their shields and thrust with short swords, felling another cluster of enemies. They stepped back, closed their shields, and reformed the line.

Thus, the dwarves fell into a rhythm with Gortch issuing orders to his squad and Vargan leading the other squad. All the while, monsters came at them and the citizens of Krotal raced across the bridge...at least those who had survived.

ARANGOLI FOUGHT IN A RHYTHM, his hammer felling attackers with each forward and backward swing. He kicked enemies trying to come between merlons, sending them falling off the wall. The steady stream of monsters kept coming until Ian used cones of flames to set them ablaze and the fire created a barrier at the bottom of the tower. The respite allowed Arangoli to check on the soldiers posted along the walls to the left and right of the tower.

The Head Thumpers fought with frantic fury, the orcs repeatedly cresting the walls only to be sent off with the slam of a shield, thrust of a sword, or hack of an axe. Dead orcs lay on the ground both inside and outside of the wall. A handful of dwarves had fallen as well, but the numbers were steeply skewed in the direction of the castle defenders.

The Krotal soldiers manning the other three walls fought off their own attackers. Captain Ludwin's squad was beginning to thin, just as were the dwarven defenders. As Arangoli came around, completing his turn, he noticed Ian staring into the distance. Following his gaze, he peered out over the city as a giant form emerged from the mist.

The demon stomped across the burning city, straight toward the castle, its head and upper body towering above the two-story buildings it walked past. The unfamiliar shiver of fear shook Arangoli's spine. Little truly frightened him, and nothing did so as powerfully as the demon, not after what he had witnessed.

They needed to prepare for a retreat, so Arangoli bellowed the command to the soldiers fighting on the wall below him. Caught up in the heat of battle, nobody reacted other than a young dwarf standing right below him. As he dwarf looked up, his eyes meeting Arangoli's, an orc burst over the wall and attacked from behind. The dwarf cried out, fell to his knees, and tumbled over the edge. His limp body landed on a pile of dead monsters inside the castle yard.

Knowing he had to act, Arangoli climbed between two merlons and jumped down. He landed on the orc's back, driving it down face-first to the wall. A kick to the monster's face sent it tumbling off the edge and into the castle yard, three stories below.

Pazacar, who fought just strides away, spun his staff and drove its butt into the face of an orc trying to crest the wall. "What are you doing?"

"We need to get out of here." Arangoli turned to the pole sticking up from the outer wall.

A rope ran from a hook at the bottom of the pole to an eyelet at the top. The rope had been strung from one end of the wall to a pole at the other end. Along the rope were six buckets, each pulling down on the rope with the weight of the kerosene inside them.

Quickly, Arangoli untied the rope, the line rapidly sliding through the ring at the top of the pole. The buckets and the rope dropped out of sight. He then pulled a torch from its mounting as an orc crawled over the wall and attacked.

Caught off guard, Arangoli ducked to avoid the monster's poisonous talons. Pazacar was there, his spinning staff striking the monster on the head. It fell to the wall and he drove the butt of his staff into its face. A kick sent the enemy off and into the castle yard.

"Thanks." Arangoli stood upright, leaned over the wall, and spied dozens of orcs climbing up.

He dropped the torch between two monsters. It fell in a streak of light and hit the ground. The kerosene ignited with a whoosh. The fire spread along the base of the wall, setting numerous orcs ablaze and releasing a wave of intense heat. A barrier of flames had been created, holding the enemy at bay.

Arangoli raised his hammer and drove it down as the orc below him crested the wall. The hammer struck it in the head, and the enemy fell, taking the monsters below with it on its way down.

With the area clear, Arangoli turned to Pazacar. "Send the call to retreat. We are to gather in the castle yard."

Even as the words came out, he spun away and raced into the upper chamber of the tower. He crossed the room and ran out onto the opposite wall, intent on dropping the next batch of buckets and setting them ablaze.

REVITA HELD tight to the crest before her as the dragon soared over the city. Ahead of her sat Vic, somehow communicating with the creature. Lint hid inside her coat with one hand on the lapel and the other holding the laces of her corset. She considered chastising him for what might be seen as advances, but the thought was lost to the thrill of their epic flight.

Again, Umbracan dove, flew over a square, and set fire to the fountain in its center. The kerosene erupted in a bloom of light and heat. The dragon fed its cone of flames, setting fire to any orc unlucky enough to be in its path. It flew beyond the edge of the square and rose up as the barrels in the fountain ignited. The thump of the concussion passed over her, followed immediately by a wave of heat. Flames and smoke swirled high above the city before receding. The dragon soared out over the river, banked, and flew back toward the city, allowing Revita her first good view since they began.

Fires burned throughout the city, none larger than those in and surrounding the five squares. The sight left Revita wondering if anything would remain of Krotal when daylight broke.

THE DEMON STOMPED across the city, its weight crushing orcs, and everything else in the way. It came toward the castle with focus, ignoring the fires, screams, and other chaos consuming the city. As the towering demon reached the base of the hill, fear climbed Ian's spine, slid around his neck, and constricted his throat. He froze, his heart thumping so loud in his ear, he heard nothing else. The plan to slow the advance of the monsters, in hope of sparing the lives of innocents, now felt wrong.

A deep, rumbling and unnatural voice shook the night. "You think to defy Az'Ianzar? Your puny warriors and weak fires cannot harm a demon lord born of flames and fed on the torment of fallen souls."

The demon climbed up the hillside, its muscles flexing with each stride. It bent and grabbed a burning wagon from the side of a roadway, lifted the wagon over its head, the flames rippling around its massive hands, and threw it. The wagon sped toward the wall to Ian's right. He urgently crafted a shield. The wagon struck the invisible barrier and blasted into pieces just feet from the dwarves manning the wall. Burning parts tumbled down onto the orcs below.

"So," the demon's voice rumbled as it climbed up the hillside. "You are the one wielding magic." Its evil, yellow eyes focused on Ian. "You will be the first to die."

Knowing he was now the demon lord's target, Ian fully opened himself to his magic while recalling H'Deesengar's warning. *Souls feed my kind, sustain us, and increase our might.*

Raw, unequaled power rushed in like a raging river, causing Ian to stumble before regaining control. He crafted a construct and thrust his arms toward the demon lord. Lightning burst forth, thick, powerful, and blinding. The bolts struck the demon full in the chest. Sizzling and crackling energy spread across its torso and then it sank into the creature. Ian fed the spell, seeking to make it stronger until he was forced to squeeze his eyes shut against the intense light. The electricity crackled and sizzled, the aura around it causing Ian's hair to stand on end. Even with the belt boosting his magic, his energy began to wane. He released his spell and opened his eyes to view the damage.

The demon still stood, its body shaking with terrible violence. Ripples ran beneath its flesh and then, it began to expand. The head swelled, its muscular body jerking, distending, and stretching. The creature convulsed. Its muscles bulged until it appeared they might pop. All the while, it grew larger and larger. By the time the process ceased, the demon stood taller than the gate tower.

The demon lord boomed laughter as it stomped up the hillside, toward the castle. "Oh, yes. Your soul will be a delicious feast."

Stunned and terrified, Ian backed across the tower rooftop. The giant lifted a hand bigger than Ian and reached for him. Urgently, he cast a shield over himself. The demon's hand struck the shield, the impact causing him to stumble backward.

Az'Ianzar growled, brows furrowed in anger. "Your puny magic cannot save you."

The demon raised its fist above the tower and slammed it down. Ian held fast to his shield and braced himself. The massive fist struck the shield with tremendous power. The shield held, but the force transferred to the base of the shield and drove it into the stone floor of the tower rooftop, cracking the stone as the entire tower shook.

Again, the demon pounded its fist down, the impulse of the blow causing Ian to wince and the tower to shake. The stone cracked further and then broke off. The center section of the rooftop collapsed, taking

Ian with it as it imploded into the winch room. He landed on his back and banged the back of his head. His magic and the shield slipped away as shards of rock and dust rained down on him. A stone block fell onto his leg and pinned it against the chunk of stone beneath him.

Eyes closed, Ian gritted his teeth from the pain in his head and leg. He blinked them open to a blur and wiped the dust from his face. The demon appeared through the hole above and laughed. It then reached down toward him. Desperate, Ian opened himself to his magic and tried to cast another shield, but the construct would not form. Panic struck as he realized he was going to die.

CHAPTER 50
RETREAT

The dragon flew out over the harbor and turned toward the city, the sky above it filled with black smoke that mixed with the evil cloud. Upon entering a massive plume of smoke rising from the burning city, Vic buried his nose and mouth in the crook of his arm. His eyes burned from the haze, so he closed them tightly and sent a message. *Get clear of the smoke.*

We are almost beyond it. A beat later, the dragon added, *We are clear.*

Vic opened his eyes and took a deep breath that turned to a gasp.

A towering giant with reddish skin covering its muscular frame stood on top of the hill, right before the castle's gate tower. It raised a fist and pounded down, destroying part of the tower and sending a cloud of dust into the air.

As Vic realized what he was looking at, the dragon sent confirmation, *It is the demon.*

My brother is at the castle. We must help him.

The dragon flew toward the behemoth as the demon reached toward the hole in the tower. A cone of flames burst from Umbracan's open maw and struck the side of the demon's face. The monster flinched and spun around, crushing monsters and trees on the hillside as its yellow-eyed gaze followed Umbracan.

"Is this a dragon I see?" The demon growled.

Umbracan banked back toward the demon, and bellowed, "You do not belong here, spawn of evil."

Even as the dragon circled around it, the demon laughed. "This world is mine, dragon. Your soul will soon be as well."

When the dragon came back around for another attack, the demon lashed out with shocking quickness. A hand the size of a wagon struck the dragon's wing as it tried to dodge. The blow sent Umbracan twirling. Vic, Revita, and Lint all screamed as the sky and ground spun past in a terrifying, twisting blur.

PANTING from the pain in his pinned leg, Ian lay on his back and stared up at a smoke-filled sky illuminated by the glow of a burning city. The demon, distracted by something, was beyond view. However, Ian's ability to cast spells relied on clear thought, and his thumping, rattled brain made that near impossible. He closed his eyes and tried to meditate, but the required peace was lost in the haze of pain emanating from his crushed leg. Then, he felt a presence in the back of his mind. *Lionel.*

Eyes closed, Ian reached out to Lionel. The drake was northeast of the castle, where the city met the forest edge. *Fly back toward the castle.* Lionel flapped his wings and flew back. *Stay low, below the smoke.*

For once, Lionel did exactly as Ian requested. It flew above the buildings and then, through Lionel's eyes, Ian spied the demon. *See the giant? Go toward it.*

The drake circled the hilltop in the middle of the city. The demon came back into view as it swung a giant arm. Its hand struck Umbracan and sent the dragon spinning off into a plume of smoke. While Ian was concerned for Vic, he forced himself to set those worries aside. *Rise higher. Go for its head.* Lionel flapped hard, rising higher as the demon lord turned back toward the castle.

Lionel flew through a cloud of smoke, obscuring the demon for a moment. The smoke cleared as Lionel emerged and flew toward the behemoth, its head fifty times larger than the drake. *The ear. Fly into its ear.* The drake leveled, flew into the dark recess of the demon's ear, and landed. Use your fire. Blow it into the depths of the demon's head.

A tremor shook Ian's body and the rock on his leg. The sharp agony caused his eyes to flash open and lose his connection.

Az'Ianzar stood over the hole again, reaching for Ian with an evil grin on its face. The demon's eyes widened, and it jerked its head to the side. It winced and struck the side of its head numerous times while releasing a roar that shook the castle.

Suddenly, Arangoli was standing over Ian. "Are you well?"

"Help me," Ian said. "My leg."

The dwarf walked over to the pile of rubble and slid the handle of his weapon in the gap between Ian's leg and the chunk of stone. He then gripped the hammer head with both hands, squatted, and lifted. The rock raised up and then toppled over, away from Ian. The pressure released from Ian's leg, allowing him to move, but his leg was unusable.

Arangoli slid an arm beneath Ian's and helped him stand. "Can you walk?"

With the movement, intense pain flared, causing Ian to gasp. "I can limp if you can help me."

"Come we must get down to the castle yard. The stairs here are blocked, so we will have to go to another tower."

With his arm around the dwarf's shoulders, Ian hopped and limped over the rubble and through the open doorway. They emerged on the castle wall, which was all but empty of defenders. Outside the castle, orc corpses, foliage, and buildings burned. The demon stomped around at the foot of the hill, still trying to clear out its ear.

"Come on!" Pazacar shouted from the far end of the wall as the last of his squad raced through the tower door at the far end of the wall.

Ian realized that the other walls were being vacated. The call for a retreat had been issued and none too soon. He closed his eyes and sent a call to Lionel. *Come. Hurry.*

Vic held on tight as Umbracan spun and spun. They flew into a thick plume of smoke and burst from it. The dragon extended its wings, slowed its rotation, and leveled. Its lower body bounced off a rooftop, struck the top of the city wall and then dropped while sailing out over the harbor. The dragon splashed down into the water, drenching Vic, Revita, and Lint, the force of impact tearing them from its back.

A wet chill enveloped Vic as water filled with bubbles surrounded him. He let his body go limp as he tumbled through the water. His momentum stopped and he began to rise. Confident he had determined the direction of the sky, he swam up and burst from the surface. A deep breath of air filled his lungs. He treaded water and spun, searching for Revita.

Lint popped up from the water ten feet from him, his body held up by a hand. An arm and head followed as Revita raised her face above the surface and gasped for air.

Vic swam over to her and wrapped an arm around her before paddling toward the nearest dock. Having grown up beside a lake, he was a strong swimmer and the sea water was pleasantly warm compared to the cold lake water of his childhood.

He reached the dock and grabbed ahold with one hand. Straining, he pulled himself and Revita up until his chin was above the edge. She placed Lint on the dock and then crawled up the rest of the way. Vic dropped down into the water and kicked while pulling up with both arms, rising with a burst. He slid onto his stomach, rolled, and lay on his back, panting for a few seconds before rolling over to see how she fared.

Revita crawled to her hands and knees while looking down at Lint. "Pipsqueak?"

When she shook the brownie, he did not move.

Concerned, Vic crawled over.

"Lint?" Revita gently shook him again. "Please, Lint." Her face was wet, so it was difficult to tell if it was water dripping from her eyes or tears.

Despite not always seeing eye to eye with the brownie, Vic had never wanted him dead. He also knew she felt something strong for Lint and seeing her in pain caused Vic pain as well. He slid an arm around her and pulled her against him. Rather than resist, she buried her head in the crook of his neck and began to weep. Her sorrow caused his eyes to tear up, so he closed them to squeeze off the tears.

A tiny cough came from nearby. Vic opened his eyes and stared at Lint. The brownie's body shook as he coughed again.

Hope and urgency had Vic let go of Revita and roll the brownie on his side. When he tapped Lint on the back, the brownie coughed and water came out of his mouth, onto the dock. "He is alive!"

She blinked. "What?'

Lint pushed himself to a side sitting position. "That water tastes horrible."

Revita laughed and scooped the brownie off the dock. "You are alive."

"You are skilled at stating the obvious." The brownie groaned. "You are squeezing me too hard."

"Oh. Sorry." She opened her hand, so he was sitting on it.

Vic looked around. The docks were empty, the water dark while the city beyond the harbor wall burned, creating a glow across the smoke-filled sky. There was no sign of Umbracan.

A RELENTLESS FLOW of orcs rushed out from the city, climbed over the corpses of their dead brethren, and attacked. Again, Gortch called for the shield bearers to absorb the impact and then dropped to one knee. The dwarves wielding pikes thrust, spearing dozens of monsters before those with shields pushed them off and then met the next wave with swords.

A few of his soldiers lay dead, and each time that occurred, he would call for the others to collapse the line and fill the gap. Although most of his squad members were young and many had never seen combat, they were well trained. He had Vargan to thank for that. The thought had him turning to look down the road, where Vargan and his squad fought off their own attackers. Like Gortch's squad, Vargan's had yielded ground but they still held the road leading to the bridge.

A deep roar came from the distance. Through the haze of smoke and in the light of the fires, a towering giant became visible. It swatted at the air around it and pounded the side of its head. Near the creature, fires surrounded the castle. In that moment, Gortch knew it was time to retreat.

He drew a breath and bellowed. "Shields ready! We prepare to retreat!"

Another wave of orcs slammed into them.

"Pikes attack!"

The shield bearers dropped down, pikes thrust through, shield bearers pushed the dead off the pikes.

"Archers ready!" Gortch waited a beat. "Loose!"

Arrows pelted orcs racing toward them.

"Retreat to the bridge!"

Gortch stood aside while his squad turned and ran down the road. An orc scrambled over the pile of corpses. He swung, and his mace took the monster in the face, blasting it off its feet. Others burst from the darkness and came at him, forcing him to turn and flee.

Having been overweight for his entire adult life, running was not an activity Gortch embraced. As a Head Thumper, it was also rarely needed until as of late. Despite this, he ran for all he was worth, knowing that the monsters were gaining on him and if they caught up, a mere scratch could be his end. The shrieks, hoots, and howls of the monsters grew closer and closer.

Ahead of him, his squad ran onto the bridge, stopped, and reformed with shields along the foot of the bridge. Gortch, huffing and puffing mightily, raced toward a gap between the shield bearers. The moment he passed through, the warriors closed the gap. Monsters slammed into the shields, eliciting grunts from the dwarves holding point. Gortch stopped between the warriors with pikes and the archers who stood farther along the bridge. There, he issued orders again, his squad dispatching the latest batch of monsters in moments.

Vargan and his squad broke and ran toward the bridge while orcs gave chase.

As the running dwarves drew near, Gortch shouted, "Open a gap! Let them through!"

Shield bearers and pikemen alike moved aside. Vargan's squad ran through the opening.

"To the far bank!" Vargan shouted as he raced past, leading his squad.

When the squad of retreating warriors was on the bridge, the gap closed again. The pursuing orcs crashed in, their talons claiming a shield bearer. Gortch called for pikes, but the gap did not fill fast enough. Two more shield bearers went down, followed by a pair of pikemen. The warriors surrounding the gap slashed and stabbed, killing the orcs, but the ranks were broken, and chaos ensued.

When an enemy burst beyond the dwarves Gortch met it with his mace. Another followed. Again, he smashed the creature before it reached him. Orcs swarmed the road and riverbank. If he didn't act fast, things would only grow worse.

"Archers!" He shouted. "Loose at will!"

Arrows filled the air, claiming enemies to the sides and beyond the foot of the bridge. The onslaught slowed. Dwarves fought off the last of the wave, and when the last attacker was down, Gortch shouted again.

"To the far bank! Run!"

Again, Gortch moved aside to allow his warriors to run past. Although the bridge was as wide as the road, he did not want to slow down their escape. He glanced back at the dead by the foot of the bridge. Among the pile of orcs lay a dozen armored bodies. As squad leader, those deaths were his responsibility. The acknowledgement and the sorrow that came with it passed in a flash, forced aside as an enemy burst from the darkness and raced toward him.

Gortch readied himself as the orc leapt and swiped. The strike missed when Gortch spun to the side with his arm extended. His mace struck the creature in the leg as it flew past, causing it to fall on its side and tumble against the bridge railing. The orc made to rise but was met by an underhand blow, the mace shattering its jaw and snapping its head back. It slammed into the side of the bridge and limply slid down its head dangling to one side.

Shrieks and howls came from the city. Gortch turned to find hundreds of monsters racing in from all directions. He spun and bolted.

The bridge had been constructed north of where the river widened and met the bay. Despite this, it was still a long run to cross it, far longer than Gortch preferred. He ran and ran, his breath coming in gasps, his armor clanking, the thump of his footsteps against the wooden bridge like thunder. The noises of wild, eager, and angry monsters came from behind him, urging him forward.

He glanced back to find pursuit just strides away. The toe of his boot hit something, and he tripped as the monster leapt. Gortch fell to the bridge with talons sweeping past his face. The orc landed past Gortch, who rolled with his momentum. The monster quickly shot to its feet as Gortch made a desperate swing. The mace clipped the creature's ankle and took its leg out from beneath it. The creature landed on its side. Gortch came up on his knees, and an overhead strike to the monster's skull ended the fight.

Shouts came from the dwarves at the end of the bridge. He climbed to his feet and turned to find a wave of enemies closing in quickly. Outnumbered, Gortch turned to run, but he knew he was not fast enough. A flurry of arrows sped past him, followed by shrieks from his pursuers. However, his mere presence shielded the monsters directly behind him, making it impossible for the archers to dispatch them all.

He glanced over his shoulder and found five orcs still chasing him. Worse, they were close. Too close. When the nearest lunged, Gortch swung a desperate backhand strike. His mace struck the creature in the arm, sending it falling to the side and through a gap in the bridge railing, but the momentum of the swing caused Gortch's feet to tangle with each other. He fell onto his back and rolled once. The monsters rushed in, and he knew he was dead.

CHAPTER 51

DESPAIR

With an arm around Ian, Arangoli helped the young wizard down the last run of stairs. They stumbled out into the castle yard to join the surviving Head Thumpers. Human soldiers poured out from doors below the towers at the opposite end of the yard. Hundreds of orc corpses surrounded the perimeter of the yard with dwarf and human remains among them.

Arangoli led Ian past the cluster of dwarves and toward the middle of the yard. The dwarves followed while Captain Ludwin led his soldiers in to meet them.

"The city burns," Ludwin said. "The castle burns. Please tell me you can get us out as you promised."

Ian's face was twisted in agony. "I will…"

A roar interrupted him. All eyes turned toward the sound as a massive head and shoulders appeared above the southern wall.

"There you are, my little prize," the demon laughed. "There is nowhere to run."

The demon's massive hand clamped onto the top of the six-foot-thick wall. It snapped off a chunk ten feet in diameter and tossed it aside while debris rained down.

Arangoli turned to Ian. "Hurry!"

Ian set his jaw and held out his arm. Nothing happened.

The demon tore off another piece of wall.

Urgency spurred Arangoli to urge Ian again. "Please, Ian. We need to leave. Now."

With a deep breath, Ian tried again. A ribbon of light split the air and spread to create a gateway fifteen feet in diameter and intersecting with the ground. The familiar sight of Ra'Tahal's central keep waited beyond it.

"Go!" Arangoli shouted. As the dwarves rushed through the gateway, Arangoli turned to Ian. "Can you hold it while I help you through?"

Ian nodded. "I think so, but I must wait."

"Wait? For what?" Arangoli looked back as the demon tore another chunk of wall away.

A dark shape flew in and landed on Ian's shoulder.

The drake settled and Ian nodded. "Now, we can go."

Arangoli helped him limp through the opening. The demon bellowed in anger as Captain Ludwin and his soldiers started running through. A massive fist came down, crushing four men while felling others nearby. Cries of pain and terror came from the fleeing soldiers. The demon burst through the remainder of the wall and reached for the crowd. It scooped up a handful of men and lifted them to its mouth. With a single bite, it tore the heads and upper bodies off the soldiers. That was the last thing Arangoli witnessed before the portal snapped closed and Ian fell limp against him.

Five orcs rushed toward Gortch, who lay on his back on a torchlit bridge. Even if he could get up before they struck, there were too many.

An armored figure leapt over him and chopped with an axe, severing the arm from one of the monsters. A broad swing followed, sliced across the torsos of two orcs before driving into the ribs of the one-armed monster. Although the dwarf was facing the other direction, Gortch immediately knew it was Vargan.

While stumbling to his feet, Gortch swung his mace and clipped the shoulder of an orc attempting to come at Vargan from the side. The impact spun the monster around, and before it could turn back toward him, Gortch finished it with a blow to the skull.

Suddenly, there was a gap of fifty feet between the two dwarves and the nearest upright monster.

"Thanks," Gortch said.

Vargan clapped him on the shoulder. "Let's go!"

They ran along the bridge and through a gap between shield bearers, not slowing until they were beyond Vargan's squad.

Gortch bent over with his free hand on his knee while panting in relief. He then stood upright and peered across the river. Thousands of orcs swarmed in from the harbor and streets. The mob flowed onto the bridge and charged across.

Vargan clapped Gortch on the shoulder. "Time to set the trap."

"Your men are already in position. Take command of them and mine as well. I'll set the fire."

Gortch rounded the wall of dwarf warriors and lifted a torch from its mount on the post at the corner of the bridge. He then descended the riverbank, the flickering light revealing reeds growing along the water's edge. Hidden in the shadows under the bridge was a stack of six barrels surrounded by sticks and twigs. When Gortch held the torch to the sticks, they caught fire. He stepped back to monitor the flames as they slowly spread from twig to twig. The moment the fire reached the base of the first barrel, he turned and hurried back up the bank.

The monsters reached the shield bearers. Vargan called out orders. Pikes and swords cut through the first wave. Arrows followed and warriors turned and ran to join Gortch's squad, who had taken position just before the first row of trees, a hundred feet away. With the torch in hand, Gortch ran after them.

The two squads melded together with shield bearers at the fore. The wave of psychotic monsters raced off the bridge and gave chase. Just before Gortch reached the waiting dwarven warriors, the barrels below the bridge exploded.

A sudden jolt and an intense wave of heat pressed against Gortch's back, causing him to stumble headfirst through a gap in the shields. He tucked his head and did a somersault before skidding to a stop. There, he lay on his back and gasped for air. The amber glow of a massive fire illuminated the trees above him. Splintered boards rained down from the sky and landed among the warriors and trees.

Vargan's voice rang out, issuing orders for his squad to attack the monsters that had made it beyond the bridge. The squad advanced past Gortch and the sounds of battle arose only to end seconds later.

From the shadows of the trees, Vargan approached, stood over Gortch, and extended a hand. "Another close call. I swear, you've the luck of the Dark Lord on your side tonight."

Gortch gripped Vargan's hand, sat up, and climbed to his feet. "I'll take any luck I can get, Dark Lord or not."

Vargan laughed and clapped Gortch on the back. "Well said."

Turning toward the city, Gortch examined the result of his efforts.

A massive section of the bridge was gone, part of it lost in the blast, another part tipped down into the river. What little remained on the near shore burned. Thousands of orcs were clustered on the intact portion of the bridge and along the far bank.

The giant form of the demon turned from what was left of the castle and stomped through the burning city. The monster appeared even larger and more imposing as it drew closer, the sight causing the fierce dwarven warriors to back away. Gortch did not blame them, for he did the same.

When the demon lord drew near the river, it released a guttural growl that shook the trees around it. "You think you have won. You know nothing, puny mortals. I am Az'Ianzar, Lord of the Fourth Realm. Death means nothing to me."

The demon lord held its arms out wide, palms up. A purple mist swirled down from his hands and snaked toward the corpses below him. Then, the dead monsters began to rise. The corpses moved in spurts and fits, their bones snapping back into place and wounds healing. The ground around them split. Arms appeared from those holes, and new orcs climbed out, as if emerging from a womb. In moments, thousands of monsters became tens of thousands.

"This is bad," Vargan said.

"Very bad," Gortch agreed. "Perhaps we should leave."

"I agree. Let's..." Vargan's jaw dropped.

The demon extended a long arm above the river. Purple light appeared above the water, shifting from a blur to something solid. In seconds, a bridge of light spanned from riverbank to riverbank, parallel to the destroyed one. Orcs rushed out onto the bridge.

Gortch bellowed. "Run!"

He turned and raced down the road. The clanking of armor came from behind, and soon, other dwarfs began to pass him.

The plan was to destroy the bridge and strand the horde of monsters north of the river. The demon's unsuspected magic had blown that plan to shreds. So, he ran and ran, hoping for a miracle.

Vic knelt on the dock with his arm around Revita. The two of them, along with Lint, stared toward the burning city. Fires and smoke were everywhere except along the waterfront. That left them blanketed in darkness, especially since the smoke and unnatural cloud blotted out the moon and starlight.

Orcs ran along the city wall, heading toward the river, oblivious to the three people watching in the darkness. The giant demon stomped in the same direction. What remained of the castle was impossible to tell. Vic prayed that Ian had escaped before it fell, as they had planned.

He turned back toward the harbor, searching the black water. There was no sign of the dragon. For the tenth time, he sent thoughts out, calling to Umbracan. With each passing attempt, his hope for a response waned.

But this time was different.

I wake. The words echoed in Vic's head.

Stunned and uncertain if he was imagining it, Vic peered into the darkness.

Revita reacted to his sudden turn. "What is it?"

He pointed out into the dark waters. "Look."

Bubbles roiled in the harbor beyond the dock. The bubbles turned to surging rapids. The dragon's head burst from the surface and it shook, spraying water as far as fifty feet in all directions. Umbracan drew a deep breath and then began swimming toward the dock.

Vic said, "I feared you were dead."

The dragon swam past. "It will take more than a crash landing to kill this dragon."

After casting a quick glance at Revita, Vic headed down the dock, trailing the swimming dragon. Umbracan's body began to rise from the water as it entered the shallows and then climbed onto shore.

Vic ran along the dock and slowed when he neared the dragon. "Are you well enough to fly?"

"I am unharmed."

"I need to know if my brother got out."

"Climb up." The dragon turned, its tail sweeping around and stopping short of Vic.

When Vic glanced at Revita, she pointed toward the dragon. "What are you waiting for? Climb up."

Vic placed a boot on the dragon's thick tail and found it slippery. Carefully using the crests for grip and footholds, he scaled up. By the time he settled between two crests near the base of its neck, Revita, with Lint in her hand, had caught up and sat behind him.

Umbracan took a few steps and launched into flight over the bay. The dragon turned while ascending and flew through the smoke-filled sky, over the burning city.

The castle loomed at the top of the hilltop, the foliage surrounding it on fire. A massive section of the southern wall was destroyed and corpses lay both within and surrounding its fortifications. At Vic's direction, the dragon landed in the castle yard. Without getting down, Vic looked from side to side, searching for signs of his brother among the dead. While there were a handful of armored dwarves and ten times that number of human soldiers among the piled-up dead, he saw no sign of Ian.

The dragon took to the sky again and flew east, through a haze of dark smoke, forcing Vic and Revita to cover their faces. It flew higher and the smoke fell away.

"What is that?" Revita pointed over the dragon's left side.

Below them was the dark river, the bridge that had spanned it burning. Beside the burning structure was a bridge of dark purple light. Orcs raced across it and poured into the gravel road east of the river. On the western bank stood the demon, its back turned to the river as it faced the city. The demon held out its hands and tendrils of magic flowed out from them. What it was doing, Vic had no idea. Frankly he wanted nothing to do with the demon. The orcs, however, posed another problem.

"The monsters made it across the river. There is nothing to stop them from reaching Greavesport."

Revita leaned over his shoulder. "What of Gortch and Vargan? Did your brother get them out as planned?"

"I don't know." Vic sent a thought to Umbracan. *Fly over the road until you are beyond the orcs.*

I am on my way. The dragon spread its wings and glided east, following the pale ribbon of gravel visible through gaps in the surrounding forest.

Now beyond the smoke and unnatural cloud created by the demon, Gortch ran along the forest road. Shadows loomed in the trees to either side while the light of the full moon painted the road in pale blue light. His breath came in rasping gasps, but he forged on, doing his best to keep up with the other dwarves running with him. The road took them down into a low spot before climbing a hill, toward a saddle between two rocky crags that appeared like dark sentinels watching over the fleeing dwarves. All the while, the hoots and howls of the pursuing orcs drew closer.

The taxing ascent sapped much of Gortch's remaining energy, and by the time he approached the top of the hill, he knew he could not run much farther. As he crested the rise and the ground leveled, Vargan came into view.

Standing in the middle of the road, Vargan shouted. "We can run no longer! Here, we form up and fight!"

Gortch slowed to a stop and glanced from side to side. Steep, rocky ground began just beyond the edges of the roadway, the uneven slopes ascending to peaks over a hundred feet above them. The narrow point would greatly reduce the monsters' advantage of superior numbers.

Vargan called out, "Squad one take the fore first. We will rotate in squad two. Shields in front. Pikes behind the shields. Archers find footing on the slopes to either side of the road."

Even as he issued the commands and the warriors shifted into position, orcs burst into the moonlight and raced up the hillside.

To Gortch, Vargan said, "I need you to resume command of squad two. Have them ready for when we fall back."

His breathing still heavy, Gortch nodded. He turned to the remaining squad members. "You heard him. Shield bearers take position ten strides behind squad one. Pikes at the rear. Archers find spots along the upslope."

As he finished issuing the order, the orcs struck squad one. The archers loosed, picking off monsters attempting to climb the slope to the sides of the shield line. The monsters attacked in their frantic, wild bloodlust while the dwarves responded with practiced efficiency. Wave after wave came at the stout dwarven warriors. Orcs died by the dozens, but they claimed two shield bearers, a pikeman, and a trio of archers by the time Vargan barked the order to retreat. The archers climbed down and hurried past Gortch and his warriors. The rest of squad one turned and fled, seeking safety behind squad two. When one of the dwarves tripped and went down, an orc rushed in for the kill. Just before it reached the fallen dwarf, Vargan was there with his axe flashing. The orc's arm flew off to the side of the road.

"Go!" Vargan shouted as the dwarf climbed to his feet.

Three more monsters ran in as Vargan turned to face them. He hacked and slashed while backing away, cutting across the torso of one and the leg of another. In the process, he stumbled over a dead monster. He landed on his back as a live one rushed in. Vargan rolled, barely avoiding the deadly talons, but as he rose to his knees and swung his axe, another came in from the side and slashed, its talons raking across Vargan's shoulder plates right before Gortch reached him. His mace smashed into the monster's face, lifting it off its feet, its body limp as it fell to the road.

Gortch slid an arm under Vargan's, helping him to his feet and the two of them darted through the opening in the shield line. The gap closed behind them right as another wave of monsters struck. The moment they were beyond the warriors, Gortch began shouting commands, the warriors responding as they repelled and dispatched the monsters.

He then glanced toward Vargan, who stood a stride away with his legs wide, his shoulders slumped, his face white. "What's wrong?"

"I..." Foam bubbled from Vargan's mouth. He stiffened and then fell to the ground.

"Vargan!" Gortch cried.

He knelt and noted the dark line of blood on Vargan's neck. Even if Vargan had not been staring into space with white spittle drooling from his mouth, Gortch would have known the worst had occurred. A mere scratch from orc talons meant death. His friend was gone.

Another realization struck – the monsters would not stop coming. Even if each dwarf in his party killed one hundred enemies before falling, every one of them would fall. The orcs outnumbered them a thousand to one and the demon lord would simply resurrect those that died and the fight would resume.

Despair gripped him in a way he had never experienced it. He was about to die and it would be for nothing.

As he turned to face the enemy attacking his squad, a dark silhouette dove down from the sky and a burst of flames lit up the night. The orcs on the hillside were engulfed by fire while those on the top of the hill turned toward the bright flames like so many moths, unable to deny the attraction.

A dragon flew overhead, and with its appearance, Gortch found hope.

He bellowed orders, commanding his squad to advance and cut down the distracted orcs from behind.

Revita held on tight as the dragon flew between the two crags, right over the dwarven warriors blocking the pass. She leaned forward and gripped Vic by the shoulder, turning him toward her. "Tell Umbracan to land. I will relay the plan while you deal with the orcs."

He frowned, appearing unhappy about the idea and then nodded.

Umbracan tilted and made a tight turn before fluttering its wings, slowing to land a few hundred strides from the fracas. Revita shoved Lint into her coat pocket, lifted her leg over the dragon crest, and slid down the scaly side. She dropped a dozen feet to the land on the gravel road, bent her legs with the fall, and rolled with her momentum. In a flash, she was on her feet and running along the road.

The sounds of battle drew closer, along with the screams of dying orcs. As she drew near, she spied a rather heavyset dwarf standing between two squads.

"Gortch!" She shouted.

Dwarves turned toward her, one of them with a familiar face. "Revita!"

She slowed to a walk as she wove between his warriors. "We are here to help."

"Help, we could use."

"Vic is on the dragon. They are going to set the forest aflame. You are to hold this point until the trees are burning and the dragon turns back in this direction. Then, you are to run."

Gortch raked a hand down his face. "More running?" He released a heavy sigh and nodded. "We will do it."

"And I will be with you."

"Good. Every blade counts right now."

She looked down at a dwarf lying at the side of the road, staring toward the bright, round moon. "Is that…"

Gortch nodded. "Vargan."

"Oh, poor Vargan." Revita had always liked the headstrong dwarf, and the sight of his corpse brought on an uncharacteristic sense of loss. She turned toward the fight and wiped her eye. "Be ready to call a hasty retreat."

As Umbracan took to the sky, Vic peered northwest, toward the burning city of Krotal, now miles away. Even at that distance, he could see the tall form of the demon walking among the ruins. What it was doing, he had no idea. He wanted nothing to do with the creature after what had occurred.

The dragon flew out over the sea and turned north, heading over the dark forest. It blasted a cone of flames that licked the trees, setting them ablaze. Again and again, it blasted fire, targeting the forest south of the road and allowing the breeze off the sea to spread the blaze northeast. When Vic was convinced that the fire was broad and intense enough to create an impassible barrier, he reached out to Umbracan.

Return to the army. It is time to finish the plan.

The monsters will suffer.

The dragon turned and flew through the night. It rounded one of the two peaks beside the road and the warriors below turned and fled. Umbracan flew out toward the sea and turned again, this time heading straight toward the nearest peak. Vic held on tight, bracing himself as the dragon headed toward the rocky crag, tilted back, extended its legs and struck. The force sent a mighty jolt through its body that just about shook Vic loose from his perch. The top of the crag broke off and tumbled down the steep hillside. The massive boulder crashed down toward the monsters running along the road. A wall of rocks and dirt rained down after the boulder as it hit the bottom and crushed the monsters unlucky enough to be in the way. The landslide poured down on the creatures as the pile at the bottom rose to fill in the gap between the two slopes.

"Good," Vic said aloud. "Let's give the monsters another fire bath and then we will go find Revita."

As the dragon again took flight, Vic glanced down the road, where dwarves fought off the last of their pursuers. The forest fire would buy them time, but he worried that nothing could stop the demon and its horde from eventually claiming the entire world.

I pray you are well, Ian.

I pray your plan, whatever it is, will work.

CHAPTER 52
EVACUATION

Shria-Li and a host of palace guards stood beside a road at the western end of Havenfall. The island city had been her home, and that of the Sylvan, for as long anyone could remember. Thus, it had been difficult to come to grips with their new reality. She suspected the same of her people, but it was better to survive than to fade into history.

That statement had been part of the proclamation she had sent out the day earlier. She didn't know if everyone would heed her warning, but as she watched her subjects march past with full carts, wagons, and human slaves carrying heavy sacks filled with goods, it had become clear that most had chosen life over a piece of land. *You cannot save everyone*, she told herself. As queen, her responsibility was to lead and short of placing those who chose not to follow under arrest, there was nothing else she could do. When death came for them, those too stubborn to flee might change their mind. It also might be too late.

The steady stream of people flowed past, and when they reached the two bridges that connected the island city to the north and south banks of the river, every single one of them chose the latter. Their journey would not take them far, but getting clear of the city before sunset was paramount. With that thought, she lifted her gaze to the western sky, where the sun lingered high above the mountain range that divided Sylvanar in half. Tree-covered hills, thriving forests, and country farms covered that land. *Would any of the farmers be willing to abandon their homes?* Most were cultivators, a skill her people would need if they were to thrive in their new habitat.

She turned to the guards. "My people have seen me. They will know that I am in this with them. Let's return to the palace. The day wanes, and there is much yet to prepare."

She climbed into the palanquin and sat back as the porters lifted it onto their shoulders. With her guards split up, half leading and half trailing, the porters marched the palanquin through the city.

Soon, they were off the busy streets that led out of Havenfall and passing through quiet, abandoned neighborhoods. It was odd to see nobody near the fountains, to find no carts selling goods in commerce square, and to hear no laughter or chatter or anything else that indicated a thriving populace. Instead, the windows were all closed, the doors locked. The people who had lived and worked in those buildings likely held hope that they would return one day. Shria-Li held no such delusions. The prophecy was coming to fruition. Havenfall was a city on the brink of death. She just never would have guessed that death would come at the hand of her friend.

The palanquin crested a rise and the palace came into view. Sunlight shone off the copper dome above the throne room and the alabaster columns outside the main entrance while glinting off the golden leaves of the massive tree rising above the structure. It was a glorious sight that instilled sorrow for the first time she could recall. Soon, she would no longer be able to gaze upon those graceful arches surrounding the Tree of Life. *Soon, it would all be a memory. Yet, the Sylvan will go on. This is only a place. As old trees die, new ones replace them. So, it will be with Havenfall.*

The porters stopped outside the palace front entrance. They set the palanquin on the ground, and Shria-Li climbed out. She stood tall, held her chin high, and headed up the stairs, following a pair of guards while the others trailed behind. Those in the fore opened the doors and waited as she passed by.

Inside, she was met by silence. Everyone other than the guards had abandoned the building, even the servants. *Well, not everyone.* With that thought, she decided it was time for her to address another issue.

She turned to the guards. "I wish to visit the dungeon."

The guards exchanged questioning looks, nobody responding.

"Now," she hoped her firm tone would prevent any resistance.

"Yes, My Queen," said Daisha-Lu, the squad leader.

When Daisha-Lu and another guard headed across the hall, Shria-Li followed. A side corridor brought them to a staircase and they descended, their surroundings dark other than the lantern on the landing ten stairs down. They rounded the corner and continued down, the air growing steadily more dank. A lantern waited at the bottom, which Daisha-Lu lifted off its hook before heading down a dark corridor.

Shria-Li followed in silence. Only once had she visited the palace's underbelly, a brief adventure that had stoked her father's anger. Getting lost in those underground warrens did not help the matter, nor did the nightmares that followed.

They turned down another corridor and came to a dark stairwell, where they descended again, the air growing cooler and mustier with each step. Another corridor took them past storage rooms and branching hallways. When they rounded a turn, light came from ahead. They made their way toward it and entered a large, round chamber surrounded by cells with barred doors. A small room with a desk and lantern beside its doorway occupied the chamber's center.

Daisha-Lu approached the open door to the center room. "Hello?"

Noise came from inside and a towering, overweight human

emerged. "Oh. Sorry. I didn't know anyone was coming." He wiped his hands on his stained tunic. The man smelled unwashed. "What can I do for you?"

The scowl on Daisha-Lu's face made her mood clear. "You are in the presence of Queen Shria-Li. Show some respect."

The man's eyes widened and he turned toward Shria-Li. "I...I am sorry...your Highness."

"Majesty," Daisha-Lu snapped.

"Ah. Right. Your Majesty." He wiped his forehead with the back of his hand. "Hardly nobody comes to see Remy."

"Remy?" Shria-Li asked.

"Yeah?"

She sighed inwardly. "Is that your name?"

"Yeah."

"Alright, Remy, I am looking for a prisoner named Evarian."

"Ah. That one." He pointed. "He is in that cell."

"What of Captain Chavell?"

The man pointed in the other direction. "He is in there."

"Tell me, Remy, do you have a place where I could have a private conversation with both prisoners?"

The man scratched his head, bald on top with greasy, brown hair hanging down the sides. "I guess the terrigate room."

Shria-Li frowned. "Terrigate room?"

Daisha-Lu said, "I think he means the interrogation chamber."

"Where is that?"

The man pointed toward the closed door across the room, the only door lacking a barred window opening.

"Fine." Shria-Li gave a firm nod. "Rouse those two prisoners and these guards will escort them to the room."

"Um. Alright." Remy lifted a ring of keys from a hook on his belt, fumbled with them, and headed toward one of the closed doors.

Daisha-Lu sidled up beside Shria-Li and spoke in a soft voice. "Are you certain this is wise?"

"Wise or not, this needs to happen."

Before the guard could argue the point, Shria-Li was walking away. She headed toward the interrogation room's door; the wood aged to a dark gray. Turning the knob, she pushed the door open. Light bled in as the door swung wide. The hinges emitted a low groan until the door stopped three quarters of the way open. The room smelled of blood and death. Dark chains and shackles hung from the opposite wall while a blood-stained table with ropes and cranks occupied the center of the room. Other tools of torture lurked in the shadows to the left and right, but Shria-Li avoided looking at them. As it stood, the room was likely to haunt her for a very long time.

Footsteps drew her attention as Daisha-Lu approached with the lantern held high. A pair of guards trailed her while gripping the elbows of a male elf. Another trio of elves, consisting of two guards and a prisoner, came from across the room.

"Leave the lantern on the table." Shria-Li said.

"Leave it?"

"Yes. I wish to speak with Evarian and Chavell alone."

The guards brought the first prisoner into the room.

"That is against protocol, and I fear..."

"You will do as I say. I am queen." While unused to asserting herself in that manner, Shria-Li was determined and did not have time to argue.

When the second prisoner was brought into the room, Daisha-Lu waved the guards out and pulled the door closed behind her.

Shria-Li turned and looked at the two male elves who had conspired to commit murder. Both stood tall with broad shoulders for their kind. Evarian had brown hair and bright green eyes while Chavell wore his lighter hair cropped. Both of them appeared worn and ragged, their clothing stained and torn, their faces dirty, their wrists shackled behind their backs.

She drew a breath of courage and focused on keeping her emotions at bay. "I suspect you know little of what has happened since your incarceration. The king has abdicated his throne. The queen has died. I have been coronated and must guide my people. It is my duty, and despite my own desires, I am obligated to do so. I seek to ensure the future of my people, which is why the city is being evacuated."

Chavell's blue eyes blinked. "Things have gotten so bad in such a little time?"

Evarian asked, "You are leaving Havenfall?"

"The Sylvan must leave if they are to survive."

"I was correct." He nodded. "The barrier has failed and the monsters of the Vale have grown too dangerous."

"While true, that is the least of my concerns at this time."

His brow furrowed. "What could be worse than that?'

"An army of darkness marches across the land. These monsters cannot be reasoned with. They seek to end all life, for they originate from the underworld itself."

Evarian guffawed. "You can't be serious."

"I am deadly serious."

Chavell asked, "Where is this army?"

"They are quite distant as of now."

"Havenfall is highly defensible. Nobody could approach from the Vale and the river protects the city's flanks. If we destroy the bridges, our archers can pick them off without fear of them drawing near."

"One might think so, but I know for a fact that is not what will happen."

"How do you know?'

"Because someone I know and trust is bringing this army directly to Havenfall using magic."

"What? Why would anyone do that?"

"Because it is the only way to save our world."

Chavell shook his head. "I don't understand."

"You don't need to understand. You only need to believe in your queen and have the desire to save your people."

"That is all I ever wanted."

Evarian nodded. "I as well."

"As I thought." Shria-Li softened her hard tone. "While your actions were reprehensible, your intent was in earnest. I see that, now. Even if this army never came to Havenfall, the city will never be safe, not with the barrier gone. This is why we must relocate. Our time here has ended."

"What of the Tree of Life?"

"We will plant a new grove using seeds I have harvested from the roots below the tree. Priestess Valaria and her retinue travel with those seeds now."

"Why are you telling us this?"

"Because I need your help." She looked at Evarian. "You are our best warrior. If you pledge your loyalty to me, I will release you and place you back at the head of the Blue Spears."

He blinked. "You are offering a pardon?"

"Fight for me. Fight for your people. Earn your redemption."

"I will do it."

She turned her attention to Chavell. "Would you do the same if I return you to captain of the palace guard? I need competent, skilled people who have the respect of those they lead. Most important of all, I believe I can trust you."

Chavell shook his head as a tear tracked down his cheek. "I betrayed my king and queen. How could you ever trust me?"

She reached out and wiped the tear from his cheek. "The guilt you bear for that act answers the question. The steps I take now might be seen as a betrayal to others, but I take them for the good of my people. The path that led you to a dungeon cell was of a similar nature." She peered into his eyes, hoping he would see the conviction in hers. "What say you? I could use a good warrior at my side to protect me in the days to come."

Another tear emerged as he nodded. "May Vandasal bless, you, Shria-Li. You have my pledge, heart and soul."

Shria-Li stepped back and exhaled in relief. "Let's get you freed, cleaned up, and fed. I will have someone retrieve your armor and weapons. I fear we are in for a long night."

CHAPTER 53

A LATE RESCUE

Asoft hand stroked Ian's face, waking him. He opened his eyes to find Winnie staring down at him, her brow furrowed in concern. Indirect sunlight illuminated his bedroom, informing him that it was past morning.

"There you are," Winnie said. "I was hoping you would wake soon."

Ian's mouth felt like he'd been sucking on cloth, his throat dry, his thirst raging. "Water?" he whispered.

"Oh. Yes." She reached for a glass on the nightstand. "I will help you."

With her hand under his neck, he sat up and drank, not stopping until the entire cup was drained.

With a sigh, he lay back down. "What time is it?"

"Late afternoon."

"Already."

He rubbed his eyes and tried to remember what had happened. Like reliving a nightmare, an image of the demon lord flashed in his head, the creature reaching for Ian, eager to consume his soul. Opening his eyes, he banished the thought. If that came to be, the world was doomed.

"How did I get here?" he asked.

"You were hurt when you arrived in Ra'Tahal. Your leg looked..." She shook her head. "Very bad. Arangoli brought you here and a healer came to see you. When the healer left, your leg was better, but he said you had exhausted your energy and would need sleep. A lot of sleep."

"So, you let me sleep the day away."

"Not the entire day."

"Which is why I am starving." He sat up. The room tilted from side to side. He realized he was not wearing a shirt. When he lifted his covers, he discovered that more than his shirt was missing. "Why am I naked?"

"The healer had you lay in a tub. He said that the water would enhance your recovery. Afterward, I dried you off and the two of us carried you to bed."

"Naked?" Although he had been unconscious at the time, Ian found himself embarrassed as he imagined it all happening.

She smirked. "It's not as if I haven't seen you that way before."

"That was different. We were, um, you know." He felt his cheeks warming.

Winnie laughed, leaned in, and kissed him. "You are so cute when you are embarrassed."

"I'm not embarrassed. It's just that I prefer to..." he considered how to explain. "I'd rather not seem so weak and vulnerable. Especially in front of you."

She took his hand. "To others, you might have to appear as a great wizard, someone who seeks to save the world. Such things don't matter to me. When we are together, you can just be you, and if the weight of responsibility is too much, I am here to help in any way I can."

He shook his head. "You are too good for me."

"Nonsense." She grinned. "If you like, I can show you how bad I can be."

It was his turn to laugh. "I'll admit that is tempting, but I need food, or I might pass out."

Winnie stood and smoothed her dress, which was tight in all the right places. He drank in her shapely figure and wondered how he had paid her so little attention back when they lived in the same small village hundreds of miles to the south.

"I expected you would be hungry," she said, "which is why dinner is cooking in the kitchen. Let me finish up there while you get dressed. By the time you come down, it will be ready."

As she turned away, he snatched her by the wrist, stopping her.

"What is it?" she asked.

"Thank you for taking care of me."

"You took care of me in my time of need. It is only right for me to do the same for you."

In that moment, he realized something striking. "I want to be with you."

"You are with me, silly."

"No. I mean... Forever."

Her eyes widened. "What are you saying?"

"This might not be the best way to ask, but I was hoping you would be my wife."

She squealed and burst toward him, her arms wrapping around him as she bent and hugged him tightly. Ian hugged her back, waiting for her to say something. Instead, she pulled back and wiped tears from her eyes.

"Are you going to answer?"

She chuckled. "Sorry. Yes. Yes. I would love nothing more than to be your wife."

"Good." He slid out of bed and stood. "That makes me feel better about walking around naked in front of you."

At that moment, Rina appeared in the doorway. "Dinner is read…" Her eyes just about popped out of her head when she saw Ian.

He hastily grabbed a pillow from the bed and held it over his groin. "Rina! I… um…"

Her cheeks turned red and she spun away. Over her shoulder, she said, "The roast is out of the oven. Come and eat when you are ready." Without waiting for a reply, she fled down the stairs.

Winnie grunted. "I am still getting used to someone else living here."

Last Ian had seen of Rina, she had been despondent. "At least she is talking."

"Yes. Today has been a better day, but I still find her staring numbly into space from time to time."

"I guess it's better than weeping."

"I am not so sure. While I cannot imagine going through what she did, the emotions connected to it will haunt her forever unless she finds a way to work through it." She stepped out into the corridor. "Get dressed and come join us when you are ready."

Ian said, "Please close the door."

She chuckled. "We will see you soon."

The door closed and Ian sat on the bed with a sigh. He pressed his palm to his forehead. *How am I supposed to face Rina, now?* Dinner would either be filled with uncomfortable silence or a steady discussion on topics focused on what was taking place in the world. He was determined to ensure it was the latter.

Dressed in black robes with gold embroidered runes on the collar, the hem, and the cuffs, Ian connected the magical belt around his waist and descended to the main floor of his tower. When Lionel, who was perched on the back of a chair, saw him, he released an urgent squawk and began to shuffle his feet while bobbing back and forth in excitement.

Ian laughed and approached the drake. "Yes. I'm happy to you see you, too."

Air rasped in Lionel's throat, making it sound as if he were purring as Ian stroked the drake's neck. He lifted Lionel to his shoulder and continued to stroke his back while staring toward the window. Ian considered taking Lionel with him but thought better of it. Although he would be dead without Lionel's help against the demon, he preferred to avoid the added distraction. What he planned would require every ounce of his attention. A rustling from across the room had him turn to find Winnie standing on the staircase, staring at him.

"What's wrong?" he asked.

"I am worried. I wish you didn't have to go."

"I would love to stay, but if I did that, more people would die. Eventually, the demon and its twisted army would come to Ra'Tahal. The only way to avoid a dark ending for everyone is to take a chance."

She descended. "But why you?"

He sighed. "You know why."

"I guess, but I don't have to like it."

"No, you don't. Is that why you came down here?"

"I came down to say goodbye."

"We already said goodbye."

She approached him. "Can I at least ask for one more kiss?"

That was one request he could not deny. She slid in close, their lips meeting. Her arms wrapped around him and hugged him against her tightly. His body reacted to the contact, his pulse rising and he might have lost himself to the passion if Lionel had not nipped at her hair.

Winnie yelped and yanked away from the drake before waggling a finger at him. "You be nice."

"Um. Sorry."

She smoothed her hair. "Just when I thought he and I were friends, he does something like this."

"He is protective of me."

"It is not like I was attacking you."

"Well, you sort of were." Ian grinned. "Had we gone on much longer, we were likely to end up back in my bedroom."

A smirk turned her lips up. "Would that be so bad?"

"I much prefer it to what I must do now." He glanced toward the window and noted the city outside draped in shadow. "I wish it were otherwise, but I must go."

"Please come back to me."

"I will do everything in my power to make it so."

He set Lionel on the back of a chair and opened himself to the source. Magic flowed into him like a dam bursting, yet he held himself steady. A gateway opened before him, the rush of crashing waves filling the room. He stepped through and dismissed it.

Ian stood on a rocky point beside a seaside cove. To the west, the sun lingered above the open sea, but it was evident that it would set within the hour. Although out of his view, the city of Greavesport waited just south of where Ian stood, but Ian's focus was north. He peered in that direction, seeking the dark cloud connected to the demon lord and his horde, and spied a black smudge in the distance. With that goal in mind, he picked out a location he was able to see well enough to picture in his mind. The portal he cast opened before him with the same boulder, a mile distant, now just a stride away. He stepped through and sought another target as he traveled north.

THE SHORELINE TOOK Ian north twenty miles before turning west where a river met an open bay. South of the bay, he spied a camp consisting of thousands and instantly knew they were refugees from Krotal. He cast a gateway taking him beyond the cluster of thousands and stepped out to find a small, peaceful town hugging the sea near the river's mouth. Just a half mile inland from there, a wooden bridge spanned the river. It was there, sixteen gateway hops into his journey, each time choosing an elevated target to give him a clear view, when Ian came across something unexpected.

While the dark cloud remained miles west of his position, an army marched along the road leading to the bridge. The squat, armored figures were easily recognizable as dwarves. Relief and joy came over him in equal measure. He cast a gateway and stepped through onto the bridge. There he waited as the dwarves approached.

When he saw a notably large dwarf in the lead, he shouted. "Gortch!"

The dwarf, who had been looking at the ground in front of him, lifted his gaze. He wiped his eyes and shook his head as he drew nearer. "Ian. Is that you?"

Ian stepped off the bridge. "I am so glad to find you. I feared what had become of you." He looked over the gathering dwarves. "Where is Vargan?"

Gortch shook his head. "We lost Vargan, along with a third of our force."

The joy slid away, replaced by sorrow. He clapped a hand on Gortch's shoulder, the metal plate clanking from the impact. "I am sorry."

"As am I." The dwarf frowned. "What happened? You were supposed to get us out. Instead, we have been fleeing that blasted demon since last night." He thrust a finger into Ian's chest. "Had you been there, Vargan would still be alive."

Guilt and regret tore at Ian's soul. It had been his plan to come for the dwarves and return them to Ra'Tahal. He shook his head. "I am so sorry. The defense of the castle didn't go as planned. I was injured. We were lucky to get out at all. The gateway to Ra'Tahal was my last act before succumbing to my injuries. I was unconscious until late today."

The dwarf surveyed Ian from head to toe. "You look well enough."

"One of your healers cared for me last night, healing my wounds."

Gortch grimaced. He glanced back at the worn and weary warriors behind him. "My squad needs food and rest. Can you bring us home?"

Ian nodded. "Of course." He turned toward the bridge, memorizing it. "But before I cast a gateway," he turned back toward Gortch. While fearing the answer to his question, he had to ask. "Have you seen my brother?"

"Not since last night."

Ian's hopes sank.

"He, Revita, and that dragon saved our arses."

"What happened?"

"After we destroyed the bridge as planned, the demon lord used magic to craft another. The blazing orcs raced across the river, and we bolted. When it became clear we could not outrun them, we found a defensible location and took a stand, but their numbers were too many. We were going to die. It was only a matter of how long we could hold out. That's when Vic, Revita, and the dragon showed up and bought us time. We have been marching east ever since."

Ian was relieved to know that Vic and Revita had survived the battle.

"There is one more thing," Gortch said. "The demon resurrected dead orcs and spawned others." He shook his head. "No matter how many we kill, it brings them back to life or creates more."

The statement aligned with something Arangoli had said.

"Which is why I must deal with the demon." Ian cast a gateway that opened to the square outside Ra'Tahal's central keep. "Go on. Eat. Rest. Your role in this war is over, so long as things go as planned."

"Things never go as planned in war."

"Which is why I must end it as soon as possible."

"Be well, Ian. We will pray you are successful."

"Thanks."

Gortch led the dwarves through the portal, their numbers north of two hundred. When all were through, Ian released the gateway and cast another. He stepped through, into a dark temple, its floor illuminated by four simmering braziers. He walked straight for the stairs leading to an open doorway with daylight waiting beyond it. He was determined to see his plan through.

CHAPTER 54

BAIT

Resolute, Ian stood in the center of Sacrumi, surrounded by villagers armed with spears, hatchets, and bows. Those with the hatchets held shields almost as tall as themselves, the face of each shield painted in garish colors. Their expressions reflected his mood, somber yet determined.

Ahni walked through a gap in the crowd, took position beside Ian, and thrust her spear into the air. "Crumi! Tonight, we fight against an evil that would seek to claim us all. Tonight, we make our god proud! Shout with me! Crumi! Crumi! Crumi…"

Two hundred fifty Crumi warriors joined her chant. When the noise subsided, she turned to Ian with a nod. "We are ready."

"Very well. Just remember, the orcs are our enemies. Save the bloodshed for the spawn of darkness. In this, all others are our allies."

"Understood."

Ian crafted a gateway. It opened to a shadowed crater with a lake in its center. Ahni led her people through the portal, and when the last warrior was gone, Ian joined them and dismissed his magic.

A force equal to the Crumi contingent stood waiting for them, their members consisting of elves, dark elves, and dwarves. All were armed and wielded a broad variety of weapons. A single elf broke from their ranks and approached Ian.

"We were anticipating your return," Draxan said. "We are prepared to die."

Ian frowned. "I would prefer if you were prepared to fight for your lives."

"We have grown weary of our lives, but rather than simply fade away, we seek to do something meaningful with them before we pass from this world."

Unable to imagine what it might be like to live for thousands of years, Ian found it difficult to argue. He also welcomed their assistance. Every weapon would be needed in this conflict. Like the Crumi, he knew they would fight with the passion that could only exist when one believes in a cause. He did not care about their motives, only their commitment.

"Alright," Ian said loudly in Dwarvish. "We will now face the enemy. It is critical that you retreat when you see the signal. We want them to follow. No matter what happens, do not attempt to fight the demon. He will come for me and that is what we want. I am the bait."

Ahni relayed the commands in her native tongue to ensure the humans clearly understood the plan.

The Crumi warriors pressed their weapons to their foreheads while those from the Valley of Gold gave a firm nod.

Ian turned to Draxan and Ahni. "I am counting on you to lead your squads. Keep me safe. Remember, we are fighting with a specific purpose. All else is insignificant." He did not wish to say that the lives of individuals did not matter, such detail was left to interpretation.

Again, Ian crafted a gateway, this one larger than the last two. A bridge spanning a river appeared on the other side. Beyond the bridge, a thick, black cloud loomed. Ian realized that the monsters were charging toward the bridge. He could not allow them to destroy the seaside village on his side of the river, not if he wished to sleep at night.

Ian turned to Ahni. "Go! Cross the bridge and set up a defense. We need to hold point until we are ready for the next phase."

Ahni raised her spear and shouted before racing toward the river's west bank even as the fore of the cloud slid over them, casting everything in shadow. The Crumi reached the bridge's far end. Those with shields crafted a blockade at the foot of the bridge while warriors holding spears and bows took position behind them. The orcs raced in. A flurry of arrows filled the air. Dozens of monsters collapsed while others smashed into the shields. Spears thrust through gaps in the line to skewer their attackers.

Ian turned to Draxan. "I am going to unleash a spell that will disrupt their attack and draw the demon. When it appears, the Crumi will retreat to this side of the river. You are to intervene and hold the monsters while I destroy the bridge."

"Then what?"

"We hope the demon comes for me."

"You are certain about this?"

"No," Ian admitted. "But I don't know what else to do."

He walked across the bridge as more and more monsters clustered on the other side. When he neared the Crumi, who fought with fury, Ian opened himself to his magic, boosted many times over by the enchanted belt around his waist. Now was not the time for restraint, but he also wanted to avoid using fire due to its unpredictable nature and the lasting devastation. The utter destruction of Krotal was proof of that. As he had once in the previous battle, he chose to combine elements of two spells into one that was untested.

Weaves of air magic flowed through the construct. Those weaves split from one to two, from two to four, from four to eight, and eight to sixteen separate threads, each forming into a swirling funnel of wind with a drastically lower pressure at its center. These creations formed funnels that grew until they were towering tornadoes taller than the surrounding trees. The wind buffeted the human warriors and Ian alike while the cyclones tore into the enemy army.

Orcs were yanked into the air by the dozens, their bodies darkening the funnel clouds as they whipped around and rose higher and higher. The tornadoes began flinging orcs from the top of the spouts, launching them in all directions. Squealing monsters sailed through the sky and rained down hundreds of feet away.

The tornadoes ravaged trees, shrubs, monsters, and anything else in their random, weaving paths of destruction. When some began to turn and come back toward him, Ian hurriedly crafted another spell. A gale of hard, driving wind burst forth, causing the Crumi warriors to stumble forward, many of them falling on those in front of them. Likewise, the orcs tripped over their dead brethren while others crouched and shielded their faces against the debris pelting them. The tornadoes headed away from the river and from Ian's position, gouging the orc army and turning the scene into total chaos.

Ian released his spell, intent on saving his strength. Small clusters of orcs remained and railed against the Crumi blockade only to fall to arrows or spears. All the while, the twisters chased after and ripped through the opposing army. The storms tore up and toppled trees, many of them crushing enemies. It was a terrifying display of power that left even Ian stunned.

Then came the deep, booming roar and boom of massive footsteps he had expected and feared.

Above the distant treetops, through the haze of the dark cloud, the glow of yellow eyes appeared. The crack of breaking trees joined the thunder of each step by the giant demon. As it drew closer to the cyclones terrorizing its army, a dark purple aura bloomed around the demon's body. It stopped a quarter mile from the bridge and spread its arms, its hands sweeping across the treetops. When the hands slapped together, a thunderclap shook the area and a mighty burst of wind blasted forth. The trees bent in the gale while the tornadoes disintegrated. The orcs in the way were blasted from their feet. The wave of air reached the Crumi and sent the entire force toppling backward. Ian shielded himself while crouching low. Even then, he was buffeted as if in a hurricane.

The demon stomped toward him, its voice rumbling. "This time, there will be no escape."

"Ahni!" Ian shouted. "Retreat!" He turned and bolted. The thunder of footsteps on the wooden bridge followed.

Ian reached the bridge's far end, where Draxan and the others were waiting with weapons drawn. He raced through a gap in the warriors, turned, and surveyed the scene.

The Crumi ran in a long trail, chased by orcs. A warrior carrying a shield tripped and fell, causing a trio of shield bearers behind him to stumble over him. The enemies were on them before they could rise, talons flashing, screams erupting. The accidental sacrifice slowed the pursuers, giving the rest of the Crumi relief as they raced off the bridge. Draxan's crew filled the gap as the elf and others armed with bows began to loose.

Channeling his magic, Ian crafted a gateway, anchoring it to the near side of the bridge. The companion gateway opened at the far end of the bridge, both expanding beyond the width of the structure and below its base. As he had seen in practice, the gateway sliced through the wood like a hot knife through butter, severing it from both ends. The entire span and the orcs attempting to cross fell into the water with a thump. The bridge tilted, one side submerging. The monsters fought to climb over each other, toward the higher edge. The structure drifted downstream, toward the sea with the trapped creatures riding it. A few of the monsters jumped toward shore, but rather than swim, they flopped and flailed before sinking.

Monsters crowded along the far side of the river while their master stomped toward them.

The demon laughed. "Your puny efforts cannot stop the might of Az'Ianzar."

"This is it," Ian said. "Back away. He must come after us."

The two squads backed from the river, toward the sleepy little village.

A purple light came from the demon and stretched across the river. As Gortch had described, the demon was crafting a bridge of sorts. Turning from it, Ian ran ahead, stopped a few hundred feet away, and gathered himself. He firmly pictured his destination and crafted a gateway unlike any other, channeling every bit of magic he could muster, boosted ten times over by the enchanted belt around his waist.

The ribbon of light began eighty feet above him and stretched downward, not stopping until it was deep below the ground. It spread open to reveal a quiet public square beneath a sky in the grip of dusk. When complete, the portal stood a hundred feet wide and just as tall. By then, the bridge of light had fully formed, and it was thrice the width of the one Ian had just destroyed.

The demon lord roared. "You shall not escape!"

The orcs poured across the bridge, their red eyes wild with hunger. Thousands upon thousands of monsters rushed Ian and his small army of warriors. The demon took a step onto the bridge while clenching fists large enough to crush half a dozen men at once.

"Run!" Ian cried as he raced through the gateway.

CHAPTER 55
LAST STAND

In the dim light dusk, the sun lost somewhere beyond the mountains to the west, Shria-Li traversed the empty streets of Havenfall for the last time. In her mind, she said goodbye to the trees, domes, arches, and spires that graced her home city. Without people, the buildings felt like empty, lifeless husks, the squares desolate wastelands, the fountains containing tears rather than the water that was so critical to sustaining life.

Her retinue, consisting of a dozen palace guards, approached commerce square and found it occupied. Four hundred Valeguard, one hundred eighty Blue Spears, and one hundred twenty palace guards gathered. Their numbers were not great, for compared to humans or even dwarves, her warriors were few but their long lives allowed for years, if not decades, more training than their counterparts. Blessed with unmatched quickness and honed skills, she knew their worth in battle equated to a far larger force.

They stood in quiet. Waiting. As a patient people, the waiting was a part of life they embraced. Even then, the silence carried an uncomfortable edge. Worse for Shria-Li, whispers could be heard in the back of her mind as the staff in her hand taunted her, demanded she use its might to perform a myriad of magical feats. She ignored those whispers and told herself she was master over the Staff of Life, not the other way around.

Chavell, now back in his former position as head of the palace guard, leaned in from beside her and whispered. "Pardon, Your Majesty."

"Yes?" Shria-Li stared out at the empty square, her stomach knotted in fear and anticipation.

"Are you certain this friend of yours will come?"

"He said to expect him at dusk. Light still lingers in the sky. I'll not cast doubt yet."

"And you believe his tale about these...these creatures from the underworld?"

"It is not a tale. It is prophecy, a glance cast into the future. He has the gift. I saw it for myself."

"If he does not appear?"

She had considered that possibility. "Then, he likely is dead, and I fear what will become of us. We need him if we wish to survive."

He stared at her for a beat. "You truly believe that don't you?"

"I do, which is why every shock lance, spear, sword, and bow we can muster awaits his arrival."

"Then, what?"

"Then, we fight." She turned toward him. "You and Evarian were clear on the orders I gave you, correct?"

"Yes. We will hold them until you give us the command to retreat toward the bridges."

Arching a brow, she asked, "The palace?"

"Leave it to the enemy."

"The demon?"

"Do not engage."

"Good. Stick to those commands and do what you can to keep your squad alive. That is all I ask...for now." Shria-Li turned back toward the empty center of the square.

"What does that mean?"

"We shall see."

A ripping sound came from across the square. The air split and stretched into a massive, shimmering blur eighty feet in diameter. Ian raced out onto the plaza and stopped twenty strides from the portal to glance back, his gaze scanning the square until his eyes met Shria-Li's. He gave a firm nod, turned, and ran off toward Havenfall Palace as hundreds of warriors rushed out onto the plaza and followed him. Elves, dwarves, dark elves, and dark-skinned humans, all carrying weapons, ran off as monsters burst from the gateway.

"Orcs," Shria-Li said aloud, stunned by the sight of them despite all she had heard.

The human-like monsters moved faster than she had anticipated as they hopped and scurried out in all directions. Hundreds soon turned to thousands, a sizable chunk of them chasing after Ian while others rounded the gateway and rushed toward Shria-Li and her warriors.

Ready, Shria-Li raised her staff, opened her mind to it, and brought it down in a sweeping motion. A strip of plaza tiles spanning from one end of the square to the other, three hundred feet away, shook and cracked. Vines burst up, a foot thick at the base and covered in massive thorns. The vines wrapped around orcs attempting to run past and lifted them off the ground. In seconds, vines had created a wall thick with writhing orcs while dividing the horde from the waiting Sylvan Army.

She nodded. "Attack."

The three squad leaders, Captain Rozenne of the Valeguard, Captain Evarian of the Blue Spears, and Captain Chavell of the Palace Guard, relayed the command and launched their assault.

Arrows sailed through the sky and rained down on the monsters beyond the wall of vines. Warriors raced in on foot with shock lances, spears, and swords flashing as they clashed with the enemies bound in the vines and those seeking to slip through their gaps. Orcs died by the hundreds, but more and more emerged from the gateway, flooding the square and pouring into connecting streets.

Shria-Li and her captains had expected as much, but the monsters would find the city empty.

A roar came from somewhere beyond the portal. A towering creature unlike anything she had seen before emerged from the doorway and pounded its chest. *The demon*, she knew with certainty. Despite her belief in Ian and the prophecy, this one aspect of his tale had been too much for her to accept. Until now.

Shria-Li shouted above the fracas, "Chavell. Call for the retreat!"

Ian, still channeling as much magic as he could handle, his head buzzing with it as he fueled the immense gateway behind him, ran past buildings, reached the end of the street, and stopped. "Draxan. Ahni. Hold the monsters here until the demon comes this way."

From his position, Ian had a clear view of the massive portal in the square at the far end of the street.

The two squad leaders began issuing commands. In seconds, the Crumi created a shield wall running from building to building. Elves and Crumi warriors with bows drew arrows and loosed, killing enemies rushing toward the wall of shields. The creatures able to avoid arrows crashed into the shields and were quickly dispatched. Orcs then began to scale the buildings, but arrows targeting those creatures knocked them loose again and again.

The demon emerged from the portal and pounded its chest. Ian, channeling the last of his bandwidth, released a blast of lightning toward the behemoth, striking it full in the chest. He now knew the monster fed off the attack, drinking in the energy as if it were the sweetest nectar. That taste of power was intentional, one he hoped would leave it longing for more.

Lumps danced beneath the giant's skin, causing its muscles to bulge, its arms and legs to stretch, and in seconds, it stood ten feet taller. The demon released a terrifying laugh and when it came toward him, Ian dismissed the gateway.

He turned toward Ahni. "Give me ten seconds, and then call for the retreat."

"Where do we go next?"

Ian pointed toward the palace entrance. "That should be defensible. Fight there. Leave the demon to me."

He raced toward the palace and turned to follow an uphill side path bordered by golden, glowing trees and a rainbow of flowers. The path opened to the fountain that fed the city's aquafer. There, he stopped to watch the demon stomping down the street. Draxan's squad and the Crumi ran toward the palace front entrance. Orcs gave chase, hundreds of them rushing past the path, oblivious to Ian.

When the demon reached the end of the street, Ian loosed another bolt of lightning. As expected, the demon absorbed the attack and grew even larger. Eager and hot on the trail of its prey, the giant fiend crashed through the foliage, knocking over trees and flattening shrubs. Ian bolted. He ran along the curving path, passed beneath a wall of open arches, and entered the famed palace garden.

The tree of life, many hundreds of feet tall, the golden glow from its trunk glinting off its metallic leaves, called to him. It was the most sacred symbol to the Sylvan, thousands of years old and the origin of the staff Shria-Li wielded. Despite this, she had agreed to his insane plan. He only prayed it would work.

Ian raced along the path, toward the tree and past it, not stopping until he reached the stairs leading to the palace garden entrance. At the top of the stairs and standing below a high arch, he turned and caught his breath while watching the giant come for him.

The demon reached the wall of arches at the garden's far end. Made of blue-tinted stone blocks, three feet thick and twenty feet tall, the wall was both imposing and a thing of beauty. The demon smashed through it as if it were made of paper. Debris blasted into the foliage and tumbled down the walkway as the monster stomped into the garden, its gaze fixed on Ian until it drew near the towering tree.

"What is this?" The demon's eyes widened. Mesmerized, it slowly approached the tree and placed a paw the size of a carriage on its trunk. "So much life…" The demon raised its face to the sky and laughed. "I will be a god!"

The fiend clapped both hands on the thick trunk. A purple glow shone from the demon's skin, its yellow eyes rolling up in its skull. The creature's distended jaw dropped in ecstasy as the tree began to shrivel.

Shria-Li and her warriors ran through the outskirts of Havenfall, passed beyond the glow of the golden trees that illuminated the city, and raced onto the tongue of rock where two bridges connected the island city to the north and south riverbanks. As her people did while fleeing the city, she and her warriors made for the south bank. They ran up and over the arching, stone bridge, passing the enchanted globes sticking up from the ends and center of the bridge, their pale aura adding to the light of the full moon. Upon reaching the gravel road on the other side, her warriors reformed with the Blue Spears creating a column in the middle, the Valeguard and their shock Lances splitting into two columns beside them, and the palace guard taking the flanks. Shria-Li took position to the side of her force, to get a clear view.

The orcs rushed out onto the open rock and spilled onto the bridge, their red eyes wild with fury as they mindlessly raced toward the small but fierce Sylvan army. The two forces clashed with monsters dying by the dozens in seconds. Arrows loosed into the enemy force clustered on the bridge while swords, spears and shock lances bit into the vanguard.

Then, elves began to fall, forcing Shria-Li to act.

She held her staff up and called out to its magic. Wisps of golden light swirled out from the staff and snaked toward the tongue of rock below the far end of the bridge. The rock shook, cracked, and split wide open. A pair of thick, muscular vines burst from the ground. One vine snaked beneath the bridge while the other rose up beyond the bridge's rail and wrapped around the upper side, plowing through monsters and shoving others aside. The vines continued to grow and extend, winding around the bridge to create a complete loop. Like twin boa constrictors, the vines then began to squeeze.

The stone bridge rails cracked, snapped, and chunks fell into the dark river. As the cracks spread and the pressure increased, debris rained down into the water. The bridge shuddered, the pressure intense. With a mighty crack, it snapped, the vine-wrapped end breaking off completely. The bridge creaked, cracked, and collapsed, taking hundreds of orcs with it. Both broken structure and monsters splashed down into the river, its swiftly flowing waters sweeping the shrieking creatures away. The banks were wet and steep, so even if they could swim, escape would be difficult. Less a mile downstream were the falls, dropping down to the depths of the Vale. Those monsters would trouble the world no longer.

The orcs trapped on the other side hooted and howled in anger as they paced back and forth, seeking a way across.

Shria-Li lowered her staff and turned to Chavell. "Captain. You are in charge. Lead our warriors to the portal stone. I will meet you there when I am finished."

"When you are finished?"

"I am not going with you."

"You are queen. We are sworn to protect you."

"You are also sworn to obey. In this, you can do nothing else."

She raised her staff and called upon its magic again. A vine burst from the ground, wrapped around her waist, and lifted her toward the sky. Across the river, another vine rose in the darkness, both climbing and climbing until they were each hundreds of feet in length. Then, at her command, the vines began to bend over the river until they met, fifty feet above the flowing waters. The second vine wound itself around her waist. The first vine released her, and she was carried to the north riverbank.

With her feet on the ground, Shria-Li peered across the river, toward her stunned people. She then turned away and ran north. The shrieks and howls coming from the direction of the city informed her of the orcs now in pursuit. Her mother's voice echoed in her head. *Your duty is to your people. You must ensure their safety.* Shria-Li sent a silent reply. *I will see this through, Mother. We will persevere.*

GOLDEN LEAVES RAINED DOWN as the Tree of Life shook, bent, and contracted. All the while, the demon's body twitched, and stretched, growing larger and larger. A hundred feet, one fifty, two hundred, the demon grew and grew while the tree shrank in on itself. When Az'Ianzar stood three hundred feet tall, the transformation stopped. The demon gripped a hand the size of a house around the tree trunk and tore the withered remains of the dead tree from the ground. The pool at the tree's base erupted as a massive root ball burst up from the ground, spraying water in all directions. The demon then tossed the tree and its roots aside, destroying much of what remained of the wall of arches across the garden from where Ian stood.

"I am now a god!" The demon boomed. It looked down at Ian with a grin. "And your power will make me an even greater god." Then it bent toward him.

Ian stared up at the behemoth, awestruck by the creature's size. The tree of life had caused the demon to grow many times more than Ian's magic. He then recalled the last aspect of H'Deesengar's instructions – *seek a means to pierce its flesh*. With that in mind, Ian cast a spell of physical manipulation, a lash of magic whipping out and wrapping around a young tree. He raised the whip, tore the tree from the ground, and launched the tree at the demon, intent on impaling it. The tree struck the demon's leg and blasted into a thousand splinters and leaves that rained down. Yet, the demon remained unharmed.

Ian tried again, casting a gateway before him, the other end of the gateway forming in front of the massive hand reaching for him. Fingers as thick as a wine barrel passed through the opening and Ian dismissed the spell. The gateway slammed shut, severing the fingers in an instant. Even as the severed body parts tumbled down the stairs, the giant hand above him began to heal. In less than two seconds, new fingers grew back to replace the old. Right before the demon's massive hand reached him, Ian crafted a shield around himself.

The demon's hand wrapped around the ten-foot diameter bubble protecting Ian, engulfing it with ease. It scooped him up and lifted him toward the sky. His plan suddenly seemed massively foolish, and he wondered if H'Deesengar had lied to him. *What have I done?*

CHAPTER 56
THE DEAD WALK

Shria-Li ran along a forest road, the glow of the staff in her hand fending off surrounding shadows. The monsters trailed behind her by a few hundred feet, pursuing her like rabid dogs, their noises constantly reminding her of her fate if she faltered.

The trees around her began to appear different, their branches barren and lifeless. She turned off the road and ran into the dead forest. With her mind, she called out. *Rise, my warriors. I am the death speaker. I demand you wake from your rest and fight.*

The trees around her shuddered. *Why do you wake us?*

I call upon you to fight. Creatures from the underworld seek to destroy this one. Rise and fight, so you have a world to return to when your sleep is over.

The oaks around her shook with a mighty tremor. The ground blasted open around their trunks as roots burst up. In fits and spurts, the oaks climbed out of the earth and swung their branches in low sweeps, scooping up charging orcs and tossing them into the air. Their flailing bodies crashed into trees and rocks before falling to the ground.

The thick branches of fallen trees bent and pushed their trunks up off the mossy turf. Once upright, they joined their brethren to battle the inrushing enemies.

THE DEMON LIFTED Ian high above the palace garden. It opened its palm and looked down at him, each of the teeth jutting up from its lower jaw the size of Ian's entire body. The monster furrowed its heavy brow, lifted its other hand toward Ian and poked a finger at him. A massive black talon struck the shield, sending a tremor through it.

"Do you think your puny magic can stand against me?" Az'Ianzar boomed.

The demon's fingers wrapped around the shield and squeezed. Intense pressure caused the shield to contract. Ian fed it more magic, fighting against the demon's immense strength. Undaunted, the demon squeezed harder, and soon, Ian found himself trembling to hold the shield. Sweat ran down his face and dampened his robes. The bubble of protection shuddered and began to fold in. Ian was able to stop the collapse and reinforce the shield, but at half the diameter. With all of his energy focused on maintaining the spell, he could not cast another. *I am going to die.*

Worse, he realized, he had failed the world.

AHNI'S WARRIORS fought for their lives, for their people, and for their god. Positioned on the stairs before the palace, those with shields held steady while warriors with spears stood on the top stair and thrust through gaps, skewering attacking orcs. Her archers and Draxan's warriors attacked from the flanks. Despite each warrior killing dozens of enemies before falling, it soon became clear that their position was unsustainable. The monsters were too many.

"Retreat!" She bellowed. "We go inside!"

The archers moved to the sides and continued to loose while the other warriors ran in through the double doors. Ahni waited for the last surviving archer to run inside before joining them. The doors slammed closed, the bar dropped, and a heavy thud shook them as the enemy crashed against it. Angry shrieks came from outside as they pounded and scratched at the doors.

She turned to Draxan. "Find a defensible location. Continue to whittle away their numbers but try to keep everyone alive."

"Where are you going?" Draxan asked.

"I am going to find Ian. We need his magic, or we will not leave here alive." She raced off down a dark corridor.

The palace was massive, the complex of rooms, terraces, and corridors larger than her entire village. She ran and ran, taking turns while attempting to find another way out until she came to a long corridor with moonlight at the far end. Racing along it, she found the corridor opened on one side to reveal a sprawling garden beyond a row of arches. She slowed to a stop and stared, stunned.

Standing in that garden was the demon, towering at a height three or four times what it was when she last saw it. The monster bent and lifted something up into the air. When upright, it opened its hand, the light of the moon shining down to reveal a robed human. It was Ian.

Ahni ran along the corridor, to a staircase leading down to the garden. The demon clenched a fist around the person in his hand. She gasped in fear, but the demon appeared to struggle to crush his captive.

With a hand cupped to her mouth, she shouted. "Ian!"

In response, Ian cried, "Ahni! Help!"

"What do I do?"

"Pierce the demon's flesh!"

She looked up at the monster, the idea of her attacking such a colossus beyond ridiculous. Yet, her friend, her people, and the world required action. With a belly full of fear, she raced down the stairs, along the garden path, and charged toward the demon's foot, its toes six to seven feet tall with curled and pointed claws hanging over them. The sacred spear had been entrusted to her. It was a symbol of her people, reputed to one day save them from certain doom. If the prophecy were true, she could not say, but she prayed to Urvadan that it was so.

Raising the spear overhead as she closed in on him, she drove the spear into the demon's big toe with all of her might. The spear tip bounced off the demon's thick hide. A shudder came through the spear, the force sending her staggering backward as if she had attempted to attack a mountain. She regained her balance and looked at the toe. Her attack had not even left a mark.

Shrieks of excitement came from the direction of the palace as orcs rushed into view. The monsters leapt through the arches, into the garden, and came for her.

Caught between the giant demon and the psychotic monsters, Ahni saw no way to escape. She was likely to die, and her friend was in trouble. The world was on the brink. She could not fail.

Ahni looked up at the claw above her and at the dark gap where the nail met the flesh of the toe. Determined, she cocked her arm back and took aim. With a mighty strike, she drove the sacred spear into the gap. It slid in and then stopped with half of the shaft sticking out.

The demon howled, the timbre of its voice shaking the plants around Ahni. The flesh around the spear began to glow with an amber hue. She turned and ran, clearing the area right before the toe exploded. The blast knocked her off her feet and tossed her into a flowering shrub. Chunks of flesh pelted the surrounding bushes and a terrible, ear-splitting scream echoed throughout the city.

Ahni scrambled to her feet and found the demon's toe blown wide open. A bright, golden glow emerged from the massive wound, bathing Ahni, the garden, and the palace in its light. Nearby orcs cowered from the light, shrieked in pain, and began to smoke like a smoldering bonfire.

IAN STRAINED to hold the shield as the demon tried to crush him in its massive palm. An explosion came from below, followed by a tremor that shook the demon's entire body. The massive fist opened as the demon raised its face to the sky and howled in pain. The noise of the howl vibrated through Ian's head and left his ears ringing. The demon's hand dropped to its side, releasing Ian, who fell toward the garden over a hundred feet down.

Ian cast a spell, wrapping a loop of magic around his waist while the other end lashed around the demon's knee. The slack pulled tight, swinging Ian down toward the ground, over the demon's destroyed foot, and out over the garden. His momentum stopped and he swung back. As he reached the low point of his arc, he released the spell and crafted another bubble. Like a ball tumbling through grass, he rolled over and through shrubs before coming to a stop against the palace wall. He released the spell, climbed from the shrubs, and stood in the golden light emitted from the demon's wound.

Orcs surrounding him screamed and huddled in pain as their bodies dried up to skeletons that turned to dust.

The demon began to shrink, its body contracting in all directions as it jerked and writhed as if in terrible pain. All the while, the golden light streaming from the demon's wound shined like a tiny sun. Pale, ghostly shadows began to emerge from the destroyed toe. A steady wave of hundreds of souls rushed out, fanning in all directions before fading into the night. One of the souls came straight for Ian, flitted around him, and touched his cheek. It hovered before him, the mist gathering to resemble a familiar and desperately missed person.

"Mother." Ian stared into her ghostly eyes as tears emerged from his. She stroked his cheek softly and then flitted off, fading into the ether.

The flow of souls continued as the demon's body contorted and contracted. When the demon was roughly the size of a very large human, the glow faded and it collapsed into the mud with a thud.

Inhuman growls, grunts, and howls came from the palace right before dozens of monsters raced into the open corridor beyond the arches facing the garden. At the same time, similar sounds echoed across the garden as monsters rushed in from the direction of the city.

STANDING among the branches of a mighty, leafless oak, Shria-Li and an army of dead trees marched along the road. Before them, orcs ran in fear while others attempted to fight, but their poisonous talons could do no harm against wood that was already dead. Instead, the trees stomped on or swept up and tossed any monster that came too close.

The bridge came into view, thick with enemies, some charging toward the oncoming trees, others seeking to return to the city. The chaos served to slow both, and when the trees reached them, a brutal and decisive bloodbath ensued.

In moments, the bridge was cleared of living enemies and the trees were heading toward the heart of Havenfall.

A bright, golden light bloomed from across the city, coming from the direction of the palace. It was then that Shria-Li realized the towering Tree of Life was gone. In its stead stood the demon, who belted a terrible shriek likely heard miles away. Even as the dead trees mowed down any orc in their path, Shria-Li watched the demon shrink until it was blocked from her view.

"He did it. Ian did it!" Relief and joy came in equal measure, but the orcs remained. She was determined to see them all dead. Thrusting her arm forward, she shouted, "Kill the spawn of darkness. Kill them all!"

In the heart of the Garden of Life, Ian found himself surrounded by monsters seeking to deliver death. The beasts charged in from opposite directions. He considered what to do and was struck by an idea he had not ever considered.

Ian grabbed Ahni by the wrist. "Back away." They stepped back until reaching the edge of the muddy hole in the ground where the tree had once stood. The demon lay in the mud beside them while the orcs converged and raced in. At the last moment, Ian cast a gateway twenty feet in diameter. The orcs, fed by their own momentum rushed through the gateway, their noises turning to fading screams. The flow of the mindless, bloodthirsty creatures did not stop. More and more monsters ran in from the direction of the city, their red eyes wide with insane hunger.

Massive, leafless trees stomped into view, chasing after the evil creatures. The trees swatted at orcs, tossing multiple monsters dozens of feet away with a single swipe. Those orcs unlucky enough to lose their footing were crushed beneath the weight of trees weighing thousands of pounds. The trees tromped over the fallen wall and through the garden, flattening shrubs in pursuit of the monsters. All the while, creatures fled through Ian's portal. When the last of the surviving monsters disappeared through the opening, Ian dismissed it. Yet, the trees kept coming.

Tensed and prepared to act if the oaks came for them, Ian and Ahni remained still. A female voice called out from the direction of the trees. All stopped save for one oak that stood even larger than the others. The tree stomped over the fallen wall and through the garden before stopping thirty feet from where Ian and Ahni stood. The tree bent low, extending a thick limb to the ground. A female gripping a glowing wooden staff shimmied along that branch and jumped down to the ground. When he saw her, Ian felt a wave of relief.

He approached the elf queen. "I am glad to see you survived."

Shria-Li stopped, her gaze sweeping across the garden. "Where did the rest of the monsters go?"

"I created a gateway and placed the other end of it just beyond the edge of the bluff overlooking the Vale."

She nodded. "Clever."

Ahni asked, "What is the Vale?"

"A valley below his city. The drop is quite daunting and impossible to survive."

Her brow furrowed. "Why did you not do this before?"

Ian shrugged. "I only just thought of it."

Shria-Li looked down at the still form lying in the mud. "This is the demon?"

Ian's gaze followed hers. Even at its natural size and lying prone on the ground, the demon was an imposing figure. "Its name is Az'Ianzar. It thought to make itself a god of our world, doing so by consuming all life. It may have succeeded, too, if not for Ahni."

Ahni walked over to the nearby shrubs, bent, and lifted her spear up to look upon it. "The sacred spear was prophesized to save the world one day. I was simply the vessel that brought the spear to its destiny."

"Spear or not, I thank you. The world thanks you."

Just then, Draxan's voice carried over the garden. "There you are!"

Ian turned to find the elf descending the stairs from the palace, trailed by his surviving warriors and two hundred Crumi.

Ian asked, "Where did you go?"

"When Ahni came this way, we took refuge in a large room with a glowing tree and thrones in the center."

"The throne room," Shria-Li said.

"We killed many monsters who tried to enter. Some of my warriors and Ahni's fell to their attacks, and I began to worry about how long we could hold out. Then, they stopped coming. That's when we left in search of you."

Ian nodded. Lives had been lost, but it could have been far, far worse. Still, he had one thing to deal with. "I must bring the demon to the Temple of Tenebri. But first, I will return you to your homes."

Shria-Li looked over her shoulder, into the forest of dead trees. "You may return to your sleep."

The trees shuddered. Several of them toppled over while the rest simply stood in place.

She turned back to Ian. "I must go join my people. I wish you well, but I do not know if I will see you again."

"Where will you go?"

"To our new home." Her eyes warily flicked from side to side. "I fear I must keep that location a secret. If need requires you to seek the Sylvan out, begin at the portal stone you visited last."

Ian recalled the location, deep in an untouched forest in the distant southeast. "I understand."

He approached and wrapped his arms around her. She returned the embrace.

"The sacrifice your people made will not be forgotten," he said.

She stepped back. "Nor will yours. Be well, Ian."

Shria-Li turned and walked off with her glowing staff in hand.

Ian turned toward Ahni. "I can now return you to your village."

She clapped a hand on his shoulder. "You were truly the one, Ian. I am honored to have fought at your side."

He nodded. "As am I."

The gateway opened with the dim interior of the Crumi temple on the other side. The warriors rushed through with Ahni leaving last. She stopped just beyond the gateway, looked back at Ian, and touched her weapon to her forehead. The gateway snapped shut, and Ian turned to Draxan.

"Your turn." Ian opened a gateway to the Valley of Sol and Draxan's warriors rushed through.

Draxan clasped Ian's forearm and peered into his eyes. "My people thank you for saving us."

"What will you do, now?"

"I do not know. I suspect we will leave the crater but where we will go, I cannot guess. We were trapped in an endless nightmare for far too long. Your quest to save the world gave us purpose for a short time, but now..." he shook his head. "I just don't know."

"Well, wherever your road leads, I wish you the best."

"You as well." Draxan stepped through the portal and was gone.

Alone, Ian turned back toward the demon. Although the creature lay still, it was not dead. Even had H'Deesengar not told him that it was impossible to kill a demon lord, he would have taken additional precautions.

He cast a spell, wrapped a thread of magic around the demon, and lifted it off the ground. The next spell opened a gateway to the chamber in the heart of a massive pyramid. Ian moved the demon through and then followed before dismissing the gateway.

Noises came from down the dark corridor, where goblins gathered in the cavern outside the temple. Strangely, the fried ogre remains were gone, but Ian pushed that thought aside and turned back toward the dais at the heart of the temple. He waved his arm, using his magic to move the demon with him as he climbed the dais. His surroundings shimmered, a dizziness washing over him as he climbed the rest of the stairs. Upon reaching the top, Ian dropped the demon on the floor and looked up at the large, muscular form lounging on the oversized throne.

H'Deesengar stood with a grin. "I knew you were the one."

Ian frowned, for the demon's voice lacked the guttural, gravel quality from his prior meeting. In fact, the voice sounded familiar. "Do I know you?"

H'Deesengar shimmered, shrank, and morphed into a human form dressed in black with a red cape draped down his back. His handsome face and blonde hair were instantly recognizable.

"Master?"

Truhan smiled. "The need for subterfuge has passed." The air around him wavered, his hair suddenly combed back, his doublet donning red panels with golden trim and gilded buttons, his appearance regal and somehow larger than life. "You did well, my prized disciple."

"Disciple?" Ian numbly muttered.

"That is the proper term for one who serves a god." A wry smile twisted his lips. "You may know me by my other name. Urvadan."

The air wavered again, his surroundings changing dramatically.

CHAPTER 57

A COMPLEX DESIGN

I an suddenly found himself in a temple twice the size of how it had previously appeared. The throne that had stood before Ian was now gone, the top of the dais open until it reached a thick column of red light streaming down from the apex of the sloped ceiling, fifty feet away. In that column of light was a throne of black stone even larger than the one that was now gone. The muscular figure of a black-skinned demon sat on that throne, its elbows on its knees, its head slumped forward.

"I don't understand," Ian said.

"I just gave you my true identity." His master touched his own chest. "I am Urvadan, the rightful god of this world." He slid his arm around Ian's shoulders. "Come. I will explain."

Stunned and confused, Ian allowed his master to guide him across the dais.

"You see, very long ago, my brother and I worked together, him guiding his people, me guiding mine. The races of magic were born of Vandasal, while humans and animals that lack magic were my children. While my worshipers were superior in number and reproduced much more rapidly, his were blessed with enhanced gifts and extended lives. There were disagreements among the mortals, but all in all, things were balanced. Then, my brother betrayed me.

"Vandasal's power is connected to sunlight. Mine is tied to the moon, which waxes and wanes, and during those times when the moon is at its weakest, my power wanes as well. This was not always the case, not until my brother destroyed the moonstone."

"Moonstone?"

"Yes. It was a crystal akin to the one from where you draw the source of your magic. The moonstone absorbed energy from the moon and fed my powers regardless of its phase. After my brother destroyed the moonstone, he smote me and cast me out. Twelve hundred years passed before I woke from my unintended sleep. By then, the races of magic had risen while mankind suffered, many of them living as slaves. Worse, he had spread lies about me, turning my worshipers against me by calling me the Dark Lord."

Ian shook his head. "I can't believe I have been working for the Dark Lord."

Urvadan gripped him by the shoulders and looked him in the eyes. "Were you not listening, Ian? That name is pure falsehood, an identity created by my brother to pit my own people against me. You should know by now that I am not evil. I do not seek to pray upon innocents and cast the world in darkness. Anything I do is for the good of my people. You see, I need them. We gods gain power from prayers. We require followers just as mortals need us for spiritual guidance."

"Why are you telling me this?"

"Because. I need you to understand. I need you to believe. I need you to help me with one more task."

"You lied to me."

"When I told you that people call me Truhan? That was no lie. People do call me that."

"But you had me believe..."

Urvadan held up a finger. "What you believe is of your own doing Ian. I only promised to train you to use your magic, and if you recall, that was after you pledged fealty to me for saving your life."

When Ian considered it, he realized that Urvadan had taken care to avoid outright lies. The worst of it seemed to be him choosing not to correct Ian's assumptions. He then recalled the prophecy. "I stopped the horde of monsters. There are still some out there, but without the demon, they are no longer immortal." He turned toward Az'Ianzar, the demon still lying near the stairs leading up to the dais. "The demon has been captured. You told me it could be trapped here, so it could no longer trouble our world."

"Ah. And so you have. For this, I owe you a debt of gratitude."

Urvadan pointed toward the demon. Its body floated up into the air and then sailed across the dais, directly over Ian's head as it headed toward the column of light. The demon's body slid into the beam and stopped when above the throne of stone.

"There," Urvadan lowered his hand. "Should Az'Ianzar wake before tomorrow night, which I find unlikely, at least the demon can cause no harm."

"What is that light?"

"That is my power, Ian. If you recall, when masquerading as H'Deesengar, you were told that Urvadan visits once a month to reinforce the demon's prison." He pointed toward the throne. "That is the prison, and it now holds two demons, one that will give its essence to make a new future possible, the other to ensure that the new world order remains in place forever."

Ian shook his head. "I have no idea what you are talking about."

"I am talking about justice, Ian. I am talking about vengeance. The time of the races of magic draws to a close. Even now, the Sylvan go into hiding, as the Drow have already done. The dwarves will eventually do the same. When the dust settles and the world embraces its new future, humans will flourish. Their numbers will swell as they spread across the land, and those with the Gift will rule over them."

"The Gift?"

"Your magic, Ian." He tapped Ian's chest. "It is my gift to mankind, a glorious gift as important as anything I do. This gift will further fuel the prayers of my people, and as I said, we gods require such devotion to feed our power."

Ian frowned. "The people only know the name Urvadan from fireside tales intended to frighten children. They will never worship you."

"Other than the Crumi."

"And their numbers are few."

Urvadan patted Ian on the back. "You make a fair point. That is a solvable problem, and one I intend to address once you have assisted me in completing my plan."

Although Ian had a bad feeling about it, he could not see another option other than complying. "What would you have of me?"

"Come. I will show you."

Again, the god slid his arm around Ian's shoulder. Together, they rounded the beam of light, the demon on the throne beneath it still slouched over and appearing unaware of Ian's presence. They then headed toward a thick stone column at the far end of the dais. An alcove in the column was occupied by a lift similar to the one found in the Tower of Solitude.

The god gestured for Ian to climb on the platform. Once he did, Urvadan joined him and pressed his hand to a panel on the pedestal. The lift began to rise, and soon, the smooth stone interior of the column blocked the temple from view.

THE PLATFORM PASSED MANY FLOORS, some of them offering tantalizing glimpses of objects and chambers that left Ian increasingly more curious. Up and up, it climbed until finally emerging to a sprawling rooftop beneath the night sky.

Urvadan stepped off the lift and headed across the rooftop without a word. Knowing he was expected to follow, Ian did so. They passed through a ring of brass posts three feet tall. The top of each post had been crafted in the shape of a clawed hand. In each hand was a crystal the size of a grapefruit. A dais rising above the rooftop graced the center of that ring and an altar made of milky white quartz stood upon the dais.

The god climbed the dais stairs, approached the altar, and ran his hand across the smooth surface. "This is where it will happen."

Ian frowned. "Where what will happen?"

Urvadan pointed west. "The moon travels across the sky."

A glance in that direction revealed the moon, halfway between them and the horizon. "Everyone knows that."

"Like the sun, it sets and then rises the next day, but unlike the sun, its light is crippled for weeks at a time before returning to its glory."

Again, the god was stating the obvious. "Yes. I know."

With his arm moving in a slow circle, Urvadan said, "The moon will travel around this world, and tomorrow evening, it will rise again," he pointed east. "It will then move across the sky until it is directly above this tower." He turned toward Ian. "The moon will then stop and will never move across our skies again."

"What? How could that be?"

"As I told you, the demons trapped in the temple below will help me make this possible. This is why I have gone through such efforts."

Ian digested the god's statement and came to a shocking, terrible conclusion. "Az'Ianzar and his horde of monsters came from the underworld."

"That is correct."

"How did they get here?"

"Through a hole torn in the veil."

"Who created this hole?"

Urvadan smiled. "Very good, Ian." He nodded. "Yes. I tore the veil."

"Why would you do such a thing?"

"I am a god, Ian, a god lacking worshipers. My people need me, just as I need them. This is the way. You see, not even the power of a god can affect a celestial body such as the moon. Two demons, each a demigod, along with what remains of my ability, will enable this otherwise impossible feat to become...possible. With the moon held firmly in place, forever fueling my power, I will be even mightier than before the moonstone was destroyed."

Ian ran his hand through his hair as he tried to imagine what it would be like to see the moon forever hanging in the same place, night or day. Although strange, he could not imagine the amount of magic required to perform such an act. Moreso, he had learned that magic does not occur without consequences. "What are you not telling me?"

The god smiled. "Your cleverness was the most important of your traits that made me decide to choose you." He shrugged. "Of course, the timing was critical as well since the hole in the veil had grown to the point where the demon would soon slip through."

Frustrated by Urvadan's lackadaisical manner of answering, Ian's lips tightened. "Tell me. What will happen?"

"The moon's gravity affects much, including the ebbs and flows of the tides in seas and oceans across our world. When the moon stops, it will draw those bodies of water toward it, and in order for me to secure the power I require, I will also draw the moon closer to our world." He shook his head. "Seaside cities and lands will drown, particularly those closer to where we now stand."

"What? You mean like Bard's Bay and Greavesport?"

"Those cities will be at the bottom of the sea. The Free Cities and more will suffer this fate."

Struck by the breadth of the devastation, Ian fell to his knees. "Why?"

"I told you, Ian. This will come to pass. I will return to power, and the human race will dominate our world with you and your kind leading them."

Unwilling to allow something so terrible to happen, Ian opened himself to his magic. It flowed in as he cast a construct. Lightning burst forth and blasted Urvadan in the chest, only to fizzle away.

The god laughed. "Your magic is part of me, Ian. Nothing you do can harm me."

Releasing his magic, his body and mind weary from such a stressful day, Ian's head dropped to his chest. Heavy breaths filled his lungs before he lifted his gaze. "You cannot do this."

"The die has been cast. The design I put in motion centuries ago will soon come to fruition. There is no turning back."

His heart breaking, Ian pleaded, "But so many will die, and humans live in those cities."

"Which is why you must save them."

"What?" He blinked. "How?"

"Gateways. Transport them to high ground, away from the sea but not anywhere near here. You see, I fear that the land beneath the moon will be impacted as well, and the destruction could be widespread."

"You expect me to evacuate full cities using my magic?"

"I know you will do your best."

Ian shook his head, "But I am already exhausted."

Urvadan patted the altar. "Come. Sleep here tonight. At daybreak, the relocation begins."

"You wish me to sleep upon an altar of stone?"

"Just do it. You will find tonight's rest unlike any other."

Overwhelmed by everything he had heard and what was yet to come, Ian staggered to his feet and stumbled over to the altar. He turned and laid down on his back, his face toward the night sky. A warmth came over him, his body tingling, his head buzzing as if he were channeling magic.

"What is happening?" Ian asked.

"Your blood shares elements with mine. The altar gathers moonlight and feeds the metals in that blood and charges you with raw power. By the time the moon sets, you will be stronger than anything you ever imagined. Such power wanes, but it will last for a day, and that is what you have."

Turning from Ian, Urvadan walked away.

Alone, Ian closed his eyes and drifted while his body recovered and his magic roiled with newly found energy.

CHAPTER 58

RELOCATION

B
ard's castle stood upon a hillside overlooking an open bay and the seaside city that shared its name. Armed guards paced along the castle wall while others loitered inside of the closed gate. The castle stood in the center of a broad yard surrounded by walls. While much of the building remained intact, a third of it lay in charred ruins, a remnant of a desperate battle to reclaim control of the city. The wreckage provided a stark contrast to a peaceful morning with the sun yet to edge over the hills east of the city.

A ribbon of light tore through the air in the castle yard, spreading until a window to another place was visible through it. A young man in black and gold robes stepped out and the portal disappeared with a pop.

Startled guards drew weapons while those on the wall nocked bows.

Ian turned toward them. "Try to attack me, and you will regret it. I am here to speak with Commander Essex."

The soldiers did not attack, nor did they sheath their weapons until one of the men at the gate shouted. "Stand down." The man slid his sword into the scabbard on his hip. "This is Barsequa Illian. He was with Essex when retaking the city. He is a hero, not a threat."

"Thank you." Ian could not recall the man's name. "Can you take me to Essex?"

"The commander is inside, breaking his fast." The man guided Ian toward the main entrance, opened the door, and led him in.

The scents of eggs, sausage, and fresh bread greeted Ian as he crossed a parlor, the seating in the room unoccupied. The parlor connected to a dining hall where twelve men sat around a long table, their forks clanking off plates as they ate. At the head of the table sat Essex, his hair shorn, his beard tightly trimmed. Although he now ruled Bard's Bay, he still wore a military coat, pressed and buttoned up.

"Commander," Ian's escort said aloud.

Essex looked up, his brow furrowing. "Ian?"

"I have no time for niceties," Ian said. "I am here to warn you. A natural disaster unlike any other is about to take place. It will completely destroy your city and any other that resides near the sea. You must pass this on to your people. Have them gather what food, clothing, and other valuables they can carry and meet near the harbor two hours prior to sunset. We must evacuate and it must happen today."

The man wiped his mouth with a cloth napkin and set it aside. "I don't know what this is about, but..."

Ian lashed his hand toward the man. A thread of magic wound around his torso and lifted him up above the table, not stopping until his back was pinned against the ceiling. The guards around the table burst to their feet, their chairs toppling over. Many drew weapons.

"Stop!" Ian shouted. "Attack me, and I will end you! Time is your enemy. Not me. I am trying to save lives. Believe me when I tell you, by midnight, Bard's Bay will no longer exist."

Essex grimaced. "Why should we believe you?"

"Because I am the only one who can save you. My power is a

hundred times what it was when I helped you defeat Creskin, but even I cannot stop what is coming. Do as I say. If I am wrong, and I am not, you can return to your city tomorrow." He lowered his arm and set Essex down, releasing his bond as the man regained his footing. "Two hours prior to sunset, I will meet you at the harbor."

Ian cast another gateway, stepped through it, and was gone.

When Ian emerged from the gateway, he walked through the small seaside village and found it empty. He cast a glance upriver and found the bridge he had destroyed gone, as was the magical bridge crafted by the demon the prior evening. He saw nothing of orcs but had no doubt that some had survived and were hiding somewhere in the shadows.

He walked along the dirt road that ran past the village and headed south, toward the camp of refugees who had fled Krotal. With wagons being loaded and others lined up along the road, it appeared that they were breaking camp.

People watched with furrowed brows as Ian walked past. He suspected none would have heard of him, so he assumed their scrutiny was mere curiosity. Spying a carriage made of black leather, he made for it. A quartet of armed guards stood beside the carriage while three others were posted outside a nearby tent. One by one, their attention turned toward Ian, their hands drifting to the pommels of the swords on their hips. None drew a weapon, but one of those near the carriage approached and stopped before Ian.

"I recognize you. You were among those riding the dragon."

Dragon? Ian realized that he didn't know what had become of Vic and Revita. When concern for his brother bubbled up, he shoved it aside. *Focus, Ian. One thing at a time.*

"I need to speak with the Duke."

The guard glanced toward a nearby white tent. "The Duke is preparing for the next leg of our journey."

"This cannot wait." When Ian moved toward the tent, the man clamped a hand around his wrist. "Remove your hand," Ian growled.

"I am not supposed to allow you to pass until the Duke is ready."

Ian lashed a thread of magic around the man's waist and whipped it away from him, lifting the man off his feet and dropping him on the roof of the carriage. He pulled the tent flap aside and ducked in.

With his back to Ian, Duke Gastwick stood over a young woman who was curled up in a blanket on the ground. Her bare shoulders, arms, and legs stuck out from the blanket while she sobbed.

The duke, wearing only a robe, spun around. "What are you doing here?"

Angered, Ian lashed out, wrapped threads of magic around the duke's neck, and lifted him off the ground. The duke gagged, twisted, and kicked.

A trio of guards burst in with weapons drawn, but Ian was ready. They swung at him. Their swords bounced harmlessly off the shield he had cast.

"Put down your weapons, or the duke dies," Ian said.

The men looked at the duke and then at each other before dropping the swords to the ground.

Ian turned toward the girl. "Did he force himself on you?"

"He said that he would leave my parents behind for those monsters to kill unless I...unless I..."

"You don't have to say it." Ian pointed. "Wrap the blanket around yourself. Take your things. Go to your family. I will deal with him."

The young woman crawled to her knees, held the blanket around herself while scooping clothing and a pair of shoes off the ground. She then burst to her feet and raced out of the tent.

Ian turned his attention toward the duke, whose complexion had turned pale, his lips purple. "I am going to set you down. You will listen and do as I say. Understand?"

When the duke gave Ian a slight nod, he dismissed the magic rope. Gastwick fell to the ground and then to his knees as he gasped and wheezed, his breaths deep and desperate.

"The monsters that destroyed your city have been dealt with, but another problem has emerged. Come nightfall, a major disaster will strike, and unless you are far from here, you will die."

The duke lifted his head, replying in a strained voice. "What are you talking about?"

"I am saying that you need to get dressed and be outside in five minutes. I am sending your people far from here, but your lives will be difficult for a time. Strong and honest leadership will be required to guide the citizens of Krotal as they begin their new life." He made a fist and shook it in front of the duke's face. "But if I ever hear that you have forced yourself on another woman, I'll come back and split you right down the middle."

He turned, stomped past the guards, and stopped outside the tent, where he took a few long, calming breaths.

The guards posted at the carriage looked at each other, including the one Ian had used his magic upon. The man pressed his lips together and approached Ian. "I apologize. I was simply obeying the duke's orders."

Ian grunted. "Never mind."

The guard's brow furrowed. "Is everything alright?"

"Other than your duke's lack of honor?"

The man scratched his head. "Yeah. He has a thing for girls. I never liked it much, but...what can I do?"

"If it ever happens again, tell me. I will deal with him."

"If you say so."

Ian glanced toward the village. "Can you tell me what happened to the people who lived there?"

"They were warned about the monsters, packed up their things, and joined us this morning. After the battle they witnessed by the bridge last night, they want to be far from here as much as anyone."

"In that case, do me a favor." He pointed. "One of you can watch the carriage. The others need to spread out and tell everyone that we are leaving. I'll be just up the road, waiting for you."

"Yes, Sir." The man waved to his men and pointed out one to remain behind before the other three of them marched off in different directions.

His anger cooling, Ian walked along the road, passing thousands of people before reaching the south end of camp. There, he stood and stared out over the sea. Waves gently crashed along the rocky shoreline while white gulls flew out over the bay. It was a serene moment that felt like a nasty lie when Ian considered what was to come. *How have I become part of something like this?* Worse, he felt helpless. As a god, Urvadan was immune to Ian's magic, and despite having applied considerable thought to the problem, there was nothing Ian could do to stop him. *It is best if you focus on saving those you can save, he told himself,* hoping to believe the lie. Noise on the road stirred him from his reverie.

People, wagons, and carts came toward him. Fear, hope, trepidation, determination, and a dozen other emotions were written on the faces of the refugees. *Deliver them to safety, Ian.* Where to go, though? It had to be somewhere beyond the destruction, somewhere livable, somewhere they could begin again. He tried to imagine being in their position, traveling with his family, uncertain of the future. When younger, he had always relied on his mother and father, one for caring and affection, the other for wisdom and guidance. The answer came to him.

"We are leaving the sea," He announced. "Something bad is coming, and we must be far from here before nightfall. I am taking you to the village where I grew up. It may be abandoned, but it resides beside a lake with a constant source of fresh water and plenty of land to farm."

Picturing Shillings was easily done. He cast a gateway through which a village was seen, the grass overgrown, the buildings around it quiet. A crystal blue lake and snow-capped mountains in the distance completed the view.

"Go on. Your new home awaits."

The people, wagons, and animals trudged past, their heads looking left and right as they spread out across the green. Thousands of people passed through the gateway, their eyes wide as they began a new life in another part of the world. Horse and oxen-drawn wagons rolled past as did carts, pigs, chickens, and cattle. When the crowd thinned with only dozens of people remaining, a pair of familiar faces came into view, one short and muscular with a shock of auburn hair, the other well over six feet tall with thick shoulders and brown curls.

"Ian?" Brady looked Ian up and down. "Why are you dressed like that?"

Terrick, who stood a full head taller than Brady, stopped beside him. "Is this magic your doing?"

"I...Yes. What are you doing here?" Ian briefly glanced at the citizens still passing through the gateway.

Brady said, "We were working on the docks of Hooked Point when we heard that the criminals who had been running Bard's Bay were gone."

Terrick added, "We took a ship back and arrived just this morning, but when we went looking for work, we were told to meet here at sunset instead." He peered through the portal. "That looks like Shillings."

"A disaster comes tonight, and when the sun rises tomorrow, Bard's Bay will be gone." He gestured toward the crowds of people in the village green and beyond. "Go on, Terrick. I suspect your father's farm awaits if you two would like to reclaim it. Shillings is about to become a full-blown city."

"How is this possible?"

"There is no time to explain. I'll visit Shillings soon and will seek you out. Until then, be well and help Essex get everyone settled."

The two childhood companions walked off, leaving Ian alone. He dismissed the gateway and considered his next destination.

GREAVESPORT PRESENTED AN ENTIRELY DIFFERENT CHALLENGE. Ian had no connection with the man who ruled the city, so he chose to take a different approach that was very time consuming but also far more personal.

Up and down the streets, he knocked on door after door, explained the situation, and begged the people he spoke with to allow him to help. He stood in squares and spoke before crowds after using brief displays of magic to get their attention. Many dismissed him or turned him away, despite anything he did or said. Others seemed eager to start over while the bulk of the people landed somewhere in between.

When asked where they would go if they could choose, some opted to join the citizens of Krotal in Ian's old hometown. Others chose to join the dwarves in Ra'Tahal, Norstan, or Westhold. A handful decided they would find or build their own new home in some untamed land. The latter, Ian brought to the heights of Mount Tiadd. While the sea might claim some or all of the flatlands of the Agrosi, the mountain's elevation would be safe, and when the seas settled, its temperate climate would likely create a nice island to live on.

This continued on and on as he worked his way through Greavesport, and when the sun was low in the western sky, he knew he had done what he could even if he had relocated fewer than half of the population. Weary, he transported himself back to Bard's Bay and stepped out onto the city wall overlooking the harbor.

A throng of people filled the harbor square while others crowded the area between the city wall and the waterfront.

To Ian's surprise, Essex stood on the wall a dozen strides from where Ian had appeared.

The city commander jerked with a start. "Ian? Where'd you come from?"

"I just left Greavesport and have relocated all save for those who refuse to leave their homes."

Essex nodded. "We ran into the same thing. I understand. People worked hard to build up their shops or to purchase their homes. They don't wish to give up on that dream."

Ian sighed. "I can't save everyone."

The man frowned. "You truly believe something horrible is going to happen, don't you?"

"I know it will happen."

"How do you know?"

"Our god told me himself."

Essex laughed. "We are not like the elves and dwarves. We have no god."

"Even if I told you that Urvadan was real?"

"The Dark Lord?" Essex shook his head. "Only a fool would serve the Dark Lord."

"Yes." Ian's shoulders slumped. "I am a fool."

"What do you mean?"

"Never mind. The day wanes, and I must get you out of here. The question is, where to send you?"

"We've over five thousand people here. Wherever we go, we need to house that many."

Ian considered and frowned. "Have you heard of Havenfall?"

"The city of elves?"

"It was until last night. Much of the island city was destroyed in battle, but it can be rebuilt. If I bring you somewhere nearby, you can resettle there, assuming the city survives what is coming. Rich farmland surrounds the city and the weather is mild."

"All I ask is that it is near fresh water."

"The river feeding the city is born from snowmelt and the island is littered with fountains."

"Do it." He nodded.

Ian lashed a loop of magic around his waist and the other end around a merlon beside him. He used the magical rope to lift himself up, out and over the crowd, extending the rope until he was over the foot of the nearest pier. The crowd fell silent, many jaws dropping with eyes and fingers pointing in his direction. When Ian's feet touched down, he cast a gateway a few feet from the shoreline and opened it until it was forty feet in diameter. An open meadow waited on the other side, the trees surrounding it hundreds of feet apart. A circular stone platform stood in the center of the glade.

In a loud voice, Ian said, "Follow me."

He rounded the edge of the portal and stepped through. The salty air was replaced by the scent of pines, the warm breeze by a cool one. The people hesitated before following, but once the caravan began, it did not stop until the harbor and the square were cleared. Last came Essex and three dozen guards.

The city commander approached Ian and nodded. "That is the last of us." He glanced around. "Where are we?"

Ian pointed. "Havenfall, or what is left of it, lies five or six miles east of here. The route is all downhill." He turned and pointed north. "Do you hear that rush? A river lies less than a quarter mile in that direction. Follow the river, and it will take you to the city, but I recommend you wait here until the day after tomorrow before you make the journey, just to be safe."

Essex narrowed his eyes. "I still cannot tell if this is real, if you are playing me a fool, or if you are crazy."

"Perhaps all three are true."

The man laughed. "Could be."

"Be well, Essex. I hope we will meet again one day." Ian cast a gateway, stepped through, and was gone.

THE TEMPLE of Urvadan in the village of Sacrumi sat empty. Ian stood in the center of the temple floor and recalled being tied to a post and thinking he was about to die. Truhan had appeared and pretended to be the god to whom Ian was to be sacrificed. Ironically, Ian's master had told the truth at the time while pretending otherwise. *When I thought he was lying, he was telling the truth. When he was to give me truth, it was so twisted and masked, the implications were buried beneath layers of scheming.*

A female voice came from across the temple. "We were wondering when you would come."

Ian turned to find Ahni standing in the doorway at the top of the stairs leading outside. Chieftess Orahna and High Priest Chutakka stood at her side.

"Ahni!" Ian crossed the floor and began up the stairs. "Something bad is going to happen. We have little time, but we must evacuate your village."

Orahna nodded. "We know."

He stopped two stairs below them. "You know?"

Ahni said, "The sacred spear saved the world and, like the monsters it destroyed, passed into legend."

Orahna spoke in a deep, knowing tone. "As foretold in prophecy, this event will lead to a cataclysm unlike any the world has ever seen. The Crumi, who have been loyal to Urvadan since the dawn of creation, have remained prepared for this moment."

Chutakka raised his hands high. "As written in the stars long, long ago, Urvadan will send a savior to deliver us to salvation." He lowered his hands, pressed them together and touched them to his forehead while nodding toward Ian. "You are that savior."

The three Crumi backed from the doorway. Curious, Ian climbed the last two stairs and stepped onto the platform leading outside.

At the base of the temple stood the entire village, all staring up at him in the light of the setting sun.

From his side, Orahna said, "Take us to our new home, Savior."

"You knew this would happen?"

"Of course. Why do you think our buildings are made of sticks and mud?" She gestured toward the open doorway. "Only the temple of Urvadan did we bother to build with stone. The rest will wash away in the coming destruction. When we find our true home, our permanent home, it will be a city made of stone."

The idea that they had lived in mud huts for centuries simply because of a prophecy seemed bizarre, but Ian was too tired to press the issue. "Let's get you out of here." He descended the stairs to the bottom of the pyramid with Ahni, her chieftess, and the high priest trailing.

The people at the bottom parted for Ian, all watching him in expectation. When he reached the far end of the crowd, he opened a gateway to the Valley of Gold and turned to find Ahni standing behind him. "It is good that you and Draxan get along. Together, you can ensure your people and his coexist. There, you should have everything you need for now." The Crumi deserved something special, and the crater and the city within was among the most beautiful places Ian had ever visited. With fresh water, fields, fruit trees, fish, and housing, it had everything they would need. "Whether it is your true home, I cannot say. I just know that Urvadan sent me to save you, and that is what I intend to do."

Orahna turned toward her people. "Crumi! Our time at Sacrumi has come to an end. A new beginning awaits." She walked through and the villagers followed.

Hundreds of dark-skinned, resolute faces walked past. Joining them were two dozen pigs, bleating goats, and carts loaded with caged chickens. The parade continued until only Ian and Ahni remained.

She lifted the sacred spear to her forehead. "Thank you, Ian. You saved the world, and now, you have rescued my people. We are in your debt."

"We saved the world together, Ahni. As for your people, I only ask that you treat others with kindness until they give you reason to do otherwise. Oh, and no more sacrifices."

She laughed. "No more sacrifices."

When she was through the opening, Ian dismissed it. A heavy silence crashed in. He was alone in the middle of swampland, far from anyone else. The solitude felt symbolic to his own position in the world. As the only human to wield magic, as the first wizard, the weight of responsibility often made him feel alone even when surrounded by others.

With a sigh of resignation, he cast a gateway and stepped onto the rooftop of a tower overlooking a world that would soon forever change.

CHAPTER 59

CATACLYSM

T he wind ruffled Ian's hair and the hem of his robes. The soft
light of dusk illuminated his surroundings, the sun hidden
behind mountains to the west, the stars just beginning to
pierce the canvas of sky above him. High atop a tower surrounded by
open, barren land, he approached his mentor, his master, his god.

Urvadan peered toward the heavens, the moon a beacon in a sky
teetering between daylight and night. "You have arrived just in time to
witness the greatest magic seen since the dawn of creation itself." He
lowered his gaze, his intense, blue eyes staring into Ian's. "What of your
quest?"

"The refugees from Krotal, the citizens of Bard's Bay, and many
people from Greavesport have been relocated. Not everyone would
leave, though."

"Free will is a dual-edged sword, and it determines one's fate more
than any other factor. What of the other Free Cities?"

"I have never been to Hooked Point or Sea Gate, so I was unable to
transport myself to either city. Even if I had, I would not have had
enough time."

"Not everyone can be saved, but the human race breeds well and their seed will spread in given time. However, you did not mention the one people who remained loyal to me all this time."

"The Crumi?"

"Yes. What of them?"

"They have been moved to the Valley of Gold."

"Ah." Urvadan nodded. "That is a good choice. It will keep them near me while I figure out how to bring the rest of the humans into the fold. One day, the human population will expand to cover the land and all will worship me, their devotion feeding my power. It will be glorious."

The statement caused Ian to frown. It was clear that Urvadan resented Vandasal, fueling a hunger for power. While he claimed that humans would benefit from his rise, Ian worried about the elves and dwarves he had befriended. They had families, hopes, and dreams just as he did. The elves had decided to relocate far from everyone else, but that answered only part of the question.

"What of the dwarves?" Ian asked.

"Their time of rule has come to an end."

"But what will happen to them?"

"At some point, I suspect human armies will go after the dwarves just as Gahagar did to the humans."

Ian shook his head. "I will not allow that to happen."

Urvadan grimaced. "You pledged yourself to me and will do as I say."

"Not in this. I'll not be a party to genocide or the persecution of someone simply due to their race. I know many dwarves and they are good, honest people who do not pray on the weakness of others."

"I see." Urvadan stroked his jaw. "What do you propose?"

"Allow them to live as they wish, so long as they do not seek to deny the same of others."

The god turned and strolled a few strides before turning back. "The dwarves do possess skills that would be useful. Perhaps we can come to an accommodation."

"What do you mean?"

"Their ability to shape stone is a skill no other race possesses. If they agree to help construct our new cities, I will agree to give them places of refuge, sheltered from human influence. They will be allowed to live free and as they wish."

Ian considered the offer. He suspected it would take decades or longer to construct new cities, but dwarves lived twice as long as humans, and so long as they had a path toward freedom, it was a better choice than death. "I can agree to that."

"Splendid. To tell you the truth, this path might prove far more beneficial to the new world order, anyway." Urvadan peered up toward the sky. "The time has come. Step back beyond the ring of crystals, or the magic I am about to wield will destroy you."

Heeding his master's warning, Ian backed from the dais, moved beyond the ring of crystals, and stopped near the tower's outer rim. The god climbed the dais stairs and laid down on the altar. Uncertain of what to expect, other than something spectacular, Ian held his breath. He did not have to wait long.

The ring of crystals began to glow with angry light. A wave of energy rippled out from the altar and spread across the dais, turning its surface from opaque stone to transparent glass. A red light shone through the glass, and Ian knew it was coming from the same column of light spanning all the way down to the temple below the tower, where the two demons remain trapped. That column of light shone up along the core of the tower and through the rooftop. The crimson glow grew brighter and brighter, joined by the light of the surrounding crystals.

A ray of light burst up from the rooftop and shot toward the heavens. It extended and extended into the distance, far beyond clouds or anything else of Ian's world.

A tiny spot of red appeared on the moon's surface, the distance making it seem like a glowing grain of sand. The crimson aura then began to spread. Like ripples expanding from a rock dropped into a still lake, the moon's soft light shifted to an angry red. In moments, the infection spread until the pale light was gone.

When the entire globe of the full moon had changed, a massive tremor shook the tower, causing Ian to stumble. Another quake struck, and Ian lost his footing. He fell to one knee as gravity pressed against him, forcing him to his hands and knees and then flat against his stomach. With effort, he rolled onto his back, his breathing labored, the pressure on his chest and the rest of this body akin to someone very heavy sitting on him.

The beam of magic connecting the tower to the distant heavenly body began to draw the moon closer, making it appear as if it were growing. The tower trembled, as did Ian. The force pressing upon him grew stronger and stronger until he was unable to breathe and feared he would be crushed. Lacking oxygen, his vision began to narrow. He fought for air, but it would not come. The blood moon was the last thing he saw before he slipped into oblivion.

Vic, Revita, and Lint walked along a winding road, toward the city of Bard's Bay. He glanced toward the sea, the water crashing against the rocks below the roadway. The white of a distant sail marked a westbound ship, heading toward the setting sun, which dangled over the horizon like a giant ball of fire.

It had been another long day, consisting of frustration, disappointment, and travel. Vic was hopeful for a better reception in Bard's Bay than what they received in Greavesport.

Lint piped, "How much farther to this city?"

Revita replied, "It should come into view when we round this bend."

"You should have had the dragon drop us off closer."

She looked down at him. "Are you complaining about a bit of travel?"

Vic nodded. "Yeah. What happened to Lint the great explorer?"

The brownie thrust his chin. "I still like to explore, but there is no shame in doing it smartly."

"Well," Vic said. "I didn't think it would be very smart to fly in on a dragon and upset the people who live here for no reason."

"If there is no reason, why visit Bard's Bay at all?"

Vic glanced over his shoulder and peered up the coastline. "While that dark cloud disappeared and the demon is likely now gone, who knows how many orcs still threaten this area?"

"So, we warn this sex guy, and then what?"

"Sex guy?" Revita chuckled. "His name is *Essex*."

Grinning at the brownie's interpretation of the name, Vic added, "And after that, hopefully he will offer us a meal and a soft bed for the night. I just hope Essex will listen to good sense."

Revita peered up at the hillside above them, where the ramparts of Bard's Castle were visible through the trees. "Thus far, he has shown more sense than most men."

Vic gave her a flat look. "What is that supposed to mean?"

She smirked. "That depends if you have the sense to figure it out."

They began up a gravel road climbing the tree-covered slope. "So, you think women have more sense than men?"

The comment made her snort. "I thought that much was obvious."

"Based on what?"

"Based on the fact that men go around causing problems that we women are forced to fix."

"Such as what?"

Revita shrugged. "Starting fights, for instance."

"I have seen you start a fight."

"Only ones I can finish."

"I see. What else?"

When they reached a switchback, Vic and Revita rounded it and resumed their uphill climb.

She tapped on her lips before speaking. "Well, look at how a man turns to jelly when a pretty woman bats her eyes and flashes him a little skin."

Vic harumphed. "That is just our nature."

"Yes. To not have sense."

He frowned. "I don't like where this conversation is headed."

"Serves you right for trying to argue with me."

"I have won arguments with you plenty of times."

She patted his cheek. "You keep telling yourself that."

Vic's frown deepened. "I told you not to patronize me."

Revita gripped his hand, stopping him. "That was not my intention. It just sort of...happened. I am sorry."

He nodded. "Old habits are difficult to break. I'll have patience with you if you can do the same for me."

The offer earned him a kiss, which he eagerly returned.

She then held his chin and looked into his eyes. "Best if we stop now. The child is watching."

Vic glanced down at Lint, who stood with his hands on his hips. "Yeah. Right."

The brownie waved a fist at him. "I am no child."

"Why are you cross with me? She was the one who said it."

"I don't have to make sense." Lint thumbed his chest. "I am a brownie." He then walked off.

Although Lint's comment begged for a snide reply, Vic let it go. Shockingly, so did Revita, the two of them instead following Lint along the gravel, hillside road. They rounded a bend and the castle came back into view.

As they continued toward the top of the bluff, Vic began to get a bad feeling. "Why are there no guards at the gate or on the wall?"

"Good question."

They approached the closed portcullis and peered through it.

"I don't see anyone," Revita said.

"Me neither." Vic drew a breath and shouted. "Ho! Is anyone here?!"

No response.

"I'll go inside and look around." Lint slid between gaps in the iron bars, hurried across the castle yard, and rounded the building.

The ground shook as a wave of energy passed beneath them and continued toward the city.

"What was that?" Vic blurted.

He turned as the tremor reached the shore, where massive waves appeared, tossing water high into the air and washing over the piers.

Another quake passed through, this time rattling the portcullis and the chain in the tower. He backed from the gate as a wall amid the burned portion of the castle collapsed in a thunderous boom.

"Something is wrong," Vic knew it with a certainty.

"Look at the moon!" Revita pointed toward the sky to the northeast.

The moon had turned the color of blood, the sight giving Vic a chill. "Something is very wrong."

He turned from the castle, walked over to the edge of the bluff, and peered down into the city. Although cast in shadow, there was still enough light for him to see that the streets were empty, as was the harbor. "Where are the people? Where are the ships?"

Another quake shook the ground, this one severe enough to cause him to stumble, his head buzzing and stomach twisting with nausea. The tremor lasted far longer than the first two. Cracks formed in the castle wall while the sound of breaking windows came from inside the grounds. When the shaking subsided, Vic lifted his face to the sky and gasped.

The red moon appeared larger than before.

Lint came running into view and leapt through a gap in the

portcullis. He slowed to a stop. "Something bad is happening. Did you see the moon?"

Revita said, "We know, but what was it?"

The brownie yipped and pointed. "Look!"

Following Lint's motion, Vic looked toward the city, his gaze shifting to the rough, sloshing water in the harbor, and then to the sea beyond. In the distance, a line of white with a dark shadow below it rose, until only the top quarter of the setting sun was visible. The water formation extended to the north and south as far as the eye could see. A distant roar arose as the tidal wave advanced and blocked the sun completely.

Revita gripped Vic by the shoulders and turned him toward her. "We need to get out of here. Fast."

Lint said, "We can't outrun that."

"No," Vic admitted. "We need help." He cast his thoughts out. *Umbracan. Please come to me. This is urgent.*

He glanced toward the wall of water, which seemed to grow taller as it advanced. Worse, it seemed to move faster and faster. The ship on the horizon was swallowed up and gone in an instant. Although the trio stood a hundred fifty feet above the city, the wall of water extended much, much higher. It blotted out the horizon, the roar growing increasingly louder.

"Should we hide?" Lint asked.

Vic shook his head. "There is no hiding from that. Not unless we were far from here and on much higher ground."

He tried one more time. *Please, Umbracan. Come this one last time. I beg you.*

The dragon burst from somewhere beyond the castle, its silhouette dark against the twilight sky. It banked inland and came around as it descended. Wings fluttering, the dragon landed on the road, its feet skidding across the gravel in a swirl of dust.

"Come, my friends," The dragon boomed. "There is little time."

Vic cast one last glance toward the wall of water, now standing easily a thousand feet tall and charging toward him. Revita scooped Lint off the ground and raced toward the dragon with Vic in close pursuit. They jumped onto the base of the tail and scrambled up. Before they could even get seated, the dragon crouched, extended its wings, and leapt into the sky as the crimson moon faded to pink.

When Revita slid into sitting position, Vic stretched past her, gripped the next dragon crest, and pulled himself into his seat.

The dragon turned as it climbed toward the sky, attempting to rise above the massive wall of water. Up and up, they went as the roaring wave came at them from behind. The front of the wave charged through the harbor, smashing through the piers, and blasting through the harbor wall. The city was engulfed instantly. The tsunami blasted into the bluff and tore the castle to pieces, drowning it, along with the hillside, and the trees, all the while chasing after the ascending dragon. The wall of water closed in quickly, despite the dragon's speed. The upper crest of the wave caught up to the dragon's tail, dousing it and sending spray through the air. With the next flap of its wings, the dragon took itself and its riders even higher. The wave passed under them and bowled through the forest, destroying everything in its path.

The energy of the tsunami was impossible to withstand. Trees, buildings, and even hillsides were flattened as it charged inland, toward a distant, lonely mountaintop.

THE PRESSURE on Ian's chest dissipated, and sweet, precious air filled his lungs. He breathed deeply again and again before opening his eyes. The moon, appearing larger than he had ever seen it, had returned to white. He pushed himself to a sitting position and took stock of the situation.

Across the rooftop, the glass dais had returned to stone, the glow of magic gone. Urvadan lay still, the night quiet, and in that stillness came a distant explosion. Ian climbed to his feet and looked over the tower edge, toward the pale light in the western sky.

Miles west of the city of Murvaran, the ground had been fractured into a branching web of deep fissures. To the distant south, the land was torn open with numerous spouts of molten lava spewing into the sky. It was a terrible yet awestriking sight that left him concerned for the rest of the world.

A cool light came from behind Ian, who spun around to find a churning blue cloud across the rooftop. The aura of the cloud brightened until he had to hold his hand up to shield his eyes. When the glow faded, Ian lowered his arm to find an elderly man with a gray beard standing on the rooftop. The man wore white robes, his posture tall and certain. Most notable was the fury in his gray eyes.

Urvadan stood from the altar. "Welcome, brother. I was expecting you."

Brother? Ian blinked. *This is Vandasal?*

The god in white approached the dais. "What have you done?"

With a smug smirk, Urvadan gestured toward the moon. "I have shifted the balance in my favor, just as you did long ago. The moon will remain over my tower, its light shining in full every night."

Vandasal pointed toward the spewing volcanoes. "Your actions have torn this world asunder. Entire cities drown. The Vale is destroyed, as are the creatures who called it home."

Ian gasped. *The Fae!* The fairies and brownies lacked souls, their lives like sparks that, when doused, would never rekindle. The realization made him feel even more horrible.

Urvadan stepped off the dais. "We crafted this world together and were to govern it as such. Your choices destroyed that vision. Rather than sit back and allow you to sit upon your throne while I linger in the background, I have taken my own actions." He stepped close to the other god, meeting him eye to eye as he poked him in the chest. "Humans will no longer bend knee to the races of magic, for they now wield magic as well. With superior numbers, they will dominate this world, and their prayers will feed my might. You will be forgotten while I rise to heights never imagined."

"If you think I will allow this to happen, you..."

Urvadan struck Vandasal with a backhand blow, the force of it sending the elder brother across the rooftop, crashing through the wall, and soaring out into the open air. As Vandasal dropped out of sight, Urvadan yanked his hand back. The other god reversed direction and shot back to the tower. He came to a sudden stop and floated a few feet above the rooftop, his head and arms hanging limply.

With a sneer, Urvadan said, "You have enjoyed two thousand years of sitting atop your tower and basking in the prayers of your people while I lingered in obscurity. That time is over. As you did so long ago, I sentence you to wander the world as a nothing more than a mere beggar. You will watch as the human race and their wizards rise in a new era. The world has been reborn and I intend to reform it in my image. Enjoy your time in the shadows. I'll not see you again."

Urvadan thrust his arm toward Vandasal. The elder god shot across the sky and was gone.

CHAPTER 60
A NEW ERA

The thrill of victory Ian had experienced after defeating the demon and its army seemed a distant memory. He sat alone on the altar atop the Dark Lord's tower while watching dozens of lava flows in the distant south, the warm light of the molten earth easily seen despite the dark of night.

Again and again, he racked his brain, attempting to figure out if there had been anything he could have done to prevent the devastation. His magic was something unique and unseen by his world, yet he found himself absolutely helpless when compared to a mighty god.

For most of his life, Ian had wished he could be a hero, someone who made a difference, someone whom others idolized. When he had been gifted with magic, he did not know that gift had come from a god. The choice between pledging himself to Truhan or dying had seemed simple at the time, despite any strings that might be attached. The abilities he had gained through that transaction had brought him into power beyond his wildest dreams. How could he have guessed the consequences that came with such power?

He had done his best to spare lives and to save the world from an army of darkness, clueless to the fact that the army and the demon driving it had entered his world only because his master had allowed it. Despite his intentions and efforts to do the right thing, guilt twisted his stomach. Intentions would not bring back the people who had died.

After hours upon hours of dwelling on the issue and staring into the distance in a numb state of denial and disbelief, the rising sun shone in the corner of Ian's eyes and stirred him from his musings. Somehow, he had spent the entire night awake on the tower rooftop.

As the sun edged into the sky, a sense of peace came over Ian. A massive cataclysm had rocked the world, resulting in untold devastation. Yet, the sun still rose, oblivious to the turmoil gripping the land it shone upon. With that realization came a different perspective.

The gods perceived the world much as the sun and moon might. Days or even years were brief moments in time to them. Humans, dwarves, and elves all saw time differently, their life spans differing greatly, yet none approached the eons witnessed by the rising sun.

Given time, the volcanoes would cool, and new mountains would stand in their place. The sea would settle, and new cities would be constructed along its shores. Generations of people would replace the old. Those populations would grow and thrive. All would be well, given time, and Ian had a hand in that. Regardless of Urvadan's selfish scheme, he had given thousands of people a chance to survive. He had left a meaningful mark, but there was more he could do, for Ian had his own life in front of him.

With the sun hovering above the eastern horizon and a sense of newfound hope filling his heart, Ian crafted a gateway.

He stepped through the opening into the sitting room on the main floor of his tower in Ra'Tahal. When the gateway disappeared with a pop, he heard a squawk behind him and spun around.

Lionel burst from the back of the chair he was perched upon and flew toward Ian, striking him full in the chest. The drake climbed his robes and eagerly licked and nipped at Ian's neck and ear.

"Alright, alright," Ian laughed. "I missed you, too."

He lifted Lionel with one hand and stroked its head and neck with the other. Waves of love and joy came through his connection with the drake, the affection further soothing the ache in his heart.

After a few minutes with Lionel, he placed him back on the chair. "Stay here. I need to go see Winnie. I'll be back soon with your breakfast."

The drake perked up with the mention of food.

"Stay," Ian waggled a finger before climbing the stairs.

He continued to the fourth floor and heard retching coming from the bedroom. Concerned, he ran in to find Winnie in a filmy night gown, bent over a bowl. Rina stood over Winnie, holding her red hair back as she vomited.

"Winnie! What's wrong?" Ian blurted.

She lifted her head and gave him a level stare. "I am being sick."

"I can see that. Did you eat something that had gone bad?"

"No." She sat back and looked up at Rina. "I am done. Thank you."

Rina gave her a sad smile. "Happy to help." She approached the door and placed a hand on Ian's chest. "I am glad you are well. I feared...we feared what had become of you. The entire city shook like thunder last night. It was as if the world might end."

"It almost did."

She bit her lip. "Ian. I never thanked you for saving me." A tear tracked down her cheek. "I was selfish and focused on what I lost. I never considered what you risked when you came for me."

"There is no need to thank me, Rina. We are friends, and that will never change."

Rina flashed him a weak smile. As her smiles had done since they were both young, it felt as if the sun was shining upon his heart. She then slid past and was gone.

Ian turned to find Winnie sitting on the bed. Although she appeared a bit worn from whatever had made her ill, the sight of her warmed his heart further. The way she sat, wearing a rather tight gown made of thin material, caused his blood to heat despite his lack of sleep.

He approached her and pulled a stray curl from her face. "I am sorry that you feel ill."

"I am fine now, I think. At least until tomorrow morning."

Frowning, he asked, "Why do you say that?"

"Because I plan to be sick again."

"Why would you plan to be sick again? Nobody plans to be sick."

"You do when you are in my condition."

"What are you talking about?"

"Think, Ian." She smirked. "Why would I be ill in the morning today, just as I was yesterday and will be tomorrow?"

He blinked. "A baby?"

Her smile broadened. "You just won a prize."

"What? How?"

"Well, one of those times when we were both naked and in bed, you..."

He covered her mouth. "I know how it works. I just...didn't expect this. Are you certain?"

"A dwarven healer visited yesterday and confirmed as much. You are going to be a father."

Shock and disbelief turned to joy. Ian whooped, wrapped his arms around her, and lifted her off the bed, hugging her tightly while spinning her around. "This is wonderful!"

He set her down, kissed her, and then pulled back to stare into her eyes.

"Are you certain you are happy?" She asked.

"I couldn't imagine anything that would make me happier."

Winnie smiled. "I am so relieved. Since we aren't yet married, I wasn't certain."

"But we are getting married, right?"

"Yes."

"Well, there is no need to wait on that. I'll talk to Korrigan and arrange for a wedding within the week...if that is alright with you."

She beamed. "I would love that." Her smile faltered. "But I will need a dress. And flowers. And there will be a party, of course." She pulled away, her face reflecting concern. "There is much to do."

He grabbed her by the hand and pulled her toward him, his arms wrapping around her. "All of that can wait."

"Wait for what?"

"I thought we might celebrate." He flicked his hand and the door across the room slammed shut. "Alone."

She gave him a naughty smile. "I would like that."

He pinched his face. "But first, could you drink some water or something? Maybe chew on a bit of mint as well? I was just reminded that you recently vomited."

Winnie laughed. "Of course." She pulled the lace on the neck of her gown and slid it off her shoulder. "But while you go fetch me something, I thought I would remind you of what awaits your return. The other shoulder was bared, and then she pulled the gown down past her chest. Ian's heart thumped like thunder as the gown slid down her torso, eased over her hips, and dropped to the floor.

With an impulse impossible to deny, he reached for her, but she planted a hand on his chest and shook a finger in front of his face.

"Oh, no. Don't get distracted. Remember your run to the kitchen." She sashayed around him, his eyes following as she slid into bed and pulled the covers up. "Remember that I am waiting."

Ian rushed to the door and down the stairs with the image affixed in his mind urging him to hurry.

Soap suds bubbled along Revita's arms and chest, disappearing when she dunked herself in the hot spring. She came up and cleared the water from her eyes. Across the cavern, Vic climbed from the pool and dried himself off. Rather than continue washing herself, she stared overtly in his direction, enjoying his lean, yet muscular body. He bent and rubbed the towel down his legs, looking up at her as he stood.

"Why are you staring at me?" he asked.

"I am enjoying the view." She stood upright, the water only reaching her navel.

He wrapped the towel around his waist. "Well, it feels a bit weird."

"You stare at me." She ran her hands down her torso. "See. You are doing it right now."

"Um. That is different."

"A woman can't enjoy the sight of a man?"

"I didn't say that."

"And why are you wearing that towel? By now, I know well what hides beneath it."

The last comment turned his cheeks red, which brought her a smile in victory.

"I...um...well," he stammered. "What if Lint came back?"

"Lint has seen you naked as well. Besides, it's not as if you can't compete with him. His entire body is roughly the size of your..."

"Revita!" He gasped.

She laughed, laid back in the water, and swam into the hotter portion of the pool. *I may never tire of that*, she thought to herself.

Vic headed for the tunnel. "I am going to the kitchen to get our clothes. I'll bring them back to our room before I get dressed."

Floating on her back, she said, "Go on. I won't be long."

The hot water was soothing, and she was happy to be clean once again. Riding a dragon had been just about everything she hoped it would be, but she had underestimated the odor one acquired when doing so. Besides, her thick, raven hair had grown greasy and had absorbed the scent of smoke during their recent adventures. Being doused in Krotal harbor hadn't helped either. Rather than leaving the harbor feeling clean, her clothes had taken on a slightly fishy odor, which is why she had washed them diligently before turning her attention to her own body.

Her clothes, along with those of Vic had been then hung on a string over the oven. With its grate open, hot air wafting out, she suspected they would dry quickly. While waiting for that to happen, she and Vic had spent two hours in the baths. Of course, much of that time was focused on activities other than actually getting clean.

When the heat became too much, Revita stood and waded to the cooler end of the pool. She climbed from the water, grabbed the towel left for her, and began to dry her hair. Although the tunnels under Mount Tiadd were generally chilly, she felt none of it after a long, hot soak. Thus, she wrapped the towel around her head and tied it, allowing her body to drip dry as she lifted the globe of light from the sconce on the wall and headed down the tunnel.

Just before reaching her room, someone came around the corner, stopped, and gaped.

"Ian!" She blurted. "I am so glad to see you."

Vic, still pulling his breeches on, hopped over to the open doorway leading to their room. "Ian! You are alive!"

"I...I..." Ian stammered, his cheeks red and eyes bulging.

Vic turned to Revita, who stood a stride away wearing nothing but a towel on her head.

"Are you staring at my wife?" Vic asked.

Somehow, that seemed to straighten Ian's thoughts. He turned away from Revita to stare down the empty corridor. "Wife?"

At the same time, it was Revita who was now stunned. "Wife?"

Vic turned toward her and hastily explained, "With half the world destroyed and everything we have been through, I thought...well...I was hoping we would stay together. Forever."

She planted a hand on her hip, her voice flat. "I see."

"You are mad."

"You could say that."

He appeared crestfallen. "I was hoping..."

Revita interjected. "You never asked."

"What?"

"You never asked me."

He frowned and then nodded. Dropping to one knee, he took her hand. "Revita Shalaan, will you take my hand in marriage? Will you be my partner for life?"

Despite her display of anger, she found herself surprised and overwhelmed. *I had no idea how it would feel to hear those words.* The role of wife was one Revita had never considered for herself, yet with Vic, she felt as if anything were possible. Surprisingly, she felt like she could be herself and not be forced to always play the part of the edgy, headstrong thief she had constructed for the rest of the world to see.

Without conscious thought, her heart somehow took control and the words came out. "I would love nothing more."

He burst to his feet while wrapping his arms around her waist, lifting her up as he spun. When his embrace relaxed, her wet body slid down his torso, and as her toes touched down, their lips met. The kiss was heated yet gentle, lasting only for moments, yet so, so satisfying.

Ian spoke over his shoulder. "I would love to congratulate you two, but it will be very awkward before you are dressed."

"Yeah." Vic released Revita. "We will finish dressing and meet you in the study."

"Fine. If you don't mind, close the curtain. I need to get a few things from my room."

Revita walked past Vic, who followed, pulled the curtain closed, and continued dressing.

∽

FULLY DRESSED, Vic scooped his weapon off the floor, stood, and glanced over at Revita, who sat on the bed in only a tunic and small clothes while attempting to pull on her tight breeches.

"This is easier when they are not wet," she complained.

"Yes. Mine were still damp. I had the same issue." He smiled.

She stopped and gave him a flat look. "This is not funny."

"It's not that. I am just happy. I had hoped..." Vic struggled to express himself. "I was afraid you might flee when you heard the word *wife*."

Revita stood while buttoning her breeches. "Not long ago, I'd have stabbed you for saying it, but things have changed. I have changed." She tilted her head in thought. "I guess that the whole world has changed. I don't know what the future holds, but I'd rather not face it alone."

His smile faltered, a pang of disappointment piercing through his joy. "Is that all I..." Her finger pressed his lips, stopping him.

"That came out wrong." She sighed, "I am not good at this stuff. You know that."

"If you didn't mean it, why did you say it?"

"I spent my life looking out for myself, and everyone else came a distant second. I thought that was how it would be and accepted long ago that it would never change. Now, I find myself worried about you as much as about myself. I even find myself wanting your help rather than doing something alone. Not anyone's help. Just yours."

A smile spread across his face as the joy returned in full force. "For someone who claims they are not good at this stuff, that was awfully well said."

She smirked. "It was painful, so don't get used to it.

He chuckled. "I am going to meet Ian. Join us when you are dressed." Another, heavier chuckle shook his shoulders. "Twice, now he has stumbled in while you were naked. Each time, his eyes bulged a bit more. If it happens a third time, we might be scooping his eyes off the floor."

She laughed. "He is even more fun to embarrass than you are."

"That sounds like something you might say." He pulled the curtain aside and headed down the tunnel.

When he reached the study, he found Ian sitting at the desk while staring up at the wall of books behind it.

"What are you doing?" Vic asked as he approached the desk.

Ian turned toward him. "Thinking. The last few days have been a bit overwhelming, and I am still coming to terms with all the changes."

"I know some of what you mean. After all, it looks like I am getting married."

"Congratulations, Vic." Ian stood and hugged his brother. "I am happy that you two found each other." He then glanced toward the tunnel. "Take care of him for me."

Vic turned as Revita crossed the room.

She shrugged. "It sounds like a full-time job, but I've nothing better to do for the next fifty years."

"Only fifty?" Vic asked.

"If we live that long." She nodded toward Ian. "You were right, Vic. He did show up."

Ian frowned. "Right about what?"

Vic said, "I told her that you would come here. Eventually."

"Is that why you are here?"

"Yes and no. In part, Umbracan wanted to rest, and once he brought us here, I told him that he had done more than enough. Dragons were not meant to be harnessed, so he flew off this morning. Who knows when or if I will see him again."

"What happened to bring you here?"

"Have you been outside?"

"No," Ian admitted.

"Come. We will show you."

Ian scooped up a pack from the desk and led Vic out of the room. They crossed the Chamber of Testing and took the tunnel leading outside. Once they passed the secret doorway, Ian closed it, sealing the entrance. They then slid past the boulder blocking the cavern mouth and were greeted by the rush of water.

When they emerged, rather than being greeted by the sprawling plains of the Agrosi, they stood on a shelf of rock overlooking the sea. Waves crashed in, washed around a boulder jutting fifteen feet above the water, and sloshed in the small protective cove below them. Perhaps fifteen miles to the east stood what remained of the grassy plains, the area in between now covered by dark blue water.

Ian stared over the sea and shook his head. "I wondered if the water had come this far inland."

Vic nodded. "I am thankful that the water leveled. When we first got to Mount Tiadd, we feared coming this low and thought the tunnels might end up being filled. Not until this morning, when the sun rose and we saw that the waves had calmed and the tsunami was no longer a threat, did we dare enter them." He looked at Ian. "What happened to cause this?"

"You are not likely to believe it."

"Try me."

"Truhan turned out to be the god, Urvadan. He explained that he had brought the demon and the orcs to our world for a purpose. He needed the demon's power added to his own, so he could capture the moon and hold it over his tower in Murvaran. That act caused all of this." Ian swept his arm toward the water.

Despite the outlandish nature of the tale, Vic knew his brother and had seen enough to believe in the outlandish. "Why would he do such a thing?"

"Power."

Vic frowned. "That's it?"

Ian shrugged. "To a god, what else is there?"

"How should I know?'

"You aren't expected to know. None of us are. We must accept what lies beyond our control and do our best to positively affect the things we can change."

"Seems like wise words."

"They should be. I stole that bit of wisdom from Parsigar."

Vic nodded. "The dwarf was a bit odd, but he always seemed wise."

"I should get back to Ra'Tahal. I assume you would like to come with me."

Revita nodded. "This island is great and all, but it would be boring with only the three of us, even if we didn't exhaust the food stores."

"Three of you?" Ian asked with a furrowed brow.

"Yes. Lint is here as well."

Grinning, Ian looked around. "I'm glad he survived. Where is he?"

"Exploring," Vic said. "We asked him to give us some time alone."

Ian smirked. "I now see why Revita was naked."

"Ian!" Vic exclaimed.

Revita laughed and slid a hand across Vic's back. "It looks like your brother is not quite as prim as I thought, Vic."

"Oh," Ian said. "I have some good news."

"We are listening," Vic replied.

"You two are not the only ones getting married."

"You and Winnie?"

"Yes." Ian grinned.

Vic thumped his brother on the back. "That is wonderful. When?"

"In three days. That's why I need to get back. There is much yet to prepare."

"Three days?" Rubbing his jaw, Vic considered the news and turned to Revita. "What if we had a dual wedding?"

Her coppery cheeks turned pale. "In three days?"

He took her hand. "Why wait? It'll be less work if Ian and Winnie are already planning everything. Besides, we know all the same people. It will be one big party."

She stared at him for a beat before nodding. "Let's do it."

Vic slid his hand up her back, into her damp hair, and pulled her toward him for a kiss.

"There is one other thing," Ian said, interrupting the moment.

Turning toward his brother, Vic asked, "What, now?"

"You are going to be an uncle."

Vic frowned. "Uncle? But that would mean..." His eyes widened. "Winnie is pregnant?"

Ian beamed. "I am going to be a father."

"That is fantastic!"

From the hillside behind them came a small voice. "You three are noisier than a pair of griffins in heat."

They all turned to find Lint standing above the cavern entrance.

"There you are, pipsqueak," Revita said.

"Everywhere I go, there I am." Lint walked along the slope and jumped down to a boulder beside Vic. "What is this about Ian?"

"He is going to be a father," Vic explained.

Lint turned to Ian. "How many are in your nest?"

Ian frowned. "Nest? What nest?"

"You didn't make a nest yet?" Lint threw his arms up. "How are they ever going to hatch?"

"Hatch what?"

"Your eggs, of course."

"What are you talking about?"

Lint rolled his eyes. "Don't you know anything? First, you eat the flower of conception. Then, your innards warm and eggs come out. Then, you must coat the eggs with honey and lick them every morning. Do it right, and you'll have a brood of new children in a few hundred years."

The three humans laughed and laughed.

Arms crossed, Lint scowled until the laughter quelled. "I would like to know what is so funny."

Revita said, "I would like to know from where eggs are going to come out of Ian."

"From his arse, of course."

Their laughter echoed across the new sea. The memory of that laughter remained even after they stepped through the portal and were gone.

The world had changed forever, but the hope found in the spirit of the survivors would become the foundation of a long and fruitful future...until the balance of magic was once again tilted in the other direction.

This tale has drawn to a conclusion, but additional stories await in the same world, set thousands of years in the future, when wizards rule and scheme for thrones that grant the power of a god.

Those adventures begin with **Eye of Obscurance**, the first book in **Fate of Wizardoms**, a COMPLETE six-book series ready to welcome new Wizardom readers

NOTE FROM THE AUTHOR

I hope you enjoyed the **Dawn of Wizards**, a tale that peers into the distant past in the world of Wizardoms.

If you have not yet read **Fate of Wizardoms, Fall of Wizardoms,** and **Wizardom Legends** (*The Outrageous Exploits of Jerrell Landish* and *Tor the Dungeon Crawler*), those 18 novels are set in the same world, some 2,000 years AFTER the Dawn of Wizards saga concludes. I suggest you check them out.

I invite you to join my author newsletter. As a way to show my appreciation, I offer character sides stories including a new tale featuring Revita and the Head Thumpers, set before **Dawn of Wizards**.

I am grateful to have you join in my wild adventures.

Best Wishes, *Jeff*

Follow me on:
Amazon
Bookbub
Facebook

ALSO BY JEFFREY L. KOHANEK

Dawn of Wizards

The First Wizard

Paragon of Solitude

The Dark Lord's Design

Fate of Wizardoms

Eye of Obscurance

Balance of Magic

Temple of the Oracle

Objects of Power

Rise of a Wizard Queen

A Contest of Gods

* * *

Fate of Wizardoms Boxed Set: Books 1-3

Fate of Wizardoms Box Set: Books 4-6

Fall of Wizardoms

God King Rising

Legend of the Sky Sword

Curse of the Elf Queen

Shadow of a Dragon Priest

Advent of the Drow

A Sundered Realm

Fall of Wizardoms Boxed Set: Books 1-3

Fall of Wizardoms Box Set: Books 4-6

Wizardom Legends

The Outrageous Exploits of Jerrell Landish

Thief for Hire

Trickster for Hire

Charlatan for Hire

Tor the Dungeon Crawler

Temple of the Unknown

Castles of Legend

Shrine of the Undead

Runes of Issalia

The Buried Symbol

The Emblem Throne

An Empire in Runes

* * *

Runes of Issalia Bonus Box

Wardens of Issalia

A Warden's Purpose

The Arcane Ward:

An Imperial Gambit

A Kingdom Under Siege

* * *

Wardens of Issalia Boxed Set

Made in United States
Troutdale, OR
06/01/2025